EVENING GAMES

Other anthologies by Alberto Manguel

BLACK WATER: The Book of Fantastic Literature
OTHER FIRES: Short Fiction by Latin American Women
DARK ARROWS: Great Stories of Revenge

EVENING GAMES

TALES OF PARENTS
AND CHILDREN

EDITED BY ALBERTO MANGUEL

Clarkson N. Potter, Inc./Publishers

DISTRIBUTED BY CROWN PUBLISHERS, INC.,
NEW YORK

Published in 1987 in the United States by
Clarkson N. Potter, Inc., 225 Park Avenue South,
New York, New York 10003
Originally published in 1986 in Canada by Penguin Books
Canada Limited.

CLARKSON N. POTTER, POTTER, and colophon are
trademarks of Clarkson N. Potter, Inc.

Manufactured in the United States of America

Library of Congress Cataloging-in-Publication Data

Evening games.

1. Parent and child—Fiction. 2. Short stories.
I. Manguel, Alberto.
PN6120.95.P28E94   1988   808.83'9355   87-22372
ISBN 0-517-56737-7
10 9 8 7 6 5 4 3 2 1

First American Edition

Acknowledgements

Apple, Max, "Bridging" from *Free Agents*. Copyright © 1984 by Max Apple. Reprinted by permission of Harper & Row, Publishers, Inc.

Birdsell, Sandra, "The Rock Garden" from *Night Travellers*. "The Rock Garden" was first published in *Night Travellers* (Turnstone Press Limited, 1982) and is reprinted by permission of Turnstone Press.

Dagerman, Stig, "The Games of the Night" from *The Games of the Night*, translated by Naomi Walford. Reprinted by permission of The Bodley Head Ltd.

Denevi, Marco, "Secret Ceremony" from *Prize Stories from Latin America*, translated by Harriet de Onis. Translation copyright © 1963 by Time Inc. Reprinted by permission of Doubleday & Co., Inc.

Déry, Tibor, "The Circus," translated by Elizabeth Csicsery-Rónay. This translation originally printed in *Hungarian Short Stories*, edited by Paul Varnai, 1982, and published by Exile Editions Ltd.

Dinesen, Isak, "The Dreaming Child" from *Winter's Tales*, by Isak Dinesen. Copyright 1942 by Random House, Inc., and renewed 1970 by Johan Philip Thomas Ingerslev c/o The Rungstedlund Foundation. Reprinted by permission of Random House, Inc.

Godwin, Gail, "Over the Mountain." "Over the Mountain" first appeared in *Antaeus* no. 49/50. Reprinted by permission of the author.

Heker, Liliana, "Jocasta." Copyright © Liliana Heker, 1967. Reprinted by permission of the author. English translation © Alberto Manguel, 1986.

Hemingway, Ernest, "Indian Camp" from *In Our Time*. Copyright 1925 Charles Scribner's Sons; copyright renewed 1953 Ernest Hemingway. Reprinted with the permission of Charles Scribner's Sons.

Minot, Susan, "Hiding" from *Monkeys*. Copyright © 1986 by Susan Minot. Published first in *Grand Street*. Reprinted by permission of the publisher, E. P. Dutton/Seymour Lawrence, a division of NAL Penguin Inc.

Moriconi, Virginia, "Simple Aritthmetic." © Virginia Moriconi, 1963. Reprinted by permission of the author.

Muschg, Adolf, "The Scythe Hand or The Homestead," translated by Michael Hamburger. Published in *Blue Man and Other Stories* (Manchester: Carcanet New Press, 1983). Reprinted by permission of Michael Hamburger. Original title "Der Zusenn oder Das Heimat" from "Liebesgeschichten" © Suhrkamp Verlag, Frankfurt am Main 1972.

Pirandello, Luigi, "The Other Son." Reprinted by permission of the Pirandello Estate and Toby Cole, agent.

Purdy, James, "Why Can't They Tell You Why?" from *Color of Darkness*. Copyright © 1956 by James Purdy. Reprinted by permission of New Directions Publishing Corp.

For Arthur Gelgoot, because
of his unrelenting generosity

"Happy the son whose father is in Hell."
Mateo Alemán, *Guzmán de Alfarache*

"What the mother sings to the cradle goes all the way down to the coffin."
Henry Ward Beecher

"Do you think that I care for my soul if my boy be gone to the fire?"
Tennyson, "Rizpah"

Contents

Introduction

What man has bent o'er his son's sleep, to brood
How that face shall watch his when cold it lies?—
Or thought, as his own mother kissed his eyes,
Of what her kiss was when his father wooed?

Dante Gabriel Rossetti

Of the four evangelists, only Luke tells the story. The younger of two sons is in a foreign land. He has spent his fortune, and is hungry, and has taken on a job feeding pigs. He looks at the corn husks the pigs are eating and thinks of his hunger, and realizes how absurd it is for him to suffer when all he needs to do is return to his father's house and eat at his father's table. He decides to go home. While he is still a way down the road, his father sees him and runs to meet him, and kisses him, and orders that the fattened calf which was to become proverbial, be slaughtered and cooked. Hearing all this, the elder son is enraged and asks his father why he, who never gave cause to lament, had no calf slaughtered for him. The father replies that while the elder son was always with him, the young prodigal son had been as dead, and was now alive again. We will never know whether the elder son was satisfied with this answer.

The story is disturbing because it leans on one commonly

accepted and undisputed convention: that parents and
children are morally bonded to one another. Or rather, as
the Commandments make it clear, that the children owe
their parents a debt of honour which the youngest son had
not kept. Because of this, the father's welcome is seen as
wonderfully magnanimous. We have no commandment
which states that the debt is reciprocal.

The bonds of blood have become (perhaps have always
been) a literary convention, like the faithfulness of dogs or
the nobility of oak trees. Cain is seen as a disgrace to his
parents, and Oedipus is a monster only because we know
the identities of the murdered traveller and the widowed
queen. Would Hamlet's doubt be equally poignant if Ger-
trude, instead of being his mother, were a somewhat racy
twice-married next-door neighbour? In all these cases, the
reader's belief in the bonds of blood is necessary for the
effectiveness of the pathos.

The Marquis de Sade, with his superb talent for scandal,
questioned in *Juliette* the truth of such a convention. "It is
false," he says, "to suppose you owe anything to the being
from whence you came forth; even falser to suppose you
owe any feeling to the one issued from you; absurd to
imagine that you owe it to your brothers, sisters, nephews,
nieces. By what reason should blood establish obligations?"

Literature, in its wisdom, has always sought to explore
not the reason, but the bond itself: the different kinds of
knots with which we tie ourselves to our parents and to our
children. It takes the archetype of family ties for granted,
like our memory of the moon or our sense of fleeting time,
and builds its stories upon it. The parents and children of
literature appear in seemingly numberless combinations:
in this anthology alone we have samples of fathers who lust
after their children, fathers who abhor their children, a
mother who learns how not to love her daughter, a mother
who loves her child with dangerous intensity, a daughter
who enslaves herself to the memory of her mother, a son
whose lack of affection destroys the life of the parents. . . .

The variety of relationships between parents and children makes it nonsensical to blanket them under one name. What monstrously distended word would encompass Medea, murdering her sons to prove a point, and the anonymous mother of a Jewish folktale which my own mother told me as an exercise in guilt:

A spoiled young man falls into bad company and in love with an evil woman. He asks her to live with him, she agrees on one condition: that he bring her his mother's heart. Blind with passion, the boy runs home, kills his mother, and rips the steaming heart out of her breast. As he races back to his love, he stumbles and falls, and from the ground his mother's heart speaks to him in a whisper: "My son, have you hurt yourself?"

And how can we use the word "father" to define both the stern, brutish Hermann Kafka immortalized in his son's letter as a frightful and unjust God, and the the generous-minded Henry James, Sr., writing to his sons Henry and William, when both were in their early adolescence:

"Every man who has reached even his intellectual teens begins to suspect that life is no farce; that it is not genteel comedy even; that it flowers and fructifies on the contrary out of the profoundest tragic depths of the essential dearth in which its subject's roots are plunged. The natural inheritance of everyone who is capable of spiritual life is an unsubdued forest where the wolf howls and the obscene bird of night chatters."

Oscar Wilde noted this astounding diversity of character not only in a variety of individuals, but in every single person. "Children," he said, "begin by loving their parents. After a time they judge them. Rarely, if ever, do they forgive them." Ernest Hemingway's story illustrates the first stage, Pirandello's the second, Gail Godwin's and James Purdy's the third and last.

Not the least of the pleasures of reading is recognizing mirrors: images that reflect a moment of ourselves, of the way we think we are, of what we want to be, or fear we might become. If we catch a glimpse of ourselves in Susan Minot's "Hiding," we can console ourselves with Stig

Dagerman's "The Games of the Night" or Max Apple's "Bridging." As readers, we have a chance few actors have: that of being all the characters in *Lear,* even Cordelia. And yet I find it bewildering that so few examples of consolation have crossed my path in stories about parents and children. It is as if the old dictum about misery breeding art were true, and that writers are indeed better craftsmen of bad times than of happiness.

A note on the title: Among American writers, William Saroyan explored the relationship between parents and children with perseverant optimism. In 1968, after having read *The Human Comedy,* I looked him up in Paris, where he was living at the time. He introduced me to hot red wine, and in a café not far from the Eiffel Tower talked for a long afternoon about that early novel and about memories of his childhood. He talked about being a son, and then about being a father. Among the notes I kept from that conversation is this one:

Saroyan (dipping his finger in the wine, then sucking it): "I sometimes think that the only reason parents put up with children and children put up with parents, is to play a game in the evening and forget their battle of the day."

Saroyan died in 1981. Eighteen years after our meeting, I want to thank him for the title of this anthology which he gave me long before I thought of collecting these stories.

Alberto Manguel
Toronto, 1986

Hiding
Susan Minot

Susan Minot
(USA, b. 1956)

A few writers choose one corner of the world and make that their entire universe. J. D. Salinger chose the Glass family's New York country and chronicled their lives with determined minuteness; Susan Minot's specialty is the suburban kingdom of the Vincents of Boston. All her stories to date have looked into some aspect of the Vincents' life—of Gus and Rosie and their six children—and many of them have come together as the chapters of her novel, *Monkeys.*

Daniel Defoe was perhaps the first to discover the possibilities of an island world inhabited by a single character who is both actor and witness of everything. Minot has multiplied this viewpoint and made her island an urban one, but equally isolated and inescapable. In "Hiding"—which became the first chapter in *Monkeys*—the witness, ten-year-old Sophie, is unaware that she is telling a tragic story. Like Crusoe's hero, hers is an aloof description, and Minot has achieved in it a wonderfully oblique style. The novelist Penelope Gilliatt has called Minot's prose "a rarity in this windy age. It is clean, shapely, with the directness and precision of a child's letter. Explosive things occur, griefs, related in so calm and matter-of-fact a fashion that the even surface of the writing is never broken. The control of the narrative allows the true happening of tragedy."

Hiding

Our father doesn't go to church with us but we're all downstairs in the hall at the same time, bumbling, getting ready to go. Mum knuckles the buttons of Chicky's snowsuit till he's knot-tight, crouching, her heels lifted out of the backs of her shoes, her nylons creased at the ankles. She wears a black lace veil that stays on her hair like magic. Sherman ripples by, coat flapping, and Mum grabs him by the hood, reeling him in, and zips him up with a pinch at his chin. Gus stands there with his bottom lip out, waiting, looking like someone's smacked him except not that hard. Even though he's nine, he still wants Mum to do him up. Delilah comes half-hurrying down the stairs, late, looking like a ragamuffin with her skirt slid down to her hips and her hair all slept on wrong. Caitlin says, "It's about time." Delilah sweeps along the curve of the banister, looks at Caitlin who's all ready to go herself with her pea jacket on and her loafers and bare legs, and tells her, "You're going to freeze." Everyone's in a bad mood because we just woke up.

Dad's outside already on the other side of the French doors, waiting for us to go. You can tell it's cold out there by his white breath blowing by his cheek in spurts. He just stands on the porch, hands shoved in his black parka, feet pressed together, looking at the crusty snow on the lawn.

He doesn't wear a hat but that's because he barely feels the cold. Mum's the one who's warm-blooded. At skiing, she'll take you in when your toes get numb. You sit there with hot chocolate and a carton of french fries and the other mothers and she rubs your foot to get the circulation back. Down on the driveway the car is warming up and the exhaust goes straight up, disappearing in thin white curls.

"Okay, Monkeys," says Mum, filing us out the door. Chicky starts down the steps one red boot at a time till Mum whisks him up under a wing. The driveway is wrinkled over with ice so we take little shuffle steps across it, blinking at how bright it is, still only half-awake. Only the station wagon can fit everybody. Gus and Sherman scamper in across the huge backseat. Caitlin's head is the only one that shows over the front. (Caitlin is the oldest and she's twelve. I'm next, then Delilah, then the boys.) Mum rubs her thumbs on the steering wheel so that her gloves are shiny and round at the knuckles. Dad is doing things like checking the gutters, waiting till we leave. When we finally barrel down the hill, he turns and goes back into the house which is big and empty now and quiet.

We keep our coats on in church. Except for the O'Shaunesseys, we have the most children in one pew. Dad only comes on Christmas and Easter, because he's not Catholic. A lot of times you only see the mothers there. When Dad stays at home, he does things like cuts prickles in the woods or tears up thorns, or rakes leaves for burning, or just stands around on the other side of the house by the lilacs, surveying his garden, wondering what to do next. We usually sit up near the front and there's a lot of kneeling near the end. One time Gus got his finger stuck in the diamond-shaped holes of the heating vent and Mum had to yank it out. When the man comes around for the collection, we each put in a nickel or a dime and the handle goes by like a rake. If Mum drops in a five-dollar bill, she'll pluck out a couple of bills for her change.

The church is huge. Out loud in the dead quiet, a baby blares out *DAH-DEE*. We giggle and Mum goes *Ssshhh* but smiles too. A baby always yells at the quietest part. Only the girls are old enough to go to Communion; you're not allowed to chew it. The priest's neck is peeling and I try not to look. "He leaves me cold," Mum says when we leave, touching her forehead with a fingertip after dipping it into the holy water.

On the way home, we pick up the paper at Cage's and a bag of eight lollipops—one for each of us, plus Mum and Dad, even though Dad never eats his. I choose root beer. Sherman crinkles his wrapper, flicking his eyes around to see if anyone's looking. Gus says, "Sherman, you have to wait till after breakfast." Sherman gives a fierce look and shoves it in his mouth. Up in front, Mum, flicking on the blinker, says, "Take that out," with eyes in the back of her head.

Depending on what time of year it is, we do different things on the weekends. In the fall we might go to Castle Hill and stop by the orchard in Ipswich for cider and apples and red licorice. Castle Hill is closed after the summer so there's nobody else there and it's all covered with leaves. Mum goes up to the windows on the terrace and tries to peer in, cupping her hands around her eyes and seeing curtains. We do things like roll down the hills, making our arms stiff like mummies, or climb around on the marble statues which are really cold, or balance along the edge of the fountains without falling. Mum says *Be careful* even though there's no water in them, just red leaves plastered against the sides. When Dad notices us he yells *Get down*.

One garden has a ghost, according to Mum. A lady used to sneak out and meet her lover in the garden behind the grape trellis. Or she'd hide in the garden somewhere and he'd look for her and find her. But one night she crept out and he didn't come and didn't come and finally when she couldn't stand it any longer, she went crazy and ran off the cliff and killed herself and now her ghost comes back and keeps waiting. We creep into the boxed-in place smelling the yellow berries and the wet bark and Delilah jumps— "What was that?"—trying to scare us. Dad shakes the wood to see if it's rotten. We run ahead and hide in a pile of leaves. Little twigs get in your mouth and your nostrils; we hold still underneath listening to the brittle ticking leaves. When we hear Mum and Dad get close, we burst up to surprise them, all the leaves fluttering down, sputtering from the dust and tiny grits that get all over your face like grey ash, like Ash Wednesday. Mum and Dad just keep walking. She brushes a pine needle from his collar and he jerks his head, thinking of something else, probably that it's a fly. We follow them back to the car in a line all scruffy with leaf scraps.

After church, we have breakfast because you're not allowed to eat before. Dad comes in for the paper or a sliver of bacon. One thing about Dad, he has the weirdest taste. Spam is his favorite thing or this cheese that no one can stand the smell of. He barely sits down at all, glancing at the paper with his feet flat down on either side of him, ready to get up any minute to go back outside and sprinkle white fertilizer on the lawn. After, it looks like frost.

This Sunday we get to go skating at Ice House Pond. Dad drives. "Pipe down," he says into the back seat. Mum faces him with white fur around her hood. She calls him Uncs, short for Uncle, a kind of joke, I guess, calling him Uncs while he calls her Mum, same as we do. We are making a racket.

"Will you quit it?" Caitlin elbows Gus.

"What? I'm not doing anything."

"Just taking up all the room."

Sherman's in the way back. "How come Chicky always gets the front?"

"Cause he's the baby." Delilah is always explaining everything.

"I am not a baby," says Chicky without turning around. Caitlin frowns at me. "Who said you could wear my scarf?"

I ask into the front seat, "Can we go to the Fairy Garden?" even though I know we won't.

"Why couldn't Rummy come?"

Delilah says, "Because Dad didn't want him to."

Sherman wants to know how old Dad was when he learned how to skate.

Dad says, "About your age." He has a deep voice.

"Really?" I think about that for a minute, about Dad being Sherman's age.

"What about Mum?" says Caitlin.

This isn't his department so he just keeps driving. Mum shifts her shoulders more toward us but still looks at Dad.

"When I was a little girl on the Boston Common." Her teeth are white and she wears fuchsia lipstick. "We used to have skating parties."

Caitlin leans close to Mum's fur hood, crossing her arms into a pillow. "What? With dates?"

Mum bats her eyelashes. "Oh sure. Lots of beaux." She smiles, acting like a flirt. I look at Dad but he's concentrating on the road.

We saw one at a football game once. He had a huge mustard overcoat and bow tie and a pink face like a ham. He bent down to shake our tiny hands, half-looking at Mum the whole time. Dad was someplace else getting the tickets. His name was Hank. After he went, Mum put her sunglasses on her head and told us she used to watch him play football at BC. Dad never wears a tie except to work. One time Gus got lost. We waited until the last people had trickled out and the stadium was practically empty. It had started to get dark and the headlights were crisscrossing out of the parking field. Finally Dad came back carrying him, walking fast, Gus's head bobbing around and his face all blotchy. Dad rolled his eyes and made a kidding groan to Mum and we laughed because Gus was always getting lost. When Mum took him, he rammed his head onto her shoulder and hid his face while we walked back to the car, and under Mum's hand you could see his back twitching, trying to hide his crying.

We have Ice House Pond all to ourselves. In certain places the ice is bumpy and if you glide on it going *Aauuuuhhhh* in a low tone, your voice wobbles and vibrates. Every once in a while, a crack shoots across the pond, echoing just beneath the surface, and you feel something drop in the hollow of your back. It sounds like someone's jumped off a steel wire and left it twanging in the air.

I try to teach Delilah how to skate backwards but she's flopping all over the ice, making me laugh, with her hat lopsided and her mittens dangling out of her sleeves. When Gus falls, he just stays there, polishing the ice with his mitten. Dad sees him and says, "I don't care if my son is a violin player," kidding.

Dad played hockey in college and was so good his name is on a plaque that's right as you walk into the Harvard rink. He can go really fast. He takes off—*whooosh*—whizzing, circling at the edge of the pond, taking long strides, then gliding, chopping his skates, crossing over in little jumps. He goes zipping by and we watch him: his hands behind him in a tight clasp, his face as calm as if he were just walking along, only slightly forward. When he sweeps a corner, he tips in, then rolls into a hunch, and starts the long side-pushing again. After he stops, his face is red and the tears leak from the sides of his eyes and there's a white smudge around his mouth like frostbite. Sherman, copying, goes chopping forward on collapsed ankles and it sounds like someone sharpening knives.

Mum practices her 3s from when she used to figure skate. She pushes forward on one skate, turning in the middle like a petal flipped suddenly in the wind. We always make her do a spin. First she does backwards crossovers, holding her wrists like a tulip in her fluorescent pink parka, then stops straight up on her toes, sucking in her breath and dips, twisted, following her own tight circle, faster and faster, drawing her feet together. Whirring around, she lowers into a crouch, ventures out one balanced leg, a twirling whirl-pool, hot pink, rises again, spinning, into a blurred pillar or a tornado, her arms going above her head and her hands like the eye of a needle. Then suddenly: stop. Hiss of ice shavings, stopped. We clap our mittens. Her hood has slipped off and her hair is spread across her shoulders like when she's reading in bed, and she takes white breaths with her teeth showing and her pink mouth smiling. She squints over our heads. Dad is way off at the car, unlacing his skates on the tailgate but he doesn't turn. Mum's face means that it's time to go.

Chicky stands in the front seat leaning against Dad. Our parkas crinkle in the cold car. Sherman has been chewing on his thumb and it's a pointed black witch's hat. A rumble goes through the car like a monster growl and before we back up Dad lifts Chicky and sets him leaning against Mum instead.

The speed bumps are marked with yellow stripes and it's like sea serpents have crawled under the tar. When we bounce, Mum says, "Thank-you-Ma'am" with a lilt in her voice. If it was only Mum, the radio would be on and she'd turn it up on the good ones. Dad snaps it off because there's enough racket already. He used to listen to opera when he got home from work but not anymore. Now we give him hard hugs and he changes upstairs then goes into the TV room to the same place on the couch, propping his book on his crossed knees and reaching for his drink without looking up. At supper, he comes in for a handful of onion-flavored bacon crisps or a dish of miniature corn-on-the-cobs pickled. Mum keeps us in the kitchen longer so he can have a little peace and quiet. Ask him what he wants for Christmas and he'll say *No more arguing*. When Mum clears our plates, she takes a bite of someone's hot dog or a quick spoonful of peas before dumping the rest down the pig.

In the car, we ask Dad if we can stop at Shucker's for candy. When he doesn't answer, it means *No*. Mum's eyes mean *Not today*. She says, "It's treat night anyway." Treats are ginger ale and vanilla ice cream.

On Sunday nights we have treats and BLTs and get to watch Ted Mack and Ed Sullivan. There are circus people on almost every time, doing cartwheels or flips or balancing. We stand up in our socks and try some of it. Delilah does an imitation of Elvis by making jump rope handles into a microphone. Girls come on with silver shoes and their stomachs showing and do clappity tap dances. "That's a cinch," says Mum behind us.

"Let's see you then," we say and she goes over to the brick in front of the fireplace to show us. She bangs the floor with her sneakers, pumping and kicking, thudding her heels in smacks, not like clicking at all, swinging her arms out in front of her like she's wading through the jungle. She speeds up, staring straight at Dad who's reading his book, making us laugh even harder. He's always like that. Sometimes for no reason, he'll snap out of it going, "What? What? What's all this? What's going on?" as if he's emerged from a dark tunnel, looking like he does when we wake him up and he hasn't put on his glasses yet, sort of angry. He sits there before dinner, popping black olives into his mouth one at a time, eyes never leaving his book. His huge glass mug is from college and in the lamplight you can see the liquid separate. One layer is beer, the rest is gin. Even smelling it makes you gag.

Dad would never take us to Shucker's for candy. With him, we do things outside. If there's a storm we go down to the rocks to see the waves—you have to yell—and get sopped. Or if Mum needs a nap, we go to the beach. In the spring it's wild and windy as anything, which I love. The wind presses against you and you kind of choke but in a good way. Sherman and I run, run, run! Couples at the end are so far away you can hardly tell they're moving. Rummy races around with other dogs, flipping his rear like a goldfish, snapping at the air, or careening in big looping circles across the beach. Caitlin jabs a stick into the wet part and draws flowers. Chicky smells the seaweed by smushing it all over his face. Delilah's dark bangs jitter across her forehead like magnets and she yells back to Gus lagging behind. Dad looks at things far away. He points out birds— a great blue heron near the breakers as thin as a safety pin or an osprey in the sky, tilting like a paper cutout. We collect little things. Delilah holds out a razor shell on one sandy palm for Dad to take and he says *Uh-huh* and calls Rummy. When Sherman, grinning, carries a dead seagull to him,

Dad says, "Cut that out." Once in Maine, I found a triangle of blue and white china and showed it to Dad. "Ah, yes, a bit of crockery," he said.

"Do you think it's from the Indians?" I whispered. They had made the arrowheads we found on the beach.

"I think it's probably debris," he said and handed it back to me. According to Mum, debris is the same thing as litter, as in Don't Be a Litter Bug.

When we get home from skating, it's already started to get dark. Sherman runs up first and beats us to the door but can't open it himself. We are all used to how warm it was in the car so everybody's going *Brrrr,* or *Hurry up,* banging our feet on the porch so it thunders. The sky is dark blue glass and the railing seems whiter and the fur on Mum's hood glows. From the driveway Dad yells, "I'm going downtown. Be right back," slamming the door and starting the car again.

Delilah yells, "Can I come?" and Gus goes, "Me too!" as we watch the car back up.

"Right back," says his deep voice through the crack in the window and he rounds the side of the house.

"How come he didn't stop on the way home?" asks Caitlin, sticking out her chin.

"Yah," says Delilah. "How come?" We look at Mum.

She kicks the door with her boot. "In we go, Totsies," she says instead of answering and drops someone's skate on the porch because she's carrying so much stuff.

Gus gets in a bad mood, standing by the door with his coat on, not moving a muscle. His hat has flaps over the ears. Delilah flops onto the hall sofa, her neck bent, ramming her chin into her chest. "Why don't you take off your coat and stay awhile?" she says, drumming her fingers as slow as a spider on her stomach.

"I don't have to."

"Yah," Sherman butts in. "Who says you're the boss?" He's lying on the marble tile with Rummy, scissor-kicking his legs like windshield wipers.

"No one," says Delilah, her fingers rippling along.

On the piano bench, Caitlin is picking at her split ends. We can hear Mum in the kitchen putting the dishes away.

Banging on the piano fast because she knows it by heart, Caitlin plays "Walking in a Winter Wonderland." Delilah sits up and imitates her behind her back, shifting her hips from side to side, making us all laugh. Caitlin whips around, "What?"

"Nothing." But we can't help laughing.

"Nothing what?" says Mum coming around the corner, picking up mittens and socks from the floor, snapping on the lights.

Delilah stiffens her legs. "We weren't doing anything," she says.

We make room for Mum on the couch and huddle. Gus perches at the edge, sideways.

"When's Dad coming back?" he says.

"You know your father," says Mum vaguely, smoothing Delilah's hair on her lap, daydreaming at the floor but thinking about something. When Dad goes to the store, he only gets one thing, like a can of black bean soup or watermelon rind.

"What shall we play?" says Sherman, strangling Rummy in a hug.

"Yah. Yah. Let's do something," we say and turn to Mum.

She narrows her eyes into spying slits. "All rightee. I might have a little idea."

"What?" we all shout, excited. "What?" Mum hardly ever plays with us because she has to do everything else.

She rises, slowly, lifting her eyebrows, hinting. "You'll see."

"What?" says Gus and his bottom lip loosens nervously.

Delilah's dark eyes flash like jumping beans. "Yah, Mum. What?"

"Just come with me," says Mum in a singsong and we scamper after her. At the bottom of the stairs, she crouches in the middle of us. Upstairs behind her, it's dark.

"Where are we going?" asks Caitlin and everybody

watches Mum's face, thinking of the darkness up there.

"Hee hee hee," she says in her witch voice. "We're going to surprise your father, play a little trick."

"What?" asks Caitlin again, getting ready to worry but Mum's already creeping up the stairs so we follow, going one mile per hour like her, not making a peep even though there's no one in the house to hear us.

Suddenly she wheels around. "We're going to hide," she cackles.

"Where?" we all want to know, sneaking along like burglars.

Her voice is hushed. "Just come with me."

At the top of the stairs it is dark and we whisper.

"How about your room?" says Delilah. "Maybe under the bed."

"No," says Sherman breathlessly. "In the fireplace." We all laugh because we could never fit in there.

Standing in the hall, Mum opens the door to the linen closet and pulls the light string. "How about right here?" The light falls across our faces. On the shelves are stacks of bed covers and rolled puffs, red and white striped sheets and pink towels, everything clean and folded and smelling of soap.

All of a sudden Caitlin gasps, "Wait—I hear the car!"

Quickly we all jumble and scramble around, bumbling and knocking and trying to cram ourselves inside. Sherman makes whimpering noises like an excited dog. *Sshhhh*, we say or *Hurry Hurry*, or *Wait*. I knee up to a top shelf and Sherman gets a boost after me and then Delilah comes grunting up. We play in here sometimes. Gus and Chicky crawl into the shelf underneath, wedging themselves in sideways. Caitlin half-sits on molding with her legs dangling and one hand braced against the door frame. When the rushing settles, Mum pulls out the light and hikes herself up on the other ledge. Everyone is off the ground then, and quiet.

Delilah giggles. Caitlin says *Ssshhhh* and I say *Come on* in a whisper. Only when Mum says *Hush* do we all stop and listen. Everyone is breathing; a shelf creaks. Chicky knocks a towel off and it hits the ground like a pillow. Gus says, "I don't hear anything." *Sshhh*, we say. Mum touches the door and light widens and we listen. Nothing.

"False alarm," says Sherman.

Our eyes start to get used to the dark. Next to me Delilah gurgles her spit.

"What do you think he'll do?" whispers Caitlin. We all smile, curled up in the darkness with Mum thinking how fooled he'll be, coming back and not a soul anywhere, standing in the hall with all the lights glaring not hearing a sound.

"Where will he think we've gone?" We picture him looking around for a long time, till finally we all pour out of the closet.

"He'll find out," Mum whispers. Someone laughs at the back of his throat, like a cricket quietly ticking.

Delilah hisses, "Wait—"

"Forget it," says Caitlin who knows it's a false alarm.

"What will he do?" we ask Mum.

She's in the darkest part of the closet, on the other side of the light slant. We hear her voice. "We'll see."

"My foot's completely fallen asleep," says Caitlin.

"Kick it," says Mum's voice.

"Ssshhh," lisps Chicky and we laugh at him copying everybody.

Gus's muffled voice comes from under the shelf. "My head's getting squished."

"Move it," says Delilah.

"Quiet!"

And then we really do hear the car.

"Silence, Monkeys," says Mum and we all hush, holding our breaths. The car hums up the hill.

The motor dies and the car shuts off. We hear the door crack, then clip shut. Footsteps bang up the echoing porch, loud, toe-hard and scuffing. The glass panes rattle when the door opens, resounding in the empty hall, and then the door slams in the dead quiet, reverberating through the whole side of the house. Someone in the closet squeaks like a hamster. Downstairs there isn't a sound.

"Anybody home?" he bellows, and we try not to giggle.

Now what will he do? He strides across the deep hall, going by the foot of the stairs, obviously wondering where everybody's gone, stopping at the hooks to hang up his parka.

"What's he doing?" whispers Caitlin to herself.

"He's by the mitten basket," says Sherman. We all have smiles, our teeth like watermelon wedges, grinning in the dark.

He yells toward the kitchen, "Hello?" and we hunch our shoulders to keep from laughing, holding onto something tight like our toes or the shelf, or biting the side of our mouths.

He starts back into the hall.

"He's getting warmer," whispers Mum's voice, far away. We all wait for his footsteps on the stairs.

But he stops by the TV room doorway. We hear him rustling something, a paper bag, taking out what he's bought, the bag crinkling, setting something down on the hall table, then crumpling up the bag and pitching it in the wastebasket. Gus says, "Why doesn't he—?" *Ssshhh*, says Mum like spitting and we all freeze. He moves again—his footsteps turn and bang on the hollow threshold into the TV room where the rug pads the sound.

Next we hear the TV click on, the sound swelling and the dial switching *tick-ah tikka tikka tick* till it lands on a crowd roar, a football game. We can hear the announcer's voice and the hiss-breath behind it of cheering.

Then it's the only sound in the house.

"What do we do now?" says Delilah only half-whispering. Mum slips down from her shelf and her legs appear in the light, touching down.

Still hushed, Sherman goes, "Let's keep hiding."

The loud thud is from Caitlin jumping down. She uses her regular voice. "Forget it. I'm sick of this anyway." Everyone starts to rustle. Chicky panics, "I can't get down" as if we're about to desert him.

"Stop being such a baby," says Delilah, disgusted.

Mum doesn't say anything, just opens the door all the way. Past the banister in the hall it is yellow and bright. We climb out of the closet, feet-feeling our way down backwards, bumping out one at a time, knocking down blankets and washcloths by mistake. Mum guides our backs and checks our landings. We don't leave the narrow hallway. The light from downstairs shines up through the railing and casts shadows on the wall—bars of light and dark like a fence. Standing in it we have stripes all over us. *Hey look*, we say whispering, with the football drone in the background, even though this isn't anything new—we always see this, holding out your arms and seeing the stripes. Lingering near the linen closet we wait. Mum picks up the tumbled things, restacking the stuff we knocked down, folding things, clinching a towel with her chin, smoothing it over her stomach and then matching the corners left and right, like crossing herself, patting everything into neat piles. The light gets like this every night after we've gone to bed and we creep into the hall to listen to Mum and Dad downstairs. The bands of shadows go across our nightgowns and pajamas and we press our foreheads against the railing trying to hear the mumbling of what Mum and Dad are saying down there. Then we hear the deep boom of Dad clearing his throat and look up at Mum. Though she is turned away, we can still see the wince on her face like when you are waiting to be hit or right after you have been. So we keep standing there, our hearts pounding, waving our hands through the flickered stripes, suddenly interested the way you get when it's time to take a bath and you are mesmerized by something. We're stalling, waiting for Mum to finish folding, waiting to see what she's going to do next because we don't want to go downstairs yet, where Dad is, without her.

The Circus
Tibor Déry

Tibor Déry
(Hungary, 1894-1977)

A story collected by the brothers Grimm tells of a woodcutter who decided to feed his father out of a wooden bowl for fear that the old man, whose hands trembled with age, would break the clay dishes. The woodcutter's little son, seeing this, took hold of a large log and asked his father for tools to make it hollow. The woodcutter enquired what he meant to do with it. "I want to build a pig's trough," said the boy, "for you to eat out of when you're as old as grandfather." Children's play reflects the games of society: the business and manners of adults become the rituals of childhood, much like certain forms of popular theatre. We read into their games at our risk, as in Tibor Déry's "The Circus."

Perhaps Hungary's greatest modern writer, Tibor Déry had a keen eye for these "savage mirrors of society," as he called the games of children. Though he was a member of the Communist party between the wars, he despised the propaganda of social realism and turned instead to the French surrealists and to Dada. After the Hungarian uprising of 1956 he was imprisoned for three years, an experience that led him to write his brilliant novel of black humour, *Mr. G.A. in the City of X* (1964), a nightmarish utopia. Déry's *oeuvre* includes *Unfinished Sentence* (1948), *The Excommunicator* (1966) and *Imaginary Report on an American Rock Festival* (1971); but he is best known for his 1958 novel, *Niki: The Story of a Dog,* which has been translated into every major language.

The Circus

The children were bored. It was a stifling, hot, and dusty Sunday afternoon. The children's bare feet sank ankle-deep into the dust of the great courtyard enclosed by the flour mill to the left and the house on the right. Their eyebrows were grey with dust, and when they spat, dust grated in their teeth.

"What should we play now?" asked Manci. She was sitting on the porch steps staring at the dust in front of her. The other children hung lazily around her, standing first on one leg and then on the other; they were silent. Kalman, the watchmaker's son, wiped dust off his glasses with a large walnut leaf.

The house belonged to them now. The chief miller had left for Pest; his wife had gone to the farm to visit grandmother who was gravely ill. The mill was at a standstill. A Sunday stillness hung over the street outside; not even barking dogs could be heard. Traffic had been suspended since noon when a Catholic priest had passed the house, bells of the altar-boys growing louder, then dying away in the dense village silence. If anyone went down the street, the cloud of dust balling up behind him as it drifted toward the board fence betrayed his presence no matter how noiselessly he ambled along. All along the street, houses were shuttered against the burning sun, which drove everyone indoors. Only the mill yard was full of children and dogs.

"What should we play?" asked Manci.

They were all alone in the house. They could tear it down, or, if they felt like it, burn it to the ground. There were nine or ten little children and older ones from the neighborhood, as well as Manci, the fourteen-year-old daughter of the chief miller and her twin brother, Gyula. Until nightfall when their mother came home, nobody would know if they had axed every piece of furniture in the house or drowned every hen. But for the time being, they were sitting quietly, standing about in the dust eyeing each other.

"What should we play?" asked Manci. "Now we can play anything."

She had large grey eyes whose cold and sleepy stare flustered even some adults as she fixed them with her languidly searching gaze. Not even her mother had ever seen her cry, except from impotent rage. She bore every punishment in silence. But once when she was ten years old, at a taunt from her father, she had grabbed the kitchen knife on the table and with all her strength plunged it into the palm of her hand. The scar was visible to this day. This summer for the first time she sat alone in the yard underneath the mulberry tree and with her sleepy cold eyes she stared at the yard bathed in moonlight until her mother chased her off to bed.

"What should we play?"

The children were silent.

"We can play anything we want."

"Let's pretend we're having an Olympics," said Pista Deli, the son of the neighbor, a fairly prosperous peasant. A hot-blooded child with a short neck and red face, famous because he would soundly trounce even much older children if they dared look askance at his shortness. He had not yet tried his strength against Gyula, the chief miller's son who was the same age.

"Olympics?" said a girl's thin voice. "It's too hot."

"It'll be hot in Rome, too."

"No, let's not," said Dezso Trenka, the stonemason's son who lived next door. "Besides, it's boring."

Pista Deli turned toward Manci sitting on the porch steps. She fixed her large, brooding, cold grey eyes on him, looked at him for a while, then shook her head.

"Let's play doctor," said another girl.

"That'll be all right. The patient will die."

"Then we'll bury him."

"Where?"

Again they looked at Manci. The young girl's ivory neck and reddish-brown hair were impervious to the sun. Her face had only a faint pinkish glow below her long, tightly combed hair. And young bespectacled Kalman, scrawny son of the local watchmaker, stood behind the girl, leaning on one of the porch columns and studying the downy nape of her neck in rapt absorption; then a minute later, turning pale, he tore his gaze from her. It was obvious, even from behind, that the girl had nixed the idea.

"Let's play grocer's," said someone.

"Let's play ball."

"Let's play Tarzan."

Manci said nothing. "Let's play Tarzan," repeated a boy's voice. The young girl shook her head. "Today we can play anything," she said impatiently, "even something special."

"Let's give the brood-hen a bath."

"Let's go up to the attic."

The children grew silent. They stared ahead blankly, downcast. Three spotted dogs were lying side by side in the shade of the mulberry tree. One scrambled to its feet, circled the others, then threw itself on its side, tongue lolling, and sighed.

Young Kalman with the glasses stepped down from the porch, taking a deep breath. "Let's start the mill," he said with lowered eyes. "If we get it started, we can grind 20 sacks full."

"What for?"

Kalman blushed and said nothing. The girl looked disdainfully at the silent children. "You're all stupid," she said quietly to the dust at her feet. "You can't find anything to do."

"Go to hell!" said Pista Deli. "Don't you tell us what to do!"

Manci got up, slowly and lazily stretched herself. She smiled and shrugged her shoulders. "Where are you going?" asked Piri Trenka, alarmed. "Wait! I'm coming with you."

"You don't have to," said Manci without turning around. Her legs, covered only to the knees by the short cotton cambric skirt, were girlishly round and as white as her arms and neck. "I'm going inside to read."

Although Busan, largest of the three dogs, was lying with his hindside to the porch, he raised his head and looked back. He pondered for a moment, then got up and, tail wagging, set off after the girl. At this moment, the sharp cracking of a whip was heard from the other end of the porch, short and hard like a gunshot. "You're staying here!" said Gyula, the head miller's son, and again he cracked his short-handled, leather-thonged whip. It was impossible to tell whether the command was meant for his sister or the dog. Both stopped. "You're idiots," said the boy, turning his pale face with the great blaze of red hair toward the children. "Idiots."

"Who's an idiot?" asked Pista Deli.

"You're one too."

The squat, short-necked child bowed his head; blood rushed to his forehead. "Why am I an idiot?" he said in a muffled voice.

"Ask your Papa," said Gyula, smiling disdainfully and squinting. He turned his long freckled face toward the sun. "Manci is right. If I weren't here, no one would know what to do."

"I know," said Pista Deli.

He turned and started for the gate. With his disproportionately wide back, short legs and arms, he seemed shorter than he really was. Gyula waited till he reached the gate. "Wait, idiot!" he shouted after him in his rather thin, rasping voice. "I need you, come back!"

Pista Deli stopped, but did not turn around. The other children listened silently without moving. On the porch, Manci was also standing with her back to the group, only her head turned out of curiosity.

"Come back!" said Gyula. "I've found something to do."

The circus game the gang was going to play for the first time required every hand, every head. The oppressive heat seemed to suddenly give way; unseen sweat poured down the high-spirited children's backs. Mozsi Beck, the poultry contractor's son, ran home with two companions to fetch empty chicken coops in which to put the menagerie. "Hey, bring your little brother too!" shouted Gyula. "Your youngest brother!"

"Why him?" said Mozsi Beck, "he still wets his pants."

"Just bring him!"

"What for?"

"He'll be the ape," said Gyula.

They had to get a handcart, at least two of them, to transport the menagerie. Dezso brought a little trap-like two-wheeled handcart from home; assistants had to help bring it over. Pista Deli stole rabbits from the courtyards, complete with pens whenever possible. If he couldn't find pens, he brought them naked under his coat; they were put in Beck's chicken coops. There were plenty of cats, dogs, even pigeons in the mill yard. But it wouldn't hurt to add one or two. The mill yard, wearily on the verge of slumber a moment ago, in an eye-wink roused itself from dusty summer sleep and man and beast began to whirl around the leader, Gyula, like electrons. The initial excited shouting was succeeded by the tense silence of creative work, broken only by the joyous yelping of dogs thrown into confusion and rushing about in every direction. Young Kalman leaned against the porch, and wiped his glasses.

"What did you bring from home?"

"Nothing," said Kalman.

In the village, one seldom came across suitable raw materials for a circus in the household of the watchmaker's widow. Gyula, sinking his hands into his pants pockets, looked the thin, round-shouldered boy up and down scornfully.

"Go help Pista Deli!"

"No."

"Why not?"

"I don't want to," said Kalman.

Blinking, Gyula turned his long, freckled face toward the sun. "I can't hear you. Speak up!"

"I don't want to," repeated Kalman.

"You don't want to?" asked Gyula, incredulous in a sing-song. "You don't want to. What do you mean you don't want to? I don't understand. I said, go help Pista Deli."

He raised his whip and slashed it into the dust, exactly an inch from Kalman's naked toes. A tiny round cloud of dust rose suddenly in its wake. The boy with the glasses involuntarily stepped back.

"Stop jumping!" said Gyula. "What are you jumping for? I tell you, go help Pista Deli."

The boy with glasses, his face pale, stared at the tiny cloud of dust whirling at his feet.

"Well, what are you going to do?" asked Gyula and his face was still full of surprise.

"He can't go," said Manci, behind his back at this moment. "I need Kalman."

"What for?"

Rather than answer, the girl laughed softly. She had a clear, bell-like laugh. The thick crystal vase that her father had taken in the war from an Arrow-Cross member's house, a man who'd fled the country, rang with the sound of her laughter. Gyula looked at his sister and screwed up his face.

"You need him?"

"What of it?"

Gyula stood for a moment longer, then turned without a word and walked away.

"Are you coming?"

"I'm coming," said Kalman, his ears burning. The young girl had already turned around; she could not see the boy's enraptured look beneath his self-conscious glasses.

"Oh, what a fine game it will be!"

"Yes," said Kalman. "What do you need me for?

"Oh, they'll be delicious," shouted the girl. "We'll eat heaps of cold, sweet melons."

Kalman quickened his pace. "What do you need me for?"

The girl laughed. "For all kinds of things. Don't you want to come?"

"Yes."

"Then why do you ask?"

Suddenly she shot off. The dust her feet stirred rose toward her tiny waist like a long, light train. Reaching the porch, she turned and waited for the boy striding along slowly and manfully.

"Or don't you want to come?" she said, fixing her coldly pensive, sleepy gaze on the boy's face.

"Now what do we do?" asked the boy.

In the room darkened by the shuttered windows, Piri Trenka knelt in front of the bottom drawer of the large dresser and cautiously lifted the heavy cool sheets and eiderdown cases placed one on top of the other. The plank floor was covered with linoleum; two rows of preserve jars stood on the dresser top, half their contents dried up. The air was cool, musty and made one shiver with pleasure. Kalman had never been in this room before.

"Not there!" said Manci. "There's nothing there."

Even in the gloomy room it was apparent that his face was flushed with excitement. Piri Trenka's groping hands were shaking, her tousled black hair kept falling into her sweating forehead.

"I tell you, there's nothing there."

"Well, where then?"

"In the wardrobe. Maybe on the top drawer."

"Can I help?" asked Kalman, who had visibly drawn courage from Piri Trenka's presence. "What should

I look for?"

"As a matter of fact, I'm going to be a bride," said Manci, opening the wardrobe. "There's a bride in every circus; she rides a black horse and leads the procession. The groom follows her on horseback or on foot. Then come the animals and the clowns."

Kalman swallowed hard.

"What am I going to be?" he asked after a while.

"I don't know yet. Do you want to be a clown?"

"No," said Kalman firmly.

"You don't want to be the groom, do you?"

The girl laughed a thin laugh. Her eyes sparkled in the gloom. Piri Trenka giggled. "All right, we'll see," said Manci. "Now come here and take down Papa's linen suit. This will be Gyula's because the ringmaster always wears a white suit."

Kalman was allowed to stay in the room, but he had to face the wall while Manci changed. Among her mother's things, she could not find a white dress to serve as a wedding gown. She had to make do with a grey silk dress for which they dug up a little white lace collar from the top drawer of the dresser. Piri Trenka pinned the dress up all around because it was too long. While Kalman stared at the stains on the whitewashed wall, the young girls were whispering ceaselessly behind his back. From time to time, a suppressed, titillating giggle would burst from the cloud of whispers, tickle his neck and make it break out into goosebumps. The clomping of shoes could be heard on the linoleum. A pair of white stockings and old-fashioned high-heeled black leather pumps from the dresser turned up on the young girl's white feet, of course, after a thorough foot washing.

"Don't you turn around!" shrieked Piri Trenka.

"I won't," said Kalman standing stiffly beside the wall with burning red ears.

They ransacked the house for a bridal veil in vain; finally they had to make do with the dirty tulle curtain that Piri Trenka pinned with a few wire hairpins to Manci's reddish-brown curls. But when the bride in the grey silk dress, with the curtain on her head reaching to her waist and her loudly thumping patent-leather shoes slipping off her feet, finally marched onto the porch with shining eyes, there was such a hullaballoo raging in the mill yard that no one noticed her enchanting presence; even less Kalman's wide-brimmed black felt hat, emblem of his rank as groom, which, though it was stuffed with straw, kept slipping over his ears.

Now fifteen or twenty children were rushing about in the yard beneath the burning sun, screaming at the top of their lungs, red faces shiny with sweat. Three handcarts stood in front of the rusty fly-wheel leaning against the wall of the mill. The two-wheeled street barrow which Dezso Trenka had surreptitiously sneaked out of his father's house was behind the carts. In the corner of the courtyard, where three or four old millstones were lying about in burnt-out yellow grass, chicken coops and wicker baskets and larger goose pens were piling up; with tireless zeal, Mozsi Beck and his pals had transported them from the poultry contractor's courtyard. Also, on the millstone slabs the other indispensable paraphernalia of the circus were gathered together—ropes, chains, a box of red minium paint, a washbasin, cooking-pots and lids, wooden spoons, a sausage stuffer and a large brass trumpet glittering like gold that a member of the volunteer fire department band had, unbeknownst to him, donated to the circus.

Gyula, in his blindingly white linen suit, stood whip in hand on the well-curb and directed troop movements. A pair of dogs had already been harnessed to the handcarts and most of the members of the menagerie were in place. A large red cat was huddled in one of the cages bearing this sign: LION, BE CAREFUL: HE BITES! BEWARE OF LION!

Two large white rabbits posing as polar bears were lying on their stomachs in a small wicker basket, restlessly twitching their noses. There were plenty of birds of prey, eagles, vultures and falcons, exactly as many chickens, geese, ducks as the children could carry to the mill yard. A

parrot was screeching in a frenzy of joy above the tiger. The
most splendid specimen of the menagerie, the anthropoid
ape, was at that moment being led by hand toward the
ringmaster by Mozsi Beck when Manci, Kalman and Piri
Trenka stepped onto the porch.

"Undress him!" said Gyula appraising the flawless
superb specimen.

"But he's only wearing these drawers," said Mozsi Beck.

"Those too!"

Mozsi Beck looked ahead, frowning, a worried look on
his face. "What are you going to do with him?"

"Nothing," said Gyula. "We'll lock him up in a cage and
we'll put him on exhibit."

"That's not a good idea!"

Pista Deli laughed so hard he had to hold his sides. "Why
isn't it a good idea?"

"He'll cry," said Mozsi Beck.

"So?"

"Why should my little brother be the ape?" said Mozsi
Beck. "There's lots of little kids around here. I brought ten
cages for the circus."

Gyula impatiently cracked his whip. "What are you
haggling for! Everybody brings what they have. If you don't
like it, you can go to hell."

Pista Deli guffawed with laughter. Even his neck turned
red.

"What are you laughing at?" said Gyula. "It's not funny.
Grab him and take off his clothes. We're going to put him
in this cage."

They had left the largest wicker cage empty for the ape.
Pista Deli jerked the little black pants off the child, then
picked him up under the arms and lowered him into the
cage through the narrow opening of the lid. All the *artistes*
and other employees of the circus gathered around the cage;
having heard news of the recent acquisition they yelled
wildly and watched the spectacle. The ape stood up to his
armpits in the cage, motionless, clutching the willow twigs
of the lid, and mutely he ran his astonished, frightened eyes

over the screaming crowd. His tiny, pale face was twisted
with fright, but he did not cry.

"Oh! He won't fit," said Piri Trenka.

"Of course he'll fit! All he has to do is pull in his neck."

Manci arranged her bridal veil, which kept slipping onto
her nose. With an unconscious, wan smile on her face, her
eyes were shining.

"He won't fit if he sits down," said a boy's voice. "Only if
he lies down curled up."

Kalman was standing behind Manci. "This should not
be allowed," he said surprised and indignant.

The girl kept staring at the cage.

" Do you hear, Manci?"

"Be quiet," said the girl without turning around. "Be
quiet!"

Pista Deli clutched the ape, still half-protruding from the
cage, and pushed him down by the shoulders. "Sit down,"
he shouted in his ear as if he were deaf. "Squat down, don't
you understand? Damn you, sit down!"

"Slap him!" yelled a voice from behind. "Then he'll sit
down.

The excitement spread to the dogs. Busan began to howl,
a long-drawn-out sound like a wolf. A smaller dog named
Didujka who could not free himself from his harness
emitted ear-splitting yelps and threw his body to and fro
like an epileptic. The two dogs harnessed in front of the
second cart also barked and growled in alarm. The eagles
and vultures in the cages were gabbling mightily. The lion,
its hair on end, stared out into the dust with round green
eyes.

The sun had long passed its zenith by the time the
procession got underway. Though inside the courtyard it
had provided an edifying spectacle, it reached full splendor
only when it could unfold its entire length on the street in
thick clouds of dust. Andris Kiss, the herald, led the way.
His naked upper body had been smeared from neck to navel
with dazzling red minium paint. With the gleaming brass
trumpet raised to his lips and his father's fireman's hat on

his head, he looked like an archangel. On either side of him, a step or two behind, followed drummers who accompanied the trumpet air by beating rhythmically on pots hung around their necks. Meanwhile, they strained their throats carrying out their duties as town criers. At the sound of their voices, the gates opened and filled and along the length of the street, more and more children, as from a frayed string of pearls, twirled on both sides of the procession.

A few steps behind the herald, the ringmaster marched alone in his blindingly white suit, cracking his whip. He was wearing white lady's gloves and a woman's straw hat, an attached wide red silk ribbon hanging down to his shoulders. The bride followed him, also alone in the procession. Unfortunately, her sleek bay steed had gone lame so she had to wobble in the dust on foot. She stepped along with downcast eyes, befitting a bride, looking neither right nor left. Directly behind her, barely a few steps away, marched Kalman the bridegroom, his glasses glittering bravely under his huge black hat. Unfortunately, apart from his dignified bearing and triumphant look, no clear outward sign indicated his status as bridegroom.

Following the vanguard came vehicles, interspersed here and there with an *artiste* walking by himself. Here, the noise and dust were greatest. The dogs pulling vehicles were barking vociferously; birds of prey were crying and crowing; the personnel designated to care for the lion, tiger and polar bears were yelling at the top of their lungs. Heading the line was the little two-wheeled street barrow carrying Eszti Bodor, the fortune-teller, hanging onto the sides of the cart with both hands. She was dressed in a flour sack held together under her arms by a thick rope; her head was covered with a large black silk scarf. Four short assistants pushed the heavy cart.

"What's this?" asked the onlookers.

"This is Robinson, the world-famous fortune-teller," shouted the herald who marched beside the cart, waving a national flag above his head. "She tells fortunes night and day and she'll tell your fortune for only ten cents. A week ago she stated the score of the Hungarian-English game, six to three, and she prophesied the flood. This is Robinson, the world-famous fortune-teller."

The news of the circus far preceded its coming. Old women stood before the gates, shaking their heads disapprovingly and shutting smaller children up in the house. Older girls ran out into the street and, giggling, they watched the pack of children growing more and more enthusiastic marching down the middle of the road. "Of course, it's that chief miller's boy who put them up to it," said a woman. "That brat should be given a good lickin'."

"The girl's the villain," said another woman. "She's the one that stirs them up."

"That's the one!"

"She'll be a great whore someday, that one will!" said the first woman, watching the girl in the white veil.

The head of the procession had already turned onto Rakoczi street, when the sound of the bugle suddenly faded away. One wheel of the fortune-teller's cart turned into the ditch with a great thud and Pythia swayed back and forth in the cart. The geese shut up in the crates gaggled piteously as they cooked in the merciless sun.

"They should never have been left alone!"

"The head miller went up to Pest. I saw him at the station this morning. His wife went to the farm to see her desperately ill mother."

Behind the fortune-teller's cart marched Pista Deli. His chest was thrust out and he was swinging his torso stripped to the waist and flexing his arm muscles, showing them off as boxers do. Around his neck he wore a rusty well-chain that he could break in two with one yank. Unfortunately, the terrifying rattle of the chain was muffled by the howls of the caged wild beasts. Behind him in a separate cart pulled by two dogs, the greatest attraction of the circus approached, the anthropomorphic ape. Hiding his face in his arms, legs drawn up to his belly, the thin brown body lay motionless in the cage.

"Hey, Laci," shouted a country lad leaning on one of the

gates. "What's in that cage?"

"An ape."

"What's its name?"

"Ape."

"But what's its real name?"

"It doesn't have a real name," said a little girl.

The young fellow laughed. "Have you ever seen a cart push the horses?"

Standing in the middle of the street, the children looked at each other. As a matter of fact, the dogs were not really pulling the cart; on the contrary, to make the cart go at all they had to be pushed by their behinds. But this was so only in reality and reality doesn't count.

"These are good horses!" shouted Sanyi Brio, one of the cart pushers, pertly. "These are good pulling horses. I can barely hold the cart back so they don't run off with it."

The band marched next to the ape cage. Two children on both sides of the cage were using pot lids as crashing cymbals. Two more were carrying a large enamel washbasin on which a third child was drumming as hard as he could with a sausage stuffer, disregarding pieces of enamel flying around. Members of the band who were not so adept at music kept the rhythm by beating on pots and pans or trumpeting into funnels.

When a pack of gypsy children on one of the street corners attached themselves to the procession, the ringmaster beckoned to a drummer in front of him.

"Run back, Peter," he ordered him, "and tell the men to keep an eye on the gypsies or else they'll steal the eagles and vultures from the cages."

"What eagles?"

"Idiot!"

"Oh, I understand," said the drummer.

"I will whip anyone to a pulp who dares steal anything," said the ringmaster, turning his long freckled face and fiery red hair covered by a little straw hat. He glared severely at the messenger. "Then get back to your place immediately."

"I'm going," said the boy. "Shouldn't we pass the hat?"

The ringmaster gave him a withering look. "Whoever dares to beg," he shouted in his thin, rasping, adolescent's voice, "will be expelled from the procession. And then I will whip him bloody," he added for greater emphasis while he pulled up his white pants with both hands since, in spite of the tight belt, they were continually slipping down to his bare feet. "Come on, move!"

Mozsi Beck marched beside the ape cage. Hangdog, he looked neither right nor left, his ears standing out from his head were burning red from shame. Beside him, one of the acrobats, who had taken a wide red velvet ribbon from the head miller's dresser and tied it around his neck as an emblem of his craft, was uttering cries and turning cart wheels. A seven- or eight-year-old little girl whirled around her own axis until she got dizzy and laughing uproariously, fell headlong into the dust.

The more the troupe advanced, the more easily and enthusiastically it showed off feats and stunts before the wonder-struck audience lining the length of the street. It almost seemed as if the *artistes* were infected with genuine enthusiasm beyond professional skill, and now they were performing difficult and highly responsible work for the sake of the game, as it were, free of charge. When they'd set off, they had timidly sidestepped the council president's wagon and the trotting cow tied behind it. However, by the time they reached the school, they very nearly trampled Kalman Tapodi, the old cowherd of the Petofi Collective Farm who, unsuspecting and defenceless, rode his bicycle toward them down the middle of the road. A few men, pushing wheelbarrows on their way back to the threshing machine after Sunday rest, shook their heads as they drew over to the side of the road to avoid the procession which was growing by leaps and bounds, having absorbed half the village children.

Mozsi Beck, walking beside the ape cage, suddenly broke into a run and passing the strong man, the carriage of the fortune-teller, the Bridegroom and the Bride, ran up to the ringmaster.

"Gyula," he panted, "we have to take the child out of the cage."

"Address me as ringmaster."

Mozsi Beck's face twitched nervously.

"Don't you hear?"

"Ringmaster, sir," said Moszi Beck. "We have to let the child out of the cage."

"I don't know what you're talking about. What child?"

"Well, the child."

"I don't hear you. Which child?" repeated the ringmaster.

"The ape," said Mozsi Beck, having pondered a while.

The ringmaster looked him up and down without saying a word. "How dare you step out of line!" he shouted, knitting his brows sternly. "Get out! Go back to your place, on the double." In the heat of the discussion, both children had unconsciously slowed down and the bride and groom walking behind caught up with them. "What's the matter with you?" asked Manci.

"We have to let the child out of the cage," said Mozsi Beck.

"Which child?" asked Manci, fixing her lazily pensive eyes on the boy's face.

"The ape,"pleaded Mozsi Beck.

"Why?"

"He's crying."

There was a silence for a moment.

"He's crying?" asked Manci.

"His whole body is shaking," said Mozsi Beck. "Even his legs are trembling."

The girl's large grey eyes immediately filled with tears. "Poor little ape," she said softly to herself. "I've never seen an ape cry."

"Get back to your place," said the ringmaster, lashing his whip in front of Mozsi Beck's feet. "If you don't take your place immediately I'll hit you in the face. About face!"

The boy jumped back and raised his trembling hands protectively. "That's not an ape; he's a child," he said, deathly pale. "He must be taken out of the cage!"

"What did you say?" asked the ringmaster.

"That's not an ape," said the boy defiantly. "My little brother is not an ape."

Gyula raised his whip and struck Mozsi Beck. Calculating the blow, the leather thong whistled in front of the child's face and struck his naked neck. Mozsi Beck cried out in pain, helplessly clutching his naked neck. Again Gyula raised his whip. But before he could strike, Mozsi Beck turned and ran off crying loudly.

"Still, the child should be released!" said Kalman the Groom.

Meanwhile, the fortune-teller's cart and Pista Deli, the strong man walking behind her, caught up to the ring-master's group. In front, the herald with his minium-red torso and golden archangel's trumpet also stopped and turned around, and the two drummers stopped drumming. The procession piled up.

"We must release the child!" said Kalman slowly, firmly, turning his pale bespectacled face toward the ringmaster. "A human being should not be shut up in a cage!"

The ringmaster was occupied with his pants: owing to the sudden movements they had slipped down again. Kalman looked at Manci standing beside him. The girl was smiling mysteriously.

"What are you interfering for?" said Gyula. "You all should have stayed in Auschwitz. Now, come on, everybody go back to your places. Let's go!"

Kalman shook his head. "No. First, release the child!"

"It's none of your business!" shouted the ringmaster, and snatching his whip from under his arm, he whirled it in a wide circle above his head. "Back to your place!"

"First, release the child!" said Kalman in a trembling voice. "I'm not going back until you let him out."

"You're not going?"

Unblinking, the two boys stared at each other. Gyula was taller by a head than the young bespectacled boy; his grey eyes were colder, his muscles more resolute. If it came to a fight, he could obviously make short work of his opponent.

Kalman was deathly pale, his knees shaking. He looked at Manci. The young girl with her mysterious smile fixed her dreamy lazy eyes on his face.

"Manci?" said Kalman, swallowing hard. His mouth was full of dust, his back bathed in sweat. He looked at the young girl, who nodded imperceptibly.

"Release the child, Gyula!" said Kalman. "You must not lock a human being in a cage!"

All the children had gathered around the opponents. There was such a silence that even the last row could hear a little girl's excited whisper. Gyula glanced around at the silently waiting children. "Everyone back to their places!" he shouted, and smiling scornfully, he raised his whip. Those standing up front flinched and moved back. The circle widened, thinned out and began to disperse.

"What are you waiting for?" asked Gyula maliciously of the bespectacled boy standing before him. Suddenly he lashed his whip at Kalman's feet and the thick dust puffed up in a dense little cloud over Kalman's naked toes. Kalman looked around. The others were slinking away. Only Manci was still beside him, standing a few steps away. Obviously, the command didn't affect her. Pista Deli's broad, indifferent back was visible as he slowly ambled by the fortune-teller's cart.

"Release the child!" said Kalman, swallowing hard, his head lowered as though trying to protect his glasses from the raised whip. "I'm not leaving until you release him."

A wagon stopped unnoticed on the side of the road, directly beside them; the dust and the excitement had swallowed the rumbling wheels. A tall woman dressed in black was sitting in the back of the wagon on a plank.

"Gyula!" whispered Manci, covering her face with her hands. "It's Mama!"

The boy suddenly lowered his raised whip and turned around. Shoulders hunched, blinking in fright, he looked at the wagon enveloped in the dense cloud of dust. "Get on!" said the woman sitting on the wagon. Her eyes were red with weeping. She glanced quickly at the grey silk bridal gown, the white linen suit, then turned away without a word. The two children huddled around her feet in the straw and the wagon set off. None said a word. Instead of the high-laced shoes she'd been wearing when she left home, grandma's loose, comfortable slipper was flopping on their mother's aching, swollen foot. Manci stared at it for a while with wide eyes, then suddenly burst into tears.

"Did she die?" she asked sobbing.

She loved her grandmother even more than her parents. Gyula too grew pale; all his freckles stood out on his face. The wagon rumbled by the disintegrating circus procession leaving the monkey cage lingering behind, the sobbing ape sitting beside it in the dust; then, in a few moments, it turned into the mill yard.

Translated from the Hungarian by Elizabeth Csicsery-Rónay

A Mother in India
Sara Jeannette Duncan

Sara Jeannette Duncan

(Canada, 1861-1922)

Canadian literature suffers from introspection, but the exceptions outshine the rule. Next to the sagas of life in the frozen north, we have Margaret Laurence's Africa, Mavis Gallant's Paris, Timothy Findley's Europe, Sara Jeannette Duncan's India. Born in Brantford over a century ago, in what is now the province of Ontario, Duncan decided at a very early age to become a writer. Rosemary Sullivan, in her introduction to a collection of Duncan's stories, *The Pool in the Desert*, quotes the author herself: "I remember once entertaining, and unguardedly expressing, at the age of nine, a wild desire to write a novel. 'Put it out of your mind, my dear,' nodded a placid old lady of the last century over her knitting. 'Novel-making women always come to some bad end.' " Before writing novels, Duncan became a journalist. In quick succession, she wrote for the Toronto *Globe*, the Washington *Post* and the Montreal *Star*. Together with another journalist, Lily Lewis, she travelled to Vancouver, Japan, Ceylon, India, Suez and Cairo, and collected her travel writing in *A Social Departure* (1890). Duncan's best fiction is set in India: *The Simple Adventures of a Memsahib* (1893), *Set in Authority* (1906) and *The Burnt Offering* (1909), but Canadian school curricula have preferred her portrait of Brantford (alias Elgin) in *The Imperialist* (1904).

"A Mother in India" has the complicated subtlety of Henry James, to whom she has been often, and accurately, compared, and offers to the curious reader an illuminating contrast with the present-day renegade mother in Sandra Birdsell's "The Rock Garden."

A Mother in India

CHAPTER I

There were times when we had to go without puddings to pay John's uniform bills, and always I did the facings myself with a cloth-ball to save getting new ones. I would have polished his sword, too, if I had been allowed; I adored his sword. And once, I remember, we painted and varnished our own dog-cart, and very smart it looked, to save fifty rupees. We had nothing but our pay—John had his company when we were married, but what is that?—and life was made up of small knowing economies, much more amusing in recollection than in practise. We were sodden poor, and that is a fact, poor and conscientious, which was worse. A big fat spider of a money-lender came one day into the veranda and tempted us—we lived in a hut, but it had a veranda—and John threatened to report him to the police. Poor when everybody else had enough to live in the open-handed Indian fashion, that was what made it so hard; we were alone in our sordid little ways. When the expectation of Cecily came to us we made out to be delighted, knowing that the whole station pitied us, and when Cecily came herself, with a swamping burst of expense, we kept up the pretense splendidly. She was peevish, poor little thing, and she threatened convulsions from the beginning, but we

both knew that it was abnormal not to love her a great deal,
more than life, immediately and increasingly; and we
applied ourselves honestly to do it, with the thermometer at
a hundred and two, and the nurse leaving at the end of a
fortnight because she discovered that I had only six of
everything for the table. To find out a husband's virtues,
you must marry a poor man. The regiment was under-
officered as usual, and John had to take parade at daylight
quite three times a week; but he walked up and down the
veranda with Cecily constantly till two in the morning,
when a little coolness came. I usually lay awake the rest of
the night in fear that a scorpion would drop from the
ceiling on her. Nevertheless, we were of excellent mind
towards Cecily; we were in such terror, not so much of
failing in our duty towards her as towards the ideal standard
of mankind. We were very anxious indeed not to come
short. To be found too small for one's place in nature would
have been odious. We would talk about her for an hour at a
time, even when John's charger was threatening glanders
and I could see his mind perpetually wandering to the
stable. I would say to John that she had brought a new
element into our lives—she had indeed!—and John would
reply, "I know what you mean," and go on to prophesy that
she would "bind us together." We didn't need binding
together; we were more to each other, there in the desolation
of that arid frontier outpost, than most husbands and wives;
but it seemed a proper and hopeful thing to believe, so we
believed it. Of course, the real experience would have come,
we weren't monsters; but fate curtailed the opportunity. She
was just five weeks old when the doctor told us that we must
either pack her home immediately or lose her, and the very
next day John went down with enteric. So Cecily was sent to
England with a sergeant's wife who had lost her twins, and I
settled down under the direction of a native doctor, to fight
for my husband's life, without ice or proper food, or
sickroom comforts of any sort. Ah! Fort Samila, with the
sun glaring up from the sand! — however, it is a long time
ago now. I trusted the baby willingly to Mrs Berry and to

Providence, and did not fret; my capacity for worry, I
suppose, was completely absorbed. Mrs Berry's letter,
describing the child's improvement on the voyage and safe
arrival came, I remember, the day on which John was
allowed his first solid mouthful; it had been a long siege.
"Poor little wretch!" he said when I read it aloud; and after
that Cecily became an episode.

She had gone to my husband's people; it was the best
arrangement. We were lucky that it was possible; so many
children had to be sent to strangers and hirelings. Since an
unfortunate infant must be brought into the world and set
adrift, the haven of its grandmother and its Aunt Emma and
its Aunt Alice certainly seemed providential. I had absolutely no cause for anxiety, as I often told people,
wondering that I did not feel a little all the same. Nothing, I
knew, could exceed the conscientious devotion of all three
Farnham ladies to the child. She would appear upon their
somewhat barren horizon as a new and interesting duty,
and the small additional income she also represented would
be almost nominal compensation for the care she would
receive. They were excellent persons of the kind that talk
about matins and vespers, and attend both. They helped
little charities and gave little teas, and wrote little notes, and
made deprecating allowance for the eccentricities of their
titled or moneyed acquaintances. They were the subdued,
smiling, unimaginatively dressed women on a small de-
finite income that you meet at every rectory garden-party in
the country, a little snobbish, a little priggish, wholly conventional, but apart from these weaknesses, sound and
simple and dignified, managing their two small servants
with a display of the most exact traditions, and keeping a
somewhat vague and belated but constant eye upon the
doings of their country as chronicled in a bi-weekly paper.
They were all immensely interested in royalty, and would
read paragraphs aloud to each other about how the Princess
Beatrice or the Princess Maud had opened a fancy bazaar,
looking remarkably well in plain grey poplin trimmed
with Irish lace—an industry which, as is well known, the

Royal Family has set its heart on rehabilitating. Upon which Mrs Farnham's comment invariably would be, "How thoughtful of them, dear!" and Alice would usually say, "Well, if I were a princess, I should like something nicer than plain grey poplin." Alice, being the youngest, was not always expected to think before she spoke. Alice painted in water-colours, but Emma was supposed to have the most common sense.

They took turns in writing to us with the greatest regularity about Cecily; only once, I think, did they miss the weekly mail, and that was when she threatened diphtheria and they thought we had better be kept in ignorance. The kind and affectionate terms of these letters never altered except with the facts they described—teething, creeping, measles, cheeks growing round and rosy, all were conveyed in the same smooth, pat, and proper phrases, so absolutely empty of any glimpse of the child's personality that after the first few months it was like reading about a somewhat uninteresting infant in a book. I was sure Cecily was not uninteresting, but her chroniclers were. We used to wade through the long, thin sheets and saw how much more satisfactory it would be when Cecily could write to us herself. Meanwhile we noted her weekly progress with much the feeling one would have about a far-away little bit of property that was giving no trouble and coming on exceedingly well. We would take possession of Cecily at our convenience; till then, it was gratifying to hear of our unearned increment in dear little dimples and sweet little curls.

She was nearly four when I saw her again. We were home on three months' leave; John had just got his first brevet for doing something which he does not allow me to talk about in the Black Mountain country; and we were fearfully pleased with ourselves. I remember that excitement lasted well up to Port Said. As far as the Canal, Cecily was only one of the pleasures and interests we were going home to: John's majority was the thing that really gave savour to life. But the first faint line of Europe brought my child to my horizon; and all the rest of the way she kept her place, holding out her little arms to me, beckoning me on. Her four motherless years brought compunction to my heart and tears to my eyes; she should have all the compensation that could be. I suddenly realized how ready I was—how ready! —to have her back. I rebelled fiercely against John's decision that we must not take her with us on our return to the frontier; privately, I resolved to dispute it, and, if necessary, I saw myself abducting the child—my own child. My days and nights as the ship crept on were full of a long ache to possess her; the defrauded tenderness of the last four years rose up in me and sometimes caught at my throat. I could think and talk and dream of nothing else. John indulged me as much as was reasonable, and only once betrayed by a yawn that the subject was not for him endlessly absorbing. Then I cried and he apologized. "You know," he said, "it isn't exactly the same thing. I'm not her mother." At which I dried my tears and expanded, proud and pacified. I was her mother!

Then the rainy little station and Alice, all-embracing in a damp waterproof, and the drive in the fly, and John's mother at the gate and a necessary pause while I kissed John's mother. Dear thing, she wanted to hold our hands and look into our faces and tell us how little we had changed for all our hardships; and on the way to the house she actually stopped to point out some alterations in the flower-borders. At last the drawing-room door and the smiling housemaid turning the handle and the unforget-table picture of a little girl, a little girl unlike anything we had imagined, starting bravely to trot across the room with the little speech that had been taught her. Half-way she came; I suppose our regards were too fixed, too absorbed, for there she stopped with a wail of terror at the strange faces, and ran straight back to the outstretched arms of her Aunt Emma. The most natural thing in the world, no doubt. I walked over to a chair opposite with my hand-bag and umbrella and sat down—a spectator, aloof and silent. Aunt Emma fondled and quieted the child, apologizing for her to me, coaxing her to look up, but the little figure still shook with sobs, hiding its face in the bosom that it knew. I smiled politely, like any other stranger, at Emma's deprecations, and sat impassive, looking at my alleged baby breaking her heart at the sight of her mother. It is not amusing even now to remember the anger that I felt. I did not touch her or speak to her; I simply sat observing my alien possession, in the frock I had not made and the sash I had not chosen, being coaxed and kissed and protected and petted by its Aunt Emma. Presently I asked to be taken to my room, and there I locked myself in for two atrocious hours. Just once my heart beat high, when a tiny knock came and a timid, docile little voice said that tea was ready. But I heard the rustle of a skirt, and guessed the directing angel in Aunt Emma, and responded, "Thank you, dear, run away and say that I am coming," with a pleasant visitor's inflection which I was able to sustain for the rest of the afternoon.

"She goes to bed at seven," said Emma.

"Oh, does she?" said I. "A very good hour, I should think."

"She sleeps in my room," said Mrs Farnham.

"We give her mutton broth very often, but seldom stock soup," said Aunt Emma. "Mamma thinks it is too stimulating."

"Indeed?" said I, to all of it.

They took me up to see her in her crib, and pointed out, as she lay asleep, that though she had "a general look" of me, her features were distinctively Farnham.

"Won't you kiss her?" asked Alice. "You haven't kissed her yet, and she is used to so much affection."

"I don't think I could take such an advantage of her," I said.

They looked at each other, and Mrs. Farnham said that I was plainly worn out. I mustn't sit up to prayers.

If I had been given anything like reasonable time I might have made a fight for it, but four weeks—it took a month each way in those days—was too absurdly little; I could do nothing. But I would not stay at mamma's. It was more than I would ask of myself, that daily disappointment under the mask of gratified discovery, for long.

I spent an approving, unnatural week, in my farcical character, bridling my resentment and hiding my mortification with pretty phrases; and then I went up to town and drowned my sorrows in the summer sales. I took John with me. I may have been Cecily's mother in theory, but I was John's wife in fact.

We went back to the frontier, and the regiment saw a lot of service. That meant medals and fun for my husband, but economy and anxiety for me, though I managed to be allowed as close to the firing line as any woman.

Once the Colonel's wife and I, sitting in Fort Samila, actually heard the rifles of a punitive expedition cracking on the other side of the river—that was a bad moment. My man came in after fifteen hours' fighting, and went sound asleep, sitting before his food with his knife and fork in his hands. But service makes heavy demands besides those on your wife's nerves. We had saved two thousand rupees, I remember, against another run home, and it all went like powder, in the Mirzai expedition; and the run home diminished to a month in a boarding-house in the hills.

Meanwhile, however, we had begun to correspond with our daughter, in large round words of one syllable, behind which, of course, was plain the patient guiding hand of Aunt Emma. One could hear Aunt Emma suggesting what would be nice to say, trying to instil a little pale affection for the far-off papa and mamma. There was so little Cecily and so much Emma—of course, it could not be otherwise—that I used to take, I fear, but a perfunctory joy in these letters. When we went home again I stipulated absolutely that she was to write to us without any sort of supervision—the child was ten.

"But the spelling!" cried Aunt Emma, with lifted eyebrows.

"Her letters aren't exercises," I was obliged to retort; "she will do the best she can."

We found her a docile little girl, with nice manners, a

thoroughly unobjectionable child. I saw quite clearly that I could not have brought her up so well; indeed, there were moments when I fancied that Cecily, contrasting me with her aunts, wondered a little what my bringing up could have been like. With this reserve of criticism on Cecily's part, however, we got on very tolerably, largely because I found it impossible to assume any responsibility towards her, and in moments of doubt or discipline referred her to her aunts. We spent a pleasant summer with a little girl in the house whose interest in us was amusing, and whose outings it was gratifying to arrange; but when we went back, I had no desire to take her with us. I thought her very much better where she was.

Then came the period which is filled, in a subordinate degree, with Cecily's letters. I do not wish to claim more than I ought; they were not my only or even my principal interest in life. It was a long period; it lasted till she was twenty-one. John had had promotion in the meantime, and there was rather more money, but he had earned his second brevet with a bullet through one lung, and the doctors ordered our leave to be spent in South Africa. We had photographs, we knew she had grown tall and athletic and comely, and the letters were always very creditable. I had the unusual and qualified privilege of watching my daughter's development from ten to twenty-one, at a distance of four thousand miles, by means of the written word. I wrote myself as provocatively as possible; I sought for every string, but the vibration that came back across the seas to me was always other than the one I looked for, and sometimes there was none. Nevertheless, Mrs Farnham wrote me that Cecily very much valued my communications. Once when I had described an unusual excursion in a native state, I learned that she had read my letter aloud to the sewing circle. After that I abandoned description, and confined myself to such intimate personal details as no sewing circle could find amusing. The child's own letters were simply a mirror of the ideas of the Farnham ladies; that must have been so, it was not altogether my jaundiced eye. Alice and Emma and grandmamma paraded the pages in turn. I very early gave up hope of discoveries in my daughter, though as much of the original as I could detect was satisfactorily simple and sturdy. I found little things to criticize, of course, tendencies to correct; and by return post I criticized and corrected, but the distance and the deliberation seemed to touch my maxims with a kind of arid frivolity, and sometimes I tore them up. One quick, warm-blooded scolding would have been worth a sheaf of them. My studied little phrases could only inoculate her with a dislike for me without protecting her from anything under the sun.

However, I found she didn't dislike me, when John and I went home at last to bring her out. She received me with just a hint of kindness, perhaps, but on the whole very well.

CHAPTER II

John was recalled, of course, before the end of our furlough, which knocked various things on the head; but that is the sort of thing one learned to take with philosophy in any lengthened term of Her Majesty's service. Besides, there is usually sugar for the pill; and in this case it was a Staff command bigger than anything we expected for at least five years to come. The excitement of it when it was explained to her gave Cecily a charming color. She took a good deal of interest in the General, her papa; I think she had an idea that his distinction would alleviate the situation in India, however it might present itself. She accepted that prospective situation calmly; it had been placed before her all her life. There would always be a time when she should go and live with papa and mamma in India, and so long as she was of an age to receive the idea with rebel tears she was assured that papa and mamma would give her a pony. The pony was no longer added to the prospect; it was absorbed no doubt in the general list of attractions calculated to reconcile a young lady to a parental roof with which she had no practical acquaintance. At all events, when I feared the embarrassment and dismay of a pathetic parting with darling grandmamma and the aunties, and the sweet cat and the dear vicar and all the other objects of affection, I found an agreeable unexpected philosophy.

I may add that while I anticipated such broken-hearted farewells I was quite prepared to take them easily. Time, I imagined, had brought philosophy to me also, equally agreeable and equally unexpected.

It was a Bombay ship, full of returning Anglo-Indians. I looked up and down the long saloon tables with a sense of relief and of solace; I was again among my own people. They belonged to Bengal and to Burma, to Madras and to the Punjab, but they were all my people. I could pick out a score that I knew in fact, and there were none that in imagination I didn't know. The look of wider seas and skies, the casual experienced glance, the touch of irony and of tolerance, how well I knew it and how well I liked it! Dear old England, sitting in our wake, seemed to hold by comparison a great many soft, unsophisticated people, immensely occupied about very particular trifles. How difficult it had been, all the summer, to be interested! These of my long acquaintance belonged to my country's Executive, acute, alert, with the marks of travail on them. Gladly I went in and out of the women's cabins and listened to the argot of the men; my own ruling, administering, soldiering little lot.

Cecily looked at them askance. To her the atmosphere was alien, and I perceived that gently and privately she registered objections. She cast a disapproving eye upon the wife of a Conservator of Forests, who scanned with interest a distant funnel and laid a small wager that it belonged to the *Messageries Maritimes*. She looked with a straightened lip at the crisply stepping women who walked the deck in short and rather shabby skirts with their hands in their jacket-pockets talking transfers and promotions; and having got up at six to make a water-colour sketch of the sunrise, she came to me in profound indignation to say that she had met a man in his pyjamas; no doubt, poor wretch, on his way to be shaved. I was unable to convince her that he was not expected to visit the barber in all his clothes.

At the end of the third day she told me that she wished these people wouldn't talk to her; she didn't like them. I had turned in the hour we left the Channel and had not left my berth since, so possibly I was not in the most amiable mood to receive a douche of cold water. "I must try to remember, dear," I said, "that you have been brought up altogether in the society of pussies and vicars and elderly ladies, and of course you miss them. But you must have a little patience. I shall be up tomorrow, if this beastly sea continues to go down; and then we will try to find somebody suitable to introduce to you."

"Thank you, mamma," said my daughter, without a ray of suspicion. Then she added consideringly, "Aunt Emma and Aunt Alice do seem quite elderly ladies beside you, and yet you are older than either of them, aren't you? I wonder how that is."

It was so innocent, so admirable, that I laughed at my own expense; while Cecily, doing her hair, considered me gravely. "I wish you would tell me why you laugh, mamma," quoth she; "you laugh so often."

We had not to wait after all for my good offices of the next morning. Cecily came down at ten o'clock that night quite happy and excited; she had been talking to a bishop, such a dear bishop. The bishop had been showing her his collection of photographs, and she had promised to play the harmonium for him at the eleven-o'clock service in the morning. "Bless me!" said I. "Is it Sunday?" It seemed she had got on very well indeed with the bishop, who knew the married sister, at Tunbridge, of her very greatest friend. Cecily herself did not know the married sister, but that didn't matter—it was a link. The bishop was charming. "Well, my love," said I—I was teaching myself to use these forms of address for fear she would feel an unkind lack of them, but it was difficult— "I am glad that somebody from my part of the world has impressed you favourably at last. I wish we had more bishops."

"Oh, but my bishop doesn't belong to your part of the

world," responded my daughter sleepily. "He is travelling
for his health."

It was the most unexpected and delightful thing to be
packed into one's chair next morning by Dacres Tottenham.
As I emerged from the music saloon after breakfast—Cecily
had stayed below to look over her hymns and consider with
her bishop the possibility of an anthem—Dacres's face was
the first I saw; it simply illuminated, for me, that portion of
the deck. I noticed with pleasure the quick toss of the cigar
overboard as he recognized and bore down upon me. We
were immense friends; John liked him too. He was one of
those people who make a tremendous difference; in all our
three hundred passengers there could be no one like him,
certainly no one whom I could be more glad to see. We
plunged at once into immediate personal affairs, we would
get at the heart of them later. He gave his vivid word to
everything he had seen and done; we laughed and exclaimed
and were silent in a concert of admirable understanding.
We were still unravelling, still demanding and explaining
when the ship's bell began to ring for church, and almost
simultaneously Cecily advanced towards us. She had a
proper Sunday hat on, with flowers under the brim, and a
church-going frock; she wore gloves and clasped a prayer-
book. Most of the women who filed past to the summons of
the bell were going down as they were, in cotton blouses and
serge skirts, in tweed caps or anything, as to a kind of family
prayers. I knew exactly how they would lean against the
pillars of the saloon during the psalms. This young lady
would be little less than a rebuke to them. I surveyed her
approach; she positively walked as if it were Sunday.

"My dear," I said, "how *endimanchée* you look! The
bishop will be very pleased with you. This gentleman is Mr
Tottenham, who administers Her Majesty's pleasure in
parts of India about Allahabad. My daughter, Dacres." She
was certainly looking very fresh, and her calm grey eyes had
the repose in them that has never known itself to be
disturbed about anything. I wondered whether she bowed
so distantly also because it was Sunday, and then I

remembered that Dacres was a young man, and that the Farnham ladies had probably taught her that it was right to be very distant with young men.

"It is almost eleven, mamma."

"Yes, dear. I see you are going to church."

"Are you not coming, mamma?"

I was well wrapped up in an extremely comfortable corner. I had *La Duchesse Bleue* uncut in my lap, and an agreeable person to talk to. I fear that in any case I should not have been inclined to attend the service, but there was something in my daughter's intonation that made me distinctly hostile to the idea. I am putting things down as they were, extenuating nothing.

"I think not, dear."

"I've turned up two such nice seats."

"Stay, Miss Farnham, and keep us in countenance," said Dacres, with his charming smile. The smile displaced a look of discreet and amused observation. Dacres had an eye always for a situation, and this one was even newer to him than to me.

"No, no. She must run away and not bully her mamma," I said. "When she comes back we will see how much she remembers of the sermon," and as the flat tinkle from the companion began to show signs of diminishing, Cecily, with one grieved glance, hastened down.

"You amazing lady!" said Dacres. "A daughter—and such a tall daughter! I somehow never—"

"You knew we had one?"

"There was theory of that kind, I remember, about ten years ago. Since then—excuse me—I don't think you've mentioned her."

"You talk as if she were a skeleton in the closet!"

"You *didn't* talk—as if she were."

"I think she was, in a way, poor child. But the resurrection day hasn't confounded me as I deserved. She's a very good girl."

"If you had asked me to pick out your daughter—"

"She would have been the last you would indicate!

Quite so," I said. "She is like her father's people. I can't help that."

"I shouldn't think you would if you could," Dacres remarked absently; but the sea air, perhaps, enabled me to digest his thoughtlessness with a smile.

"No," I said, "I am just as well pleased. I think a resemblance to me would confuse me, often."

There was a trace of scrutiny in Dacres's glance. "Don't you find yourself in sympathy with her?" he asked.

"My dear boy, I have seen her just twice in twenty-one years! You see, I've always stuck to John."

"But between mother and daughter—I may be old-fashioned, but I had an idea that there was an instinct that might be depended on."

"I am depending on it," I said, and let my eyes follow the little blue waves that chased past the hand-rail. "We are making very good speed, aren't we? Thirty-five knots since last night at ten. Are you in the sweep?"

"I never bet on the way out—can't afford it. Am I old-fashioned?" he insisted.

"Probably. Men are very slow in changing their philosophy about women. I fancy their idea of the maternal relation is firmest fixed of all."

"We see it a beatitude!" he cried.

"I know," I said wearily, "and you never modify the view."

Dacres contemplated the portion of the deck that lay between us. His eyes were discreetly lowered, but I saw embarrassment and speculation and a hint of criticism in them.

"Tell me more about it," said he.

"Oh, for heaven's sake don't be sympathetic!" I exclaimed. "Lend me a little philosophy instead. There is nothing to tell. There she is and there I am, in the most intimate relation in the world, constituted when she is twenty-one and I am forty." Dacres started slightly at the ominous word; so little do men realize that the women they like can ever pass out of the constated years of attraction. "I find the young lady very tolerable, very creditable, very nice. I find the relation atrocious. There you have it. I would like to break the relation into pieces," I went on recklessly, "and throw it into the sea. Such things should be tempered to one. I should feel it much less if she occupied another cabin, and would consent to call me Elizabeth or Jane. It is not as if I had been her mother always. One grows fastidious at forty—new intimacies are only possible then on a basis of temperament —"

I paused; it seemed to me that I was making excuses, and I had not the least desire in the world to do that.

"How awfully rough on the girl!" said Dacres Tottenham.

"That consideration has also occurred to me," I said candidly, "though I have perhaps been even more struck by its converse."

"You had no earthly business to be her mother," said my friend, with irritation.

I shrugged my shoulders—what would you have done?—and opened *La Duchesse Bleue.*

CHAPTER III

Mrs Morgan, wife of a judge of the High Court of Bombay, and I sat amidships on the cool side in the Suez Canal. She was outlining "Soiled Linen" in chain-stitch on a green canvas bag; I was admiring the Egyptian sands. "How charming," said I, "is this solitary desert in the endless oasis we are compelled to cross!"

"Oasis in the desert, you mean," said Mrs Morgan; "I haven't noticed any, but I happened to look up this morning as I was putting on my stockings, and I saw through my port-hole the most lovely mirage."

I had been at school with Mrs Morgan more than twenty years agone, but she had come to the special enjoyment of the dignities of life while I still liked doing things. Mrs Morgan was the kind of person to make one realize how distressing a medium is middle age. Contemplating her precipitous lap, to which conventional attitudes were certainly more becoming, I crossed my own knees with energy, and once more resolved to be young until I was old.

"How perfectly delightful for you to be taking Cecily out!" said Mrs Morgan placidly.

"Isn't it?" I responded, watching the gliding sands.

"But she was born in sixty-nine—that makes her twenty-one. Quite time, I should say."

"Oh, we couldn't put it off any longer. I mean—her father has such a horror of early débuts. He simply would not hear of her coming before."

"Doesn't want her to marry in India, I dare say—the only one," purred Mrs Morgan.

"Oh, I don't know. It isn't such a bad place. I was brought out there to marry, and I married. I've found it very satisfactory."

"You always did say exactly what you thought, Helena," said Mrs Morgan excusingly.

"I haven't much patience with people who bring their daughters out to give them the chance they never would have in England, and then go about devoutly hoping they won't marry in India," I said. "I shall be very pleased if Cecily does as well as your girls have done."

"Mary in the Indian Civil and Jessie in the Imperial Service Troops," sighed Mrs Morgan complacently. "And both, my dear, within a year. It *was* a blow."

"Oh, it must have been!" I said civilly.

There was no use in bandying words with Emily Morgan.

"There is nothing in the world like the satisfaction and pleasure one takes in one's daughters," Mrs Morgan went on limpidly. "And one can be in such *close* sympathy with one's girls. I have never regretted having no sons."

"Dear me, yes. To watch oneself growing up again— call back the lovely April of one's prime, etcetera—to read every thought and anticipate every wish—there is no more golden privilege in life, dear Emily. Such a direct and natural avenue for affection, such a wide field for interest!"

I paused, lost in the volume of my admirable sentiments.

"How beautifully you talk, Helena! I wish I had the gift."

"It doesn't mean very much," I said truthfully.

"Oh, I think it's everything! And how companionable a girl is! I quite envy you, this season, having Cecily constantly with you and taking her about everywhere. Something quite new for you, isn't it?"

"Absolutely," said I; "I am looking forward to it immensely. But it is likely she will make her own friends, don't you think?" I added anxiously.

"Hardly the first season. My girls didn't. I was practically their only intimate for months. Don't be afraid; you won't be obliged to go shares in Cecily with anybody for a good long while," added Mrs Morgan kindly. "I know just how you feel about *that.*"

The muddy water of the Ditch chafed up from under us against its banks with a smell that enabled me to hide the emotions Mrs Morgan evoked behind my handkerchief. The pale desert was pictorial with the drifting, deepening purple shadows of clouds, and in the midst a blue glimmer of the Bitter Lakes, with a white sail on them. A little frantic Arab boy ran alongside keeping pace with the ship. Except for the smell, it was like a dream, we moved so quietly; on, gently on and on between the ridgy clay banks and the rows of piles. Peace was on the ship; you could hear what the Fourth in his white ducks said to the quartermaster in his blue denims; you could count the strokes of the electric bell in the wheel-house; peace was on the ship as she pushed on, an ever-venturing, double-funneled impertinence, through the sands of the ages. My eyes wandered along a plank-line in the deck till they were arrested by a petticoat I knew, when they returned of their own accord. I seemed to be always seeing that petticoat.

"I think," resumed Mrs. Morgan, whose glance had wandered in the same direction, "that Cecily is a very fine type of our English girls. With those dark grey eyes, a *little* prominent possibly, and that good colour—it's rather high now perhaps, but she will lose quite enough of it in India—and those regular features, she would make a splendid Britannia. Do you know, I fancy she must have a great deal of character. Has she?"

"Any amount. And all of it good," I responded, with private dejection.

"No faults at all?" chaffed Mrs Morgan.

I shook my head. "Nothing," I said sadly, "that I can put my finger on. But I hope to discover a few later. The sun may bring them out."

"Like freckles. Well, you are a lucky woman. Mine had plenty, I assure you. Untidiness was no name for Jessie, and Mary—I'm *sorry* to say that Mary sometimes fibbed."

"How lovable of her! Cecily's neatness is a painful example to me, and I don't believe she would tell a fib to save my life."

"Tell me," said Mrs Morgan, as the lunch-bell rang and she gathered her occupation into her work-basket, "who is that talking to her?"

"Oh, an old friend," I replied easily; "Dacres Tottenham, a dear fellow, and most benevolent. He is trying on my behalf to reconcile her to the life she'll have to lead in India."

"She won't need much reconciling, if she's like most girls," observed Mrs Morgan, "but he seems to be trying very hard."

That was quite the way I took it—on my behalf—for several days. When people have understood you very adequately for ten years you do not expect them to boggle at any problem you may present at the end of the decade. I thought Dacres was moved by a fine sense of compassion. I thought that with his admirable perception he had put a finger on the little comedy of fruitfulness in my life that laughed so bitterly at the tragedy of the barren woman, and was attempting, by delicate manipulation, to make it easier. I really thought so. Then I observed that myself had preposterously deceived me, that it wasn't like that at all. When Mr Tottenham joined us, Cecily and me, I saw that he listened more than he talked, with an ear specially cocked to register any small irony which might appear in my remarks to my daughter. Naturally he registered more than there were, to make up perhaps for dear Cecily's obviously not registering any. I could see, too, that he was suspicious of any flavour of kindness; finally, to avoid the strictures of his upper lip, which really, dear fellow, began to bore me, I talked exclusively about the distant sails and the Red Sea littoral. When he no longer joined us as we sat or walked together, I perceived that his hostility was fixed and his *parti pris*. He was brimful of compassion, but it was all for Cecily, none for the situation or for me. (She would have marvelled, placidly, why he pitied her. I am glad I can say that.) The primitive man in him rose up as Pope of nature and excommunicated me as a creature recusant to her functions. Then deliberately Dacres undertook an office of consolation; and I fell to wondering, while Mrs Morgan spoke her convictions plainly out, how far an impulse of reparation for a misfortune with which he had nothing to do might carry a man.

I began to watch the affair with an interest which even to me seemed queer. It was not detached, but it was semi-detached, and, of course, on the side for which I seem, in this history, to be perpetually apologizing. With certain limitations it didn't matter an atom whom Cecily married. So that he was sound and decent, with reasonable prospects, her simple requirements and ours for her would be quite met. There was the ghost of a consolation in that; one needn't be anxious or exacting.

I could predict with a certain amount of confidence that in her first season she would probably receive three or four proposals, any one of which she might accept with as much propriety and satisfaction as any other one. For Cecily it was so simple; prearranged by nature like her digestion, one could not see any logical basis for difficulties. A nice upstanding sapper, a dashing Bengal Lancer—oh, I could think of half a dozen types that would answer excellently. She was the kind of young person, and that was the summing up of it, to marry a type and be typically happy. I hoped and expected that she would. But Dacres!

Dacres should exercise the greatest possible discretion. He was not a person who could throw the dice indifferently with fate. He could respond to so much, and he would inevitably, sooner or later, demand so much response! He was governed by a preposterously exacting temperament, and he wore his nerves outside. And what vision he had! How he explored the world he lived in and drew out of it all there was, all there was! I could see him in the years to come ranging alone the fields that were sweet and the horizons that lifted for him, and ever returning to pace the common dusty mortal road by the side of a purblind wife. On general principles, as a case to point at, it would be a conspicuous pity. Nor would it lack the aspect of a particular, a personal misfortune. Dacres was occupied in quite the natural normal degree with his charming self; he would pass his misery on, and who would deserve to escape it less than his mother-in-law?

I listened to Emily Morgan, who gleaned in the ship more information about Dacres Tottenham's people, pay, and prospects than I had ever acquired, and I kept an eye upon the pair which was, I flattered myself, quite maternal. I watched them without acute anxiety, deploring the threatening destiny, but hardly nearer to it than one is in the stalls to the stage. My moments of real concern for Dacres were mingled more with anger than with sorrow—it seemed inexcusable that he, with his infallible divining-rod for temperament, should be on the point of making such an ass of himself. Though I talk of the stage

there was nothing at all dramatic to reward my attention,
mine and Emily Morgan's. To my imagination, excited
by its idea of what Dacres Tottenham's courtship ought
to be, the attentions he paid to Cecily were most humdrum. He threw rings into buckets with her—she was
good at that—and quoits upon the "bull" board; he
found her chair after the decks were swabbed in the morning and established her in it; he paced the deck with her
at convenient times and seasons. They were humdrum,
but they were constant and cumulative. Cecily took them
with an even breath that perfectly matched. There was
hardly anything, on her part, to note—a little discreet
observation of his comings and goings, eyes scarcely lifted
from her book, and later just a hint of proprietorship, as
the evening she came up to me on deck, our first night in
the Indian Ocean. I was lying in my long chair looking
at the thick, low stars and thinking it was a long time
since I had seen John.

"Dearest mamma, out here and nothing over your
shoulders! You *are* imprudent. Where is your wrap? Mr
Tottenham, will you please fetch mamma's wrap for
her?"

"If mamma so instructs me," he said audaciously.

"Do as Cecily tells you," I laughed, and he went and
did it, while I by the light of a quartermaster's lantern
distinctly saw my daughter blush.

Another time, when Cecily came down to undress, she
bent over me as I lay in the lower berth with unusual
solicitude. I had been dozing, and I jumped.

"What is it, child?" I said. "Is the ship on fire?"

"No, mamma, the ship is not on fire. There is nothing
wrong. I'm so sorry I startled you. But Mr Tottenham has
been telling me all about what you did for the soldiers the
time plague broke out in the lines at Mian-Mir. I think it
was splendid, mamma, and so does he."

"Oh, *Lord!*" I groaned. "Good night."

CHAPTER IV

It remained in my mind, that little thing that Dacres had taken the trouble to tell my daughter; I thought about it a good deal. It seemed to me the most serious and convincing circumstances that had yet offered itself to my consideration. Dacres was no longer content to bring solace and support to the more appealing figure of the situation; he must set to work, bless him! to improve the situation itself. He must try to induce Miss Farnham, by telling her everything he could remember to my credit, to think as well of her mother as possible, in spite of the strange and secret blows which that mother might be supposed to sit up at night to deliver to her. Cecily thought very well of me already; indeed, with private reservations as to my manners and—no, *not* my morals, I believe I exceeded her expectations of what a perfectly new and untrained mother would be likely to prove. It was my theory that she found me all she could understand me to be. The maternal virtues of the outside were certainly mine; I put them on with care every morning and wore them with patience all day. Dacres, I assured myself, must have allowed his preconception to lead him absurdly by the nose not to see that the girl was satisfied, that my impatience, my impotence, did not at all make her miserable. Evidently, however, he had created our relations differently; evidently he had set himself to their amelioration. There was portent in it; things seemed to be closing in. I bit off a quarter of an inch of wooden pen-handle in considering whether or not I should mention it in my letter to John, and decided that it would be better just perhaps to drop a hint. Though I could not expect John to receive it with any sort of perturbation. Men are different; he would probably think Tottenham well enough able to look after himself.

I had embarked on my letter, there at the end of a corner-table of the saloon, when I saw Dacres saunter through. He wore a very conscious and elaborately purposeless air; and it jumped with my mood that he had nothing less than the crisis of his life in his pocket, and was looking for me. As he advanced towards me between the long tables doubt left me and alarm assailed me. "I'm glad to find you in a quiet corner," said he, seating himself, and confirmed my worst anticipations.

"I'm writing to John," I said, and again applied myself to my pen-handle. It is a trick Cecily has since done her best in vain to cure me of.

"I am going to interrupt you," he said. "I have not had an opportunity of talking to you for some time."

"I like that!" I exclaimed derisively.

"And I want to tell you that I am very much charmed with Cecily."

"Well," I said, "I am not going to gratify you by saying anything against her."

"You don't deserve her, you know."

"I won't dispute that. But, if you don't mind—I'm not sure that I'll stand being abused, dear boy."

"I quite see it isn't any use. Though one spoke with the tongues of men and of angels—"

"And had not charity," I continued for him. "Precisely. I won't go on, but your quotation is very apt."

"I so bow down before her simplicity. It makes a wide and beautiful margin for the rest of her character. She is a girl Ruskin would have loved."

"I wonder," said I. "He did seem fond of the simple type, didn't he?"

"Her mind is so clear, so transparent. The motive spring of everything she says and does is so direct. Don't you find you can most completely depend upon her?"

"Oh yes," I said, "certainly. I nearly always know what she is going to say before she says it, and under given circumstances I can tell precisely what she will do."

"I fancy her sense of duty is very beautifully developed."

"It is," I said. "There is hardly a day when I do not come in contact with it."

"Well, that is surely a good thing. And I find that calm poise of hers very restful."

"I would not have believed that so many virtues could reside in one young lady," I said, taking refuge in flippancy, "and to think that she should be my daughter!"

"As I believe you know, that seems to me rather a cruel stroke of destiny, Mrs Farnham."

"Oh yes, I know! You have a constructive imagination, Dacres. You don't seem to see that the girl is protected by her limitations, like a tortoise. She lives within them quite secure and happy and content. How determined you are to be sorry for her!"

Mr Tottenham looked at the end of this lively exchange as though he sought for a polite way of conveying to me that I rather was the limited person. He looked as if he wished he could say things. The first of them would be, I saw, that he had quite a different conception of Cecily, that it was illuminated by many trifles, nuances of feeling and expression, which he had noticed in his talks with her whenever they had skirted the subject of her adoption by her mother. He knew her, he was longing to say, better than I did; when it would have been natural to reply that one could not hope to compete in such a direction with an intelligent young man, and we should at once have been upon delicate and difficult ground. So it was as well perhaps that he kept silence until he said, as he had come prepared to say, "Well, I want to put that beyond a doubt—her happiness—if I'm good enough. I want her, please, and I only hope that she will be half as willing to come as you are likely to be to let her go."

It was a shock when it came, plump, like that; and I was horrified to feel how completely every other consideration was lost for the instant in the immense relief that it prefigured. To be my whole complete self again, without the feeling that a fraction of me was masquerading about in Cecily! To be freed at once, or almost, from an exacting condition and an impossible ideal! "Oh!" I exclaimed, and my eyes positively filled. "You *are* good, Dacres, but I couldn't let you do that."

His undisguised stare brought me back to a sense of the proportion of things. I saw that in the combination of influences that had brought Mr Tottenham to the point of proposing to marry my daughter consideration for me, if it had a place, would be fantastic. Inwardly I laughed at the egotism of raw nerves that had conjured it up, even for an instant, as a reason for gratitude. The situation was not so peculiar, not so interesting, as that. But I answered his stare with a smile; what I had said might very well stand.

"Do you imagine," he said, seeing that I did not mean to amplify it, "that I want to marry her out of any sort of *goodness*?"

"Benevolence is your weakness, Dacres."

"I see. You think one's motive is to withdraw her from a relation which ought to be the most natural in the world, but which is, in her particular and painful case, the most equivocal."

"Well, come," I remonstrated. "You have dropped one or two things, you know, in the heat of your indignation, not badly calculated to give one that idea. The eloquent statement you have just made, for instance—it carries all the patness of old conviction. How often have you rehearsed it?"

I am a fairly long-suffering person, but I began to feel a little annoyed with my would-be son-in-law. If the relation were achieved it would give him no prescriptive right to bully me; and we were still in very early anticipation of that.

"Ah!" he said disarmingly. "Don't let us quarrel. I'm sorry you think that; because it isn't likely to bring your favour to my project, and I want you friendly and helpful. Oh, confound it!" he exclaimed, with sudden temper. "You ought to be. I don't understand this aloofness. I half suspect it's pose. You undervalue Cecily—well, you have no business to undervalue me. You know me better than anybody in the world. Now are you going to help me to marry your daughter?"

"I don't think so," I said slowly, after a moment's silence, which he sat through like a mutinous schoolboy. "I might tell you that I don't care a button whom you marry, but that would not be true. I do care more or less. As you say, I know you pretty well. I'd a little rather you didn't make a mess of it; and if you must I should distinctly prefer not to have the spectacle under my nose for the rest of my life. I can't hinder you, but I won't help you."

"And what possesses you to imagine that in marrying Cecily I should make a mess of it? Shouldn't your first consideration be whether *she* would?"

"Perhaps it should, but, you see, it isn't. Cecily would be happy with anybody who made her comfortable. You would ask a good deal more than that, you know."

Dacres, at this, took me up promptly. Life, he said, the heart of life, had particularly little to say to temperament. By the heart of life I suppose he meant married love. He explained that its roots asked other sustenance, and that it throve best of all on simple elemental goodness. So long as a man sought in women mere casual companionship, perhaps the most exquisite thing to be experienced was the stimulus of some spiritual feminine counterpart; but when he desired of one woman that she should be always and intimately with him, the background of his life, the mother of his children, he was better advised to avoid nerves and sensibilities, and try for the repose of the common—the uncommon—domestic virtues. Ah, he said, they were sweet, like lavender. (Already, I told him, he smelled the housekeeper's linen-chest.) But I did not interrupt him much; I couldn't, he was too absorbed. To temperamental pairing, he declared, the century owed its breed of decadents. I asked him if he had ever really recognized one; and he retorted that if he hadn't he didn't wish to make a beginning in his own family. In a quarter of an hour he repudiated the theories of a lifetime, a gratifying triumph for simple elemental goodness. Having denied the value of the subtler pretensions to charm in woman as you marry her, he went artlessly on to endow Cecily with as many of them as could possibly be desirable. He actually persuaded himself to say that it was lovely to see the reflections of life in her tranquil spirit; and when I looked at him incredulously he grew angry, and hinted that Cecily's sensitiveness to reflections and other things might be a trifle beyond her mother's ken. "She responds instantly, intimately, to the beautiful everywhere," he declared.

"Aren't the opportunities of life on board ship rather limited to demonstrate that?" I inquired. "I know—you mean sunsets. Cecily is very fond of sunsets. She is always asking me to come and look at them."

"I was thinking of last night's sunset," he confessed. "We looked at it together."

"What did she say?" I asked idly.

"Nothing very much. That's just the point. Another girl would have raved and gushed."

"Oh, well, Cecily never does that," I responded. "Nevertheless she is a very ordinary human instrument. I hope I shall have no temptation ten years hence to remind you that I warned you of her quality."

"I wish, not in the least for my own profit, for I am well convinced already, but simply to win your cordiality and your approval—never did an unexceptional wooer receive such niggard encouragement!—I wish there were some sort of test for her quality. I would be proud to stand by it, and you would be convinced. I can't find words to describe my objection to your state of mind."

The thing seemed to me to be a foregone conclusion. I saw it accomplished, with all its possibilities of disastrous commonplace. I saw all that I have here taken the trouble to foreshadow. So far as I was concerned, Dacres's burden would add itself to my philosophies, *voilà tout*. I should always be a little uncomfortable about it, because it had been taken from my back; but it would not be a matter for the wringing of hands. And yet—the hatefulness of the mistake! Dacres's bold talk of a test made no suggestion. Should my invention be more fertile? I thought of something.

"You have said nothing to her yet?" I asked.

"Nothing. I don't think she suspects for a moment. She treats me as if no such fell design were possible. I'm none too confident, you know," he added, with longer face.

"We go straight to Agra. Could you come to Agra?"

"Ideal!" he cried. "The memory of Mumtaz! The garden of the Taj! I've always wanted to love under the same moon as Shah Jehan. How thoughtful of you!"

"You must spend a few days with us in Agra," I continued. "And as you say, it is the very place to shrine your happiness, if it comes to pass there."

"Well, I am glad to have extracted a word of kindness from you at last," said Dacres, as the stewards came to lay the table. "But I wish," he added regretfully, "you could have thought of a test."

CHAPTER V

Four days later we were in Agra. A time there was when the name would have been the key of dreams to me; now it stood for John's headquarters. I was rejoiced to think I would look again upon the Taj; and the prospect of living with it was a real enchantment; but I pondered most the kind of house that would be provided for the General Commanding the District, how many the dining-room would seat, and whether it would have a roof of thatch or of corrugated iron—I prayed against corrugated iron. I confess these my preoccupations. I was forty, and at forty the practical considerations of life hold their own even against domes of marble, world-renowned, and set about with gardens where the bulbul sings to the rose. I smiled across the years at the raptures of my first vision of the place at twenty-one, just Cecily's age. Would I now sit under Arjamand's cypresses till two o'clock in the morning to see the wonder of her tomb at a particular angle of the moon? Would I climb one of her tall white ministering minarets to see anything whatever? I very greatly feared that I would not. Alas for the aging of sentiment, of interest! Keep your touch with life and your seat in the saddle as long as you will, the world is no new toy at forty. But Cecily was twenty-one, Cecily who sat stolidly finishing her lunch while Dacres Tottenham talked about Akbar and his philosophy. "The sort of man," he said, "that Carlyle might have smoked a pipe with."

"But surely," said Cecily reflectively, "tobacco was not discovered in England then. Akbar came to the throne in 1526."

"Nor Carlyle either for that matter," I hastened to observe. "Nevertheless, I think Mr Tottenham's proposition must stand."

"Thanks, Mrs Farnham," said Dacres. "But imagine Miss Farnham's remembering Akbar's date! I'm sure you didn't!"

"Let us hope she doesn't know too much about him," I cried gaily, "or there will be nothing to tell!"

"Oh, really and truly very little!" said Cecily, "but as soon as we heard papa would be stationed here Aunt Emma made me read up about those old Moguls and people. I think I remember the dynasty. Baber, wasn't he the first? and then Humayon, and after him Akbar, and then Jehangir, and then Shah Jehan. But I've forgotten every date but Akbar's."

She smiled her smile of brilliant health and even spirits as she made the damaging admission, and she was so good to look at, sitting there simple and wholesome and fresh, peeling her banana with her well-shaped fingers, that we swallowed the dynasty as it were whole, and smiled back upon her. John, I may say, was extremely pleased with Cecily; he said she was a very satisfactory human accomplishment. One would have thought, positively, the way he plumed himself over his handsome daughter, that he alone was responsible for her. But John, having received his family, straightway set off with his Staff on a tour of inspection, and thereby takes himself out of this history. I sometimes think that if he had stayed—but there has never been the lightest recrimination between us about it, and I am not going to hint one now.

"Did you read," asked Dacres, "what he and the Court poet wrote over the entrance gate to the big mosque at Fattehpur-Sikri? It's rather nice. 'The world is a looking-glass, wherein the image has come and is gone—take as thine own nothing more than what thou lookest upon.' "

My daughter's thoughtful gaze was, of course, fixed upon the speaker, and in his own glance I saw a sudden ray of consciousness; but Cecily transferred her eyes to the opposite wall, deeply considering, and while Dacres and I smiled across the table, I saw that she had perceived no reason for blushing. It was a singularly narrow escape.

"No," she said, "I didn't; what a curious proverb for an emperor to make! He couldn't possibly have been able to see all his possessions at once."

"If you have finished," Dacres addressed her, "do let me show you what your plain and immediate duty is to the garden. The garden waits for you—all the roses expectant —"

"Why, there isn't one!" cried Cecily, pinning on her hat. It was pleasing, and just a trifle pathetic, the way he hurried her out of the scope of any little dart; he would not have her even within range of amused observation. Would he continue, I wondered vaguely, as, with my elbows on the table, I tore into strips the lemon-leaf that floated in my finger-bowl—would he continue, through life, to shelter her from his other clever friends as now he attempted to shelter her from her mother? In that case he would have to domicile her, poor dear, behind the curtain, like the native ladies—a good price to pay for a protection of which, bless her heart! she would be all unaware. I had quite stopped bemoaning the affair;

perhaps the comments of my husband, who treated it with broad approval and satisfaction, did something to soothe my sensibilities. At all events, I had gradually come to occupy a high fatalistic ground towards the pair. If it was written upon their foreheads that they should marry, the inscription was none of mine; and, of course, it was true, as John had indignantly stated, that Dacres might do very much worse. One's interest in Dacres Tottenham's problematical future had in no way diminished; but the young man was so positive, so full of intention, so disinclined to discussion—he had not reopened the subject since that morning in the saloon of the *Caledonia*—that one's feeling about it rather took the attenuated form of a shrug. I am afraid, too, that the pleasurable excitement of such an impending event had a little supervened; even at forty there is no disallowing the natural interests of one's sex. As I sat there pulling my lemon-leaf to pieces, I should not have been surprised or in the least put about if the two had returned radiant from the lawn to demand my blessing. As to the test of quality that I had obligingly invented for Dacres on the spur of the moment without his knowledge or connivance, it had some time ago faded into what he apprehended it to be—a mere idyllic opportunity, a charming background, a frame for his project, of prettier sentiment than the funnels and the hand-rails of a ship.

Mr Tottenham had ten days to spend with us. He knew the place well; it belonged to the province to whose service he was dedicated, and he claimed with impressive authority the privilege of showing it to Cecily by degrees—the Hall of Audience to-day, the Jessamine Tower to-morrow, the tomb of Akbar another, and the Deserted City yet another day. We arranged the expeditions in conference, Dacres insisting only upon the order of them, which I saw was to be cumulative, with the Taj at the very end, on the night precisely of the full of the moon, with a better chance of roses. I had no special views, but Cecily contributed some; that we should do the

Hall of Audience in the morning, so as not to interfere
with the club tennis in the afternoon, that we should
bicycle to Akbar's tomb and take a cold luncheon—if we
were sure there would be no snakes—to the Deserted City,
to all of which Dacres gave loyal assent. I endorsed everything; I was the encouraging chorus, only stipulating
that my number should be swelled from day to day by the
addition of such persons as I should approve. Cecily, for
instance, wanted to invite the Bakewells because we had
come out in the same ship with them; but I could not
endure the Bakewells, and it seemed to me that our having made the voyage with them was the best possible reason for declining to lay eyes on them for the rest of our
natural lives. "Mamma has such strong prejudices,"
Cecily remarked, as she reluctantly gave up the idea; and
I waited to see whether the graceless Tottenham would
unmurmuringly take down the Bakewells. How strong
must be the sentiment that turns a man into a boa-
constrictor without a pang of transmigration! But no,
this time he was faithful to the principles of his pre-
Cecilian existence. "They are rather Boojums," he
declared. "You would think so, too, if you knew them
better. It is that kind of excellent person that makes the
real burden of India." I could have patted him on the
back.

Thanks to the rest of the chorus, which proved abund-
antly available, I was no immediate witness to Cecily's
introduction to the glorious fragments which sustain in
Agra the memory of the Moguls. I may as well say that I
arranged with care that if anybody must be standing by
when Dacres disclosed them, it should not be I. If Cecily
had squinted, I should have been sorry, but I would have
found in it no personal humiliation. There were other
imperfections of vision, however, for which I felt responsible and ashamed; and with Dacres, though the situation, Heaven knows, was none of my seeking, I had a
little the feeling of a dealer who offers a defective *bibelot*
to a connoisseur. My charming daughter—I was fifty

times congratulated upon her appearance and her
manners—had many excellent qualities and capacities
which she never inherited from me; but she could see no
more than the bulk, no further than the perspective; she
could register exactly as much as a camera.

This was a curious thing, perhaps, to displease my
maternal vanity, but it did; I had really rather she
squinted; and when there was anything to look at I kept
out of the way. I can not tell precisely, therefore, what the
incidents were that contributed to make Mr Tottenham,
on our return from these expeditions, so thoughtful, with
a thoughtfulness which increased, towards the end of
them, to a positive gravity. This would disappear during
dinner under the influence of food and drink. He would
talk nightly with new enthusiasm and fresh hope—or did
I imagine it?—of the loveliness he had arranged to reveal
on the following day. If again my imagination did not
lead me astray, I fancied this occurred later and later in
the course of the meal as the week went on; as if his state
required more stimulus as time progressed. One evening,
when I expected it to flag altogether, I had a whim to
order champagne and observe the effect; but I am glad to
say that I reproved myself, and refrained.

Cecily, meanwhile, was conducting herself in a manner
which left nothing to be desired. If, as I sometimes
thought, she took Dacres very much for granted, she took
him calmly for granted; she seemed a prey to none of
those fluttering uncertainties, those suspended judge-
ments and elaborate indifferences which translate themselves so plainly in a young lady receiving addresses. She
turned herself out very freshly and very well; she was
always ready for everything, and I am sure that no glance
of Dacres Tottenham's found aught but direct and decor-
ous response. His society on these occasions gave her
solid pleasure; so did the drive and the lunch; the satisfac-
tions were apparently upon the same plane. She was
aware of the plum, if I may be permitted a brusque but
irresistible simile; and with her mouth open, her eyes

modestly closed, and her head in a convenient position, she waited, placidly, until it should fall in. The Farnham ladies would have been delighted with the result of their labours in the sweet reason and eminent propriety of this attitude. Thinking of my idiotic sufferings when John began to fix himself upon my horizon, I pondered profoundly the power of nature in differentiation.

One evening, the last, I think, but one, I had occasion to go to my daughter's room, and found her writing in her commonplace-book. She had a commonplace-book, as well as a Where is It?, an engagement-book, an account-book, a diary, a Daily Sunshine, and others with purposes too various to remember. "Dearest mamma," she said, as I was departing, "there is only one 'p' in 'opulence,' isn't there?"

"Yes," I replied, with my hand on the door-handle, and added curiously, for it was an odd word in Cecily's mouth, "Why?"

She hardly hesitated. "Oh," she said, "I am just writing down one or two things Mr Tottenham said about Agra before I forget them. They seemed so true."

"He has a descriptive touch," I remarked.

"I think he describes beautifully. Would you like to hear what he said to-day?"

"I would," I replied, sincerely.

" 'Agra,' " read this astonishing young lady, " 'is India's one pure idyll. Elsewhere she offers other things, foolish opulence, tawdry pageant, treachery of eunuchs and jealousies of harems, thefts of kings' jewels and barbaric retributions; but they are all actual, visualized, or part of a past that shows to the backward glance hardly more relief and vitality than a Persian painting'—I should like to see a Persian painting—'but here the immortal tombs and pleasure-houses rise out of color delicate and subtle; the vision holds across three hundred years; the print of the court is still in the dust of the city.' "

"Did you really let him go on like that?" I exclaimed. "It has the license of a lecture!"

"I encouraged him to. Of course he didn't say it straight off. He said it naturally; he stopped now and then to cough. I didn't understand it all; but I think I have remembered every word."

"You have a remarkable memory. I'm glad he stopped to cough. Is there any more?"

"One little bit. 'Here the Moguls wrought their passions into marble, and held them up with great refrains from their religion, and set them about with gardens; and here they stand in the twilight of the glory of those kings and the noonday splendour of their own.' "

"How clever of you?" I exclaimed. "How wonderfully clever of you to remember!"

"I had to ask him to repeat one or two sentences. He didn't like that. But this is nothing. I used to learn pages letter-perfect for Aunt Emma. She was very particular. I think it is worth preserving, don't you?"

"Dear Cecily," I responded, "you have a frugal mind."

There was nothing else to respond. I could not tell her just how practical I thought her, or how pathetic her little book.

CHAPTER VI

We drove together, after dinner, to the Taj. The moonlight lay in an empty splendor over the broad sandy road, with the acacias pricking up on each side of it and the gardens of the station bungalows stretching back into clusters of crisp shadows. It was an exquisite February night, very still. Nothing seemed abroad but two or three pariah dogs, upon vague and errant business, and the Executive Engineer going swiftly home from the club on his bicycle. Even the little shops of the bazaar were dark and empty; only here and there a light showed barred behind the carved balconies of the upper rooms, and there was hardly any tom-tomming. The last long slope of the road showed us the river curving to the left, through a silent white waste that stretched indefinitely into the moonlight on one side, and was crowned by Akbar's fort on the other. His long high line of turrets and battlements still guarded a hint of their evening rose, and dim and exquisite above them hovered the three dome-bubbles of the Pearl Mosque. It was a night of perfect illusion, and the illusion was mysterious, delicate, and faint. I sat silent as we rolled along, twenty years nearer to the original joy of things when John and I drove through the same old dream.

Dacres, too, seemed preoccupied; only Cecily was, as they say, herself. Cecily was really more than herself, she exhibited an unusual flow of spirits. She talked continually, she pointed out this and that, she asked who lived here and who lived there. At regular intervals of about four minutes she demanded if it wasn't simply too lovely. She sat straight up with her vigorous profile and her smart hat; and the silhouette of her personality sharply refused to mingle with the dust of any dynasty. She was a contrast, a protest; positively she was an indignity. "Do lean back, dear child," I exclaimed at last. "You interfere with the landscape."

She leaned back, but she went on interfering with it in terms of sincerest enthusiasm.

When we stopped at the great archway of entrance I begged to be left in the carriage. What else could one do, when the golden moment had come, but sit in the carriage and measure it? They climbed the broad stone steps together and passed under the lofty gravures into the garden, and I waited. I waited and remembered. I am not, as perhaps by this time is evident, a person of overwhelming sentiment, but I think the smile upon my lips was gentle. So plainly I could see, beyond the massive archway and across a score of years, all that they saw at that moment—Arjamand's garden, and the long straight tank of marble cleaving it full of sleeping water and the shadows of the marshaling cypresses; her wide dark garden of roses and of pomegranates, and at the end the Vision, marvellous, aerial, the soul of something—is it beauty? is it sorrow?—that great white pride of love in mourning such as only here in all the round of our little world lifts itself to the stars, the unpaintable, indescribable Taj Mahal. A gentle breath stole out with a scent of jessamine and such a memory! I closed my eyes and felt the warm luxury of a tear.

Thinking of the two in the garden, my mood was very kind, very conniving. How foolish after all were my cherry-stone theories of taste and temperament before that uncalculating thing which sways a world and builds a Taj Mahal! Was it probable that Arjamand and her Emperor had loved fastidiously, and yet how they had loved! I wandered away into consideration of the blind forces which move the world, in which comely young persons like my daughter Cecily had such a place; I speculated vaguely upon the value of the subtler gifts of sympathy and insight which seemed indeed, at that enveloping moment, to be mere flowers strewn upon the tide of deeper emotions. The garden sent me a fragrance of roses; the moon sailed higher and picked out the little kiosks set along the wall. It was a charming, charming thing to wait, there at the portal of the silvered, scented garden, for an idyll to come forth.

When they reappeared, Dacres and my daughter, they came with casual steps and cheerful voices. They might have been a couple of tourists. The moonlight fell full upon them on the platform under the arch. It showed Dacres measuring with his stick the length of the Sanskrit letters which declared the stately texts, and Cecily's expression of polite, perfunctory interest. They looked up at the height above them; they looked back at the vision behind. Then they sauntered towards the carriage, he offering a formal hand to help her down the uncertain steps, she gracefully accepting it.

"You—you have not been long," said I. "I hope you didn't hurry on my account."

"Miss Farnham found the marble a little cold under foot," replied Dacres, putting Miss Farnham in.

"You see," explained Cecily, "I stupidly forgot to change into thicker soles. I have only my slippers. But, mamma, how lovely it is! Do let us come again in the daytime. I am dying to make a sketch of it."

Mr Tottenham was to leave us on the following day. In the morning, after "little breakfast," as we say in India, he sought me in the room I had set aside to be particularly my own.

Again I was writing to John, but this time I waited for precisely his interruption. I had got no further than "My dearest husband," and my pen-handle was a fringe.

"Another fine day," I said, as if the old, old Indian joke could give him ease, poor man!

"Yes," said he, "we are having lovely weather."

He had forgotten that it was a joke. Then he lapsed into silence while I renewed my attentions to my pen.

"I say," he said at last, with so strained a look about his mouth that it was almost a contortion, "I haven't done it, you know."

"No," I responded, cheerfully, "and you're not going to. Is that it? Well!"

"Frankly—" said he.

"Dear me, yes! Anything else between you and me would be grotesque," I interrupted, "after all these years."

"I don't think it would be a success," he said, looking at me resolutely with his clear blue eyes, in which still lay, alas! the possibility of many delusions.

"No," I said, "I never did, you know. But the prospect had begun to impose upon me."

"To say how right you were would seem, under the circumstances, the most hateful form of flattery."

"Yes," I said, "I think I can dispense with your verbal endorsement." I felt a little bitter. It was, of course, better that the connoisseur should have discovered the flaw before concluding the transaction; but although I had pointed it out myself I was not entirely pleased to have the article returned.

"I am infinitely ashamed that it should have taken me all these days—day after day and each contributory—to discover what you saw so easily and so completely."

"You forget that I am her mother," I could not resist the temptation of saying.

"Oh, for God's sake don't jeer! Please be absolutely direct, and tell me if you have reason to believe that to the extent of a thought, of a breath—to any extent at all—she cares."

He was, I could see, very deeply moved; he had not arrived at this point without trouble and disorder not lightly to be put on or off. Yet I did not hurry to his relief, I was still possessed by a vague feeling of offense. I reflected that any mother would be, and I quite plumed myself upon my annoyance. It was so satisfactory, when one had a daughter, to know the sensations of even any mother. Nor was it soothing to remember that the young man's whole attitude towards Cecily had been based upon criticism of me, even though he sat before me whipped with his own lash. His temerity had been stupid and obstinate; I could not regret his punishment.

I kept him waiting long enough to think all this, and then I replied, "I have not the least means of knowing."

I can not say what he expected, but he squared his shoulders as if he had received a blow and might receive another. Then he looked at me with a flash of the old indignation. "You are not near enough to her for that!" he exclaimed.

"I am not near enough to her for that."

Silence fell between us. A crow perched upon an opened venetian and cawed lustily. For years afterward I never heard a crow caw without a sense of vain, distressing experiment. Dacres got up and began to walk about the room. I very soon put a stop to that. "I can't talk to a pendulum," I said, but I could not persuade him to sit down again.

"Candidly," he said at length, "do you think she would have me?"

"I regret to say that I think she would. But you would not dream of asking her."

"Why not? She is a dear girl," he responded inconsequently.

"You could not possibly stand it."

Then Mr Tottenham delivered himself of this remarkable phrase: "I could stand it," he said, "as well as you can."

There was far from being any joy in the irony with which I regarded him and under which I saw him gather up his resolution to go; nevertheless I did nothing to make it easy for him. I refrained from imparting my private conviction that Cecily would accept the first presentable substitute that appeared, although it was strong. I made no reference to my daughter's large fund of philosophy and small balance of sentiment. I did not even—though this was reprehensible—confess the test, the test of quality in these ten days with the marble archives of the Moguls, which I had almost wantonly suggested, which he had so unconsciously accepted, so disastrously applied. I gave him quite fifteen minutes of his bad quarter of an hour, and when it was over I wrote truthfully but furiously to John. . . .

That was ten years ago. We have since attained the shades of retirement, and our daughter is still with us when she is not with Aunt Emma and Aunt Alice—grandmamma has passed away. Mr Tottenham's dumb departure that day in February—it was the year John got his C.B.—was followed, I am thankful to say, by none of the symptoms of unrequited affection on Cecily's part. Not for ten minutes, so far as I was aware, was she the maid forlorn. I think her self-respect was of too robust a character, thanks to the Misses Farnham. Still less, of course, had she any reproaches to serve upon her mother, although for a long time I thought I detected—or was it my guilty conscience?—a spark of shrewdness in the glance she bent upon me when the talk was of Mr Tottenham and the probabilities of his return to Agra. So well did she sustain her experience, or so little did she feel it, that I believe the impression went abroad that Dacres had been sent disconsolate away. One astonishing conversation I had with her some six months later, which turned upon the point of a particularly desirable offer. She told me something then, without any sort of embarrassment, but quite lucidly and directly, that edified me much to hear. She said that while she was quite sure that Mr Tottenham thought of her only as a friend—she had never had the least reason for any other impression—he had done her a service for which she could not thank him enough—in showing her what a husband might be. He had given her a standard; it might be high, but it was unalterable. She didn't know whether she could describe it, but Mr Tottenham was different from the kind of man you seemed to meet in India. He had his own ways of looking at things, and he talked so well. He had given her an ideal, and she intended to profit by it. To know that men like Mr Tottenham existed, and to marry any other kind would be an act of folly which she did not intend to commit. No, Major the Hon. Hugh Taverel did not come near it—very far short, indeed! He had talked to her during the whole of dinner the night before about jackal-hunting with a bobbery pack—not at all an elevated mind. Yes, he might be a very good fellow, but as a companion for life she was sure he would not be at all suitable. She would wait.

And she has waited. I never thought she would, but she has. From time to time men have wished to take her from us, but the standard has been inexorable, and none of them have reached it. When Dacres married the charming American whom he caught like a butterfly upon her Eastern tour, Cecily sent them as a wedding present an alabaster model of the Taj, and I let her do it—the gift was so exquisitely appropriate. I suppose he never looks at it without being reminded that he didn't marry Miss Farnham, and I hope that he remembers that he owes it to Miss Farnham's mother. So much I think I might

claim; it is really very little considering what it stands for.
Cecily is permanently with us—I believe she considers
herself an intimate. I am very reasonable about lending
her to her aunts, but she takes no sort of advantage of my
liberality; she says she knows her duty is at home. She is
growing into a firm and solid English maiden lady, with
a good colour and great decision of character. That she
always had.

I point out to John, when she takes our crumpets away
from us, that she gets it from him. I could never take
away anybody's crumpets, merely because they were
indigestible, least of all my own parents'. She has
acquired a distinct affection for us, by some means best
known to herself; but I should have no objection to that
if she would not rearrange my bonnet-strings. That is a
fond liberty to which I take exception; but it is one thing
to take exception and another to express it.

Our daughter is with us, permanently with us. She
declares that she intends to be the prop of our declining
years; she makes the statement often, and always as if it
were humorous. Nevertheless I sometimes notice a spirit
of inquiry, a note of investigation in her encounters with
the opposite sex that suggests an expectation not yet
extinct that another and perhaps a more appreciative
Dacres Tottenham may flash across her field of vision—
alas, how improbable! Myself I can not imagine why she
should wish it; I have grown in my old age into a perfect
horror of cultivated young men; but if such a person
should by a miracle at any time appear, I think it is
extremely improbable that I will interfere on his behalf.

The Scythe Hand
or The Homestead
Adolf Muschg

Adolf Muschg
(Switzerland, b. 1934)

"Every man and woman is tormented in their own way," says
Adolf Muschg's agonizing protagonist in "The Scythe Hand,"
"and I have learned that those who are stronger will then oppress
others because of it." What we hear in this confessional story is
not the voice of the oppressed, but the voice of the oppressor, the
tormentor, the tyrant, of him who seemingly has no justification.
The family in this story is a microcosm of society, and the father's
statement a political defence of the criminal powers of the state.
And yet there is more: behind the statement, what moves us as
readers is the fact that the father is a real father; the daughters, in
his memory, real daughters. The story's poignancy lies in its
unrelenting verisimilitude.

The author of numerous novels, short stories and volumes of
poetry, Adolf Muschg remains practically unknown to English
readers. Professor of German Language and Literature at the
Swiss Institute of Technology in Zurich, his characters define
their world through a particular use of their mother tongue,
which explains perhaps in part the lack of an audience outside
the German-speaking countries. Only one of his volumes of
short stories, *The Blue Man*, is currently available in English.

The Scythe Hand
or The Homestead

Perhaps the Court of Enquiry is not aware that with my
late wife Elisabeth I farmed for fifteen years at Frogs' Well
and was of good repute there, had enough to live on, too,
till the same burned to the ground for dubious reasons in
the year 1951 with our son Christian, aged two at that time,
and I also lost all our livestock, as well as vehicles, because
the fire spread too fast and the fire brigade did not arrive in
time. Frogs' Well had been in the family for more than a
century, and my grandfather farmed it to everyone's satisfaction in his time. Consequently my father, deceased, was
even elected to the School Board, and I take the liberty of
mentioning that I was able to attend the Secondary School
at Krummbach, because my mother, deceased, skimped no
sacrifice. Water could have been drawn from the hydrant
by the well, but the fire chief insisted on his view that this
was frozen over, which was quite correct, but all that was
needed was to break the thin ice. So more than one hour
passed before the hose was laid across from Hasenrain, and
the main building too could not be saved. The death of
Christian gave rise to many ugly rumors, although he was
quite small and we had always looked after him well. That

was a great blow to us at the time. Since the indemnity was never adequate and at first we were housed at Shady Bank, that too gave rise to sharp friction, and my dear wife survived it only for one year, because she had caught cold during the conflagration, which turned out to be cancer. That also is a cause of great distress to us, when everyone knew that we used to manage well and had been punished enough as it was, and had paid our ground-rent regularly. But the indemnity was reduced out of malice, and the operation cost 5000 francs, which I could hardly raise, and it became too much for the farmeress at Shady Bank, because of my daughters, although Lina was already 22 and gave a hand everywhere, as I did in the field, while they said that I scared the cows and therefore must not milk them. It wasn't Barbara's fault that she was only three years old, though she did cause a lot of work in which as a man I could not assist enough, and the farmeress at Shady Bank was herself expecting. So we had to move out and take out a lease for Torgel Alp from the municipality, for which I had reason to be grateful too, because the previous tenant had caught his death there after running down the farm and hanging himself. The place was too lonely for him as well.

So up on Torgel Alp nothing had been done for years, but Lina and I got the homestead back into working order, and we succeeded, too, in bringing up Barbara satisfactorily, so that she kept her health. Only her way to school was so long that in winter she could not always manage it, so that she fell behind and lost much joy, even though I cleared the track each morning and this wasn't even laid down in the contract.

I cleared the road as far as the dairy farm, but didn't hang about there, nor in the village, because of the people, not even to collect money owing for milk. If that gave rise to new rumors, that's typical, but the real trouble was the great remoteness of the homestead, which often set in as early as mid-October because of snow.

Also, I had to go over completely to dairy farming,

which I should not have dreamed of doing at Frogs' Well, but carried out in the teeth of all sorts of obstacles.

Also, the ground-rent was so high that with the best will in the world we had to borrow again. At first I had the good luck to be able to graze 15-20 bullocks, privately, but then for no evident reason the number decreased, although I only asked for my due, the bullocks returned to the valley in good condition, too, but I never stayed there long enough to forestall the rumors. Furthermore, my older daughter Lina was often sick, which did not affect the running of the farm, since I kept her at her work and exertions all the same, and our younger one had had to learn early on to help her sister, even though this kept her away from school. I must add that Lina was a strong support for me without words and despite the pain she had in her belly, and would be still if she hadn't been taken into care now, for which she is not to blame, and I only hope that now she is receiving medical attention, because she has earned it. It was a blow to us when the municipality would send no more bullocks for grazing because of irregularities that were completely unfounded, or that were due only to all the special circumstances there, and because I didn't spend all my time defending myself, so that I was thrown back on my meager resources.

Sheer slander it was, their saying that I was out of my mind, only because I could no longer control a twitching in my cheek, and I'm sure that caused no inconvenience to anyone, but never allowed a bad word to cross my lips, as the Vicar can testify, as long as he came to see us, that is, for he stopped, as everyone knows, until it was too late. When people wouldn't look at me because of the twitch, I sent Barbara out with the milk, which would have done her no harm, I'm sure, and she only bought the most necessary things at the shop, because we couldn't afford more in any case, and if she sometimes stayed for a while it was only because she had to wait and other people can afford more than they could in my time.

And if they say my milk wasn't 100%, no one has proved that and none of those gentlemen saw how I looked after my cattle, they always got fed before we did, and as for sick cows, I had to telephone to report such a case if it occurred, so that the vet could get there in time, even though a jeep was put in his disposal by the municipality.

I too am a member of the municipality, but that doesn't mean that my daughters can simply be taken into care, only because they aren't to blame for anything. It is always being said, too, that I ceased to go to church or to confession, but there I should like you to consider that I should have gone when the trouble started, but it was too far away, and so we had to cope with the trouble on our own. If that is sin, my daughters couldn't help it, and you gentlemen of the Court should admit it, because of their youth for one thing, because of their poverty for another, and you should take into account that, given all those things, Barbara may have been a bit backward. Nevertheless, when it had happened, no sort of deterioration took place in the household, no, it improved if anything, since at last we lived together in peace and could raise the ground-rent for once, which was like a miracle, and I thanked God for it, until the Vicar arrived and, after him, the Justice of the Peace, all because of the slander. For it is my opinion that if you leave a family alone for so long you must allow them to solve their problems in their own way. But since she has been taken into care now, I don't want to stand in the way of my daughter's happiness, only hope that this is what's in question, not somebody's profit because my daughter has learned how to work, and I also request that there shall be no recriminations, because I did not corrupt her, although, as you know, unlawful acts did take place. These were only for the sake of her peace, as Barbara can confirm if she likes, and I forgive her in my heart, she must not fret because she got me into prison, for that was our fate, it seems, and that's all there is to it. So I will thank God that she came down from Torgel Alp, and beg the honorable Court only for some attention to her, so that she survives. I was fond of her, there's no getting away from it, and consequently could not do otherwise, and wouldn't know today what to do. And even my late wife would have had no objection, I know that, when I had the privilege to know her kind heart for twenty-four years, and she was glad, too, to be blessed with late children, first Barbara, then Christian who stayed behind in the fire. That is why, too, she departed this life and left the family to their own devices, that was a bit much all at once, when on top of it you are penalized and have to move to Torgel Alp. If my older daughter Lina hadn't taken after her late mother, hadn't been the split image of her, I don't know what would have become of us up there.

One should not forget, though, that a girl has other thoughts in her head beyond housekeeping, even an older girl.

In any case Lina was no longer ill when you separated us, that may not have suited the Rev. Vicar, because his mind boggled, but then he was clerical and past the age when a person is tormented.

But should Lina now be ailing once more, then it's those people who did that to her, for my daughter has a strong constitution and recovers every time she is needed. I myself couldn't know—could I?—that at 57 I should be tormented again, and it was a cold morning too. I was about to go out and feed the cows, and I noticed that she hadn't lit the fire, but the kitchen was empty, and your breath froze in front of your nose. I was startled, dear Court of Enquiry, for I can only say that nothing like that had happened in ten years, even when she did have a bellyache she'd drag herself downstairs and put the coffee on the stove. All the windows were covered in frost, and the place quiet as a churchyard, that's where she ought to have appeared to me, for it hadn't been as quiet as that since the death of my wife. But this didn't occur to me at that instant, I can promise you, didn't come over me till later.

Went upstairs to the bedroom, the little one was asleep for

we'd always let her sleep when it was too cold, and there was only a little boxroom for her, but a warm bed, there she was coziest, why take her anywhere else. My only thought was that there could be one fewer of us again, and that made me shake with fear, I never so much as knocked on Lina's door but tore it open. I only write this much so that you will know the circumstances, not so that you'll come to dirty conclusions again. For there in the cold bedroom my wife sat in her shift, her bare shift, honorable Court of Enquiry, never turned her head but went on as before, leaning forward a little, so as to see herself in the mirror, only a small one it was, and passed the brush over her hair. But she did that so slowly that this slowness, together with the mere shift and the breath clouding the mirror, so that she had to wipe it clear with her free hand, all this cut into my heart and made me feel quite faint, I can't describe it, when my wife had been dead all those years. What are you doing, I asked, why don't you stop, or you'll catch cold. She said, without turning round: Why not, she said, quite calm and funny. Later she said she had dreamed of her mother, and only then, I promise you, I remembered that I too had dreamed of her mother, but by then it was too late.

As long as I stood there, by the door, I saw only that she didn't so much as turn around and, in consequence, that her hair had already turned gray in places. You should bear in mind that Lina was not quite 37, which is normal, save that as her father I had never paid attention to it, also the cold, and that the shock had left me in an abnormal state of mind. That is why everything happened so fast that I can't recall how it came about, I didn't lie about that, even though you want to know the exact details, but what's the use of them now. On my honor and salvation, all I know is that suddenly I felt relieved and Lina's face, with a rosy and languid look she hadn't had since her childhood, lay beside me on the pillow, and the two of us breathed. I am sorry I cannot tell you more, save that it happened, and that was all, and you are grown-up people after all, nor was I aware of the illegality of the act at that moment, but it wasn't my age, on the contrary, 57 doesn't amount to old age, I wish it did. Next item, I went to feed the animals, and when I returned Lina was at the stove as usual, humming a tune, and the coffee was already made. That's how it went till the evening, save that I couldn't get to sleep and was cruelly tormented. I drank several glasses of brandy, fill yourself up, I said to myself, and you won't feel so sore about it. But this was not the case, the whole mood of the place was changed, too, like at Christmas, for which reason I retired for self-abuse, as in all the previous years, when tormented. The mood would not leave me, though, but you must not think that this happened often, I'd been tormented daily only in the four or five years after my wife's death, then once a month perhaps, and then it stopped completely and I lived like a decent widower. I said to myself, what's up, then, you have no right to any Christmas any more, have you, you aren't even sleepy, and so I took a walk over to the cattle, which nearly always helped.

Although by then I had only two cows of my own and six goats, and your breath froze on your nose, I got into a sweat as soon as I so much as looked at them, though I'd seen the same thing a thousand times if I'd seen it once, and they turned their heads to look at me, too, as though they wanted to do something to me, as though bewitched, so that I went out again and on and on through the snow, as far as the place where I took it into my head to lie down, thinking that will make you feel better. But then in the cold it struck me that my daughters wouldn't be able to raise the money for my funeral, but would be exposed to mockery, though behind hands held to the face as usual, I didn't want them to suffer that, couldn't get my daughters out of my mind at all, but not in the way you think, and I got up again. So I suddenly found myself back at the homestead, must have walked in a semi-circle, that happens in the snow. It wasn't my own homestead either, I'd always known that, but when you're tired and the above has occurred, you see things as though for the first time. So I stood like a stranger in front of this homestead and no longer knew what was what, was afraid to go in. I thought, something will happen of itself if you stand here long enough, sooner or later the music will stop, for I had heard music all that night, and the stars were out, it was getting colder fast, near dawn. But because the snow itself made everything bright I saw that a window upstairs was open, please, my God, don't, I said to that, but nothing helped, so I called out, shut it, then, shut it, you pig, yes that's what I called out, but don't know whether she heard me, my voice was feeble too, and all remained as it was.

If I turned my head a bit could see it more clearly, but still, couldn't tell for certain, what, if I looked at it straight it was there at one moment, gone the next, but it was something white all the time.

A man wants to know, gentlemen, whether someone his own is standing so long at an open window in such a frost and catching her death of it, so I went inside and upstairs, but it wasn't the torment, when I couldn't even feel my own feet. In Lina's bedroom everything was open, and the window too, but no one was standing there, and I began to fear what she might have done to herself. Stretched out my hand, I did, to where it was darkest, for that's where the bed was, till I felt something warm, something alive, that was there. Said, Thank God for that, without her being able to hear me, because she was under the cover and I wanted to comfort her. But she held on to my hand and said, come on, then, you idiot, you chicken, and said it quite clearly, and I responded to it, because I suddenly lost all consciousness of myself, and it must have happened for the second time, for suddenly there was peace again and no music any more. You must not hold that chicken against my daughter, it was clearly meant to be a sort of joke. I had called out pig, too, and hadn't meant it. You can call that sin, but there was this cold all the time, and I'm no chicken I'm sorry to say, so I stayed till it was warm. No one thanks you, anyway, for suffering the cold, and the need is too great to be forgiven us, as the Vicar said, whether we live as husband and wife now or not.

After that Lina was cured of her bellyache, we were kinder to each other, too, and took good care of each other, and that year I could pay off my ground-rent in time, because a blessing had been put on it. Was able to buy two more cows and have all four served, and they produced cow calves and got a prize a year later, which was made possible because the judges at Krummbach didn't know so much about my situation, and it became evident that without prejudice I could manage well, received a loan from the Small Farmers' Assistance too, which enabled me to have the roof re-thatched and to build a long-needed reservoir, but created more bad blood in the village. For, High Court of Justice, it is true, on my oath, that one can stand on one's head, bad blood can't be made any better, especially if the village is small.

It was also true that I could have a new dress bought for each of my daughters, which nowadays is no luxury even in remote places, and I waited till the sales for that and certainly did not live in splendor and affluence. When we only had just enough for us to get used to our state of affairs.

As for me, I can only add that since the death of my lamented wife I had never lived in a family, but this was now the case more than ever. My younger daughter caught me singing, too, as I whitewashed the cowshed. That was more than I deserved, I'm sure, and I give all the credit for it to my dear daughters.

After finishing her school years Barbara did not want to take any employment, since she'd had enough teasing, the spasms in her face grew more violent too, which she must have inherited, though in myself I was not always aware of them. The vet couldn't find a good reason for them either, save that they were nervous, though I should have paid him to the last penny for his pills. So it came about that Barbara stayed with us, nor expressed any desire for an apprenticeship, which I should certainly have let her have, never wanting to deprive my daughters of anything, since I am fond of them both, though not in the way you think. Nor did I know that in the shed she was subject to regular

molestation by the scythe hand, that Füllemann who is well
known to you, who took advantage of her extremity,
because she never said anything about it in public, perhaps
thinking we had enough trouble already. It would have
been better if she had, though, for in that case I should have
bashed in the scythe hand's skull without qualms. What I
am charged with, though, because the scythe hand got it out
of her, that was quite different from the gossip it gave rise to,
the reason why I am now in prison. Because I was fond of
my daughter, and concerned about her health, about which
I knew no better when even a vet wouldn't take the trouble,
I couldn't resist, but I never implanted any pride in her on
that score, so that she would go and boast to the scythe
hand about something that certainly happened as an emer-
gency measure and under the stress of too much molestation, when she was still half a child, as she is to this day.

For, High Court of Justice, you wouldn't have done any
different either if your daughter had begged for it so
urgently and you couldn't bear to see her suffer, only
because the girl doesn't know the facts of life, but was
physically mature and plagued by it, again because of the
remoteness of the homestead, which could happen only up
on Torgel Alp. Our Frogs' Well was burnt down, as you
know, my wife departed and I alone with the girls, of whom
one was now 37, the other 21, a great gap, but not with
regard to the female body, that makes it hard to show no
love when Lina is better all at once, but the younger one
sleeps just behind the thin partition and is tormented in her
fashion.

Since she slept lightly I wanted to relieve her of that, there
was no other motive, and the longer it went on the less
anyone thought anything of it, if the scythe hand hadn't got
it out of her, I bet he had his reasons. And if it is said that she
burst into tears, I'd like to have seen you if as half a child
still you'd got under the scythe hand, and that wasn't till
seven months later, the tears too came because of the Vicar,
who got there late enough, it had never happened with me.

Rather the facts of the case were as follows, my younger

daughter came to me in the spring, complaining that I
didn't esteem her, because Lina was privileged, and she was
only her sister. At first I dismissed that, till my younger girl
went to bed ill and wouldn't get up again, the twitches in
her face got so bad, too, that mine broke out again and I
feared for her sanity, and she sang so loud when I was with
Lina that I thought a sow was being struck, but she never
dared come in, because she was a decent girl. In March,
though, she developed such a bellyache that I thought, Oh,
hell, maybe it would be better for you to give her peace,
talked about it with Lina, who'd turned into a real
housewife. But it wasn't true that she advised me to do it, she
only knew, what must be, must be. So, when Lina had gone
to the road house with the milk, I took Barbara a jug of milk
warm from the cow to her bedroom, since I had to take
everything up to her, which became troublesome, and it was
March 23rd. She grabbed hold of my hand at once so that I
could feel if there wasn't a swelling there, and when I felt
her she started that cruel screaming again, as well as spasms
which ran visibly across her whole body, and I felt so sorry
for her that I couldn't help myself but allowed what
followed to occur. Then she got up quite amiable and
smiled like a rogue, but I was too fond of my daughter to
bear her any grudge, only begged her sincerely never to let it
happen again. Whereupon she quite easily drank the milk
which she had pushed far away from her before, and went
quite sensibly to the kitchen, and prepared an evening meal,
which she hadn't done for a long time, indeed started
cooking and frying so much that I got alarmed and we fed
well that evening, in great obliviousness even drank brandy
till it gave rise to new acts, and I was even the instigator,
which I would beg to have taken into account today in
my daughters' favor. That was March 23rd. For I must
add that because of constant physical labor I am still full
of sap, quite unexpectedly, nor knew any remedy for it
till Lina took the matter into her hand, but this occurred
with good will on both sides, like the relations with my
younger daughter, which I did not need any more, as

you will understand.

But let the respected Court tell me of a way to help a poor person like Barbara out of her predicament, when the partition is thin and there's no prospect of her finding a suitable man, when already at school she couldn't keep up, but only because of Torgel Alp, where one couldn't make a secret of our situation, as other people do. For, dear Court, poverty had come first, I must say that quite plainly, and poverty brings many troubles in its train, of which one can relieve only the most pressing, if no one else offers any help.

It would have been the first time I preferred one daughter to the other, that is why I had to take her on in turn, not because I was tormented. After that all went smoothly in our house, you can ask anyone, and if it was a sin and no one wants to have anything to do with us now, I do beseech you not to make too great an issue of our intercourse, for neither did we, but peace was the main thing, and we did not disturb anyone, but were never bedded on roses. And I assure you that the abomination was no unmitigated pleasure, a thing that is quite unknown on Torgel Alp, but only a kind of comfort.

Earlier on we did have a conscience about it, but that ceased because my daughters no longer suffered from a bellyache, and this was better than a deal of worrying about it and even made us quite merry at times in the winter. There are always people who talk about their conscience but don't tell a man all the same what's to be done against the cold or against pains, at least nobody told us. When the Vicar arrived at last we no longer expected him and didn't really know what to do about it, and nor did he. For he walked up quite slowly, Lina saw him from a long way off, and she said, O my God. So, when he could think of nothing to say but only asked, don't you want to confess, I could not back him up and answered quite legitimately, I wouldn't know what to confess, and he replied, he thought I did know, and he couldn't even look me straight in the eyes. For years he could have observed how Barbara's face twitched, and my daughter Lina's bellyache, but all that had been nothing to him, not so now that all was going well, though without his blessing. I told him what I thought about that. He said that he never listened to gossip but was answerable for preventing the spreading of the bacillus, which would make half the community sick at the very mention of us, and that I could bear even less to be answerable for it, either toward God or toward my daughters. I said I could bear to be answerable for many things as long as a man needs help and the ways are not always clear to him, in short I refused point-blank to make a confession of it, when he still couldn't look me in the face, but only stroked his hip with one hand.

I then offered him a glass of schnapps, whereupon he did not come in, but said: if you will not avail yourself of the secrecy of confession I must ask you as a fellow citizen to give yourself up, because otherwise you will be in trouble, you will make the village unhappy with your state of affairs, or would you prefer to have your roof set on fire one night? High Court of Justice, that give me a fright, to hear him talk of a fire, when I had lost one child in a fire before, and there too the cause had remained obscure, although I had never given offense to anyone. Whereupon my daughter Barbara rushed into the room and made our distress very great by screaming that the Vicar was a dirty old man and ought to wipe his nose after sticking it into everyone's pots, when it wasn't his business, and did the scythe hand confess too what he had done to her? So the cat was out of the bag, as far as the scythe hand was concerned, and it then came out that the same had repeatedly lain in wait for her when she was helpless because of the heavy pails she was carrying, and had grabbed hold of her in spite of her protests. Finally, at the end of June, he had gone so far as to bash her head against a stone near the milking-shed, so that she couldn't struggle, and used her, because there was no help for her nearby, and on top of that had said to her mockingly, how well the meadow had been mown already, and hadn't he hurt her? Whereupon my daughter had screamed in her half-conscious state, with his miserable stub he couldn't do

anyone any harm, let alone any good. Whereupon the same
had merely buttoned up his trousers, saying, all right, all
the more power to our buck, who had all the nanny-goats to
himself, now that the farmer had come to an agreement
with his daughters, and she was to give his regards to the
whole happy household, put on his hat and left. That was a
sad speech, since it is well known that lonely men have to
make do with animals, when for years they cannot find a
single human being, something I did not do even in my
worst plight, but only deviated from the straight and
narrow path to give my daughters peace, of which certainly
the younger one ought not to have bragged, nor did I ever
implant such arrogance in her heart.

Nevertheless, High Court of Justice, you should take into
account that she was used by the scythe hand, and this
without any understanding between them.

I have always believed that in such things there must be
an agreement, and that two are needed for that, even with
poor folk, and a little joy, which even beasts do not fail to
feel in their fashion. But between my daughters and me this
was so, because we did it for the sake of warmth and it was
not the most important thing, but so that the family would
be kept together, nor was violence ever used. But the scythe
hand confessed his crime to the Vicar and got rid of his sin
by bringing down justice upon our homestead, and we all
had to pay dearly for Barbara's little lapse into pride. Now
you want to know more than I can offer you, when the real
shock and perdition came only after everyone took such a
lively interest in the affair.

The scythe hand got off lightly because he is young and
daft as a duck, but older flesh is never forgiven when it's
tormented, and yet its trials are harder than those of any
loud-mouthed young ruffian. But if my daughter Lina had
been younger, and without my fears, I should never have
violated her, but it was because I saw her gray hairs and pity
took hold of me like a rage that this daughter of mine was
not to be taken for what she was, but must drag her
bellyache around in silence all her life, which to this day

seems more bestial to me than everything else. And this too was not because of the flesh, but because the flesh is tormented by a soul and has nothing left to hope for if it finds no warmth, something I could not bear to watch any longer. Everything else, as I have set it down, followed logically from that, because I could not slight Barbara, and never pursued those relations for their own sake, but only so that the girls should have some kindness in their lives.

And I raise no objection now if the whole responsibility falls on me, because men should always know better. I did not know better, only did what I could in those criminal acts to find the right course.

By taking my daughters into care and appointing a guardian doubtless you know better, and I only ask that my daughters, because they are girls, will be spared as much of the disgrace as possible, perhaps in another valley, where they are not known. For we have never in our lives received as much attention as after the Vicar's visit, in which connection I will name only the Justice of the Peace, then Lina's old teacher, twice the constable, and then a regular police action even with dogs, as though we had ever thought of running away, when we couldn't even have known where to. All the nets are so tightly meshed everywhere. I have never seen my daughters again since then, and enough of cross-examinations, if I may say so, don't know whether they had to undergo them too and if that was of any use, they will hardly have understood your words, but surely taken them to heart. So let me apologize at this point on their behalf. Nor do I want to receive a letter ever again from my daughters, if that could do them harm, would only like to know whether they are well cared for as far as the circumstances permit, and should be much gratified to obtain an assurance to that effect from you. I also beg for instructions as to how, once and for all, I am to express myself under interrogation, since I can see very well that I was far from satisfying the gentlemen with my way of speaking, but may well have made matters even worse, though I spoke the truth.

About the abnormality in my face which I got rid of but which has now returned, I beg of you not to be disturbed, nor to be put off by it, if that is possible. I shall manage all right.

Details of the criminal act, I am sorry to say, embarrass me, since the process is familiar enough to grown-up people, and I should only like to observe that most of those can go through the same in more favorable circumstances, nor do I believe that more is to be learned about it from my daughters than what every real man or woman knows.

Make an end of it, at last, honorable Court, because you are better off, or I could begin to say things I should be sorry about, all right, I will admit to having led my daughters into misdemeanor, if you insist on it and I can lessen the plight of those girls by saying so.

Perhaps it is possible, too, to choose a guardian for my daughters who is not a clergyman. These, I regret to say, often fall into false assumptions which their wards then have to swallow, but can't always, which leads to tragedies.

Every man and woman is tormented in their way, and I have learned that those who are stronger will then oppress others because of it, by which I don't mean to deny their good will, and please don't hold those words against me.

I have written to you only because my spoken words are not adequate for your satisfaction and because perhaps you will take the opportunity, nonetheless, to convey a greeting to my daughters, which I set down herewith, but this too not for my sake, but because in those years my daughters grew accustomed again to a little warmth.

May it please you to tell them that they are on my mind by day and by night, but not in the way the High Court of Justice thinks.

Translated from the German by Michael Hamburger

Over the Mountain
Gail Godwin

Gail Godwin
(USA, b. 1937)

Gail Godwin is best known as a novelist, author of such best-sellers as *A Mother and Two Daughters* and *The Finishing School,* but her roots are in the realm of the short story, in the poignant description of one particular moment, one action, and its origins and consequences.

Gail Godwin was born in Alabama and grew up in North Carolina, where she studied to become a journalist. She worked for a time for the Miami *Herald* and then travelled through Europe for five years before returning to the United States; she now lives in Woodstock, New York.

Godwin's language, like that of several other Southern writers, is unblushingly lyrical, careful to milk every word for its many senses and hues of meaning. Not surprisingly, she has written several librettos for the composer Robert Starer. "Over the Mountain" is a musical exercise in female voices, set against Godwin's memories of a suburban American past. Mother, daughter, grand-daughter engage in a game of power in which there are ultimately no winners, no losers. One cannot help feeling that "Over the Mountain" is but a glimpse of a contest which began before the days of Electra and hasn't yet come to a discernable end.

Over the Mountain

If you have grown to love your life, it seems ungrateful to belabor old injustices, especially those that happened in childhood, that place of sheltered perspectives where you were likely to wake up and go to bed without anyone ever disabusing you of your certainty that all days were planned around you. After all, isn't it possible that the very betrayal that flags your memory and constricts your heart led to a development in character that enabled you to forge your present life?

This is not a belaboring. I know by now that behind every story that begins "When I was a child" there exists another story in which adults are fighting for their lives. It is because I accept this that I am ready to go back and fill in some of the blank spaces in the world of a ten-year-old girl whose mother takes her on an overnight train journey. The train carries them out of their sheltered mountains to a town some thousand feet below. The mother and daughter walk around this town, whose main attraction is that the mother spent her happy girlhood years there. The mother and her little girl stay the night in a respectable boarding house. The next day, they get on the northbound version of yesterday's train and go back to the mountains.

Why do I remember nothing particular about that
journey? I, with my usually prodigious memory for
details? Except for a quality of light and atmosphere—the
lowland town throbbed with a sociable, golden-yellow
heat that made people seem closer, whereas our mountain
town had a cool, separating blue air that magnified
distances—I have no personal images of this important
twenty-four hours. I say important because it was a
landmark in my life: it was the first time I had gone away
alone with my mother.

Despite the fact that I believe I now know why that
excursion lies blank among my memory cells, there is
something worth exploring here. The feeling attached to
that event, even today, signals the kind of buried affect
that shapes a life.

We were not, our little unit of three, your ordinary
"nuclear" family, but, as I had known nothing else, we
seemed normal enough to me. Our living arrangements
were somewhat strange for a trio of females with high
conceptions of their privileges in society, but, as my
grandmother hastened to tell people, it was because of the
war. And when the war ended, and all the military personnel who had preempted the desirable dwellings had
departed from town, and we continued to stay where we
were, I accepted my mother's and grandmother's continual reminders that "it was only a matter of time now
until the right place could be found."

The three of us slept in one gigantic room, vast enough
to swallow the two full-sized Persian carpets that had
once covered my grandmother's former living room and
dining room and still reproach us with its lonely space,
even when we filled it with all the furniture from the two
bedrooms of her previous home. The rest of her furniture
crowded our tiny living room and dark, windowless kitchen and then spilled out into the shabby public entrance
hall of our building, euphemistically called "the lobby"
by our landlord and my grandmother. My grandmother

spent a lot of time trying to pounce on a tenant in the act of sitting on "our" sofa in the lobby, or winding up "our" old Victrola. She would rush out of our apartment like a fury and explain haughtily that this furniture did not belong to the lobby, it was our furniture, only biding its time in this limbo until it could be resettled into the sort of room to which it was accustomed. She actually told one woman, whom she caught smoking while sitting on "our" sofa, to please "consider this furniture invisible in the future." The woman ground out her cigarette on the floor, told my grandmother she was crazy, and went upstairs.

Our building was still known in town by its old name: The Piping Hot. During the twenties, when Asheville overflowed with land-boom speculators and relatives visiting TB patients, this brown-shingled monstrosity had been thrown up on a lot much too small for it. It had come into existence as a commercial establishment whose purpose was to make money on not-too-elegant people willing to settle for a so-so room and a hot " home-cooked " meal. Therefore it had none of those quaint redeeming features of former private residences fallen on hard times. The reason our bedroom was so huge was simple: it had been the dining room.

It was a pure and simple eyesore, our building: coarse, square, and mud-colored, it hulked miserably on its half-acre with the truculent insecurity of a social interloper. It was a building you might feel sorry for if you were not so busy feeling sorrier for yourself for living in it. Probably the reason its construction had been tolerated at all on that leafy, genteel block was because its lot faced the unsightly physical plant of the proud and stately Manor Hotel which rambled atop its generous acreage on the hill across the street; moreover, the guests at the Manor were prevented by their elevation from seeing even the roof of the lowlier establishment. Our landlord had bought Piping Hot when it went out of business just before the war, chopped it up into as many "apartments" as he could get away with legally, and now collected the rents. Whenever he was forced to drop by, breathless and red-faced, a wet cigar clamped in one corner of his mouth, he would assure my grandmother he had every intention of sowing grass in the bare front yard, of having someone come and wash the filthy windows of the lobby, of cutting down the thorny bushes with their suspicious red berries that grew on either side of the squatty, brown-shingled "shelter" at the sidewalk's edge, where Negro maids often sat down to rest on their way to the bus stop from the big houses at the upper end of the street.

The most "respectable" tenants lived on the ground floor, which must have been some consolation to my grandmother. The Catholic widow, Mrs Gannon, and her two marriageable daughters lived behind us in a rear apartment which had been made over from pantries and half of the old kitchen. (Our kitchen had been carved out of the other half.) When my grandmother or Mrs Gannon felt like chatting, either had only to tap lightly on the painted-over window above her sink; they would gossip about the upstairs tenants while snapping beans or peeling potatoes at their facing sinks. The apartment across the lobby was inhabited by another widow, the cheerful Mrs Rhinehart, who went limping off to work in a china shop every day; her numerous windowsills (her apartment was the Piping Hot's ex-sunporch) were crowded with delicate painted figurines. She suffered from a disease that made one leg twice the width of the other. Among the three widows existed a forbearing camaraderie. Mrs Rhinehart did not like to gossip, but she always stopped and listened pleasantly if my grandmother waylaid her in the lobby; and, though both my grandmother and Mrs Gannon thought Mrs Rhinehart had too many little objects in her windows for good taste, they always amended that, at any rate, she was a brave lady for standing in a shop all day on that leg; and when sailors trekked regularly past our side windows on the way to call on the Gannon girls, my grandmother did not allow her imagination to run as wild as she would have if those same sailors had been on their way to one of the apartments upstairs.

Except for the policeman and his wife, whose stormy marital life thudded and crashed directly above our bedroom, the other upstairs apartments were filled with people my grandmother referred to simply as "the transients." They didn't stay long. You would have to be pretty desperate to stay long in those rear upstairs apartments, which were weird amalgams of former guest rooms, opening into hallways or one another in inconvenient, embarrassing ways, their afterthought bathrooms and kitchens rammed into ex-closets and storage rooms. We didn't even bother to learn their names, those constantly changing combinations of women, of women and children and the occasional rare man, who occupied those awkward upper quarters. They were identified merely by their affronts: the two working girls who clopped around most of the night in their high heels; the woman with the little boy who had written the dirty word in chalk on the sidewalk shelter; the woman who sat down on "our" sofa and stomped out her cigarette on the floor.

Those were the politics of our building. There were also, within our family unit, the politics of my mother's job, the politics of my school, and the subtler triangular dynamics that underpinned life in our apartment.

"Today has been too much for my nerves," my grandmother would say as we huddled over her supper at one end of our giant mahogany dining table which, even with its center leaf removed, took up most of the kitchen. "I was out in the lobby trying to wipe some of the layers of dust off those windows when I happened to look out and there was that little boy about to eat some of the berries on those poison bushes. I rushed out to warn him, only to have his mother tell me she didn't want him frightened. Would she rather have him frightened or dead? Then, not five minutes later, the LaFarges' Negro maid came along and sat down in our shelter and I happened to see her hike her dress up and her stockings were crammed with eggs. I had to debate with myself whether I shouldn't let the LaFarges know. . . ."

"I hope you didn't," said my mother, rolling her eyes at me in that special way which my grandmother was not meant to see.

"No. You have to let them get away with murder if you're going to keep them. I remembered that. Do you remember Willy Mae, when we lived in Greenville?"

My mother laughed. Her voice was suddenly younger and she looked less tired. Greenville was the town on the other side of the mountain where, in a former incarnation, she had lived as a happy, protected young girl. But then a thought pinched her forehead, crimping the smoothness between her deep blue eyes. "I do wish that ass Dr Busey could see through that snake Lu Ann Leach," she said.

"Kathleen. Lower your voice."

My mother gave an exasperated sigh and sent me a signal: We've got to get out of here. After supper we'll go to the drugstore.

"He hasn't said anything about her staying on at the college, has he?" asked my grandmother *sotto voce*, casting her eyes balefully towards the painted-over window above our sink behind which even a good friend like Mrs Gannon might be straining to hear how other people's daughters were faring in this uncertain world without a man.

"No, but he hasn't said anything about her leaving, and now she's taken over the literary magazine. She was only supposed to fill in for Miss Pennell's operation and Miss Pennel has been back three weeks. The college can't afford to keep all three of us. There aren't that many students taking English. All the GI's want their math and science so they can go out and make *money*."

"Well, they have to keep you," declared my grand-mother, drawing herself up regally.

"They don't have to do anything, Mother." My mother was losing her temper.

"What I mean is," murmured my grandmother in a conciliatory manner to ward off a "scene" which might be overheard, "they will naturally want to keep you, because you're the only one with your MA. I'm so thank-ful that Poppy lived long enough so we could see you through your good education."

"You should see the way she plays up to him," my mother went on, as if she hadn't heard. "She has that plummy, little-girl way of talking, and she asks his *advice* before she'll even go the bathroom. If she weren't a Leach, people couldn't possibly take her seriously; she couldn't get a job in a kindergarten."

"If only Poppy had lived," moaned my grandmother, "you would never have had to work."

"My work is all I've *got*," blurted my mother passion-ately. "I mean, besides you two, of course."

"Of course," agreed my grandmother. "I only meant if he had lived. Then we could have had a nice house, and you could have worked if you wanted."

My mother's eyes got round, the way they did when someone had overlooked an important fact. She was on the verge of saying more, but then with an effort of her shoulders harnessed her outburst. She sat with her eyes still rounded, but cast down breathing rapidly through her nostrils. I thought she looked lovely at such times.

"Can we walk to the drugstore and look at the maga-zines?" I asked.

"If you like," she said neutrally. But, as soon as my grandmother rose to clear the dishes, she sneaked me a smile.

"The thing is, no matter how much I wipe at those lobby windows from the inside," my grandmother said, as much to herself as to us, "they can never be clean. They need to be washed from the outside by a man. Until they are, we will be forced to look through dirt."

"It was on the tip of my tongue to say, 'If you stay *out* of the lobby you won't have to worry about the dirt,' " my mother told me as we walked to the drugstore a block away.

"That would have been perfect!" I cried, swinging her hand. "Oh, why *didn't* you?" I was a little overexcited, as I always was when the two of us finally made it off by ourselves. Here we were escaped together at last, like two sisters from an overprotective mother. Yet even as the spring dusk purpled about our retreating figures, we both knew she was watching us from the window: she would be kneeling in the armchair, her left hand balancing her on the windowsill, her right hand discreetly parting the white curtains; she could watch us all the way to our destination. She had left the lights off in the apartment, to follow us better.

"It would have been cruel," my mother said. "That lobby is her outside world."

Though complaining about my grandmother often drew us closer, I could see my mother's point. It was not that we didn't love her; it was that the heaviness of her love confined us. She worried constantly that something would happen to us. She thought up things, described them aloud in detail, which sometimes ended up scaring us all. (The mother of the little boy about to eat the berry had been right.)

We had reached the corner of our block. As we waited for a turning car to go by, we looked up and saw the dining-room lights of the Manor Hotel twinkling at us. The handful of early spring guests would just be sitting down to eat.

I looked up at one of the timbered gables. "There's nobody in Naomi Benjamin's room yet," I said.

"The season will be starting soon. All the rooms will be filled. But never again will I ever write *anybody's* autobiography. Unless I write my own someday."

My mother and grandmother had been so excited last summer when Naomi Benjamin, an older woman from New York who had come to our mountains for her health, offered my mother $500 to "work with her on her autobiography." Someone at the Manor had told Naomi that my mother was a published writer, and she had come down from the hill to call on us at The Piping Hot and make her offer. We were impressed by her stylish clothes and her slow, gloomy way of expressing herself, as if the weight of the world lay behind her carefully chosen words. But, before the end of the summer, my mother was in a rage. Sometimes, after having "worked with" Naomi Benjamin all afternoon, and after typing up the results at night, my mother would lie back and rant while my grandmother applied a cold washcloth to her head and told her she was not too young to get a stroke. "A stroke would be something *happening*," snarled my mother, "whereas not a damn thing has happened to that woman; how dare she aspire to autobiography!" "Well, she is Jewish," reflected my grandmother. "They never have an easy time." "Ha!" spat my mother. "That's what I thought. I thought I'd learn something interesting about other ways of suffering, but there's not even that. I'd like to tell her to take her five hundred dollars and buy herself some excitement, That's what she really needs." "Kathleen, tension can burst a blood vessel . . ." "I wish to God I could make it up," my mother ranted on, growing more excited, "at least I wouldn't be dying of boredom!" "I'm going to phone her right now," announced my grandmother, taking a new tack; "I'm going to tell her you're too sick to go on." "No, no, no!" My mother sprang up, waving the cold cloth aside. "It's all right. I'm almost finished. Just let me go walk up and down the street for a while and clear my head."

We had reached the drugstore in the middle of the next block, our oasis of freedom. We passed into its brightly lit interior, safe for a time behind brick walls that even my grandmother's ardent vision could not penetrate. Barbara, the pharmacist, was doing double duty behind the soda fountain, but when she looked up and saw it was us she went on wiping the counter; she knew that, despite her sign (THESE MAGAZINES ARE FOR *BUYING*, NOT FOR BROWSING), we would first go and look through the pulp magazines to see if there was any new story by Charlotte Ashe. But we always conducted our business as quickly and unobtrusively as possible, so as not to set a bad example for other customers; we knew it pained Barbara to see her merchandise sinking in value with each browser's fingerprints, even though she admired my mother and was in on the secret that Charlotte Ashe's name had been created from the name of this street and the first half of the name of our town.

There was no new story by Charlotte Ashe. It was quite possible all of them had appeared by now, but my mother did not want to spoil our game. It had been a while since Charlotte Ashe had mailed off a story. During the war, when my mother worked on the newspaper, it had been easier to slip a paragraph or two of fiction into the typewriter on a slow-breaking news day. But now the men had come home, to reclaim their jobs at the newspaper, and fill up the seats in the classroom where my mother taught; there was less time and opportunity to find an hour alone with a typewriter and let one's romantic imagination soar—within the bounds of propriety, of course.

We sat down at the counter. It would not do to make Barbara wait on us in a booth. She was, for all her gruff tones, the way she pounced on children who tried to read the comic books, the pharmacist. As if to emphasize this to customers who might confuse her with a mere female employee, Barbara wore trousers and neckties and took deep, swinging strides around her store; she even wore men's shoes.

"Kathleen, what'll you have?"

"A Coke, please, Barbara, for each of us. Oh, and

would you put a tiny squirt of ammonia in mine? I've got a headache coming on."

"How tiny?" Barbara's large hand with its close-clipped nails hovered over the counter pump that discharged ammonia.

"Well, not too tiny."

Both women laughed. Barbara made our Cokes, giving my mother an indulgent look as she squirted the pump twice over one of the paper cups. All the other customers got glasses if they drank their beverages in the store, but my grandmother had made us promise never to drink from a drugstore glass after she saw an ex-patient of the TB sanatorium drink from one. "Your cups, ladies," said Barbara ironically, setting them ceremoniously before us. She and my mother rolled their eyes at each other. Barbara knew all about the promise; my mother had been forced to tell her after Barbara had once demanded gruffly, "Why can't you all drink out of glasses like everybody else?" But Barbara did not charge us the extra penny for the cups.

We excused ourselves and took our Cokes and adjourned to a booth, where we could have privacy. As there were no other customers, Barbara loped happily back into her rear sanctum of bottles and pills.

At last I had my mother all to myself.

"How was school today?"

"We had field day practice," I said. "Mother Donovan was showing us how to run the three-legged race and she pulled up her habit and she has really nice legs."

"That doesn't surprise me, somehow. She must have had a real vocation, because she's certainly pretty enough to have gotten married. How are you and Lisa getting along?"

"We're friends, but I hate her. I hate her and she fascinates me at the same time. What has she *got* that makes everybody do what she wants?"

"I've told you what she's got, but you always forget."

"Tell me again. I won't forget."

My mother swung her smooth pageboy forward until it half-curtained her face. She peered into the syrupy depths of her spiked Coke and rattled its crushed ice, as if summoning the noisy fragments to speak the secret of Lisa Gudger's popularity. Then, slowly, she raised her face and her beautiful dark blue eyes met mine. I waited, transfixed by our powerful intimacy.

"You are smarter than Lisa Gudger," she began, saying her words slowly. "You have more imagination than Lisa Gudger. And, feature by feature, you are prettier than Lisa Gudger . . ."

I drank in this litany, which I did remember from before.

"But Lisa likes herself better than you like yourself. Whatever Lisa has, she thinks it's best. And this communicates itself to others, and they follow her."

This was the part I always forgot. I was forgetting it again already. I stared hard at my mother's face, I could see myself reflected in the small pupils, contracted from the bright drugstore lights; I watched the movement of her lips, the way one front tooth crossed slightly over the other. The syllables trying to contain the truth about a girl named Lisa Gudger broke into smaller and smaller particles and escaped into the air as I focused on my mother, trying to show her how well I was listening.

I partially covered up by asking, after it was over, "Do you hate Lu Ann Leach the way I hate Lisa?"

"Now that's an interesting question. Now, Lisa Gudger would not have had the imagination to ask that question. I do hate Lu Ann, because she's a real threat; she can steal my job. I hate her because she's safe and smug and has a rich father to take care of her if everything else falls through. But Lu Ann Leach does not fascinate me. If I could afford it, I would feel pity for her. See, I've figured her out. When you've figured someone out, they don't fascinate you anymore. Or at least they don't when you've figured out the kind of thing I figured out about her."

"Oh, what? What have you figured out?"

"Shh." My mother looked around towards Barbara's whereabouts. She leaned forward across our table. "Lu Ann hates men, but she knows how to use them. Her hatred gives her a power over them, because she just doesn't care. But I'd rather be myself, without that power, if it means the only way I can have it is to become like Lu Ann Leach. She's thirty, for God's sake, and she still lives with her parents."

"But you live with your mother."

"That's different."

"How is it different?"

My mother got her evasive look. This dialogue had strayed into channels where she hadn't meant it to. "It's a matter of choice versus necessity," she said, going abstract on me.

"You don't hate men, then?" I could swear I'd heard her say she had: the day she got fired from the newspaper, for instance.

"Of course I don't. They're the other half of the world. *You* don't hate men, do you?" She gave me a concerned look.

I thought of Men. There was the priest at school, Father Lilley, whose black skirts whispered upon the gravel; there was Jovan, our black bus driver; there was Hal the handyman who lived in a basement apartment under the fifth-grade classroom with his old father, who drove the bus on Jovan's day off. There was Don Olson, the sailor I had selected as my favorite out of all those who passed our window on their way to see the Gannon girls; I would lie in wait for him at our middle-bedroom window, by the sewing machine, and he would look in and say, "Hi there, beautiful. I might as well just stop here." Which always made me laugh. One day my grandmother caught me in the act of giving him a long list of things I wanted him to buy me in town. "She's just playing, she doesn't mean it," she cried, rushing forward to the window. But he brought me back every item on the list. And there was my father, who had paid us one surprise visit from Florida. His body shook the floor as he strode through our bedroom to wash his hands in the bathroom. He closed the bathroom door behind him and locked it. My mother made me tell everybody he was my uncle, because she had already told people he had been killed in the war: a lie she justified because, long ago, he had stopped sending money, and because people would hire a war widow before they would a divorced woman. Still, I was rather sorry not to be able to claim him; with his good-looking face and sunburnt ankles (he wore no socks, even with his suit), he was much more glamorous than my friends' dull business fathers.

"Sure. I like men," I told my mother in the booth. I was thinking particularly of Don Olson. The Gannon girls were fools to let him get away.

"Well, good," said my mother wryly, shaking her ice in the paper cup. "I wouldn't want *that* on my conscience. That I'd brought you up to hate men."

As if we had conjured him up by our tolerant allowance of his species, a Man materialized in front of our booth.

"Well looky here what I found," he said, his dark brown eyes dancing familiarly at us.

My mother's face went through an interesting series of changes. "Why, what are *you* doing home?" she asked him.

It was Frank, one of her GI students from the year before, who was always coming by our apartment to get extra help on a term paper, or asking her to read a poem aloud so he could understand it better. Once last year, out of politeness, I had asked him to sign my autograph book; but whereas her other GIs had signed things like "Best of luck from your friend Charles," or "To a sweet girl," Frank had written in a feisty slant: "To the best daughter of my best teacher." His page troubled me, with its insinuating inclusion of himself between my mother and me; also, his handwriting made "daughter" look like "daughtlet." It was like glimpsing myself from a sudden unflattering angle: a "daughtlet." And what did he mean *best* daughter? I was my mother's only daughter. At the end of last spring, when I knew he would be transferring to Georgia Tech, I took a razor and carefully excised his page.

"I can't stay out of these mountains," said Frank, reaching for a chair from a nearby table and fitting it backwards between his legs. Barbara looked out from the window of her pharmacy, but when she saw who it was did not bother to come out.

"I should think it would be nice to get out of them for a change," said my mother.

"Well, what's stopping you?" asked Frank, teetering forward dangerously on two legs of his chair. He rested his chin on the dainty wrought-iron back of the chair and assessed us, like a playful animal looking over a fence.

My mother rolled her eyes, gave her crushed ice a fierce shake, and emptied the last shards into her mouth. They talked on for a few more minutes, my mother asking him neutral questions about his engineering courses, and then she stood up. "We've got to be getting back or Mother will start worrying that we've been kidnapped."

He stood up, too, and walked us to the door with his hands in his pockets. "Want a ride?"

"One block? Don't be silly," said my mother.

He got into a little gray coupe and raced the motor unnecessarily, I thought, and then spoiled half of our walk home by driving slowly along beside us with his lights on.

"I wish we could go off sometime, just by ourselves," I said in the few remaining steps of cool darkness. My grandmother had pulled down the shades and turned on the lamp, and we could see the shadow of the top of her head as she sat listening to the radio in her wing chair.

"Well, maybe we can," said my mother. "Let me think about it some."

We went inside and the three of us scrubbed for bed

and the women creamed their faces. I got in bed with my mother, and, across the room, my grandmother put on her chin strap and got into her bed. We heard the policeman coming home; his heavy shoes shook the whole house as he took the stairs two at a time. "He has no consideration," came my grandmother's reproachful voice from the dark. There soon followed their colorful exchange of abuses, the wife's shrieks and the policeman's blows. "It's going too far this time," said my grandmother, "he's going to kill her, I'm going to call the police." "You can't call the police on the police, Mother. Just wait, it'll soon be over." And my mother was right: about this time the sound effects subsided into the steady, accelerated knocking against our ceiling which would soon lead to silence. "If Poppy had lived, we would not be subjected to this," moaned my grandmother. "Even he couldn't keep life out," sighed my mother, and turned her back to me for sleep.

Our trip alone together came to pass. I don't know how my mother talked my grandmother out of going with us. She was a respectful daughter, if often impatient, and would not have hurt my grandmother's feelings for the world. And it would have been so natural for my grandmother to come: she was the only one of us who could ride free. The widow of a railroad man, she could go anywhere she wanted on Southern Railways until the end of her life.

But, at any rate, after what I am sure were exhaustive preparations sprinkled with my grandmother's imaginative warnings of all the mishaps that might befall us, we embarked—my mother and I—from Biltmore Train Station south of Asheville. My grandmother surely drove us there in our ten-year-old Oldsmobile, our last relic of prosperity from the days when Poppy lived. I am sure we arrived at the station much too early, and that my grandmother probably cried. Poppy had been working at Biltmore Station when my grandmother met him. His

promotions had taken them out of her girlhood mountains to a series of dusty piedmont towns which she had
never liked; and now here she was back in the home
mountains, in the altitude she loved—but old and without him. My mother and I were going to the first of the
towns to which he had been transferred when my mother
had been about the age I was now.

I do not remember our leaving from Biltmore Station or
our returning to it the next afternoon. That is the strange
thing about those twenty-four hours. I have no mental
pictures that I can truly claim I inhabited during that
timespan. Except for that palpable recollection of the
golden heat which I have already described, there are no
details. No vivid scenes. No dialogues. I know we stayed
in a boarding house, which my grandmother, I am sure,
checked out in advance. It is possible that the owner
might have been an old acquaintance, some lady fallen
on harder times, like ourselves. Was this boarding house
in the same neighbourhood as the house where my
mother had lived? I'm sure we must have walked by that
house. After all, wasn't the purpose of our trip—other
than going somewhere by ourselves—to pay a pilgrimage
to the scene of my mother's happy youth? Did we, then,
also walk past her school? It seems likely, but I don't
remember. I do have a vague remembrance of "downtown," where, I am sure, we must have walked up and
down streets, in and out of stores, perhaps buying something, some small thing that I wanted; I am sure we must
have stopped in some drugstore and bought two Cokes in
paper cups.
  Did the town still have streetcars running on tracks,
jangling their bells; or was it that my mother described
them so well, the streetcars that she used to ride when she
lived there as a girl?
  I do not know.
  We must have eaten at least three meals, perhaps four,
but I don't remember eating them.

We must have slept in the same bed. Even if there had
been two beds in the room, I would, sooner or later, have
crawled in with my mother. I always slept with her.

My amnesia comes to a stunning halt the moment the
trip is over. My grandmother has picked us up from
Biltmore Station and there I am, on Charlotte Street
again, in the bedroom *née* dining room of the old Piping
Hot.

It is late afternoon. The sun is still shining, but the
blue atmosphere of our mountains has begun to gather.
The predominant color of this memory is blue. I am
alone in the bedroom, lying catty-cornered across the bed
with my head at the foot; I am looking out the window
next to the one where I always used to lie in wait for the
sailor, Don Olson, on his way to call on the Gannon
girls. The bedspread on which I am lying is blue, a light
blue, with a raised circular pattern in white; it smells
clean. Everything in this room, in this apartment, smells
clean and womanly. There is the smell of linen which
has lain in lavender-scented drawers; the smell of my
mother's "Tweed" perfume, which she dabs on lightly
before going to teach at the college; the acerbic, medicinal
smell of my grandmother's spirits of ammonia, which she
keeps in a small green cut-glass bottle and sniffs whenever she feels faint; the smell of a furniture polish, oil-
based, which my grandmother rubs, twice a week, into
our numerous pieces of furniture.

Where are they? Perhaps my grandmother is already in
the kitchen, starting our early supper, hardly able to contain her relief that our trip without her is over. Perhaps
my mother is out by herself in the late sunshine, taking
one of her walks to clear her head; or maybe she is only
in the next room, reading the Sunday paper, grading student themes for the following day, or simply gazing out
at the same view I was gazing at, thinking her own
thoughts.

I looked out at the end of that afternoon. The cars were

turning from Charlotte Street into Kimberly, making a whishing sound. I could see the corner wall of the drugstore. But there was no chance of going there after supper, because we had already been away for more time than ever before.

An irremediable sadness gathered about me. *This time yesterday, we were there,* I thought; *and now we are here and it's all over.* How could that be? For the first time, I hovered, outside my own body, in that ghostly synapse between the anticipated event and its aftermath. I knew what all adults know: that "this time yesterday" and "this time tomorrow" are often more real than the protracted now.

It's over, I thought; and perhaps, at that blue hour, I abandoned childhood for the vaguely perceived kingdom of my future. But the knot in my chest that I felt then—its exact location and shape—I feel now, whenever I dredge up that memory.

A lot of things were over, a lot of things did come to an end that spring. My mother announced that she would not be going back to teach at the college. (Lu Ann Leach took her place, staying on into old age—until the college was incorporated into the state university.) And then, on an evening in which my grandmother rivaled the policeman's wife in her abandoned cries of protest, my mother went out for a walk and reappeared with Frank, and they announced to us that they were married. The three of us left that night, but now we are talking about a different three; my mother, Frank, and me. All that summer we lived high on a mountain—a mountain that, ironically, overlooked the red-tiled roofs of the Manor Hotel. Our mountain was called Beaucatcher, and our address was the most romantic I've ever had: One Thousand Sunset Drive. Again we were in a house with others, but these others were a far cry from the panicked widows and lonely mothers of Charlotte Street. Downstairs lived a nightclub owner and his wife and her son (my age) from

an earlier marriage; upstairs lived a gregarious woman of
questionable virtue. One night, a man on the way
upstairs blundered by accident into my room—I now had
a room, almost as large as the one we three had shared in
the life below—and Frank was so incensed that he rigged
up a complicated buzzer system: if my door opened during the night, the buzzer-alarm would go off, even if it
was I who opened it. That summer I made friends with
the nightclub owner's stepson, learned to shoot out street
lights with my own homemade slingshot, and, after seeing a stray dog dripping blood, was told about the realities of sex. First by the boy, the stepson, in his own
words; then, in a cleaned-up version, by my mother. I
invited Lisa Gudger up to play with me; we got into
Frank's bottle of Kentucky Tavern and became roaring
drunk; and I beat her up. My mother called Mrs Gudger
to come and get Lisa, and then hurriedly sewed onto
Lisa's ripped blouse all the buttons I had torn off.

My grandmother, who had screamed she would die if we
left her, lived on through the long summer. And through
another summer, during which we were reconciled. Frank
had quit Georgia Tech to marry my mother, and worked
as a trainee in Kress's. Within a year, my mother and
Frank had moved back to the old Piping Hot. They now
had the former apartment of the policemen and his wife.
My grandmother slept on in her bed downstairs, and I
divided my time between them.

    A few years later, we left my grandmother again. Frank
was being transferred to a town on the other side of the
mountain. One of those hot little towns a thousand feet
below. After we had been away for some months, my
grandmother shocked us all by getting her first job at the
age most people were thinking about retiring. At the time
most people were coming home from work, my grandmother pinned on her hat and put on her gloves and hid
all of Poppy's gold pieces and his ring and his watch in
a secret fold of her purse, and took the empty bus

downtown to her job. She worked as night housemother at the YWCA residence for working girls. It was a job made in heaven for her: she sat up waiting for the girls. If they came in after midnight, they had to ring and she let them in with an admonition. After three admonitions she reported them to the directress, a woman she despised. We heard all about the posturings and deceptions of this directress, a Mrs Malt, whenever we visited. My grandmother's politics had gone beyond the lobby into the working world; she was able to draw Social Security because of it.

When our brand new "nuclear family" arrived in the little lowland town where Frank was to be the assistant manager of Kress's, we moved into a housing development. Our yard had no grass, only an ugly red clay slope that bled into the walkway every time it rained. "I guess I'll never know what it's like to have grass in the front yard," I said, in the sorrowful, affronted, doom-laden voice of my grandmother. "Hell, honey," replied Frank with his mountain twang, "if you want grass in this world, you've got to plant it." I forgive him for his treachery now, as I recall the thrill of those first tiny green spikes, poking up out of that raw, red soil.

Years and years passed. I was home on a visit to my mother and Frank and their little daughter and their two baby sons. "You know, it's awful," I told Mother, "but I can't remember a single thing about that trip you and I took that time on the train. You know, to Greenville. Do you remember it?"

"Of course I do," she said, her eyes going that distant blue. "Mother took us to the station and we had a lovely lunch in the dining car, and then we went to all my old haunts, and we stayed the night at Mrs ————'s, and then we got back on the train and came home. It was a lovely time."

"Well, I wish I could remember more about it."

"What else would you like to know?" asked Frank,

who had been listening, his eyes as warm and eager to communicate as my mother's were cool and elegiac.

But she suddenly got an odd look on her face. "Frank," she said warningly.

"Well hell, Kathleen." He hunched his shoulders like a rebuked child.

"Frank, please," my mother said.

"Well, I was there, too," he flared up.

"You were not! That was another time we met in Greenville." But her eyes were sending desperate signals and her mouth had twisted into a guilty smirk.

"The hell it was. The second time we went, it was to get married."

Then he looked at me, those brown eyes swimming with their eager truths. She had turned away, and I didn't want to hear. Fat chance. "I drove down," he said. "I followed your train. You were sick on the train and you had to have a nap when you got there. I waited till your mother met me on the corner after you fell asleep. And then after you fell asleep that night, Well dammit, Kathleen," he said to the cool profile turned away from him, "it's the truth. Did the truth ever hurt anybody?"

He went on to me, almost pleading for me to see his side. "I don't know what we would have done without you," he said. You were our little chaperone, in a way. Don't you *know* how impossible it was, in those days, ever to get her alone?"

The Gardener
Rudyard Kipling

Rudyard Kipling
(India, 1865-1936)

In October of 1915, Rudyard Kipling's only son John was reported missing in action. The last man to see him alive, a guardsman named Michael Bowes, reported that he had seen John crying from a mouth wound "but hadn't liked to help for fear of humiliating him." The fear for John was intensified by the dread that the Germans would be especially cruel towards the son of the man who had written so vehemently against "the Hun's unspeakable atrocities." Three years later, Kipling's friend Rider Haggard (who believed in reincarnation) asked him if he thought that Earth was one of the hells. "I don't *think* so," Kipling answered. "I am certain of it." To a friend of the family, visiting after John's disappearance, Kipling said, "Down on your knees, Julia, and thank God you haven't a son."

"The Gardener" is one of the war stories Kipling wrote when he was at the height of his literary powers; it is one of his most subtle studies of social hypocrisy and private grief, told from the point of view of Helen, an unmarried Englishwoman. The identity of the gardener, in the final scene, has been variously discussed by reviewers. Alexander Woolcott, the American critic, knew someone to whom Kipling confided that the gardener was Helen's brother; others have suggested that he is the ghost of Helen's lover, father of her son. In the text, the reference is to the Gospel of St John, 20:15, when Mary Magdalene is at the tomb of Jesus and does not recognize him. Whatever the correct interpretation might be—and in this ambiguity is much of Kipling's richness—the gardener's identity is less important than the sense of loss, and pity, and untold love that so desperately reflects Kipling's own.

The Gardener

One grave to me was given,
  One watch till Judgement Day;
And God looked down from Heaven
  And rolled the stone away

One day in all the years,
  One hour in that one day,
His Angel saw my tears,
  And rolled the stone away!

Everyone in the village knew that Helen Turrell did her duty by all her world, and by none more honourably than by her only brother's unfortunate child. The village knew, too, that George Turrell had tried his family severely since early youth, and were not surprised to be told that, after many fresh starts given and thrown away, he, an Inspector of Indian Police, had entangled himself with the daughter of a retired non-commissioned officer, and had died of a fall from a horse a few weeks before his child was born. Mercifully, George's father and mother were both dead, and though Helen, thirty-five and independent, might well have washed her hands of the whole disgraceful affair, she most nobly took charge, though she was, at the time, under threat of lung trouble which had driven her to the South of France. She arranged for the passage of the child and a nurse from Bombay, met them at Marseilles, nursed the baby through an attack of infantile dysentery due to the carelessness of the nurse, whom she had had to dismiss, and at last, thin and worn but triumphant, brought the boy later in the autumn, wholly restored, to her Hampshire home.

All these details were public property, for Helen was as open as the day, and held that scandals are only increased by hushing them up. She admitted that George had always been rather a black sheep, but things might have been much worse if the mother had insisted on her right to keep the boy. Luckily, it seemed that people of that class would do almost anything for money, and, as George had always turned to her in his scrapes, she felt herself justified—her friends agreed with her—in cutting the whole non-commissioned officer connection, and giving the child every advantage. A christening, by the Rector, under the name of Michael, was the first step. So far as she knew herself, she was not, she said, a child-lover, but, for all his faults, she had been very fond of George, and she pointed out that little Michael had his father's mouth to a line; which made something to build upon.

As a matter of fact, it was the Turrell forehead, broad, low, and well-shaped, with the widely spaced eyes beneath it, that Michael had most faithfully reproduced. His mouth was somewhat better cut than the family type. But Helen, who would concede nothing good to his mother's side, vowed he was a Turrell all over, and, there being no one to contradict, the likeness was established.

In a few years Michael took his place, as accepted as Helen had always been—fearless, philosophical, and fairly good-looking. At six, he wished to know why he could not call her "Mummy," as other boys called their mothers. She explained that she was only his auntie, and that aunties were not quite the same as mummies, but that, if it gave him pleasure, he might call her "Mummy" at bedtime, for a pet-name between themselves.

Michael kept his secret most loyally, but Helen, as usual, explained the fact to her friends; which when Michael heard, he raged.

"Why did you tell? *Why* did you tell?" came at the end of the storm.

"Because it's always best to tell the truth," Helen answered, her arm round him as he shook in his cot.

"All right, but when the troof's ugly I don't think it's nice."

"Don't you, dear?"

"No, I don't, and"—she felt the small body stiffen—"now you've told, I won't call you 'Mummy' any more—not even at bedtimes."

"But isn't that rather unkind?" said Helen softly.

"I don't care! I don't care! You've hurted me in my insides and I'll hurt you back. I'll hurt you as long as I live!"

"Don't, oh, don't talk like that, dear! You don't know what—"

"I will! And when I'm dead I'll hurt you worse!"

"Thank goodness, I shall be dead long before you, darling."

"Huh! Emma says, 'Never know your luck.' " (Michael had been talking to Helen's elderly, flat-faced maid.) "Lots of little boys die quite soon. So'll I. *Then* you'll see!"

Helen caught her breath and moved towards the door, but the wail of "Mummy! Mummy!" drew her back again, and the two wept together.

At ten years old, after two terms at a prep. school, something or somebody gave him the idea that his civil status was not quite regular. He attacked Helen on the subject, breaking down her stammered defences, with the family directness.

" 'Don't believe a word of it," he said, cheerily, at the end. "People wouldn't have talked like they did if my people had been married. But don't you bother, Auntie. I've found out all about my sort in English Hist'ry and the Shakespeare bits. There was William the Conqueror to begin with, and—oh, heaps more, and they all got on first-rate. 'Twon't make any difference to you, my being *that*—will it?"

"As if anything could—" she began.

"All right. We won't talk about it any more if it makes you cry." He never mentioned the thing again of his own will, but when, two years later, he skilfully managed to have measles in the holidays, as his temperature went up to the appointed one hundred and four he muttered of nothing else, till Helen's voice, piercing at last his delirium, reached him with assurance that nothing on earth or beyond could make any difference between them.

The terms at his public school and the wonderful Christmas, Easter, and Summer holidays followed each other, variegated and glorious as jewels on a string; and as jewels Helen treasured them. In due time Michael developed his own interests, which ran their courses and gave way to others; but his interest in Helen was constant and increasing throughout. She repaid it with all that she had of affection or could command of counsel and money; and since Michael was no fool, the War took him just before what was like to have been a most promising career.

He was to have gone up to Oxford, with a scholarship, in October. At the end of August he was on the edge of joining the first holocaust of public-school boys who threw themselves into the Line; but the captain of his O.T.C., where he had been sergeant for nearly a year, headed him off and steered him directly to a commission in a battalion so new that half of it still wore the old Army red, and the other half was breeding meningitis through living overcrowdedly in damp tents. Helen had been shocked at the idea of direct enlistment.

"But it's in the family," Michael laughed.

"You don't mean to tell me that you believed that old story all this time?" said Helen. (Emma, her maid, had been dead now several years.) "I gave you my word of honour— and I give it again—that—that it's all right. It is indeed."

"Oh, *that* doesn't worry me. It never did," he replied valiantly. "What I meant was, I should have got into the show earlier if I'd enlisted—like my grandfather."

"Don't talk like that! Are you afraid of its ending so soon, then?"

"No such luck. You know what K. says."

"Yes. But my banker told me last Monday it couldn't *possibly* last beyond Christmas—for financial reasons."

"'Hope he's right, but our Colonel—and he's a Regular—says it's going to be a long job."

Michael's battalion was fortunate in that, by some chance which meant several "leaves", it was used for coast-defence among shallow trenches on the Norfolk coast; thence sent north to watch the mouth of a Scotch estuary, and, lastly, held for weeks on a baseless rumour of distant service. But, the very day that Michael was to have met Helen for four whole hours at a railway junction up the line, it was hurled out, to help make good the wastage of Loos, and he had only just time to send her a wire of farewell.

In France luck again helped the battalion. It was put down near the Salient, where it led a meritorious and unexacting life, while the Somme was being manufactured; and enjoyed the peace of the Armentieres and Laventie sectors when that battle began. Finding that it had sound views on protecting its own flanks and could dig, a prudent Commander stole it out of its own Division, under pretence of helping to lay telegraphs, and used it round Ypres at large.

A month later, and just after Michael had written Helen that there was nothing special doing and therefore no need to worry, a shell-splinter dropping out of a wet dawn killed him at once. The next shell uprooted and laid down over the body what had been the foundation of a barn wall, so neatly that none but an expert would have guessed that anything unpleasant had happened.

By this time the village was old in experience of war, and, English fashion, had evolved a ritual to meet it. When the postmistress handed her seven-year-old daughter the official telegram to take to Miss Turrell, she observed to the Rector's gardener: "It's Miss Helen's turn now." He replied, thinking of his own son: "Well, he's lasted longer than some." The child herself came to the front door weeping aloud, because Master Michael had often given her sweets. Helen, presently, found herself pulling down the house-blinds one after one with great care, and saying earnestly to each: "Missing *always* means dead." Then she took her place in the dreary procession that was impelled to go through an inevitable series of unprofitable emotions. The Rector, of course, preached hope and prophesied word, very soon, from a prison camp. Several friends, too, told her perfectly truthful tales, but always about other women, to whom, after months and months of silence, their missing had been miraculously restored. Other people urged her to communicate with infallible Secretaries of organizations who could communicate with benevolent neutrals, who could extract accurate information from the most secretive of Hun prison commandants. Helen did and wrote and signed everything that was suggested or put before her.

Once, on one of Michael's leaves, he had taken her over a munition factory, where she saw the progress of a shell from blank-iron to the all but finished article. It struck her at the time that the wretched thing was never left alone for a single second; and "I'm being manufactured into a bereaved next of kin," she told herself, as she prepared her documents.

In due course, when all the organizations had deeply or sincerely regretted their inability to trace, etc., something gave way within her and all sensation—save of thankfulness for the release—came to an end in blessed passivity. Michael had died and her world had stood still and she had been one with the full shock of that arrest. Now she was standing still and the world was going forward, but it did not concern her—in no way or relation did it touch her. She knew this by the ease with which she could slip Michael's name into talk and incline her head to the proper angle, at the proper murmur of sympathy.

In the blessed realization of that relief, the Armistice with all its bells broke over her and passed unheeded. At the end of another year she had overcome her physical loathing of the living and returned young, so that she could take them by the hand and almost sincerely wish them well. She had no interest in any aftermath, national or personal, of the war, but, moving at an immense distance, she sat on various relief committees and held strong views—she heard herself delivering them—about the site of the proposed village War Memorial.

Then there came to her, as next of kin, an official intimation, backed by a page of a letter to her in indelible pencil, a silver identity-disc, and a watch, to the effect that the body of Lieutenant Michael Turrell had been found, identified, and re-interred in Hagenzeele Third Military Cemetery—the letter of the row and the grave's number in that row duly given.

So Helen found herself moved on to another process of the manufacture—to a world full of exultant or broken relatives, now strong in the certainty that there was an altar upon earth where they might lay their love. These soon told her, and by means of time-tables made clear, how easy it was and how little it interfered with life's affairs to go and see one's grave.

"*So* different," as the Rector's wife said, "if he'd been killed in Mesopotamia, or even Gallipoli."

The agony of being waked up to some sort of second life drove Helen across the Channel, where, in a new world of abbreviated titles, she learnt that Hagenzeele Third could be comfortably reached by an afternoon train which fitted in with the morning boat, and that there was a comfortable little hotel not three kilometres from Hagenzeele itself, where one could spend quite a comfortable night and see one's grave next morning. All this she had from a Central Authority who lived in a board and tar-paper shed on the skirts of a razed city full of whirling lime-dust and blown papers.

"By the way," said he, "you know your grave, of course?"

"Yes, thank you," said Helen, and showed its row and number typed on Michael's own little typewriter. The officer would have checked it, out of one of his many books;

but a large Lancashire woman thrust between them and
bade him tell her where she might find her son, who had
been corporal in the A.S.C. His proper name, she sobbed,
was Anderson, but, coming of respectable folk, he had of
course enlisted under the name of Smith; and had been
killed at Dickiebush, in early 'Fifteen. She had not his
number nor did she know which of his two Christian names
he might have used with his alias; but her Cook's tourist
ticket expired at the end of Easter week, and if by then she
could not find her child she should go mad. Whereupon she
fell forward on Helen's breast; but the officer's wife came
out quickly from a little bedroom behind the office, and the
three of them lifted the woman on to the cot.

"They are often like this," said the officer's wife,
loosening the tight bonnet-strings. "Yesterday she said he'd
been killed at Hooge. Are you sure you know your grave? It
makes such a difference."

"Yes, thank you," said Helen, and hurried out before the
woman on the bed should begin to lament again.

Tea in a crowded mauve and blue striped wooden structure,
with a false front, carried her still further into the nightmare. She paid her bill beside a stolid, plain-featured Englishwoman, who, hearing her inquire about the train to
Hagenzeele, volunteered to come with her.

"I'm going to Hagenzeele myself," she explained. "Not
to Hagenzeele Third; mine is Sugar Factory, but they call it
La Rosière now. It's just south of Hagenzeele Three. Have
you got your room at the hotel there?"

"Oh yes, thank you. I've wired."

"That's better. Sometimes the place is quite full, and at
others there's hardly a soul. But they've put bathrooms into
the old Lion d'Or—that's the hotel on the west side of Sugar
Factory—and it draws off a lot of people, luckily."

"It's all new to me. This is the first time I've been over."

"Indeed! This is my ninth time since the Armistice. Not
on my own account. *I* haven't lost anyone, thank God—but,
like everyone else, I've a lot of friends at home who have.

Coming over as often as I do, I find it helps them to have someone just look at the—place and tell them about it afterwards. And one can take photos for them, too. I get quite a list of commissions to execute." She laughed nervously and tapped her slung Kodak. "There are two or three to see at Sugar Factory this time, and plenty of others in the cemeteries all about. My system is to save them up, and arrange them, you know. And when I've got enough commissions for one area to make it worth while, I pop over and execute them. It *does* comfort people."

"I suppose so," Helen answered, shivering as they entered the little train.

"Of course it does. (Isn't it lucky we've got window-seats?) It must do or they wouldn't ask one to do it, would they? I've a list of quite twelve or fifteen commissions here"—she tapped the Kodak again—"I must sort them out tonight. Oh, I forgot to ask you. What's yours?"

"My nephew," said Helen. "But I was very fond of him."

"Ah, yes! I sometimes wonder whether *they* know after death? What do you think?"

" Oh, I don't—I haven't dared to think much about that sort of thing," said Helen, almost lifting her hands to keep her off.

"Perhaps that's better," the woman answered. "The sense of loss must be enough, I expect. Well, I won't worry you any more."

Helen was grateful, but when they reached the hotel Mrs Scarsworth (they had exchanged names) insisted on dining at the same table with her, and after the meal, in the little, hideous salon full of low-voiced relatives, took Helen through her "commissions" with biographies of the dead, where she happened to know them, and sketches of their next of kin. Helen endured till nearly half past nine, ere she fled to her room.

Almost at once there was a knock at her door and Mrs Scarsworth entered; her hands, holding the dreadful list, clasped before her.

"Yes—yes— *I* know," she began. "You're sick of me, but I

want to tell you something. You—you aren't married, are you? Then perhaps you won't . . . . But it doesn't matter. I've *got* to tell some one. I can't go on any longer like this."

"But please—" Mrs Scarsworth had backed against the shut door, and her mouth worked dryly.

"In a minute," she said "You—you know about these graves of mine I was telling you about downstairs, just now? They really *are* commissions. At least several of them are." Her eye wandered round the room. "What extraordinary wall-papers they have in Belgium, don't you think? . . . . Yes. I swear they are commissions. But there's *one*, d'you see, and—he was more to me than anything else in the world. Do you understand?"

Helen nodded.

"More than any one else. And, of course, he oughtn't to have been. He ought to have been nothing to me. But he *was*. He *is*. That's why I do the commissions you see. That's all."

"But why do you tell me?" Helen asked desperately.

"Because I'm so tired of lying. Tired of lying—always lying—year in and year out. When I don't tell lies I've got to act 'em and I've got to think 'em, always. *You* don't know what that means. He was everything to me that he oughtn't to have been—the one real thing—the only thing that ever happened to me in all my life; and I've had to pretend he wasn't. I've had to watch every word I said, and think out what lie I'd tell next, for years and years!"

"How many years?" Helen asked.

"Six years and four months before, and two and three-quarters after. I've gone to him eight times, since. Tomorrow'll make the ninth, and—and I can't—I *can't* go to him again with nobody in the world knowing. I want to be honest with some one before I go. Do you understand? It doesn't matter about *me*. I was never truthful, even as a girl. But it isn't worthy of *him*. So—so I—I had to tell you. I can't keep it up any longer. Oh, I can't!"

She lifted her joined hands almost to the level of her mouth, and brought them down sharply, still joined, to full arms' length below her waist. Helen reached forward, caught them, bowed her head over them, and murmured: "Oh, my dear! My dear!" Mrs Scarsworth stepped back, her face all mottled.

"My God!" said she. "Is *that* how you take it?"

Helen could not speak, and the woman went out; but it was a long while before Helen was able to sleep.

Next morning Mrs Scarsworth left early on her round of commissions, and Helen walked alone to Hagenzeele Third. The place was still in the making, and stood some five or six feet above the metalled road, which it flanked for hundreds of yards. Culverts across a deep ditch served for entrances through the unfinished boundary wall. She climbed a few wooden-faced earthen steps and then met the entire crowded level of the thing in one held breath. She did not know that Hagenzeele Third counted twenty-one thousand dead already. All she saw was a merciless sea of black crosses, bearing little strips of stamped tin at all angles across their faces. She could distinguish no order or arrangement in their mass; nothing but a waist-high wilderness as of weeds stricken dead, rushing at her. She went forward, moved to the left and the right hopelessly, wondering by what guidance she should ever come to her own. A great distance away there was a line of whiteness. It proved to be a block of some two or three hundred graves whose headstones had already been set, whose flowers were planted out, and whose new-sown grass showed green. Here she could see clear-cut letters at the ends of the rows, and, referring to her slip, realized that it was not here she must look.

A man knelt behind a line of headstones—evidently a gardener, for he was firming a young plant in the soft earth. She went towards him, her paper in her hand. He rose at her approach and without prelude or salutation asked: "Who are you looking for?"

"Lieutenant Michael Turrell—my nephew," said Helen slowly and word for word, as she had many thousands of times in her life.

The man lifted his eyes and looked at her with infinite compassion before he turned from the fresh-sown grass towards the naked, black crosses.

"Come with me," he said, "and I will show you where your son lies."

When Helen left the Cemetery she turned for a last look. In the distance she saw the man bending over his young plants; and she went away, supposing him to be the gardener.

Why Can't They
Tell You Why?
James Purdy

James Purdy
(USA, b. 1923)

I met James Purdy in 1980, in an all-night coffee shop off Broadway. I had read *The Nephew,* one of the finest, most intelligent novels about—among other things—the aftermath of war, and also *Narrow Rooms,* a Southern Gothic fantasy, darkly erotic. Purdy didn't sound like the author of either book: there was no heady melancholia or gaudy display in his conversation. Instead, he quietly remembered some of his encounters with the characters who had become part of his fiction, and whose lives he had recorded to exorcise them from his dreams. The mother and son in "Why Can't They Tell You Why?" he met in Chicago, in the forties, long before the press had picked up the story of battered children. "The Press find out things so long after we all know them," he said. "And to me, this was a very American story. Fathers are often absent in America, or at least were not much there during the forties and fifties. And mothers vie for that absent love; they don't really want their children to love their father. Like all of us, really; we want love all to ourselves."

The story was written in the early fifties, at a time when Purdy could get nothing published; it was privately printed in 1956. Dame Edith Sitwell, the flamboyant English poet who discovered, among others, Dylan Thomas and Wilfred Owen, read it and was dazzled. "I think it undoubted," she wrote, "that James Purdy will come to be recognized as one of the greatest living writers of fiction in our language."

Why Can't They
Tell You Why?

Paul knew nearly nothing of his father until he found the box of photographs on the backstairs. From then on he looked at them all day and every evening, and when his mother Ethel talked to Edith Gainesworth on the telephone. He had looked amazed at his father in his different ages and stations of life, first as a boy his age, then as a young man, and finally before his death in his army uniform.

Ethel had always referred to him as *your father*, and now the photographs made him look much different from what this had suggested in Paul's mind.

Ethel never talked with Paul about why he was home sick from school and she pretended at first she did not know he had found the photographs. But she told everything she thought and felt about him to Edith Gainesworth over the telephone, and Paul heard all of the conversations from the backstairs where he sat with the photographs, which he had moved from the old shoe boxes where he had found them to two big clean empty candy boxes.

"Wouldn't you know a sick kid like him would take up with photographs," Ethel said to Edith Gainesworth. "Instead of toys or balls, old photos. And my God, I've hardly mentioned a thing to him about his father."

Edith Gainesworth, who studied psychology at an adult

center downtown, often advised Ethel about Paul, but she did not say anything tonight about the photographs.

"All mothers should have pensions," Ethel continued. "If it isn't a terrible feeling being on your feet all day before the public and then having a sick kid under your feet when you're off at night. My evenings are worse than my days."

These telephone conversations always excited Paul because they were the only times he heard himself and the photographs discussed. When the telephone bell would ring he would run to the backstairs and begin looking at the photographs and then as the conversation progressed he often ran into the front room where Ethel was talking, sometimes carrying one of the photographs with him and making sounds like a bird or an airplane.

Two months had gone by like this, with his having attended school hardly at all and his whole life seemingly spent in listening to Ethel talk to Edith Gainesworth and examining the photographs in the candy boxes.

Then in the middle of the night Ethel missed him. She rose feeling a pressure in her scalp and neck. She walked over to his cot and noticed the Indian blanket had been taken away. She called Paul and walked over to the window and looked out. She walked around the upstairs, calling him.

"God, there is always something to bother you," she said. "Where are you, Paul?" she repeated in a mad sleepy voice. She went on down into the kitchen, though it did not seem possible he would be there, he never ate anything.

Then she said *Of course*, remembering how many times he went to the backstairs with those photographs.

"Now what are you doing in here, Paul?" Ethel said, and there was a sweet but threatening sound to her voice that awoke the boy from where he had been sleeping, spread out protectively over the boxes of photographs, his Indian blanket over his back and shoulder.

Paul crouched almost greedily over the boxes when he saw this ugly pale woman in the man's bathrobe looking at him. There was a faint smell from her like that of an uncovered cistern when she put on the robe.

"Just here, Ethel," he answered her question after a while.

"What do you mean, *just here*, Paul?" she said going up closer to him.

She took hold of his hair and jerked him by it gently as though this was a kind of caress she sometimes gave him. This gentle jerking motion made him tremble in short successive starts under her hand, until she let go.

He watched how she kept looking at the boxes of photographs under his guard.

"You sleep here to be near them?" she said.

"I don't know why, Ethel," Paul said, blowing out air from his mouth as though trying to make something disappear before him.

"You don't know, Paul," she said, her sweet fake awful voice and the stale awful smell of the bathrobe stifling as she drew nearer.

"Don't, don't!" Paul cried.

"Don't what?" Ethel answered, pulling him toward her by seizing on his pajama tops.

"Don't do anything to me, Ethel, my eye hurts."

"Your eye hurts," she said with unbelief.

"I'm sick to my stomach."

Then bending over suddenly, in a second she had gathered up the two boxes of photographs in her bathrobed arms.

"Ethel!" he cried out in the strongest, clearest voice she had ever heard come from him. "Ethel, those are my candy boxes!"

She looked down at him as though she was seeing him for the first time, noting with surprise how thin and puny he was, and how disgusting was one small mole that hung from his starved-looking throat. She could not see how this was her son.

"These boxes of pictures are what makes you sick."

"No, no, Mama Ethel," Paul cried.

"What did I tell you about calling me Mama," she said,

going over to him and putting her hand on his forehead.

"I called you Mama Ethel, not Mama," he said.

"I suppose you think I'm a thousand years old." She raised her hand as though she was not sure what she wished to do with it.

"I think I know what to do with these," she said with a pretended calm.

"No, Ethel," Paul said, "give them here back. They are my boxes."

"Tell me why you slept out here on this backstairs where you know you'll make yourself even sicker. I want you to tell me and tell me right away."

"I can't, Ethel, I can't," Paul said.

"Then I'm going to burn the pictures," she replied.

He crawled hurrying over to where she stood and put his arms around her legs.

"Ethel, please don't take them, Ethel. Pretty please."

"Don't touch me," she said to him. Her nerves were so bad she felt that if he touched her again she would start as though a mouse had gotten under her clothes.

"You stand up straight and tell me like a little man why you're here," she said, but she kept her eyes half closed and turned from him.

He moved his lips to answer but then he did not really understand what she meant by *little man*. That phrase worried him whenever he heard it.

"What do you do with the pictures all the time, all day when I'm gone, and now tonight? I never heard of anything like it." Then she moved away from him, so that his hands fell from her legs where he had been grasping her, but she continued to stand near his hands as though puzzled what to do next.

"I look is all, Ethel," he began to explain.

"Don't bawl when you talk," she commanded, looking now at him in the face.

Then: "I want the truth!" she roared.

He sobbed and whined there, thinking over what it was she could want him to tell her, but everything now had begun to go away from his attention, and he had not really ever understood what had been expected of him here, and now everything was too hard to be borne.

"Do you hear me, Paul?" she said between her teeth, very close to him now and staring at him in such an angry way he closed his eyes. "If you don't answer me, do you know what I'm going to do?"

"Punish?" Paul said in his tiniest child voice.

"No, I'm not going to punish this time," Ethel said.

"You're not!" he cried, a new fear and surprise coming now into his tired eyes, and then staring at her eyes, he began to cry with panicky terror, for it seemed to him then that in the whole world there were just the two of them, him and Ethel.

"You remember where they sent Aunt Grace," Ethel said with terrible knowledge.

His crying redoubled in fury, some of his spit flying out onto the cold calcimine of the walls. He kept turning the while to look at the close confines of the staircase as though to find some place where he could see things outside.

"Do you remember where they sent her?" Ethel said in a quiet patient voice like a woman who has endured every unreasonable, disrespectful action from a child whom she still can patiently love.

"Yes, yes, Ethel," Paul cried hysterically.

"Tell Ethel where they sent Aunt Grace," she said with the same patience and kind restraint.

"I didn't know they sent little boys there," Paul said.

"You're more than a little boy now," Ethel replied. "You're old enough . . . . And if you don't tell Ethel why you look at the photographs all the time, we'll have to send you to the mental hospital with the bars."

"I don't know why I look at them, dear Ethel," he said now in a very feeble but wildly tense voice, and he began petting the fur on her houseslippers.

"I think you do, Paul," she said quietly, but he could hear her gentle, patient tone disappearing and he half raised his hands as though to protect him from anything this woman might now do.

"But I don't know why I look at them," he repeated, screaming, and he threw his arms suddenly around her legs.

She moved back, but still smiling her patient, knowing, forgiving smile.

"All right for you, Paul." When she said that *all right for you* it always meant the end of any understanding or reasoning with her.

"Where are we going?" he cried, as she ushered him through the door, into the kitchen.

"We're going to the basement, of course," she replied.

They had never gone there together before, and the terror of what might happen to him now gave him a kind of quiet that enabled him to walk steady down the long irregular steps.

"You carry the boxes of pictures, Paul," she said, "since you like them so much."

"No, no," Paul cried.

"Carry them," she commanded, giving them to him.

He held them before him and when they reached the floor of the basement, she opened the furnace and, tightening the cord of her bathrobe, she said coldly, her white face lighted up by the fire, "Throw the pictures into the furnace door, Paul."

He stared at her as though all the nightmares had come true, the complete and final fear of what may happen in living had unfolded itself at last.

"They're Daddy!" he said in a voice neither of them recognized.

"You had your choice," she said coolly. "You prefer a dead man to your own mother. Either you throw his pictures in the fire, for they're what makes you sick, or you will go where they sent Aunt Grace."

He began running around the room now, much like a small bird which has escaped from a pet shop into the confusion of a city street, and making odd little sounds that she did not recognize could come from his own lungs.

"I'm not going to stand for your clowning," she called

out, but as though to an empty room.

As he ran round and round the small room with the boxes of photographs pressed against him, some of the pictures fell upon the floor and these he stopped and tried to recapture, at the same time holding the boxes tight against him, and making, as he picked them up, frothing cries of impotence and acute grief.

Ethel herself stared at him, incredulous. He not only could not be recognized as her son, he no longer looked like a child, but in his small unmended night shirt like some crippled and dying animal running hopelessly from its pain.

"Give me those pictures!" she shouted, and she seized a few which he held in his fingers, and threw them quickly into the fire.

Then turning back, she moved to take the candy boxes from him.

But the final sight of him made her stop. He had crouched on the floor, and, bending his stomach over the boxes, hissed at her, so that she stopped short, not seeing any way to get at him, seeing no way to bring him back, while from his mouth black thick strings of something slipped out, as though he had spewed out the heart of his grief.

The Games of Night
Stig Dagerman

Stig Dagerman
(Sweden, 1923-1954)

One of the greatest Swedish writers of our century, Stig Dagerman wrote most of his work before the age of twenty-five and committed suicide in 1954. Abandoned by his mother, he was brought up by his grandparents on a farm north of Stockholm. When Dagerman was sixteen, his grandfather was murdered by a madman; his grandmother died from the shock a few weeks later. "The evening I heard about the murder," Dagerman is quoted as saying, in Michael Meyer's introduction to *The Games of Night*, "I went to the City Library and tried to write a poem to the dead man's memory. Nothing came of it but a few pitiful lines which I tore up in shame. But out of that shame, out of that impotence and grief, something was born—something which I believe was the desire to become a writer; that is to say, to be able to tell of what it is to mourn, to have been loved, to be left lonely. . . ."

Dagerman writes without explaining: he allows the facts to build up the story with relentless objectivity. Compared to other major Swedish writers of our time—Per Olov Enquist, P. C. Jersild—Dagerman is inobtrusive; he never permits himself, as the author, to intrude on his own fiction. It is up to us, the readers, to become the mourners, the loved ones, the ones left lonely.

The Games of Night

Sometimes at night, when his mother was crying in the bedroom and only unknown steps clattered on the stairs, Ake had a game which he played instead of crying. He pretended that he was invisible and that he could wish himself anywhere, just by thinking it. On those evenings there was only one place to wish oneself, and so Ake was suddenly there. He never knew how he had arrived; he just knew that he was standing in a room. What it looked like he didn't know, because he hadn't the right eyes for it, but it was full of the smoke of cigarettes and pipes, and people laughed suddenly, frighteningly, for no reason, and women who couldn't talk clearly leaned across a table and laughed in just the same, dreadful way. It cut through Ake like knives, yet he was glad to be there. On the table around which everybody was sitting were a number of bottles, and as soon as a glass was empty a hand unscrewed the screw-stopper and filled it again.

Ake who was invisible lay down on the floor and crawled under the table without anybody who sat there noticing him. In his hand he carried an invisible drill and without a moment's hesitation he set the point of it against the underside of the table-top and started drilling upwards. He soon got through the wood, but went on drilling. He drilled through glass, and suddenly, when he had pierced the bottom of a bottle, the brandy ran in a fine thin steam down through the hole in the table. He recognised his father's shoes under the table, and dared not think what would happen if he suddenly became visible again. But then with a thrill of joy he heard his father say, "Empty," and somebody else joining in, "Hell, so it is." Then everybody in the room got up.

Ake followed his father downstairs and when they reached the street he led him, though his father never noticed it, to a taxi-rank, and whispered the right address to the driver. During the whole journey he stood on the step to be sure they were really going in the right direction. When they were only a few blocks from home, Ake wished himself back—and there he lay again in the kitchen bench bed, listening to the car drawing up in the street. Not until it drove off again did he hear that it was not the right car: it had stopped next door. The right one must be still on the way; perhaps it had got into a traffic-jam, perhaps it had stopped in front of a cyclist who had fallen off; lots of things can happen to cars.

But at last one came which sounded like the right one. A few doors beyond Ake's house it began slowing down; it drove slowly past the next-door house and stopped with a slight squeak exactly opposite the right gateway. A door opened, a door banged, and somebody whistled as he rattled his money. His father never whistled, but one never knew; why shouldn't he suddenly take to whistling? The car started up and turned the corner, and afterwards the street was absolutely quiet. Ake strained his ears and listened down the stairs, but the front door never closed behind anybody coming in. The little click of the staircase light-switch never came. There was no muffled noise of footsteps on the way upstairs.

Why did I leave him so soon? Ake wondered. I might just as well have stayed with him all the way to the door, when we were so near. Now of course he's standing down there because he's lost his key and can't get in. Now perhaps he'll get angry and go away, and won't come back until the door's opened tomorrow morning. And he can't whistle, or he'd whistle to me or mum to throw down the key.

As noiselessly as he could Ake clambered over the edge of the creaking bed and bumped against the kitchen table in the darkness; he stiffened all over his body as he stood there on the cold linoleum; but his mother's sobbing was as loud and as regular as the breathing of a sleeper, so she had heard nothing. He went forward to the window, and when he reached it he pushed the roller-blind gently aside and looked out. There was not a soul in the street, but the lamp above the gateway opposite was lit. It was lit at the same time as the staircase light, so it was like the lamp above Ake's own door.

Presently Ake grew cold and he padded back to the bench bed. To avoid bumping against the table he slid his hand along the draining-board, until suddenly his finger-tips touched something cold and sharp. For a while he let his fingers explore and then gripped the handle of the carving-knife. When he crept back into bed he had the knife with him. He laid it beside him under the blanket and made himself invisible again. After that he was back in that same room, standing in the doorway and watching the men and women who held his father prisoner. He realised that if his father was to be free he must release him in the same way as Viking released the missionary, when the missionary was bound to a stake to be roasted by cannibals.

Ake crept forward, raised his invisible knife and drove it into the back of the fat man next to his father. The fat man died and Ake went on round the table. One by one they slid down off their chairs without really knowing what had happened. When his father was free Ake took him down the many stairs and as he could hear no taxi about they walked very slowly down the steps, crossed the street and boarded a tram. Ake arranged it so that his father had a seat inside, hoping that the conductor wouldn't notice that his father had been drinking and hoping that his father wouldn't say anything out of place to the conductor, or suddenly laugh out loud, just like that, without having anything to laugh at.

The song of the night tram rounding a bend forced its way inexorably into the kitchen, and Ake who had already left the tram and was lying in bed again noticed that his mother had stopped sobbing during the short time he had been away. The roller-blind in the next room flew up towards the ceiling with a fearful clatter, and when the clatter had died away his mother opened the window and Ake wished he could jump out of bed and run into their room and call out that she could quite well shut the window again, draw down the blind and go quietly to bed, for now he really was coming. "On that tram, because I helped him get on to it." But Ake knew it was no good doing that, as she would never believe him. She didn't know how much Ake did for her when they were alone at night and she thought he was asleep. She didn't know what journeys he made and what adventures he braved for her sake.

When later the tram stopped at the halt round the corner he stood by the window and looked out through the crack between the blind and the window-frame. The first people to come round the corner were two youths who must have jumped off while the tram was still moving; they were pretending to box with each other. They lived in the new house diagonally across the street. Passengers who had alighted were making a noise round the corner, and when the tram peered out with its lamp and rattled slowly across Ake's street, little groups of people came in sight and then vanished in different directions. One man with an unsteady gait, carrying his hat in his hand like a beggar, made straight for Ake's gateway, but it wasn't Ake's father; it was the porter.

But still Ake waited. He knew there were several things round the corner that might delay a tram passenger: there were shop-windows, for instance—there was a shoe-shop there. Here his father might be standing to choose a pair of shoes for himself before he came in; and the fruit-shop had a window too, with hand-painted placards in it which lots of people stopped to look at because of the funny little men painted on them. But the fruit-shop also had a slot-machine that didn't work properly and it might well be that his father had put in a twenty-öre piece for a packet of Läkerol for Ake, and now couldn't get the drawer open.

While Ake was standing by the window waiting for his father to tear himself away from the slot-machine, his mother suddenly left the bedroom next door and went past the kitchen. As she was barefoot Ake hadn't heard her, but she couldn't have noticed him because she walked on into the hall. Ake dropped the blind and stood motionless in total darkness while his mother searched for something among the coats. It must have been a handkerchief, for after a little while she blew her nose and returned to her room. Although her feet were bare, Ake noticed that she was walking especially quietly so as not to wake him. She shut her window at once and drew down the blind with a hard, quick pull. Then she lay down hastily on the bed and the sobbing began again, exactly as if she could only sob lying down, or had to start sobbing as soon as she did lie down.

When Ake had looked out at the street once again and found it empty except for a woman being embraced by a seaman in the gateway opposite, he crept back to bed, thinking—as the linoleum suddenly creaked underfoot— that it sounded as if he had dropped something. Now he was terribly tired; sleep rolled over him like mists as he walked, and through these mists he caught the clash of steps on the stairs—but going the wrong way: coming downstairs instead of up. As soon as he slipped under the covers he glided reluctantly but swiftly into the waters of sleep and the last waves that beat over his head were as soft as sobs.

Yet sleep was so brittle that it could not keep him away from all that preoccupied him when awake. Certainly he had not heard the taxi drawing up in front of the gate, the switching on of the staircase light or the steps coming upstairs, but the key that poked into the keyhole poked a hole in his sleep; instantly he was awake and joy struck down in him like a flash of lightning, sending a wave of heat through him from toes to forehead. Then the joy vanished as quickly as it had come, in a smoke of questions. Ake had a little game which he played whenever he awoke in this way. He played that his father hurried straight through the hall and stood between the kitchen and the bedroom so that both of them might hear him as he shouted.

"One of the chaps fell off a scaffolding and I had to take him to hospital; I've been sitting by him all night; I couldn't ring you because there wasn't a phone anywhere near." Or, "What do you know? We've won first prize in the lottery and I've come back late like this so's to keep you guessing as long as I could." Or, "What do you know? The boss gave me a motor-boat today and I've been out trying her, and early tomorrow morning we'll push off in her all three of us. What do you say to that, eh?"

But reality always happened much more slowly and never so surprisingly. His father couldn't find the hall light-switch. At last he gave up and knocked down a coat-hanger. He swore and tried to pick it up, but instead overturned a suitcase standing by the wall. Then he gave that up too, and tried to find a peg for his coat, but when he had found it the coat fell on the floor just the same, with a soft thud. Leaning against the wall his father walked the few steps to the lavatory, opened the door and left it open, and switched on the light; and as so many times before Ake lay quite rigid listening to the splashing on the floor. Then the man switched out the light, bumped into the door, swore and entered the room through the drawn curtain, which rattled as if it wanted to bite.

Then everything was quiet. His father stood in there without saying a word; there was a faint creaking from his shoes and his breathing was heavy and irregular, but these two things only made it all even more hideously quiet, and in this quietness another flash of lightning struck down in Ake. It was hatred, this heat that surged through him; he squeezed the handle of the knife until his palm hurt, but he felt no pain. The silence lasted only a moment. His father began to undress. Jacket and waistcoat. He threw them on a chair. He leaned back against a cupboard and let the shoes drop off his feet. His tie flapped. Then he took a few steps further into the room, that's to say towards the bed, and stood still while he wound up the clock. Then everything was quiet again, as horribly quiet as before. Only the clock crunched the silence, like a rat—the gnawing clock of the drunk.

Then the thing the silence was waiting for would happen. His mother threw herself desperately round in bed, and the scream welled out of her mouth like blood.

"You devil, you devil—devil-devil-devil!" she shrieked, until her voice died and all was silent. Only the clock nibbled and nibbled and the hand clutching the knife was quite wet with sweat. The fear in the kitchen was so great that it couldn't be endured without a weapon, but at last Ake grew so weary from his deadly fear that unresistingly he plunged headfirst into sleep. Far down in the night he woke for a moment and through the open door heard the bed in the other room creaking and a soft murmur filling the room, and didn't quite know what it meant except that these were two safe noises which meant that fear had yielded for that night. He was still holding the knife; he let it go and pushed it from him, filled with a burning lust for himself, and in the very moment of falling asleep he played the last game of the night—the one that brought him final peace.

Final—and yet there was no end. Just before six in the evening his mother came into the kitchen, where he was sitting at the table doing his homework. She just took the arithmetic book from him and pulled him up from the bench with one hand.

"Go to your dad," she said, dragging him out into the hall and standing behind him to cut off his retreat. "Go to your dad and tell him I said he was to give you the money."

The days were worse than the nights. The games of the night were much better than those of the day. At night one could be invisible and speed over the roofs to wherever one was wanted. In the daytime one was not invisible. In the daytime things took longer; it wasn't such fun to play in the daytime. Ake came out of the gateway and was not the slightest bit invisible. The porter's son pulled at his coat, wanting him to play marbles, but Ake knew his mother was standing up there at the window watching him until he should disappear round the corner, so he broke free without a word and ran away as if somebody were after him. But as soon as he turned the corner he began to walk as slowly as he could, counting the paving-stones and the splashes of spittle on them. The porter's boy caught him up but Ake didn't answer him, for one couldn't tell people that one was looking for one's father because he hadn't brought the wages home yet. At last the porter's boy tired of it, and Ake drew nearer and nearer to the place he didn't want to get nearer to. He pretended that he was getting further and further away from it, but it wasn't true at all.

The first time, though, he went right past the café, brushing so close by the doorman that the doorman muttered something after him. He turned up a little side street and stopped in front of the building where his father's workshop was. After a while he passed through the entrance into the yard, pretending that his father was still there and that he'd hidden himself somewhere behind the drums and sacks for Ake to come and look for him. Ake raised the lids of all the paint-barrels, and each time he was just as much surprised not to find his father crouching inside. After hunting through the yard for half an hour at least, he realized at last that his father couldn't have hidden himself there, and he turned back.

Next to the café were a china shop and a watchmaker's. At first Ake stood looking in at the window of the china shop. He tried to count the dogs, first the pottery ones in the window, and the ones he could see if he shaded his eyes and peered at the shelves and counters inside. The watchmaker came out just then and drew down the iron shutter in front of his window, but through the chinks in the shutter Ake could see the wrist-watches ticking away inside. He looked also at the clock with the Correct Time and decided that when the second hand had gone round ten times he would go in.

While the doorman was shouting at a fellow who was showing him something in a newspaper, Ake stole into the café and ran straight to the right table before too many people noticed him. At first his father didn't see him, but one of the other painters nodded at Ake and said,

"Your nipper's here."

His father took Ake on his knee and rubbed his bristly chin against the boy's cheek. Ake tried not to look at his eyes, but now and again he was fascinated by the red lines in the whites of them.

"What d'you want, son?" his father asked, but his tongue was soft and slurry in his mouth and he had to say the same thing two or three times before he was satisfied.

"Money."

Then his father put him gently down on the floor, leaned back and laughed so loudly that the others had to hush him. Still laughing he took the purse from his pocket, clumsily drew off the rubber band round it and hunted about for a long time until he found the shiniest one-crown piece.

"Here you are then, Ake," he said. "Off you go and get some sweets for yourself."

The other painters were not to be outdone, and Ake was given a crown by each of them. He held the money in his hand as, overwhelmed with shame and confusion, he picked his way out between the tables. He was so afraid that someone might see him running out past the doorman and tell tales at school, and say, "I saw Ake coming out of a pot-house last evening." But he paused for a moment in front of the watchmaker's window, and while the second hand swept ten times round its centre he stood pressed against the grille, knowing that he would have to play his games again tonight; but which of the two people he played for he hated more he couldn't tell.

Later, when slowly he turned the corner he met his mother's gaze from thirty feet up, and walked as lingeringly as he dared towards the gateway. Next to this was a woodmerchant's, and he was bold enough to kneel for a little and stare through the window at an old man putting coal into a black sack. Just as the old man finished Ake's mother came and stood behind him. She jerked him to his feet and took his chin in her hand, to find his eyes.

"'What did he say?" she whispered. "Did you funk it again?"

"He said he was coming back right away," Ake whispered back.

"What about the money?"

"Shut your eyes, mum," said Ake; and now he played the last of the day's games.

While his mother shut her eyes, Ake slipped into her outstretched hand the four crown-pieces, and then dashed down the street on feet that slipped on the stones because they were so frightened. A rising shout pursued him along the houses, but did not stop him. On the contrary, it made him run all the faster.

Translated from the Swedish by Naomi Walford

Jocasta
Liliana Heker

Liliana Heker
(Argentina, b. 1943)

In 1966 a twenty-three-year-old Argentinian writer won the prestigious Casa de las Americas Prize for fiction, an annual award given in Cuba to the best book in Spanish published anywhere in the world. The author was Liliana Heker; the book of short stories, *Los que vieron la zarza ("Those Who Beheld the Burning Bush")*. At the time Heker was editor-in-chief of an influential literary magazine, *El Escarabajo de Oro (The Golden Bug)* which later changed its name to *El Ornitorrinco (The Platypus)*, in keeping with Oscar Wilde's motto: "You should always be a little improbable."

Liliana Heker remained in Argentina during the military dictatorship of the seventies, writing and publishing in spite of the difficulties and dangers. Heker's theme is the social reality of Argentina, both political and psychological, and most of the witnesses of that reality are women: young girls, wives, mothers, artists, maids, teachers. English-speaking readers have grown to believe that the literature that comes from Latin American countries is all "magic realism," as in García Márquez's *One Hundred Years of Solitude*. Liliana Heker's writing proves otherwise. "Jocasta," told in the voice of a young mother, enters that borderline country in which maternal love allows itself a vast, dangerous freedom that no magic can assist.

Jocasta

When will night be over? Tomorrow all this will seem so
foolish. All I need is morning when he will come and wake
me, though God knows if I'll be able to sleep through the
night. Just like any other child in the world, isn't he?
Jumps out of bed as soon as his eyes are open and comes
running very fast, otherwise maybe Mother will have gotten up already and we'll miss the best part of the day. Only
at night can one believe something so monstrous; only at
night, and I feel sick imagining him now, jumping on my
stomach and singing Horsey, horsey, don't you stop, let
your hooves go clippety-clop; just a little longer, Mommy.
And how can one refuse, Just a little longer, Mommy,
when he's playing; who would have the courage to say no,
after he looks at you, with longing in his eyes. No, that's
enough, Daniel; it's very late. It's enough because tonight
your mother felt filthy, once and for all, and now she
knows that she'll never be able to kiss you like before, tuck
you into bed, let you climb up onto her knees whenever
you like; from now on it's not right to demand that mother
look after you alone and speak only to you, tell you stories
and nibble your nose, and tickle you so much you laugh
like crazy, and we both laugh with your funny somersaults.
He does them carefully, the imp, so you won't take your
eyes off him, and then you forget the rest of the world. I do
what I can. I told them today, I do everything possible

so he won't be around me all day. They laughed; you know, it looks funny when you're stuck with me all day, watching each of my gestures, scowling like a miniature lover every time I pay attention to one of my friends. They call you Little Oedipus, and even I laugh at the joke. Little Oedipus, I tell them, gets furious furious when I'm in bed with his father; it's terrible. But it wasn't terrible, Daniel; nothing that happens beneath the trees in the garden on a lovely summer's day during a restful afternoon with a group of friends is terrible; your odd ways even add a certain charm; we can spend the hours talking about you without the slightest uneasiness. Of course, my love; it's all right to want to be with Mommy, to enjoy her; she is young, she is pretty, she guesses our words before we say them and knows how to hold us in her arms and make us laugh more than anyone in the world; and she's silly, stupid, to feel so dirty tonight, to think that never again will she be able to stroke you, or let you climb into her arms. She'll put you away, in a school, the sooner the better. That's a lie, Daniel; it's the night, you know; it transforms even the purest things; loving you as I do becomes awful. But tomorrow it will be the same as before; you'll see when you come in, horsey, horsey, don't you stop, just like any day. Or did it ever matter? I'll let you jump in my arms even if they keep on talking, but that child, Nora; he doesn't let you out of his sight even for a second. See what I mean?, I said. But you kept on hugging my neck and putting your fingers on my lips, my little tyrant. You said, Don't talk, and then I explained: What can I do?: he's my little tyrant. Don't you think you should do *something*? I do everything I can, I swear, but there's nothing to be done, and I pushed you gently, go on, Daniel, sweetheart, trying to put you down. But it was just another joke; like calling you Little Oedipus beneath the trees in the garden, when the hideous part was far away. They're funny words we use, we like listening to: That child is in love with you, Nora; or saying to them: He's jealous of his father, the little monster. Everything proper, correct, even saying: But get

down, Daniel, you see Mommy has something to do; go
and play with Graciela, sweetheart. So that which was to
come later would have its place. Because, you know, I
myself would have put you down, I swear it; because
sometimes I do get angry and say: well Daniel, that's
enough, and I carry you in my arms over to Graciela.
Graciela, here's this little rascal for you to look after. I
don't know if she liked the gift: before she used to play
alone, quietly, and now she has to look after you, make
the effort of holding you back because you, the young
gentleman, of course want to go with me but in the end,
thank God, you stay there quietly and I can go back to
my friends who are still talking about how strange you
are. You see, I say, he has me very worried, I don't know
what to do; I try to get him to play with other children but
immediately he comes after me, running in circles around
me like something demented; did you see how he kisses me?
One would say he's making love to me, lecherous little
rascal, and I must say that for his age, he does it
wonderfully! And we all laugh because we are spending
such a splendid afternoon. All except you, my poor Daniel;
while we talk I watch you from the corner of my eye:
Graciela is trying hard to entertain you, but you won't take
your eyes off me. "What a devil, do you think he'll be alright
with Graciela? He won't take his eyes off you. . . ." Of
course; you're fighting to get away and however hard
Graciela tries to hold you back, she can't. But, now you've
freed yourself and are running towards me; the respite was
brief; you've climbed back into my arms and here you are,
and it's useless to try to get you down again. You'll stay with
me, growing quieter and quieter, until sleep comes over
you and I have to climb the stairs with you in my arms,
half asleep, and tuck you into bed. Goodnight, Daniel.
Goodnight, Mommy. But there are no good nights for
Mommy, Daniel. Never any good nights again. Never again
to kiss you and nibble at your nose and tell you stories and
wait till morning for you to climb all over me and sing
horsey, horsey. It is useless to wait for daybreak: there are

things that neither day nor night can blot out. And today, maybe just a second before taking you over to Graciela and allowing everything to happen as usual, I thought: Graciela, that devil of a child, standing there, at a distance from us. Yes, that's what I thought: Devil of a child. Yes, Daniel, the shame of thinking that, the hate that comes from seeing you make faces at her, this doesn't go out with the light. Because I knew you were looking at her: at her wicked and marvellous eyes, her black strands of hair falling this way and that, her pug nose, her naked legs all the way up to the forbidden place. You loved it, Daniel, you loved it. My God, why did I think something like that, how did I ever imagine she was provoking you with her charming cheekiness? Yet I knew she was wicked, and that she was challenging me. We were fighting over you, Daniel. And she was so far away, so free and naked; alone and something to be jealous of, telling you: I can show you my legs up to where I want, I can eat you up with kisses, if I want, we can roll around in the grass, right there, in front of everyone, because I'm a little girl and you can see my knickers, yes, without people thinking things; they'll just say: How lovely, look at them play, happy is the time when one can do those things; and you pull my hair, you tangle yourself in my legs, and I'll lift you up, and we'll both roll, both, because I'm nine years old and I'll do everything for you, so you can have fun. She stood there so invulnerable, all odds on her side, sticking her tongue out at you and calling you with her eyes: Come, Daniel. You smiled at her. The others were still saying, That child, Nora, is really in love with you, but I saw how you smiled; I knew that in a secret way, a way I couldn't reach, you two understood each other. You knew how to say Yes to her, if she accepted you as her tyrant, and she answered, Yes, you are so lovely with your blond hair, your blue eyes and your unabashed way of being tender. So here I come to Graciela, you thought: she and I are the same and we love each other.

You went, Daniel. You slid out from my arms without even looking at me; as if you'd climbed up on something

like a bush and seen Sebastian behind the hedge, and gone
off to find him. It's so easy when one knows nothing about
betrayals, isn't it Daniel? One is in mother's arms, the best
place in the world, wishing to spend one's life like this,
huddled up, letting yourself be loved; one feels one would
die if anyone tried to tear us away; and then Graciela
appears with her devilish eyes, and sticks out her tongue,
and rolls around in the grass, the best place in the world,
one feels one could live like that, rolling around in the wet
clover; nobody could ever stop us from playing together,
from pulling her hair until she screams, from making her
come running from far, far away to make me fly up in the
air; laughing out loud at her faces that no one can pull as
well as she does. They will never take me from her side; it's
useless to watch us, Mommy; it's useless to feel like you
can't take your eyes off me and that you can barely hide it
with a smile from your friends when they tease: He betrayed
you, Nora. Yes, all men are the same, and you fake a voice as
if you were saying something funny but you're not even
looking at them; you're still waiting for my eyes, just one of
my looks to let you know that everything's the same, and
you'll be calm again; so I can go on playing with Graciela
but I still love you more than anything else. But if it weren't
so? But if I loved Graciela more, Graciela who can lift her
legs? And you can't. Who can yell like Tarzan. And you
can't. Who can fight with me in the grass. And you can't.
Who can smear her whole face with orange juice. And you
can't. Who can kill herself laughing at the grown-ups all
sitting there, looking so stupid. And you can't. So it's
useless to smile every time I turn my head; and to make
funny faces to win me over. I'm not amused by those
faces; I don't even notice them. I don't see you even when
you pass by my side. And you've passed three times now;
and you've touched me; I felt how you touched me but I
didn't turn around. And I know you make noises for me
to hear and you sing that song about the bumblebee
because I like it best. But I don't like it any more. Now
you know. Graciela can sing much better songs, pretty

Graciela, nobody will take me from her side even if its
nighttime and we have to go to sleep. She'll come, earlier
today than all the other days, with more cuddles and
more promises. But I won't. And I won't. I'll resist up to
the last minute; I'll resist up to the last minute; I'll
scream and kick when Mommy wants to hold me in her
arms. Yes, Daniel, you want to be with Mommy, of
course you want Mommy to put you to bed. It's nighttime, can't you see? You must remember we love each
other so much, Daniel. That I'm the best in the world for
you, Daniel. You can't climb the stairs screaming and
kicking that way; don't you see you are betraying me, my
little monster who doesn't understand betrayal? Don't you
know that Mommy *does* understand and that her heart
aches and she can't stand letting you fall asleep in tears,
remembering Graciela? I didn't want to hurt you, my
darling. I didn't hurt you, it's not true. You fell asleep in
peace and quiet and I'm sure that you're having lovely
dreams now. Only I am not sleeping. Only I'm afraid of
the kisses I gave you, of the caresses, of the terrible way
we both played on the bed till you fell asleep, happy and
exhausted, thinking of me, I'm sure. And it's useless for
me to repeat over and over again that I always kiss you,
that I always caress you, and that we always play, both of
us, because my little Daniel must be happy. It's useless to
say that little Daniel is happy now and he's dreaming
lovely dreams; that he doesn't know anything about his
miserable mother's ugliness. It is useless to repeat that
night turns everything horrible, that tomorrow it will be
different. That you will come running to wake me, and
everything will be lovely, like every day. Horsey, horsey,
don't you stop, let your hooves go clippety-clop. Like
every day.

Translated from the Spanish by Alberto Manguel

Simple Arithmetic
Virginia Moriconi

Virginia Moriconi
(USA, 1924-1987)

The English teacher at my Buenos Aires high school was a thin, intelligent woman called Alicia Luna, who made us read short stories. Under her guidance, we discovered Saki's "Tobermory," William Saroyan's "The Daring Young Man on the Flying Trapeze," and Willa Cather's "Paul's Story." "Paul's Story" was one of my favourites and I told her so. "Really?" she said. "Read this." And she threw at me an anthology of *Best American Short Stories*, in which she had marked one called "Simple Arithmetic." I read it and then read it again, mesmerized. Who was Virginia Moriconi? I was unable, at the time, to find any information about her.

Many years later, in Toronto, literary agent Lucinda Vardey told me she had a book of short stories by a fairly unknown writer whose work she admired. The book was called *The Mark of St. Crispin*: the author was my long-lost Virginia Moriconi. I devoured the stories and found many of them as memorable as "Simple Arithmetic," especially "The Maternal Element," about a famous woman scientist who slowly turns into a national stone monument. But I still knew nothing about the author. In 1986 I finally got in touch with Virginia Moriconi herself and she sent three of her novels: *The Distant Trojans*, *Black Annis* and *The Princes of Q*. I read them with increasing delight, but before I could write and tell her how much I admired them, news reached me that she had died. With the death of Virginia Moriconi I felt I had lost a friend I had never met.

Simple Arithmetic

Geneva, January 15

Dear Father,

Well, I am back in School, as you can see, and the place is just as miserable as ever. My only friend, the one I talked to you about, Ronald Fletcher, is not coming back any more because someone persuaded his mother that she was letting him go to waste, since he was extremely photogenic, so now he is going to become a child actor. I was very surprised to hear this, as the one thing Ronnie liked to do was play basketball. He was very shy.

The flight wasn't too bad. I mean nobody had to be carried off the plane. The only thing was, we were six hours late and they forgot to give us anything to eat, so for fourteen hours we had a chance to get quite hungry but, as you say, for the money you save going tourist class, you should be prepared to make a few little sacrifices.

I did what you told me, and when we got to Idlewild I paid the taxi driver his fare and gave him a fifty-cent tip. He was very dissatisfied. In fact he wouldn't give me my suitcase. In fact I don't know what would have happened if a man hadn't come up just while the argument was going on and when he heard what it was all about he gave the taxi driver a dollar and I took my suitcase and got to the plane on time.

During the trip I thought the whole thing over. I did not come to any conclusion. I know I have been very extravagant and unreasonable about money and you have done the best you can to explain this to me. Still, while I was thinking about it, it seemed to me that there were only three possibilities. I could just have given up and let the taxi driver have the suitcase, but when you realise that if we had to buy everything over again that was in the suitcase we would probably have had to spend at least five hundred dollars, it does not seem very economical. Or I could have gone on arguing with him and missed the plane, but then we would have had to pay something like three hundred dollars for another ticket. Or else I could have given him an extra twenty-five cents which, as you say, is just throwing money around to create an impression. What would you have done?

Anyway I got here, with the suitcase, which was the main thing. They took two week-end privileges away from me because I was late for the opening of School. I tried to explain to M. Frisch that it had nothing to do with me if the weather was so bad that the plane was delayed for six hours, but he said that prudent persons allow for continjensies of this kind and make earlier reservations. I don't care about this because the next two week-ends are skiing week-ends and I have never seen any point in waking up at six o'clock in the morning just to get frozen stiff and endure terrible pain, even if sports are a part of growing up, as you say. Besides, we will save twenty-seven dollars by having me stay in my room.

In closing I want to say that I had a very nice Christmas and I apreciate everything you tried to do for me and I hope I wasn't too much of a bother. (Martha explained to me that you had had to take time off from your honeymoon in order to make Christmas for me and I am very sorry even though I do not think I am to blame if Christmas falls on the twenty-fifth of December, especially since everybody knows that it does. What I mean is, if you had wanted to have a long honeymoon you and Martha could have gotten married earlier, or you could have waited until Christmas was over, or you could just have told me not to come and I would have understood.)

I will try not to spend so much money in the future and I will keep accounts and send them to you. I will also try to remember to do the eye exercises and the exercises for fallen arches that the doctors in New York prescribed.

Love,
Stephen

Dear Stephen,

Thank you very much for the long letter of January fifteenth. I was very glad to know that you had gotten back safely, even though the flight was late. (I do not agree with M. Frisch that prudent persons allow for "continjensies" of this kind, now that air travel is as standard as it is, and the service usually so good, but we must remember that Swiss people are, by and large, the most meticulous in the world and nothing offends them more than other people who are not punctual.)

In the affair of the suitcase, I'm afraid that we were both at fault. I had forgotten that there would be an extra charge for luggage when I suggested that you should tip the driver fifty cents. You, on the other hand, might have inferred from his argument that he was simply asking that the tariff—i.e. the fare, plus the overcharge for the suitcase—should be paid in full, and regulated yourself accordingly. In any event you arrived, and I am only sorry that obviously you had no time to learn the name and address of your benefactor so that we might have paid him back for his kindness.

I will look forward to going over your accounting and I am sure you will find that in keeping a clear record of what you spend you will be able to cut your cloth according to the bolt, and that, in turn, will help you to develop a real regard for yourself. It is a common failing, as I told you, to spend too much money in order to compensate oneself for a lack of inner security, but you can easily see that a foolish purchase does not insure stability, and if you are chronically insolvent you can hardly hope for peace of mind. Your allowance is more than adequate and when you learn to make both ends meet you will have taken a decisive step ahead. I have great faith in you and I know you will find your anchor to windward in your studies, in your sports, and in your companions.

As to what you say about Christmas, you are not obliged to "apreciate" what we did for you. The important thing was that you should have a good time, and I think we had some wonderful fun together, the three of us, don't you? Until your mother decides where she wants to live and settles down, this is your *home* and you must always think of it that way. Even though I have remarried, I am still your father, first and last, and Martha is very fond of you too, and very understanding about your problems. You may not be aware of it but in fact she is one of the best friends you have. New ideas and new stepmothers take a little getting used to, of course.

Please write to me as regularly as you can, since your letters mean a great deal to me. Please try too, at all times, to keep your marks up to scratch, as college entrance is getting harder and harder in this country, and there are thousands of candidates each year for the good universities. Concentrate particularly on spelling. "Contingency" is difficult, I know, but there is no excuse for only one "p" in "appreciate"! And *do* the exercises.

Love,
Father

Geneva, January 22

Dear Mummy,

Last Sunday I had to write to Father to thank him for my Christmas vacation and to tell him that I got back all right. This Sunday I thought I would write to you even though you are on a cruze so perhaps you will never get my letter. I must say that if they didn't make us write home once a week I don't believe that I would ever write any letters at all. What I mean is that once you get to a point like this, in a place like this, you see that you are supposed to have your life and your parents are supposed to have their lives, and you have lost the connection.

Anyway I have to tell you that Father was wonderful to me and Martha was very nice too. They had thought it all out, what a child of my age might like to do in his vacation, and sometimes it was pretty strenuous, as you can imagine. At the end the School sent the bill for the first term, where they charge you for the extras which they let you have here and it seems that I had gone way over my allowance and besides I had signed for a whole lot of things I did not deserve. So there was a terrible scene and Father was very angry and Martha cried and said that if Father always made such an effort to consider me as a person I should make an effort to consider him as a person too and wake up to the fact that he was not Rockefeller and that even if he was sacrificing himself so that I could go to one of the most expensive schools in the world it did not mean that I should drag everybody down in the mud by my reckless spending. So now I have to turn over a new leaf and keep accounts of every penny and not buy anything which is out of pro-portion to our scale of living.

Except for that one time they were very affectionate to me and did everything they could for my happiness. Of course it was awful without you. It was the first time we hadn't been together and I couldn't really believe it was Christmas.

I hope you are having a wonderful time and getting the rest you need and please write me when you can.

All my love,

Stephen

Geneva, January 22

Dear Father,

Well it is your turn for a letter this week because I wrote to Mummy last Sunday. (I am sure I can say this to you without hurting your feelings because you always said that the one thing you and Mummy wanted was a civilised divorce so we could all be friends.) Anyway Mummy hasn't answered my letter so probably she doesn't aprove of my spelling any more than you do. I am beginning to wonder if maybe it wouldn't be much simpler and much cheaper to if I didn't go too college after all. I really don't know what this education is for in the first place.

There is a terrible scandal here at School which has been very interesting for the rest of us. One of the girls, who is only sixteen, has gotten pregnant and everyone knows that it is all on account of the science instructer, who is a drip. We are waiting to see if he will marry her, but in the meantime she is terrifically upset and she has been expelled from the School. She is going away on Friday.

I always liked her very much and I had a long talk with her last night. I wanted to tell her that maybe it was not the end of the world, that my stepmother was going to have a baby in May, although she never got married until December, and the sky didn't fall in or anything. I thought it might have comforted her to think that grown-ups make the same mistakes that children do (if you can call her a child) but then I was afraid that it might be disloyal to drag you and Martha into the conversation, so I just let it go.

I'm fine and things are just the same.

Love,
Stephen

New York, February 2

Dear Stephen,

It would be a great relief to think that your mother did not "aprove" of your spelling either, but I'm sure that it's not for that reason that you haven't heard from her. She was never any good as a correspondent, and now it is probably more difficult for her than ever. We did indeed try for what you call a "civilised divorce" for all our sakes, but divorce is not an easy thing for any of the persons involved, as you well know, and if you try to put yourself in your mother's place for a moment, you will see that she is in need of time and solitude to work things out for herself. She will certainly write to you as soon as she has found herself again, and meanwhile you must continue to believe in her affection for you and not let impatience get the better of you.

Again, in case you are really in doubt about it, the purpose of your education is to enable you to stand on your own feet when you are a man and make something of yourself. Inaccuracies in spelling will not *simplify* anything.

I can easily see how you might have made a parallel between your friend who has gotten into trouble, and Martha who is expecting the baby in May, but there is only a superficial similarity in the two cases.

Your friend is, or was, still a child, and would have done better to have accepted the limitations of the world of childhood—as you can clearly see for yourself, now that she is in this predicament. Martha, on the other hand, was hardly a child. She was a mature human being, responsible for her own actions and prepared to be responsible for the baby when it came. Moreover I, unlike the science "instructer" am not a drip, I too am responsible for *my* actions, and so Martha and I are married and I will do my best to live up to her and the baby.

Speaking of which, we have just found a new apartment because this one will be too small for us in May. It is right across the street from your old school and we have a kitchen, a dining alcove, a living room, two bedrooms—one for me and Martha, and one for the new baby—and another room which will be for you. Martha felt that it was very important for you to feel that you had a place of your own when you came home to us, and so it is largely thanks to her that we have taken such a big place. The room will double as a

study for me when you are not with us, but we will move all
my books and papers and paraphernalia whenever you
come, and Martha is planning to hang the Japanese silk
screen you liked at the foot of the bed. Please keep in touch,
and *please* don't forget the exercises.

Love,
Father

Geneva, February 5

Dear Father,

There is one thing which I would like to say to you which
is that if it hadn't been for you *I* would never have heard of a
"civilised divorce", but that is the way you explained it to
me. I always thought it was crazy. What I mean is, wouldn't
it have been better if you had said, "I don't like your mother
any more and I would rather live with Martha," instead of
insisting that you and Mummy were always going to be the
greatest friends? Because the way things are now Mummy
probably thinks that you still like her very much, and it
must be hard for Martha to believe that she was chosen, and
I'm pretty much confused myself, although it is really none
of my business.

You will be sorry to hear that I am not able to do any of
the exercises any longer. I cannot do the eye exercises
because my room-mate got so fassinated by the stereo gadget
that he broke it. (But the School Nurse says she thinks it
may be just as well to let the whole thing go since in her
opinion there was a good chance that I might have gotten
more cross-eyed than ever, fidgeting with the viewer.) And I
cannot do the exercises for fallen arches, at least for one foot,
because when I was decorating the Assembly Hall for the
dance last Saturday, I fell off the stepladder and broke my
ankle. So now I am in the Infirmary and the School wants to
know whether to send the doctor's bill to you or to
Mummy, because they had to call in a specialist from the
outside, since the regular School Doctor only knows how to
do a very limited number of things. So I have cost a lot of

money again and I am very very sorry, but if they were half-way decent in this School they would pay to have proper equipment and not let the students risk their lives on broken stepladders, which is something you could write to the Bookkeeping Department, if you felt like it, because I can't, but you could, and it might do some good in the end.

The girl who got into so much trouble took too many sleeping pills and died. I felt terrible about it, in fact I cried when I heard it. Life is very crewel, isn't it?

I agree with what you said, that she was a child, but I think she knew that, from her point of view. I think she did what she did because she thought of the science instructer as a grown-up, so she imagined that she was perfectly safe with him. You may think she was just bad, because she was a child and should have known better, but I think that it was not entirely her fault since here at School we are all encouraged to take the teachers seriously.

I am very glad you have found a new apartment and I hope you won't move all your books and papers when I come home, because that would only make me feel that I was more of a nuisance than ever.

Love,
Stephen

New York, February 8

Dear Stephen,

This will have to be a very short letter because we are to move into the new apartment tomorrow and Martha needs my help with the packing.

We were exceedingly shocked by the tragic death of your friend and very sorry that you should have had such a sad experience. Life can be "crewel" indeed to the people who do not learn how to live it.

When I was exactly your age I broke my ankle too—I wasn't on a defective stepladder, I was playing hockey—and it hurt like the devil. I still remember it and you have all my sympathy. (I have written to the School Physician to ask how long you will have to be immobilised, and to urge him to get you back into the athletic program as fast as possible. The specialist's bill should be sent to me.)

I have also ordered another stereo viewer because, in spite of the opinion of the School Nurse, the exercises are most important and you are to do them *religiously*. Please be more careful with this one no matter how much it may "fassinate" your room-mate.

Martha sends love and wants to know what you would like for your birthday. Let us know how the ankle is mending.

Love,
Father

Geneva, February 12

Dear Father,

I was very surprised by your letter. I was surprised that you said you were helping Martha to pack because when you and Mummy were married I do not ever remember you packing or anything like that so I guess Martha is reforming your charactor. I was also surprised by what you said about the girl who died. What I mean is, if anyone had told me a story like that I think I would just have let myself get a little worked up about the science instructer because it seems to me that he was a villan too. Of course you are much more riserved than I am.

I am out of the Infirmary and they have given me a pair of crutches, but I'm afraid it will be a long time before I can do sports again.

I hope the new apartment is nice and I do not want anything for my birthday because it will seem very funny having a birthday in School so I would rather not be reminded of it.

Love,
Stephen

New York, February 15

Dear Stephen,

This is not an answer to your letter of February twelfth, but an attempt to have a serious discussion with you, as if we were face to face.

You are almost fifteen years old. Shortly you will be up against the stiffest competition of your life when you apply for college entrance. No examiner is going to find himself favourably impressed by "charactor" or "instructer" or "villan" or "riserved" or similar errors. You will have to face the fact that in this world we succeed on our merits, and if we are unsuccessful, on account of sloppy habits of mind, we suffer for it. You are still too young to understand me entirely, but you are not too young to recognise the importance of effort. People who do not make the grade are desperately unhappy all their lives because they have no place in society. If you do not pass the college entrance examinations simply because you are unable to spell, it will be nobody's fault but your own, and you will be gravely handicapped for the rest of your life.

Every time you are in doubt about a word you are to look it up in the dictionary and *memorise* the spelling. This is the least you can do to help yourself.

We are still at sixes and sevens in the new apartment but when Martha accomplishes all she has planned it should be very nice indeed and I think you will like it.

Love,
Father

Geneva, February 19

Dear Father,

I guess we do not understand each other at all. If you immagine for one minute that just by making a little effort I could imaggine how to spell immaggine without looking it up and finding that actually it is "imagine," then you are all wrong. In other words, if you get a letter from me and there are only two or three mistakes well you just have to

take my word for it that I have had to look up practically
every single word in the dictionary and that is one reason I
hate having to write you these letters because they take so
long and in the end they are not at all spontainious, no, just
wait a second, here it is, "spontaneous," and believe me
only two or three mistakes in a letter from me is one of the
seven wonders of the world. What I'm saying is that I am
doing the best I can as you would aggree if you could see my
dictionary which is falling apart and when you say I should
memmorise the spelling I can't because it doesn't make any
sence to me and never did.

Love,
Stephen

New York, February 23

Dear Stephen,
    It is probably just as well that you have gotten everything
off your chest. We all need to blow up once in a while. It
clears the air.
    Please don't ever forget that I am aware that spelling is
difficult for you. I know you are making a great effort and I
am very proud of you. I just want to be sure that you *keep
trying*.
    I am enclosing a small cheque for your birthday because
even if you do not want to be reminded of it I wouldn't want
to forget it and you must know that we are thinking of you.

Love,
Father

Geneva, February 26

Dear Father,
    We are not allowed to cash personal cheques here in the
School, but thank you anyway for the money.
    I am not able to write any more because we are going to
have the exams and I have to study.

Love,
Stephen

New York, March 2

NIGHT LETTER
  BEST OF LUCK STOP KEEP ME POSTED EXAM RESULTS

LOVE,
FATHER

Geneva, March 12

Dear Father,

Well, the exams are over. I got a C in English because aparently I do not know how to spell which should not come as too much of a surprise to you. In Science, Mathematics, and Latin I got A, and in French and History I got a B plus. This makes me first in the class, which doesn't mean very much since none of the children here have any life of the mind, as you would say. I mean they are all jerks, more or less. What am I supposed to do in the Easter vacation? Do you want me to come to New York, or shall I just stay here and get a rest, which I could use?

Love,
Stephen

New York, March 16

Dear Stephen,

I am *immensely* pleased with the examination results. Congratulations. Pull up the spelling and our worries are over.

Just yesterday I had a letter from your mother. She has taken a little house in Majorca, which is an island off the Spanish coast, as you probably know, and she suggests that you should come to her for the Easter holidays. Of course you are always welcome here—and you could rest as much as you wanted—but Majorca is very beautiful and would certainly appeal to the artistic side of your nature. I have written to your mother, urging her to write to you immediately, and I enclose her address in case you should want to write yourself. Let me know what you would like to do.

Love,
Father

Geneva, March 19

Dear Mummy.

Father says that you have invited me to come to you in Majorca for the Easter vacation. Is that true? I would be very very happy if it were. It has been very hard to be away from you for all this time and if you wanted to see me it would mean a great deal to me. I mean if you are feeling well enough. I could do a lot of things for you so you would not get too tired.

I wonder if you will think that I have changed when you see me. As a matter of fact I have changed a lot because I have become quite bitter. I have become bitter on account of this School.

I know that you and Father wanted me to have some expearience of what the world was like outside of America but what you didn't know is that Geneva is not the world at all. I mean, if you were born here, then perhaps you would have a real life, but I do not know anyone who was born here so all the people I see are just like myself, we are just waiting not to be lost any more. I think it would have been better to have left me in some place where I belonged even if Americans are getting very loud and money conscious. Because actually most of the children here are Americans, if you come right down to it, only it seems their parents didn't know what to do with them any longer.

Mummy I have written all this because I'm afraid that I have spent too much money all over again, and M. Frisch says that Father will have a crise des nerfs when he sees what I have done, and I thought that maybe you would understand that I only bought these things because there didn't seem to be anything else to do and that you could help me somehow or other. Anyway, according to the School, we will have to pay for all these things.

Concert, Segovia (Worth it)	16.00	(Swiss francs)
School Dance	5.00	
English Drama (What do they mean?)	10.00	
Controle de l'habitant (?)	9.10	
Co-op purchases	65.90	
Ballets Russes (Disappointing)	47.00	
Librairie Prior	59.30	
Concert piano (For practicing)	61.00	
Teinturie (They ruined everything)	56.50	
Toilet and Medicine	35.00	
Escalade Ball	7.00	
Pocket Money	160.00	
77 Yoghurts (Doctor's advice)	42.40	
Book account	295.70	
Total	869.90	(Swiss francs)

Now you see the trouble is that Father told me I was to spend about fifty dollars a month, because that was my allowance, and that I was not to spend anything more. Anyway, fifty dollars a month would be about two hundred and ten Swiss francs, and then I had fifteen dollars for Christmas from Granny, and when I got back to School I found four francs in the pocket of my leather jacket and then I had seventy-nine cents left over from New York, but that doesn't help much, and then Father sent me twenty-five dollars for my birthday but I couldn't cash the cheque because they do not allow that here in School, so what shall I do?

It is a serious situation as you can see, and it is going to get a lot more serious when Father sees the bill. But whatever you do I imploar you not to write to Father because the trouble seems to be that I never had a balance foreward, and I am afraid that it is impossible to keep accounts without a balance foreward, and even more afraid that by this time the accounts have gone a little bizerk.

Do you want me to take a plane when I come to
Majorca? Who shall I say is going to pay for the ticket?

Please do write me as soon as you can, because the
holidays begin on March 30 and if you don't tell me what
to do I will be way out on a lim.

Lots and lots of love,
Stephen

Geneva, March 26

Dear Father,

I wrote to Mummy a week ago to say that I would like
very much to spend my Easter vacation in Majorca. So far
she has not answered my letter, but I guess she will pretty
soon. I hope she will because the holidays begin on
Thursday.

I am afraid you are going to be upset about the bill all
over again, but in the Spring term I will start anew and
keep you in touch with what is going on.

Love,
Stephen

P.S. If Mummy doesn't write what shall I do?

Secret Ceremony
Marco Denevi

Marco Denevi
(Argentina, b. 1922)

In 1955 an international jury awarded the Life in Spanish prize to the best Latin-American short story. The winner was "Secret Ceremony," by a little known Argentine writer whose only previous publication was an excellent detective novel, *Rose at Ten*. Denevi later confessed that he had written a longer version of "Secret Ceremony," almost a full-length novel, and then cut it down to fit the number of words demanded by the competition's rules.

The official trimming was a blessing: "Secret Ceremony" is probably Denevi's best work. It is unlike anything else written up to then in Argentina, combining detective-story elements seen through the metaphysics of a writer such as Borges, with brutal social realism. In it, the parent-child relationship is played out as if it were a long-established ritual whose meaning has been forgotten or cannot be revealed, not even to the players. The story's dramatic qualities have made it an easy prey to adaptations, at least three times: once—atrociously—for the screen, directed by Joseph Losey and starring Elizabeth Taylor; once marvellously for Argentine television; and once for the Canadian Broadcasting Corporations.

After "Secret Ceremony," Denevi went on to write short stories, plays and a collection of apocryphal pieces, *Falsifications*, attributed to various writers from Kafka to Stendhal, which still await publication in English.

Secret Ceremony

It was not yet light when Miss Leonides Arrufat left her house.

There was not a soul in the street.

Miss Leonides walked hugging the wall, her eyes low, her body stiff, her step quick, almost martial, the way a woman should walk at such an hour if alone, and decent, and, in addition, single, even though fifty-eight. For you never can tell.

(But, who would have ventured to accost her? Dressed in black from head to foot, on her head a liturgical hat in the form of a turban, under her arm a handbag which resembled a huge, rotted fig, the tall, gaunt figure of Miss Leonides took on, in the dim light, a vaguely religious air. She might have been taken for a Greek Orthodox priest who, under cover of darkness, was fleeing a Red massacre, if the smile that distended her lips had not indicated, on the contrary, that that priest was hurrying to officiate at his rites.)

She walked so quickly that her fleshless, angular knees hit against her skirt, against the hem of her coat, and dress and coat swirled around her legs like troubled waters in which she was wading and from whose splashing she seemed to be trying to protect the bouquet of

leaves and flowers which she was holding reverently with
both hands at breast level.

When she reached the house of that paralytic child who
had once smiled at her she laid on the doorstep a passion
flower, bent her head, and prayed aloud: "Oh Lord, at
whose will all the moments of our life transpire, look
with favor on the prayers and offerings of your slaves
who implore you for the health of the sick, and heal them
of all suffering."

She kept on walking.

In the balcony of the house of Ruth, Edith, and Judith
Dobransky she laid a spray of periwinkle tied with a pink
ribbon, and prayed: "May the God of Israel be the
tabernacle of your virginity, oh maiden, and save you
from the serpent's snares."

She kept on walking.

She tossed three leaves of cineraria into the garden of a
house where, several days before she had seen a funeral
procession setting out, and murmured in bold Latin:
"*Requiem aeternam dona eis, Domine,*" and "*lux
perpetua luceat eis.*"

She kept on walking.

Now Natividad González's turn was coming. For
months now every day she had been leaving that hussy a
big bouquet of nettles. Miss Leonides had decided that
the bouquet of nettles should serve as a notice to its
recipient whereby, without using dirty words, but dotting
the *i*'s and crossing the *t*'s, she was urged to move to
another neighborhood. But it would seem that Natividad
González was illiterate in the language of nettles for she
showed no signs of moving. So Miss Leonides found herself under the tiresome obligation of insisting in her net-
tling hints.

But that morning when she stopped in front of Natividad's house, as she opened her handbag, holding her
breath (with the object of keeping herself immune to the
nettle's band) and took out her message, just as she was
about to lay it on the doorstep, a bolt of lightning

flashed out and fell upon her. The lightning bolt was
Natividad.

And this Natividad, looking as though she had not
slept, as though she had spent the entire night on the
watch, pale and disheveled, squared off to Miss Leonides
and began to insult her loud and thoroughly. She called
her names that bristled with *R's* and *B's* like shards of
broken glass; she conferred upon her unsuspected origins;
she attributed to her professions sometimes classified as
sad, sometimes as gay; she upbraided her as the worst
sinners of us shall be upbraided on the Judgment Day,
and finally, she invited her to employ the poor nettles for
the most heroic and least accustomed purposes. It was as
though Natividad had been multiplied a hundredfold and
the hundred Natividads were all screaming at the same
time. Where did the woman get all those words? Miss
Leonides had the terrifying feeling that a wave of lava
was moving toward her and that if she did not make her
escape in time she would be engulfed forever like one of
the residents of Pompeii. To save herself from the river of
molten fire, she turned and with all the dignity she could
muster, took her leave.

(What I mean is that she ran like crazy, for blocks and
blocks, until she could go no further. When her legs
buckled under her like wires, she stopped. She was gasp-
ing. The drumbeat of her heart deafened her. Under her
clothes her whole body oozed a cold glue. Her feet were
throbbing like pulses. Her eyes crossed and she felt like
throwing up. It took her forever to calm down.)

She made a long detour to get to the streetcar, for there
on the spot she swore she would never again pass before
Natividad's house. Never. And as though to emphasize
that solemn oath, she threw to the ground the rest of the
flowers she was still holding in one hand, all of which
seemed suddenly to have withered, blasted undoubtedly,
by the sulphurous fumes of the insults.

Meanwhile a kind of steady lightning flash made its
appearance in the sky, and propelled by this storm, there

appeared, as though emerging from some house, the first streetcar.

Miss Leonides took it, sat down next to a window, and an infinite street, made up of pieces of many streets, began to unroll before her eyes. She knew it by heart, that route. But no matter, she always found some way of entertaining herself. Like counting the trees that lined the sidewalk (skipping an occasional one whose looks did not appeal to her), picking out the letters of her name from the posters on the walls, trying to guess how many people wearing mourning she would see before coming to the sixth cross street. A person who has imagination never gets bored.

(The truth of the matter is that these games had wound up by becoming obsessions. Miss Leonides could not sit down in her bathroom without counting the tiles on the wall. In the kitchen she ran the scale up and down the eight panes of a window. As she walked along the street, she arranged the mosaics of the pavement in crosses, stars, big polygonal figures. At times the design became so complicated that she had to stop until she had worked it out. And when this happened it was a sight to see her, standing in the middle of a river of pedestrians, sweeping the ground with a fantastic pattern of glances that aroused the curiosity of all passers-by.)

But that morning Miss Leonides was in no mood for games. As soon as she had settled herself on the wooden seat of the streetcar, the zephyrs of thought caught her up and carried her far away, transported her to the house of Natividad González.

Dear God, the language that cockatrice had used! Miss Leonides could not recall any word concretely, for all were fused in an inseparable gibberish. But that the stew was seasoned with the most shocking insults, of that she had no doubt. Just imagine, a strumpet like that daring to insult, in the middle of the street and at the top of her lungs, Miss Leonides Arrufat! And she, why on earth had she stood for it! Oh no, things would have to be put in their proper place. And mentally she began to insult Natividad. She did not have the other's vast repertoire, but what difference did it make. She was satisfied with one word. A terrible word. *Slut.* And she repeated it like a magic formula, like a spell, like a person hammering a stubborn nail. She repeated it to the point of ecstasy, vertigo, and angelic intoxication. It seemed to her that that word, intoned in that way, went flying over streets and housetops, to Natividad herself, knocked her down, threw her to the ground, and there sucked all her pride, her youth, her beauty, that vicious strength she had employed toward Miss Leonides, and finally left her the way a swarm of locusts leaves a devoured tree.

(And as she was thinking up these delightful fates for Natividad, Miss Leonides quivered in her seat and gave little starts and twitches, so that anyone sitting beside her might have thought that the lady in the abbatial turban was not quite all there. Or might have thought, as someone did, that she had recognized her and that all this pantomime was due to emotion or added up to a secret code message.)

Suddenly Miss Leonides remembered something. Yes, a little incident in the big scene with Natividad. At the time she had taken it in, and then terror had hidden it beneath its flood. But now that the muddied waters had receded, the little incident reemerged. What had happened was that Natividad, while she had been riddling Miss Leonides with indecent words, had, without noticing, moved her bare foot close to the nettle, and the nettle had stung her. As though saying to her: "Caw all you like, I'm going to stick my claws in you, for that's what my mistress told me to do. And I obey her, not you." Natividad had started back, had pulled her foot away from the nettle as though it were a live coal, and enraged more by the humiliation than the pain, she had begun to howl like a madwoman. As she recalled it, Miss Leonides had such an attack of mirth that she choked and had to put her handkerchief to her lips. But she could not keep her

shoulders from shaking and a ripple of laughter from
spurting noisily out of her nose.

Frightened by the noise, the zephyrs dropped Miss
Leonides back on the car seat. Miss Leonides squirmed a
little, coughed, put on an expression of offended dignity
and turned toward the person sitting beside her.

It was like turning around and running into the point
of a knife. Because the person seated beside her was a
young girl (vaguely she made out that she was blonde,
rather plump, and wearing mourning) and this girl,
huddled in her seat, with her hands in her coat pockets,
motionless and as though her soul had departed her body,
had her face turned straight toward Miss Leonides and
was looking at her. But she was looking at her, not with
the momentary surprise with which one looks at a person
who is laughing to himself, but like one who was expecting this laughter, knowing that after it something terrible
was going to happen, and was now waiting for this terrible thing to happen.

Miss Leonides looked away (with difficulty, as though
to do so—what an odd thing!—she had had to disengage
gears) and began to stare out of the window. She waited
awhile and then looked ahead of her. That was all she
needed to know that the girl had not changed her
position.

She looked out of the window again and then straight
ahead. The girl had not moved.

"She's a poor crazy creature," she thought.

But thinking that she is a poor crazy creature is not
much help if the poor crazy creature happens to be sitting
next to us and is staring at us hypnotically. Miss Leonides did not know what to do. She had a vague feeling
of danger. It seemed to her that that girl had begun to get
a hold on her, to compromise her. From the moment
their eyes met the girl had ceased to be a stranger. She was
taking possession of her, invading her. She was transferring to her a responsibility, a burden, a danger. The very
coincidence that they were both wearing mourning

created a mysterious bond between them which set them off, separate and apart from the others.

Miss Leonides' eyes shuttled between the window and the front door of the streetcar, and back again, and thanks to these shifts she could watch the girl. And the girl kept on looking at her.

Miss Leonides repeatedly opened and closed her bottomless handbag, cleared her throat loudly, hummed in a low voice, began to read the fascinating small print on her ticket, showing in all these ways that she was not intimidated.

And the girl went on looking at her. Looking at her. Looking at her.

"If she goes on looking at me like that" (Miss Leonides moaned mentally) "I'm going to ask her if I've got a picture painted on my face. But doesn't she realize how ridiculous she is? Or is there something wrong about me? Have I got something in my ear? Has my face turned purple? Am I getting ready to die?"

Surrendering to a kind of dizziness, she turned toward the girl. Why did she do it? She hastily withdrew her glance. For that crazy creature kept on looking at her, true, but her eyes, which had seemed to be waiting for something terrible to happen, had now broken into pieces. The girl was crying. Crying silently, without a gesture, without making a motion. She was crying with her hands in her pockets. Huddled in her seat, she was crying. Crying and looking at Miss Leonides. Looking at Miss Leonides and bitterly reproaching her for not fulfilling the pact.

The pact? What pact? Miss Leonides lost her head. Hurriedly she stood up, stepped over and on the girl, literally trampling her as she stepped on her feet. It seemed to her that the girl tried to stop her, that she was mumbling something, but she did not listen to her, for if she did she would be lost, lost forever. She rushed down the aisle, bumped into a passenger, yelled to the conductor to stop the car, and when it came to the corner she plunged out of the unoffending vehicle as though it were a burning building, stumbled, almost fell, and hurried off down the street as fast as her legs would carry her. She did not once look back.

She was on San Martín. From the intersection of San Martín and Córdoba she heard the bells of the Blessed Sacrament. The church opened its arms to her as all churches always received her, like a secret sanctuary which put her out of the reach of the infinite evils of this world.

Afterward everything happened as in a game, with one counter advancing slowly, capricously, moving here, stopping there, along a zigzag path traced upon a multi-colored board, while another counter, in the rear, follows it, also moving at intervals, until suddenly, and when chance so wills, the second counter overtakes the first, and then the two, the pursued and the pursuer, abandon the path and meet in the square where they are enclosed as in a fortress.

Miss Leonides went into the Blessed Sacrament, heard Mass (absent-mindedly, alas), went out again, cautiously surveyed the street from the portico, did not see the girl dressed in mourning (who was inside the church, stand-ing between two confessionals, in a dark corner), stepped into the street and turned north along San Martín.

Crossing the square brought her two unpleasant expe-riences. The first was that couple. How is it possible for people to feel like hugging and kissing each other in a square at eight o'clock in the morning? She passed by the disgusting spectacle as though she did not see it. But she heard. She heard the woman's laughter. Miss Leonides compressed her lips. Slut. Slut. *Slutslutslut.*

The second unpleasant experience: the boys. There is nothing, in the whole universe of galaxies and nebulae, nothing so fearsome as a gang of boys. Nobody can say how they gather, where they come from but there they are, more compact than the tubers of a plant, intertwined in a web of indecent words and gestures, linked together like a single coralline mass. Just look at them. They greet one another with cuffs. They hardly talk. They communicate by means of snickers, winks, secret codes. They assume a sly, wary air as though plotting God knows what scheme. And if a woman passes by, they all look at her, sometimes menacingly, sometimes insolently, as though they knew some secret of hers and were threatening her with exposure. But they are never more ferocious than when standing on corners like a bunch of Indians. One has to be a woman and have crossed this mine field to know the meaning of scorn and derision for one's sex. Take Miss Leonides' word for it.

Fortunately, her sharp eyes identified the danger in time. A gang of boys was coming in her direction. Miss Leonides turned and retraced her steps. She had to pass the couple again (and again the woman laughed provocatively). "Drop dead," Miss Leonides thought to herself, and descended and climbed stairs, walked several extra blocks. But anything was preferable.

It was nine o'clock when she got to the cemetery. She visited the three identical tombstones of gray marble. She read, as she always did, by way of greeting, the inscriptions that were growing blurred: Aquiles Arrufat, d. March 23, 1926; Leonides Llegat de Arrufat, d. March 23, 1926; Robertito Arrufat, d. March 23, 1926.

"I did not bring you flowers today," she explained aloud to them, "because that hussy, you know, that Natividad, dirtied those I was bringing."

She strolled about for a time among the vaults and mausoleums. As she turned a corner she saw her.

There she was, a few yards off, as though barring the way. Miss Leonides stopped and the two stood looking at each other.

Now she could size her up better. She was short, plump, with short, stocky legs. Her head, which was too big for her body, seemed bigger still because of her shock of blonde hair. Her face, which was broad and somewhat coarse-featured, radiated innocence and kindliness, like that of a peasant, and this resemblance was emphasized by a kind of flush, a curious congestion which thickened her already flabby features, as though she were carrying a huge weight on her head. On the other hand, her clothes were of good quality but she wore no jewelry. Nor gloves, purse, or hat. And that was all.

"Gracious," Miss Leonides sighed with relief, "she's just a poor harmless girl. She gives me the impression of being a stranger who is lost and wants to ask me how to get home. Honestly, I can't imagine why I had all those queer ideas in the streetcar."

That was all and yet it was not all. Someone has looked at us fixedly and has cried. One doesn't cry for nothing. Afterward she has trailed us halfway around the city, until she came face to face with us again. Then she has looked at us all over again. Now she's not weeping silly tears. Now she's just standing there, in an attitude of offering and renunciation, of imploring and resignation. And leaving the next move up to us, she waits distressfully to see what we are going to do. One would have to be made of iron to reject her and pass by. That presence there is a question that demands an answer, yes or no. One must make up one's mind. And Miss Leonides was not made of iron, but of wax and butter. So Miss Leonides, without further thought, made up her mind.

What I mean to say is that she smiled. And as though that smile had suddenly opened a crack in her soul, she plunged headlong into the abyss, and, unable to control her movements, she made several gestures by way of greeting. That was enough. A dizzy mechanism went into operation. As though flung by some giant's hand, the girl threw herself on Miss Leonides and hugged her, clasped her arms around her neck, rested her head on Miss Leonides' flat spinster's bosom, while her whole body shook as though she were being whipped. And while this was taking place, from beneath the blonde mop of hair there came a whimpering, or convulsive laughter, the panting of a terrified small animal, an in-articulate muttering which slowly became transformed into a word, a single word, repeated in a tone of frenzied delight:

" *Mom, mom, mom, mom, mom. . . .*"

Miss Leonides blinked in amazement.

Until finally the muttering died away, the shock of blonde hair moved and drew back from Miss Leonides' breast; from beneath the hair, timidly, like some wary little animal, appeared the face of the girl. In a kind of terror Miss Leonides looked at it. She looked at it, and did not see there the silky furrow of tears, nor the forehead shiny with sweat, nor the spectral smile, now sorrowful, now gay, which incessantly appeared and disappeared from the lips, nor the throat distended like a pigeon's crop. Miss Leonides saw nothing but the eyes. Like that, with those very eyes, Robertito had looked at her that twenty-third of March of 1926. An immense pity and an infinite tenderness came over her. She knew that she could no longer escape. She had fallen into a snare. She was caught, trapped, betrayed. Now they would take her wherever her captor ordered.

The girl took her by the arm and the two of them left the cemetery.

Once more they crossed the city. They walked side by side, linked to one another, like intimate friends or like mother and daughter. They did not exchange a single word. Miss Leonides moved with her soldier's stride, her eyes on the ground. She felt bewildered, excited, confusedly happy. The turn her adventure with the girl dressed in mourning was taking produced a kind of intoxication in her. What was going to happen to her? But she did not even want to guess. Come what would, she was ready for it. For often, sick with loneliness, she had dreamed that in this crowded world there was someone who was aware of her existence, who needed her, who was waiting for her, looking for her, and that sometime this person would find her and take her away. And now this dream was no longer a mad fantasy. But one must never interfere with the delicate workings of magic by seeking explanations. One must yield and let oneself be guided: Miss Leonides did not even dare to glance at the girl out of the corner of her eye for fear the spell might be broken.

But the spell was not broken, the dream continued, the fair chubby doll went trotting along beside her; she could feel under hers the plump arm continually twitching with electric shocks. And she went on, and on. Where was she going? She did not know, nor did she want to.

In this way they came to Suipacha Street. They came to that stretch of Suipacha which runs from the Diagonal Norte to the Avenida de Mayo, and has nothing but shops, shops, shops, women sniffling around the show windows.

There, in the shadow of the large modern buildings, stood a big old house which nobody ever noticed. It bears (or at least did until a short time ago) the number 78. It has two grilled windows on the first floor, a double door, with two funereal bronze knockers. On the second floor there is a large overhanging balcony, and that's all it has, unless you count a huge crack that crosses it like some evil scar or like the reproduction of a flash of lightning in some naïve water color. On its left there is a store; on its right, another. Across from it, the wall of St Michael Archangel. The house does everything in its power to avoid calling attention to itself, as though it were ashamed of its ugliness and decrepitude. But it is not necessary, for nobody notices it. They pass over it as though it were a vacant lot. If they do look at it, they've forgotten it the next minute. Perhaps some pair of lovers takes shelter there at night, but it is to kiss, and not to observe its architecture. So the house is there, and is as though it were not there; it is there by oversight, as if through a crack between the two buildings which flank it an excrescence had risen to the surface, a bit of rubble of the colonial city, which now lies buried under the sky-scrapers and towers. If the store on the right and the store on the left were to move a little closer to one another, they could obliterate this growth, as with a pair of pincers.

Miss Leonides, moving swiftly along Suipacha, stood open-mouthed when the girl stopped in front of that relic. She saw her take a key out of the pocket of her coat, unlock the stubborn door (whose knockers frightened her as though they were two barking dogs) and then step aside to let her in. But Miss Leonides could not quite make up her mind.

"Who's here, who's inside?" she asked, peering into the house's vague shadows.

The girl shook her big head back and forth.

"Nobody, nobody," she said, and her face suddenly became overcast, and she looked at Miss Leonides in distress.

With throbbing heart Miss Leonides Arrufat then walked into the house at 78 Suipacha Street.

A smell of dampness, of stale air, medicines, decay and death, a smell which was the sum and product of all the bad smells in this world, was the first thing that came out to meet her, ruining the emotion she was feeling. She would have preferred to turn back. She would have liked, at any rate, to cover her nose with her handkerchief. But the girl had already taken her by the hand and was dragging her toward the bottom of that fetid abyss.

They crossed several darkened rooms crowded with furniture. They came to a narrow vestibule illuminated by the murky gloom that filtered through a remote skylight. They ascended a black wooden staircase that squeaked and creaked under their feet. They reached another still smaller vestibule. They went down a hall. They crossed an anteroom. They stopped in front of a door. The girl opened this door and Miss Leonides found herself in a sumptuous bedroom.

At first she saw only the awe-inspiring double bed, covered with a white satin spread; the huge triple wardrobe with its long mirror; a motley of small tables and armchairs, and, in the rear, a long French door veiled by a curtain of macramé lace. Behind the curtain she could make out the light of morning, and in it the ocher silhouette of St Michael, and this sight, seen from a perspective so unusual for her, frightened her without knowing why. Suddenly the whole business struck her as being so absurd that she did not know how to go on with it.

She took a few steps around the room. She felt the girl's eyes behind her. She heard her uneven breathing. It even seemed to her that she could hear again that wheeze, that moaning. She was embarrassed. They had dragged her, she had allowed herself to be dragged, on to a stage, and now they were waiting for her to begin to play her part. What part? She had no idea. And the girl, there, like a curtain going up, like a call bell, like a pointing hand.

Trying to find some way to fill this awkward vacuum, Miss Leonides did something very funny. She began to examine with fierce interest the photographs which adorned the bedroom walls. She exchanged glances with a rosy man who had a long mustache, with faded ladies wearing hats very similar to hers, then again with the man with the mustache, with newborn infants, dressed and naked, once more with the man with the mustache. Suddenly she gave a start. A woman who looked amazingly like her, who looked a little like her, who had a remarkable, or perhaps a faint resemblance to her, was looking at her out of one of the photographs. Standing beside her a little girl exactly like the young woman dressed in mourning was leaning her head on the shoulder of Leonides Arrufat's double, and both of them, through the lens of the camera, were looking at her steadily, with guarded, stubborn eyes.

Miss Leonides was so astounded that her head swiveled mechanically toward the girl. She was evidently awaiting this move. And waiting for it as a warm invitation to give rein once more to her demonstrations of affections. For, running toward the visitor, she clasped her arm, rested her head on her shoulder, reproducing the posture of the child in the photograph and babbling again that strange word:

"*Mom, mom, mom, mom. . . .*"

For several minutes the four women scrutinized one another.

"It is a fact," reflected Miss Leonides looking at her double, "it is a fact that she has some of my features. What a pity she wears her hair parted in the middle like that. It makes her look so old-fashioned!"

(A woman who looked as though she had stepped out of a photograph album of 1920 was looking at the picture of a woman who looked as though she had stepped out of the year 1920, and found her old-fashioned. And that is as it should be. For, if this were not the case, there would be no judges or critics in the world.)

"On the other hand," Miss Leonides mused, "the girl hasn't changed at all."

(Not at all, except for the puffiness of her face.)

"So that's the key to the whole thing. She has taken me for this woman, who is undoubtedly her mother and has undoubtedly just died. That clears everything up."

This simple explanation left her with a feeling of disappointment. She had expected something different, less trite, more involved. And now what was she supposed to do? Say to her: "My dear, I am not the person you think. So, please, let me go," and go?

She freed herself from the girl's arm, bore left, then right, like a person looking for an exit, and who, not finding it, stops and rests her hand on a piece of furniture. Suddenly she saw her reflection in the wardrobe mirror. A mixture of fright and anger came over her. And turning toward the girl, she burst forth in a torrent of words which she could not hold back:

"And now what? Now what? What are you waiting for? What do you want of me? Why don't you do something? Why don't you say something? Have you swallowed your tongue?"

She bit her lips. Why had she talked like that? And why

had she used that harsh, loud tone, as though she were angry, when she wasn't? On the contrary. Her outburst was, at most, a call for help. When one can't find the exit, one screams and lashes out. And then she had found herself so ridiculous in the mirror, so graceless and grotesque in the luxurious surroundings of the bedroom! And now what? The girl would undoubtedly start crying.

But no, she didn't. Paradoxically, she not only did not start crying but gave a shrill little laugh and mumbled:

"Breakfast, breakfast."

She made a gesture as though asking Miss Leonides to wait, and rushed out of the room.

Standing there in the center of that big bedroom, Miss Leonides blinked her eyes. Had she heard right? Had the girl said "Breakfast, breakfast?" Well, she would wait a little while longer to see what those words and that protective gesture meant. And why not? After all, she wasn't doing anything wrong. If someone, a relative, a friend, say, were to appear, what could they reproach her with? Nothing. Breakfast, breakfast. All right, let's wait.

With a sudden feeling of well-being, Miss Leonides ensheathed herself in a close-fitting chair of indigo velvet. But no, we must make better use of the moment we have to ourselves. She got up, stole a glance out of the window, turned back to the room, riffled the leaves of several books piled on a kind of desk (books of poetry, some of them in a foreign language, and all with a sprawling signature on the first page: *Jan Engelhard,* and a flourish underneath like the tail of a comet and three dots like three stars), opened the wardrobe (a thousand dresses), opened a little door hidden behind a screen (the door opened into a huge bathroom with a sunken tub) and closed it quickly as though she had surprised a man there with his pants down; she admired the stone fireplace (with its andirons piled with wood, ready to be lighted), a pendulum clock (Heavens, a quarter past ten already!) innumerable statuettes of ivory, jade, strange iridescent substances, and was stroking the satin spread when the girl reappeared.

Miss Leonides straightened up instantly and blushed as though she had been caught doing something wrong. (How silly. Because as far as the girl was concerned, she was in her own home and in her own bedroom.) But the sight that met her eyes instantly drove from her mind blushes, satin bedspread, statuettes, the clock with the hour of a quarter past ten, the bathtub of the Emperor Caracalla, the thousand dresses, Suipacha Street, the room, the house, the world, everything. For the girl had come in carrying in her hands a gigantic tray. And on this tray there stood, in silver and porcelain, the most sublime breakfast service anyone in his right mind could imagine. The girl set that monument on a little table, pulled up a chair, and then turned toward Miss Leonides, as though inviting her to sit down.

Everything began to whirl around Miss Leonides, and her eyes did not focus. The voracity of a cannibal awoke in her like a fury. Her stomach, her lungs, her heart, her head became sensitized, the same scorpion was stinging them all. Without taking off her hat, tottering, she approached the table and sat down.

Her hands were shaking. She had one last moment of hesitation. She looked at the girl. But she was standing there beside her, with the respectful air of a trusted servant waiting on her mistress. With this Miss Leonides waited no longer. Hunger was stronger than good breeding, than shame, than dissimulation. Like a Hindu god, ten arms sprouted on her left, on her right, and with these tentacles all moving at the same time, she fell upon the tray. For a long time consciousness disappeared. An astral Leonides Arrufat manipulated spoons which buried themselves in pink jellies, in transparent marmalades, in fragrant tea with milk, and then rose radiantly to her mouth; she maneuvered, like little cranes, knives laden with preserves and butter; she crunched toast that filled her head with noise, croissants as tender as boned spring chickens, slices of cake that melted in her mouth and filled it with the most surprising, unexpected, delicious flavors. At times she raised unseeing eyes, eyes of mica, to the girl, who smiled at her, and she mechanically returned the smile and went on devouring.

Until the moment when all that monument was reduced to ruins. Then Miss Leonides and her spirit came together again, she leaned back in the chair, gave a mighty sigh which halfway out was metamorphosed into a belch, looked timidly at the girl, and murmured, apologetically:

"Delicious. Thank you so much."

And she felt suddenly drawn to that girl.

The girl, who looked more and more like a decent Polish or German servant, took the tray with the easy movement of someone performing a daily chore, and left the room with it. Miss Leonides stood up, took off her hat, took off her coat, loosened her belt, and went back to the velvet chair. (On the way she exchanged a glance with the Leonides in the wardrobe mirror, the two of them shrugged their shoulders, tittered, and, completely in agreement, separated.) Miss Leonides felt a sudden optimism without knowing why. Waves of abnegation and kindness laved her body. She felt like talking. Talking with the girl, with someone, anyone. The world is beautiful. People are nice. One must live. This is how profound the effects of a splendid breakfast are.

When the girl came back, Miss Leonides, swinging one leg and running her tongue over her teeth, asked:

"My dear, are we really alone?"

The doll nodded her floppy head.

"And did you prepare that breakfast all by yourself?"

Again the head moved up and down like a puppet's.

"Nobody helped you?"

A sly smile rose to the fleshy lips.

"Don't you remember? Don't you remember, mama?" she blubbered in a cottony voice, as though her mouth were full. "Don't you remember?"

"Don't I remember what, dear?"

"We fired Rosa and Amparo. Don't you remember, don't you remember?"

"Oh yes. But isn't there anybody else downstairs?"

"Nobody, nobody."

But Miss Leonides wanted to make absolutely sure.

"And later on, this afternoon, or tomorrow, or the next day, who's coming? Are you expecting visitors?"

"Nobody, nobody."

All right, nobody. Apparently, the poor creature had no relatives or friends, she lived all alone in that big house, she was alone in the world. Miss Leonides felt an inner satisfaction.

"Dearie," she asked in an insinuating voice, "would you like me to stay here and live with you?"

The words were no more than out of her mouth than she regretted them. She had made a slip. As her only answer, the girl knelt before Miss Leonides, took both her hands, looked her straight in the eye, while an expression of violent distress spread over her flaming face; and as at the same time that hateful sly little smile began to play over her lips again, this sinisterly dual face terrified the idol of whom benevolence was thus besought.

"If you want me to," stammered Miss Leonides, "if you want me to stay . . . I'll stay as long as. . . ."

And as the kneeling figure went on staring at her like a sleepwalker, she screamed:

"Forever, forever, I'll stay forever!"

At this the girl began a kind of frenzied contortion. The distress disappeared from her eyes, the perfidious smile began to well up, to spread to the corners of her lips, and burst like a paludal bubble. Miss Leonides found herself hugged, squeezed, kissed. A revolting hiccoughing clicked beside her mouth. Two damp hands stroked her hair. Miss Leonides could not bear to have anybody touch her hair. She struggled under those repulsive caresses. Then with an impulse she was unable to restrain, she gave the girl a slap in the face, and screamed:

"Let me be, let me be!"

The girl immediately fell back, let her hands drop, and turned very pale, very white (and white, like that, her face seemed a copy in pale marble of her other face, red and tanned, a peasant's face), her pupils trembled, but the ghost of the crazy smile went on dancing behind her lips.

Miss Leonides was no less pale. What had she done? Why had she given in to that attack of hysterics? Was that any way to repay that poor innocent creature for her breakfast and her devotion? Was that silly mania about not having her hair touched more important? Poor little girl, poor little doll. And when she saw the mark of the slap begin to show on the girl's cheek, she was on the verge of tears. Poor little doll, poor crazy little thing.

"Excuse me," she murmured, and stretched out her contrite hand imploring forgiveness.

(Yes, forgiveness, forgiveness. But it was impossible for her to stop smiling?)

The girl took that veined, fleshless hand and put it to her cheek, holding it there as if it were a poultice (her face was burning. "I wonder if she's got a fever, if she's sick?" Miss Leonides thought to herself). Her color quickly returned, and the cowardly trembling moisture disappeared from her eyes. Once more she was the peasant coming back after gathering grapes all day in the sun with a loaded basket on her head.

Then she sat down on the floor at Miss Leonides' feet. They sat like that, the two of them, motionless and silent, for a long time, as with lazy eyes they followed the cockchafer of their thoughts and dreams.

Every now and then Miss Leonides turned her head to look out of the corner of her eye at the big double bed. That bed fascinated her, drew like her a magnet. How wonderful it must be to lie in it, not to sleep, but to spend hours and hours resting, reading, or having tea. Often, in her own house, she had planned to spend several days in bed. For no special reason. Because when she got up, she had asked herself: What am I getting up for? Why am I repeating this meaningless routine? What for? But in her house this prospect was not at all alluring. To look at the patches of mold on the walls, to see them as monstrous diseased organs, to run the scale along the rosettes of the ceiling, to think: "In ten minutes I am going to die; in five minutes; in one minute; now," to scream, and then start all over again. But here it was different.

Finally Miss Leonides could stand it no longer. She got up, approached the bed, and stood there looking at it as though she were watching somebody lying there. Then she felt two hot hands resting on her shoulders and beginning to undress her. A minute later she was floating on the bosom of that huge bed as though in clear water, swimming between sheets of embroidered linen, with her head resting on a feather pillow, while warm blankets covered her like a down comforter of sand. And a girl who bent over her and kissed her on the forehead and then went and lighted a splendid fire.

Miss Leonides closed her eyes. Tears of happiness gathered under her lids. A thousand frozen buds melted in the depths of her soul and burst into bloom. Old paralyzed mechanisms lost their rust, and began to move, to run again. She felt herself drifting on the vortex of a thousand opposing currents but all of them equally delightful. Dear God, at last she was shielded from loneliness, poverty, women who let themselves be embraced in public places, gangs of street louts, and Natividad González. If only nobody would snatch her from that paradise. If they would let her stay there at least a day, even a few hours. And as though asserting her claim to it, she caressed with her feet and hands that enormous bed fit for an empress.

That first day went by quickly, hastened and as though crisscrossed by the surprises, the novelties, the continual tension. In any case, Miss Leonides did not have a bad time. The girl prepared a lunch for her which was breakfast multiplied by ten; then she served her a glass of some powerful liqueur which burned her throat and made her laugh for a long time (although the girl did not taste the

liqueur, she accompanied her in her laughter); then Miss
Leonides talked her head off, without giving a hoot
whether the girl was listening or not, because she was
talking to limber up her tongue, not to be heard by a
poor madwoman. Then came the afternoon, and Miss
Leonides, not to offend, gobbled down an abundant tea;
then the girl sat down at the desk with books (which
turned out to be a kind of archaic piano) and drew from
it a tintinnabulation like that of a music box which
moved Miss Leonides deeply; then all sounds died away,
night came, the girl lighted a lamp which colored the
whole bedroom pink; then Miss Leonides decided she
wanted to look out of the window for a minute and see
what Suipacha Street looked like from above at night;
then she had dinner; then the girl read out loud (with
gestures) a poem in which someone kept calling for a certain Anabel Anabelí; then, lulled by the litany, Miss Leonides fell asleep.

She could not understand how it was, if the window
was always on her left, she now saw it on the right. And
what in the devil was that reddish reflection that glim-
mered like tortoise shell where the chest of drawers stood?
She sat up bathed in sweat. Several minutes must have
elapsed before she realized that she was not in her own
house, but in the house at 78 Suipacha Street. The adventure she was living suddenly struck her as being a fantastic
nightmare, a dream which, now that she was awake, she
would dream all over again. She felt about with her
hands until she found the lamp and turned it on. She was
alone. A last ember smoldered in the fireplace. The clock
showed three.

She got up like a sleepwalker and went out of the bedroom. Downstairs, far in the distance, a light shone. She
made out the stairway, went down it to the accompani-
ment of muted creaks, and reached the hall. She walked
with her eyes fixed on that remote light. It was not she
who moved it, but the light that came to meet her. Under
her feet she could feel carpets, wooden floors, tiles. She

struck her ankle against a sharp object. Another, as light
as a cobweb, brushed her forehead. The light came
nearer, broadened and turned into the opening of a door.
Behind the door she could hear the rattle of dishes and a
woman's voice muttering unintelligible words. Miss Leonides stopped and waited, her heart pounding. Then, fur-
tively, she took several steps and stood where she could
see into the room where the talk was going on. She saw
that it was a large kitchen, and that the enigmatic girl
dressed in mourning, wearing an apron and with her hair
falling over her eyes, was moving about it. What was she
doing there at this time of night? Didn't she sleep? Whom
was she talking to? And in what language? And that vol-
uble voice, modulated, changing tone, like that of an
actress, was it hers? Miss Leonides stood there for a time
watching her. She seemed very busy. She was putting
away piles of dishes, opening and closing cupboard
doors, scouring pots, sitting down at a marble table and
writing, with a pencil she kept wetting against her
tongue, in an oilcloth-covered notebook. And all this
without interrupting her barbarous gabble. As she never
stopped, as nobody answered her, Miss Leonides realized
that she was talking to herself.

Miss Leonides shivered. She turned to go back as she
had come, but now there was no light to guide her. She
moved without knowing where she was going, bumped
into the wall, stumbled over furniture. She did not know
where she was, she was lost, she screamed.

There was a noise of running feet, two hands grasped
hers, and a voice murmured in her ear:

"Come, Mama, come."

The girl guided her slowly through that dark labyrinth; she soothed her with a kind of cooing, as one does
a child; she clasped her hand tightly.

Miss Leonides groaned and allowed herself to be led.

For two days nobody came to cast her out of paradise.

Miss Leonides was enchanted, really enchanted. But
her situation was not yet assured. She was walking the

tightrope of an hallucination. And the victim of the hallucination at moments kept staring at her steadily as she had done in the streetcar. Miss Leonides was waiting for an explosion: "Who are you? And what are you doing here in my mother's bedroom? Get out, get out of here fast," and then she would have to leave this Eden. At other times the girl smiled as though to herself, with that sly smile which aroused Miss Leonides' darkest suspicions. "Can she have something up her sleeve?" she wondered. "She may have brought me here God only knows with what intention." But what intentions could there be? Except in those rare moments when she seemed to lose herself in her own aberrations, the girl was so docile, so hard-working, so anxious to please. One only had to say to her: "My dear, my dear," and the doll was running about on her stumpy legs as though she had been wound up. And the way she looked after her! Like a queen.

But, just in case, Miss Leonides was on the alert. Just in case, she treated the keeper of paradise with the greatest politeness, asked her no questions, did not pry into anything. Just in case, she combed her hair with a part in the middle. She did not leave the bedroom again. That was her domain, her fortress, her refuge. No matter what happened on the lower floor, it was all one to her. Where did the girl sleep? She didn't know. Where did the money come from? She didn't know that either. She did not know and she did not care. There was no need for her to venture into those labyrinths which might shatter her hypostatic identification with the dead woman. She hardly left the bed, except to exchange it for the bathtub, which she filled with warm water and quantities of perfume, and where she lay for hours and hours with the water up to her neck, sighing with pleasure. When she recalled her house it was like something in a remote, sordid world to which, later on, she would have to return. But in the meantime she was living a long holiday. And, as for the bad odor, what bad odor? She didn't smell anything. Miss Leonides was enchanted, really enchanted.

The girl had served her another glass of that diabolical drink. Then she had brought in the bottle, and they both drank. A sudden spurt of energy came over Miss Leonides.

"Darling," she said, raising her shoulders and wrinkling her nose, as though about to propose some mischievous trick, "what would you think if I were to try on some of those dresses?"

The girl gave a shrill laugh (which left Miss Leonides somewhat disconcerted), moved her puppet's head from side to side, and rushed to open the wardrobe. Miss Leonides leaped out of bed and, standing before the mirror, began to try on, one after the other, the dresses which, it was apparent, had belonged to the false Leonides of the photograph. They did not look bad on her. A little short, perhaps, and a bit loose. But how pretty they were! Miss Leonides gazed at herself in the mirror, turned herself about, trying to see herself from the back and in profile, repeating over and over the same thing: "Why, it's an original!"

The girl had seated herself on the floor, watching with an ambiguous expression the successive transformations of Miss Leonides. From time to time (for no reason? or when the dress was especially becoming? or especially unbecoming? how could one tell?) she laughed screechily. She laughed stupidly. Like what she was. Like a crazy thing. "Can she be making fun of me?" Miss Leonides asked herself, with uneasiness and a touch of anger.

They poured themselves another glass.

Now Miss Leonides began to wriggle into an evening dress of black silk. Then she added to it a fur stole. Whereupon the girl, strangely excited, got a box of make-up out of a drawer, and Miss Leonides painted her lips and rouged her cheeks.

They poured themselves another glass.

"Jewelry," Miss Leonides suddenly shouted. "Where is my jewelry? I need a necklace, a bracelet, earrings."

The girl looked feverishly everywhere, Miss Leonides

helped her, they searched the room. They found an empty jewel box, several cases, empty too, but not even a modest ring turned up.

It did not matter. With a willowy walk Miss Leonides returned to the mirror and admired herself again. Was she that woman with her hair parted in the middle, all made up, with eyes like a tiger, her body squeezed into a skin-tight silk dress and wearing a fur cape that barely hid her bare shoulders?

She downed another glass.

Suddenly she began to cry. She didn't know why, but she cried. The tears ran down her cheeks, washing away the make-up, dropping down her bosom, wetting the silk of the dress.

(Now the marionette was not laughing. She stood motionless, watching Miss Leonides, her forehead puckered.)

At that moment from the distance, on the ground floor, there came the sound of knocking.

The alcoholic haze vanished like a bubble from inside Miss Leonides' head.

"What's that? What are those knocks?" she asked in a low voice.

The girl had got swiftly to her feet and ran to peer out of the window.

"Who is it? Please tell me, who is it?" Miss Leonides repeated, without venturing to move from the spot.

"Encarnación and Mercedes," whispered the girl, drawing back from the window and running across the bedroom.

"Please, please," Miss Leonides implored, "don't tell them I'm here."

But the girl had already disappeared.

Miss Leonides stood rooted to the floor. Dressed for a party, with the cape over her shoulders, and her face completely raddled, she was offering, in return for not being discovered, the sacrifice of complete immobility.

But after half an hour this corpse came back to life, and

curiosity took the place of panic. She slipped off her shoes, put down the fur scarf, and doing everything she could to make herself incorporeal, she began the descent to the Inferno. Now it was not a light that guided her steps, but the voices of several women chattering in one of the front rooms. She came to a little parlor and then to a breakfast room. From there, through a glass door covered with a net curtain, she could make out the visitors, comfortably settled in armchairs. They were two old white-haired women. The girl was sitting on the edge of a chair, her eyes stubbornly fixed on the floor, with the air of a criminal at the bar.

"Cecilia," said one of the old women, whose voice, hoarse and with a strangely metallic quality, paused after every syllable, recalling the bleating of a goat, "we were at the cemetery yesterday. There was not a single flower on your poor mother's grave. It must be a long time since you were there. Do you think that is nice?"

The other voice, slow and mellow, like a trickle of oil dripping on sand, added:

"Your poor mother is dead, Cecilia. You must realize that and not go about the streets looking for her. Are you listening to me?"

"Mercedes," the first voice rebuked her.

"But it's that . . ."

"Be still."

A silence followed. Cecilia (so her name was Cecilia!), who was fingering her skirt, shook all over. Was she crying?

The goat stamped her hoof on the floor and bleated:

"Now what are you laughing at? Don't laugh. I order you not to laugh, Cecilia. Good Heavens, it seems to me you smell of liquor. Have you been drinking? That's all you needed. To take to drink."

"You're like your parents," growled the other old hag.

"Mercedes!"

"But it's that . . ."

"Be still."

Another silence, and the bleating started up again:
"And what has happened today that you haven't
offered us tea? Come, Cecilia, get a move on."

The girl leaped up and ran to the rear of the house,
just as if Miss Leonides had said to her: "My dear, my
dear." "Apparently," Miss Leonides thought to herself,
"anybody can wind up my doll." And she felt a twinge
of jealousy.

For a while there was no sound from the dining room.
The two old women sat as stiff and silent as statues. But
all of a sudden this immobility was shattered. And Miss
Leonides witnessed in amazement a scene so perfectly
acted that she realized at once that those two actresses
had been playing it for a long time. Mercedes, chunky
and flat-footed, got up and went to the dining-room
door, alert for Cecilia's return. A pause, and now it was
Encarnación who got up, raising a long reptilian body,
and went straight to a glass case, opened it, and, with
movements as deft as the passing of a magnet, picked
something up, stowed it in her handbag, closed the case,
returned to her chair and sat down. In a moment
Mercedes had joined her. Once more the two women
transformed themselves into sphinxes. Not even the buz-
zing of a fly broke the silence.

From her hiding place the single spectator of that pantomime boiled with indignation. She took advantage of
the rejoicing of the two old women when Cecilia
appeared with the tea to slip out of the breakfast room.
For more than an hour she paced the bedroom. And if
they heard her downstairs, so much the better. She didn't
give a hoot. "Thieves, thieves," she growled. Now they
were stuffing themselves on the tea the poor child had
fixed for them. And a little while before, like two angels
of justice, they had been showering her with reproaches.
Who were they to talk! *Sluts. Sluts. Slutsslutssluts.*

She seated herself in the velvet chair and waited. She
must have waited nearly an hour for the wretched old
women did not go until it began to get dark. Out of

prudence Miss Leonides had not lighted the lamp. She was staring absent-mindedly at the fire, whose reflection, lighting her from below, turned her face into a scarlet winking skull.

Cecilia came into the bedroom, sat down on the floor, and, as seemed to have become a habit, rested her head on Miss Leonides' knees. She gave the impression of being strangely happy. Apparently the words of the visitors had bounced off her without leaving a dent.

"She's still drunk," Miss Leonides thought to herself. And she said: "Have they finally left, those two?"

The shock of blonde hair moved up and down and hatched a giggle.

"And you had told me that nobody would be coming...." Miss Leonides went on.

New twitters of hilarity came from under the blonde plumage.

"Did you say anything to them about me?"

Silence.

"Cecilia, did you talk to them about me?"

The plumage swelled, shook, raised up, tossed itself back, revealing the egg of a face.

A demented smile curved those lips. The eyes glittered. She looked at Miss Leonides with terrifying scorn, as though making her an accomplice of some hideous jest.

And in a viscous, molluscous, warped voice, she slobbered:

"They think you're dead."

Miss Leonides, terrified, averted her eyes.

Cecilia had gone out.

She had gibbered a mysterious word, something like *danerban*, and had left. Miss Leonides followed that vanishing black point with her eyes through the mesh of the curtain until it disappeared. Then she turned, looked at the other Leonides who, from the mirror, gave her back a conspiratorial gaze; they took counsel with one another, they encouraged one another, and at the same time, in different directions, the two left the bedroom.

There was the house, subdued, prostrate, for her to do her will. A feverish impatience burned in her. She descended on the lower floor as though it were a garment in whose seams she was looking for a hidden diamond. She switched on and turned off lights; she opened and closed doors, drawers, windows; she searched the furniture, piece by piece, so carried away that she hardly noticed what she picked up and had to go over the things again; she made sure she had examined every nook, looked behind every curtain, every picture, under the rugs. In sudden panic it seemed to her she heard a noise, Cecilia's returning footsteps. Her hands tingled. Her cheekbones stood out. She was sure that as she turned a corner, as she opened a door, as she switched on a light or looked inside a cupboard she would make some marvelous or macabre discovery, she would find some fabulous thing for which all the rest was nothing but the setting. But there was no trace of fire in the cold ashes.

The only thing that became clear was that that house, with its sumptuous furnishings and fittings, lay (except for the bedroom on the second floor) in a state of total neglect. The furniture was thick with dust. Suspicious gaps were visible (due, without a doubt, to the depredations of Encarnación and Mercedes). A disgusting fluff had gathered on the floor. It was not hard to imagine that at night cockroaches swarmed about. Perhaps some rat even dragged along its damp sinister tail. And the kitchen was like the rest of the house. To think that she nourished herself on the meals prepared in the midst of that dung! She noted once more the stench of putrefaction, medicines, death.

She came to the street door. She found it locked. A posthumous illusion led her to slip her hand into the mail box. She found there two envelopes, both addressed to Miss Cecilia Engelhard. One of them was small and seemed to have a visiting card inside. The other larger one bore the engraved address of the *Danish Bank*. The canceled stamps showed that the first envelope had been mailed five months before, and the second, two weeks. She looked at them for a while, shook them in her hand, put them in the pocket of her dressing gown, and returned to the inner rooms of the house. "I'll give them to Cecilia later on," she thought. And without knowing why she had the feeling that she was lying, lying to herself.

She went up the stairs. On the landing she noticed a door which she had overlooked before. She opened it and found herself in another bedroom. She saw an unmade bed; she saw a desk; she saw a shelf, and on it a collection of Dutch dolls; she saw the film of dust over everything; she saw a window whose shutters were open; she went over to it, and saw the roof of the rear of the house, covered with trash, and farther back, the high side walls of the neighboring buildings; she made several turns through that gloomy room; her fingers, almost mechanically, began their search of the furniture; inside the desk she found photographs, postcards, a letter. It read:

> *Dear Cecilia: I have just managed to get Monday off, and so I can come. I beg you to tear up this letter. The harpy now living with you might get hold of it. You're not angry, I hope. Yesterday I waited for a while on the corner of Suipacha and Bartolomé Mitre to see if you would come out. But you didn't. On the other hand, I saw the harpy looking out of the window. You can expect me on Monday for sure. I'll be on the sidewalk in front of the church. If everything is O.K., you come to the window and give me a sign. If I don't see you it's because there's been some difficulty. Yours, Fabian.*

Miss Leonides felt a twinge at the base of her spine. She threw the letter back in the desk and fled to her room. For a long time her mind was a blank. Her whole soul was a black pit where a black wind howled.

Then she began to run the scale over the books, the

pictures, the pheasants in the lace curtain.

Finally wisps of thoughts began to appear amidst these random notes like fish flickering through foam.

Doremifasolatido. So, the harpy . . . *Dotilasolfamiredo.* The harpy now living with you. *Dore.* With you. Yours, Fabian. *Dore.* So she is a cheat, a fraud. Just when she had begun to *dore dore.* And she shut up here, with that impostor. Under lock and key. A prisoner. *Domisoldo.* So she had dates with men. Yours, Fabian. At that very minute she was probably with Fabian. Where? And doing what? She knew very well what. The hypocrite. Maybe the two were cooking up something. Something against her? That was why she had dragged her here, and was treating her like a queen. A scheme. To kill her. *Solfasol solsol.* But why did they want to kill her? Why, why? But with a crazy thing and a street lout, there's no need to ask why. They wanted to kill her and that was all. And then they'd bury her in the back yard, at night. And who would be any the wiser, who would notice the disappearance of Leonides Arrufat, who would know what happened in that cursed old house? Nobody. Nobody. Ah, no, she would go to the window and call for help. But, no, wait a minute. We must be calm. Now let's see. *Dear Cecilia. I have managed to get Monday off.* Monday? When is Monday? What's today? Thursday. Or Friday? Wednesday. It's not Monday, for if it was Monday yesterday would have had to be Sunday, and it wasn't Sunday, for all the stores on Suipacha were open. And when had Fabian's letter come? Had the mailman brought it? Or maybe . . . . Letters.

Letters. She put her hand in the pocket of her dressing gown and brought out the two envelopes. Yes indeed, she would open them. Now she would open them. She was free, free from obligations, free from scruples. She would open them. Yes, sir.

The small envelope held, as she had guessed, a calling card. And there was a name engraved on the card, *Andrés Jorgensen*, and below it, in writing, three words: "My

deepest sympathy." In the other envelope there was a
note. "Miss Cecilia Engelhard. Account Number 3518.
We beg to inform you that your balance, as of July 31
last, unless there are any exceptions taken in the next ten
days, your balance is 4 . . . 4315 . . . 4315276 . . . 4,315,276
pesos. . . ."

Stupor paralyzed all Miss Leonides' muscles, obfus-
cated her brain. She could not grasp, she could not take
in the meaning of that monstrous sum. She read it again.
Four million. She had a choking sensation. She had to sit
down.

After a time the anesthesia of her stupefaction began to
fade, and little by little she could grasp it. She felt overpowered. She felt vaguely humiliated, derided, offended.
So everyone was plotting behind her back. Cecilia,
Fabian, the Danish Bank, the whole world, everybody.
And she was a poor fool. She felt like crying. (But, at the
same time, deep down in her soul, vague desires to avenge
herself began to stir, a general ire, the determination to be
henceforth implacable and sly.)

Until she heard the unmistakable steps of the doll. She
picked up a book, the first one she could lay her hands
on, and leaped into bed. She pretended that she did not see
her, as though she did not realize that she had returned.
She was so engrossed in that book! She smiled, sighed,
frowned, and concentrated her gaze, as though she had
not quite understood what she had read and had to read it
again.

Cecilia took a few steps in one direction, then in another, approached the bed, went away from the bed,
picked up a statuette, put it back in its place, went over to
the window, played with the fringes of the curtain, all
this without taking her eyes off those of Miss Leonides.
But Miss Leonides was a thousand miles off. Miss Leonides was galloping along the bridle paths of poetry.
Miss Leonides looked and looked again at certain signs
which said (if they said anything):

Du liebes Kind, komm, spiel mit mir,
Gar schöne Spiele spiel ich mit dir . . .

Cecilia sat down beside the window as though prepared to wait as long as necessary for Miss Leonides to return. But a person can't read like that. Nobody can read while being watched. The absorbed reader of Goethe rolled over on her side, turning her back on that tiresome creature, and with a regal gesture turned the page, encountering new hieroglyphics, as fascinating as the preceding.

Es war ein König in Thule,
Gar treu bis an das Grab,
Dem sterbend seine Bhule
Einemgoldnen Becher gab . . .

She, too, was prepared to wait.

But nearly a quarter of an hour went by like that. She had come to the last page of the book, and that idiot sat on without opening her mouth.

"Maybe you think I don't know where you've been," Miss Leonides suddenly shouted without interrupting her reading.

Cecilia got up as though she had been jerked by a string, but she made no answer.

"You think I don't know?" Miss Leonides repeated, throwing her a contemptuous look. Cecilia came over on the side of the bed toward which Miss Leonides' face was turned, fumbled in her pockets, and pulled out a sheaf of thousand-peso bills, holding them up, like a trophy, safe conduct.

Miss Leonides began to see daylight, but she would not give in. She would go on kicking, just for fun, among the strings of the net.

"I would like to know who gave you that money."

Cecilia's eyes swallowed up her face. She stammered:

"But Mama . . . but Mama . . . I went to the bank . . . to the bank . . . to the bank. . . ."

Miss Leonides' soul was a kaleidoscope turned by brutal hands. One blow, one picture; another blow, another picture.

"Do you swear to me that you did not go out to meet some man?"

Cecilia turn pale, trembled, seemed overwhelmed by that accusing question.

"But Mama, but Mama," she protested weakly, "what are you saying? What man?"

The kaleidoscope formed the reddish pattern of pain that seemed to spread in every direction, to consume the whole world, to devour itself.

"Who is this Fabian? Answer me. Who is he? Where do you meet? Answer me, don't pretend that you don't understand."

"Mama, Mama, calm yourself," sobbed Cecilia.

"I don't want to calm myself, I want you to answer me. I have asked you who Fabian is."

"I don't know. I don't know. . . ."

(Good Heavens, that tortured face, those eyes, those wringing hands, can that all be make-believe? But let's go on torturing, torturing ourselves. And then, by way of compensation, the joy of forgiving, making up, weeping together.)

"Hypocrite. I don't believe you. You are lying. Just so you'll know, I have found Fabian's letter and read it."

"Mama, Mama," Cecilia sobbed, "what letter?"

"So you're still denying it." She could not stand it any more, she was crying, too. "Now you just wait."

She burst violently out of the cocoon of sheets where all her chrysalides were ensheathed, but not a butterfly, an eagle took wing. And she was running like one possessed to the nearby bedroom when, all of a sudden, she stopped. For a memory, a tenuous thread of recollection, a bare sliver, a shaving, had caught fire amidst the rubbish of her disordered thoughts and had set them ablaze. The bonfire of the revelation enveloped her like a martyr. Ah Leonides, Leonides Arrufat, you fool, a thousand times a fool. What was she about to do? Why, Fabian's letter was not recent; a film of dust covered it like all the other objects in that room undoubtedly closed months ago. So the idyll with Fabian was not a recent one, the meetings with Fabian were not now, next Monday was a bygone Monday. And the harpy was not she, but another.

She passed in front of Cecilia again, and took refuge in her cocoon once more, ashamed and wildly happy. It seemed to her that she had been saved from a mortal peril. She closed her eyes. She stretched out her arms. Under the sheets her fingers came upon the two envelopes addressed to Cecilia.

"My dear," she murmured in the suffering voice of a convalescent. "Dearest."

And when Cecilia was at her side, with a sign of unconditional surrender she handed her the envelopes. But the girl did not even look at them. Her liquescent eyes were fixed on the huddled cocoon. The hateful smile was mirrored again on her lips.

"Mama," she stammered, "who is . . . who is Fabian?"

Miss Leonides blushed and did not know what to answer.

"Daughter," she said in confusion, without knowing what she was saying, to change the subject, "daughter, I'm hungry."

When she was alone she turned things over in her mind.

Who is Fabian, who is Fabian. In the letter he called her "Dear Cecilia," and the contents implied familiarity, an intimacy, dates, meetings, that arrangement about Monday. "Yours, Fabian." But, apparently, this Fabian had been expunged from Cecilia's memory. Perhaps the idyll had come to a tragic end, strewn with deaths, partings, suicides. And that was the cause of the unhappy girl's derangement. Miss Leonides promised herself that, given time, she would get to the bottom of it. Ah, yes, the coming Monday she would be on the lookout. For, in any case, one could not trust this strange girl too much.

In a word, she was staying.

The next Monday nothing happened. Cecilia hardly left her side, nor gave any sign of uneasiness. Whenever she left the bedroom, Miss Leonides hurried over to the window to peer out. Nothing. No sign, no young man waiting on the opposite sidewalk. When evening came Miss Leonides breathed a sigh of relief.

But two days later Encarnación and Mercedes turned up again, and the implacable spiral which was to drag Miss Leonides to desperate measures began to whir.

Miss Leonides was shut up in the bedroom waiting for the two old hags to leave. What would they steal this time, she wondered. And suddenly she heard the voices of the visitors close by. She barely had time to lock herself into the bathroom. From there she could hear everything.

She heard them come stomping into the bedroom, their voices raised, as though they were mad. Encarnación's bleating rose above the tumult.

"And why, may I ask, are you trying to keep us from visiting your poor mother's bedroom? Don't forget that we were her best friends. Her sisters, you might say. Or even closer. Oh, how nice. You have lighted the fire. And why a fire, when it's not cold? What a silly idea. What was I saying? Ah, yes, don't forget. Instead of letting all these dresses—excuse me—all these dresses—just look, Merceditas—hang there until they fall to pieces, you might give us a few of them. This one, for example. It's just right for me. Or this otter stole, which the moths will get at before you know it. What do you want it for? And Merceditas needs it so much. Not another word: I'm taking the stole for Merceditas and the dress for me. And I just wonder about this other one. . . . What's that? What did you say, Merceditas? What's the matter with Guirlanda's bed? It's warm? Who's warm? The bed? But how can it be warm, when it's over an hour. . . .?"

A deep silence followed. Then out of this silence came an unrecognizable voice (Encarnación's? Mercedes'?), a murmur steeped in the blackest suspicion:

"Are you alone, Cecilia?"

And on the heels of this, the same voice, or another, equally turgid with suspicion, excreted these words, which aroused in Miss Leonides a kind of prickling of horror:

"Are you alone, or are you up to your old tricks?"

Several soundless minutes elapsed, without the old women or Cecilia either talking or, apparently, moving. But suddenly Miss Leonides noticed with terror that the knob of the bathroom was turning, that a hand was trying to open the door, that the owner of the hand guessed that someone was locked in there. (At that moment Miss Leonides might have made a spectacular appearance. But she did not think of this until much later. Just then she was suffering a kind of giddiness. The tiles began to glow. The bathtub came loose and rocked in the air, like a gondola in the water. The bidet disappeared. Amidst all these optical illusions she heard again the sound of hoofs moving off. Then silence once more.)

She must have waited a good half hour before she made up her mind to come out of her hiding place. When she opened the door she stumbled over Cecilia's stare. She must have been there, standing in the middle of the bedroom, waiting for her to emerge. They looked at one another. Miss Leonides' eyes would have made those of a saint from heaven drop abashed. But the girl stood there, as cool as a cucumber. She even smiled. She smiled that sly smile, of an accomplice, which had already on one occasion given Miss Leonides goose pimples of repugnance. More than once. But now her revulsion had grown a hundredfold, it impregnated her whole soul, it made her feel almost sick. She could not get that phrase out of her ears: "You're up to your old tricks." She sensed an abyss of abjection beneath those words. And she would not, she could not look into the depths of that abyss.

She walked past Cecilia with her body as tense as though she were walking through a snake pit. Going to the other end of the room she sat down, picked up a book, pretending she was looking through it. She was thinking.

After a good while she gathered the late-blooming fruit of her meditations. With an air of indifference, still turning the pages of the book, she asked:

"Where do Encarnación and Mercedes live?"

No answer. Miss Leonides, making a great effort, had to turn around and look at her. Only then did the girl mutter between her teeth:

"On Cochabamba Street."

The peasant girl's face had a strange look, a rictus, a set expression which was new to Miss Leonides. She was afraid, and to cover this up, she feigned impatience.

"I know they live on Cochabamba Street. What I am asking is the number. I don't recall it. It's been such a long time. . . ."

She made a vague gesture, and not knowing how to continue, she became silent and looked out of the window.

Cecilia went out and came back at once, taking a position alongside Miss Leonides. Miss Leonides looked at the shoes of that suddenly frightening doll, saw out of the corner of her eye that she was holding out a piece of paper to her, took it and read: "Address of E. and M., Cochabamba 1522, Buenos Aires." The handwriting was clumsy and enormous. Miss Leonides croaked out a "Thank you," and went on turning the leaves of the book.

An awkward silence, like an invisible third presence, established itself between the two of them, and prevented Miss Leonides from uttering a single word that whole day. Cecilia, too, remained silent. (But what torture, what torture that of eyes avoiding each other, seeking, separating, pursuing, watching, lurking, spying, tiring, drowsing, awakening, coming to life, studying, provoking, defying, clashing, fighting, attacking, succumbing, asking forgiveness, fleeing, returning to seek one another to begin all over again.)

The next afternoon, after her nap, Miss Leonides began to study the pheasants in the curtain as though they were a map or a timetable, and suddenly in a determined voice which admitted of no argument she stated:

"Cecilia, I am going out."

She heard behind her that panting, eager, uneven breathing, just as that first day in the cemetery. She waited for a minute, and then added:

"I'm going out by myself, Cecilia."

She waited another minute. Nothing? No question? No objection? She wasn't going to stop her? Then, up and at them.

It was at the door, just as she was about to say good-by, that Cecilia, who had been following at her heels with a somber, taciturn air, suddenly said, in a voice so low she could barely hear her:

"Mama, come back . . . come back. . . ."

And ulcerated eyes clutched at her, while the smile seemed to give the lie to the suffering of the expression. Miss Leonides felt a tug at her heart. As best she could she improvised a calm visage and laughed.

"But, of course, I'll be back. What an idea!"

She had walked a few yards along Suipacha heading south, when Cecilia let out a scream. Good God, now what was wrong? Miss Leonides turned around, and with her, two hundred passers-by. And the reason for all this? So that poor devil could wave good-by to her with both hands. All right, good-by. Miss Leonides walked on and soon was lost in the crowd.

The farther away she got, and as, free from the beleaguerment of Cecilia, the old Leonides Arrufat came alive once more in the feigned Guirlanda Santos, her spirit took on strength. She felt increasingly intrepid, lucid, and sure of herself. She had dressed herself like the dead woman, had combed her hair like hers, so she was disguised. And like all those who put on a disguise, this gave her boldness and at the same time impunity. Moreover, she had everything all thought out.

1522 Cochabamba. A one-story house, with the front
painted an olive green asperged by rain and dogs. The
street door was open, revealing a passage at the end of
which was another door, closed. Miss Leonides rang the
bell. Nobody answered. She walked in and rang another
bell beside the second door. Inside, far away, she heard a
bell, barkings, a voice which Miss Leonides recognized at
once, singsonging:

"Coming, coming. . . ."

The door opened, and that simple soul of a Mercedes,
beatifically munching a piece of cookie, suddenly found
herself, without warning, face to face with the beyond.
Her jaw dropped; the half-chewed piece of cookie slid off
her tongue and fell to the floor, out of her throat came a
strangled gasp. She turned around and ran, lurching like
a bear and screaming:

"Encarnación! Encarnación!"

This initial triumph emboldened Miss Leonides who,
without waiting to be asked in, crossed the threshold and
made her way into the house. She found herself in an
enclosed veranda which ran along two sides of a
rectangular patio, on to which successive doors opened,
all alike and equally decrepit. One of these doors opened
and—Encarnación leading, Mercedes following—the two
culprits appeared before that figure from the other world
who had surely come to settle accounts with them.

But as soon as she came near, Encarnación's face
dissolved in a smile which looked like a repressed yawn,
and turning to Mercedes, she said something to her in a
low voice. Then she spoke to the apparition:

"What can I do for you, madam?"

Miss Leonides half-closed her eyes and said:

"I am Guirlanda Santos' cousin."

Encarnación turned again to Mercedes:

"You see?"

And again to Miss Leonides, holding out a languid,
flabby hand:

"Pleased to meet you. As you look so much like the

deceased, this silly thing was frightened."

Mercedes came forward, cowed and smiling, and she, too, stretched out a fat batrachian of a hand:

"Pleased to meet you. Yes, when I saw you, I took you for the departed."

"Except that Guirlanda was a little shorter than you," observed Encarnación with the air of a person who likes to get everything straight, "and her eyes were a different color."

Now the two of them began to itemize the differences so the stranger would not think them a pair of fools whom anybody could take in.

"Guirlanda was thinner," said Mercedes, "especially toward the end."

"That was the sickness. But Guirlanda was not thin," added Encarnación heatedly, as though being thin were a crime, and then went on amiably: "Besides you've got less hair than Guirlanda had."

"No, now that I take a good look at you, you're very different."

"Of course. I don't know how you came to make such a mistake."

"It was that at first sight. . . ."

Until they realized that they were keeping their guest standing there on the porch.

"Come in."

"Come in."

They went into a dark room that smelled of cat, Mercedes opened the shutters, the afternoon light threw into harsh relief a small parlor furnished in abominable taste. And the first thing Miss Leonides saw was a Dutch doll with its mouth open, its eyes open, its arms open, shrieking to be released from the horrible sofa where it had been seated and to be returned to its sisters, to a shelf, to a lifeless, closed bedroom where there was a desk in which there was a letter that bore a name, Fabian.

The caller and the two ladies of the house sat down on chintz-covered chairs, looked at one another, smiled, sized each other up, the doll seemed to stop crying and listen, and a juicy conversation began between the self-styled cousin and the two best friends of the late Guirlanda Santos.

ENCARNACIÓN: So you are poor Guirlanda's cousin.

POOR GUIRLANDA'S COUSIN: Second cousin.

ENCARNACIÓN: On her mother's side?

COUSIN: On her father's.

ENCARNACIÓN: So your name is Santos, too, I mean your last name.

COUSIN: Naturally.

ENCARNACIÓN: Then you must have some outlandish name, like all the Santos women. Papa used to say they took them from novels.

COUSIN: Ah, yes, From novels? But not mine. They got mine out of a book of poems. I am called Anabelí.

MERCEDES: Didn't I tell you?

ENCARNACIÓN: Mercedes! It's a beautiful name, Anabelí. And what relation does that make you to Belena?

ANABELÍ: Me? To Belena? Why. . . .

MERCEDES: Aunt. For if you are a cousin of Guirlanda's, and Guirlanda was Belena's aunt, then you, too, are an aunt of hers.

ANABELÍ: Of course. Not a real aunt though, but twice removed.

ENCARNACIÓN: I wonder why Guirlanda never happened to mention you.

ANABELÍ: My dear, you are not doubting. . . .

ENCARNACIÓN: No, of course not. One only has to look at you. But how odd, for Guirlanda said that, aside from Belena, there were no other Santos. And as Jan had come to America by himself, she said that she and Cecilia were alone in the world. For she did not count Belena, you know.

ANABELÍ: She did not count me either, my dear.

ENCARNACIÓN: Ah.

MERCEDES: Ah.

ANABELÍ: There were several misunderstandings, family matters, which I'd rather not talk about.

ENCARNACIÓN: Because of Jan? That was just what happened with Belena.

ANABELÍ: Can you imagine? They didn't even let me know that Guirlanda had died.

ENCARNACIÓN: There was just what happened with Belena.

MERCEDES: Belena found it out from the newspaper.

ANABELÍ: To be sure, I was living in Cordoba. But, anyway, Cecilia knew my address, and she could have sent me a card. You see, I had to come to Buenos Aires. Because as I was left a widow . . .

ENCARNACIÓN: Dear me! You have my sympathy.

MERCEDES: You have my sympathy.

ANABELÍ: Thank you very much, thank you very much. As I was left a widow five years ago, I decided to come to the capital. And naturally, after such a long time, I'm not a person who bears a grudge, the first thing I did was go to see Guirlanda. And I found out that she had passed away.

ENCARNACIÓN: You can't imagine what she suffered, poor Guirlanda. I don't know if Cecilia has told you.

ANABELÍ: Very little.

ENCARNACIÓN: She died of cancer. She spent her last three years shut up in that house. She didn't want to see anybody, not even us. That gives you the whole picture. Not even the doctor. She even fired the servants. She said they were trying to poison her.

ANABELÍ: And who took care of her?

MERCEDES: Cecilia.

ENCARNACIÓN: Cecilia. She was nurse, cook, housemaid, everything. She couldn't leave her alone for a single minute, because when she came back she would find her crying her eyes out and screaming that she was dying. Believe me, that girl deserves a front seat in heaven.

ANABELÍ: And did Cecilia know that her mother . . . .?

ENCARNACIÓN: How could she help knowing it! And for that reason she devoted herself to making Guirlanda's last years as pleasant as she could with an abnegation that brought tears to our eyes.

ANABELÍ: Until she died.

MERCEDES: Until she died, poor Guirlanda.

ANABELÍ: It was really a blessing for them both.

ENCARNACIÓN: It was. But, nevertheless, it was a terrible shock for Cecilia. She idolized her mother. I remember the night of the wake. She sat there beside the coffin, and the expression on her face was frightening. In my opinion it was then that she became unbalanced. I may tell you that the only persons at the wake were my sister and I. For they didn't have any friends; you know how odd Jan was, with his manias, his occult sciences, his Rosicrucianism. As for Guirlanda, I don't have to tell you. And the few they had left, what with shutting herself up and her queer ways, they drifted away. We were the only ones who stood by her. Relatives, there was you . . .

ANABELÍ: In Córdoba, without knowing a thing.

ENCARNACIÓN: . . . and Belena. We never thought that Belena would come to the wake of her mortal enemy.

ANABELÍ: But she came.

ENCARNACIÓN: She came. When I saw her come in, I was speechless.

ANABELÍ: And how is Belena?

ENCARNACIÓN: As beautiful as ever, so distinguished. . . .

MERCEDES: They can say what they like about Belena, but. . . .

ENCARNACIÓN: Mercedes! The trouble with Belena is that she is too attractive, and that always arouses envy and gossip. And excuse me, I am not referring to Guirlanda, God rest her soul, but in spite of all they have said about Belena, and they've said plenty, I have no proof of it. If you could have seen her that night. She kissed Cecilia, she kissed both of us, she looked for a long time at poor Guirlanda, she wiped her eyes over and over again. If she had been what they say she is, she would not have shed a tear over Guirlanda.

ANABELÍ: And you haven't see her since?

ENCARNACIÓN: How could we? Don't you know?

MERCEDES: Don't you know?

ANABELÍ: No. What?

ENCARNACIÓN: Didn't Cecilia tell you?

ANABELÍ: Not a word.

ENCARNACIÓN: It was like this. As Cecilia had been left all alone, and as Belena was alone, too, because she lost her husband some years ago . . .

ANABELÍ: Like me.

ENCARNACIÓN: Like you. That's life. And as, when all is said and done, and in spite of the quarrels, Cecilia and Belena were first cousins, and as Belena doesn't bear a grudge. . . .

ANABELÍ: Like me.

ENCARNACIÓN: Like you. Belena went to live with Cecilia.

ANABELÍ: Did she? Belena? She went to live with Cecilia there, in the house on Suipacha? But she's not there now.

ENCARNACIÓN: No. Not any longer.

ANABELÍ: What happened? Did they have a quarrel?

ENCARNACIÓN: You ask what happened.

MERCEDES: God in Heaven!

ANABELÍ: Gracious, you are frightening me.

ENCARNACIÓN: There are some things it's not easy to talk about, madam.

ANABELÍ: Remember, my dear. I'm one of the family. And it's as though you were, too. You are more than relatives.

ENCARNACIÓN: Well, with your permission. After Guirlanda's death, we often went to see them. Belena received us cordially.

MERCEDES: Whereas Cecilia . . .

ENCARNACIÓN: Mercedes!

ANABELÍ: Go on. What about Cecilia?

ENCARNACIÓN: What she is trying to say is that Cecilia never spoke, she didn't open her mouth even to ask how we were, or how Mama was. For you know Mama is paralyzed.

ANABELÍ: How dreadful!

ENCARNACIÓN: Never! Not a word.

MERCEDES: She takes after her father. You must have known Jan. We couldn't stand him.

ENCARNACIÓN: Mercedes!

ANABELÍ: But Belena . . .

ENCARNACIÓN: I was coming to that. We noticed that Belena looked worried. One afternoon she walked us to the corner and told us several things. First, how stingy Cecilia was. She counted out every penny she gave her. Mercedes is right about that. She takes after Jan. But the other thing was more serious. Yes, Cecilia's going out. For instance, she would go out in the afternoon and not come back until night. Belena would ask her: "Where've you been, dear?" and she wouldn't tell her. Naturally, Belena began to suspect that she was up to no good. But what could she do?

ANABELÍ: Well, if I had been in Belena's place . . .

ENCARNACIÓN: Sure you would have, my dear. But you were not living on Cecilia's bounty the way Belena was. For poor Belena doesn't have a penny to bless herself with. Besides, you're her aunt, you're a mature woman . . .

ANABELÍ: And what about Belena? She's no child, is she?

ENCARNACIÓN: No, but . . .

ANABELÍ: It was her duty to look after her cousin who is a minor.

ENCARNACIÓN: Cecilia?

MERCEDES: Cecilia a minor?

ANABELÍ: Isn't she? I can never remember ages.

ENCARNACIÓN: Cecilia is past twenty-three.

ANABELÍ: *Doremifa.*

ENCARNACIÓN: Excuse me?

ANABELÍ: No, I was just thinking.

ENCARNACIÓN: To be sure, she doesn't look it.

MERCEDES: Crazy people never look their age.

ENCARNACIÓN: Mercedes!

ANABELÍ: Go on, my dear.

ENCARNACIÓN: One day when we went to see them Cecilia was not at home. I, this one, and Belena were talking as calm as you please there in the dining room. When all of a sudden Belena began to cry. You can imagine us. She told us that as she was going over Cecilia's clothes, she had found a photograph—"this one," she said. And she showed us the picture of a young, blond fellow, not bad-looking,

but with such eyes. . . . On the back of the photograph there
was written: "F. to C."

ANABELÍ: And was that why Belena was crying?

ENCARNACIÓN: Naturally.

ANABELÍ: It was nothing to take on about. Any girl can
have a boy friend.

ENCARNACIÓN: Yes, but Cecilia is not any girl. Think of
her fortune. Think what she is like. Can't you see the bait
she is for some adventurer? And if he was the kind of boy
friend he should be, why did she hide him? Why didn't he
come to the house so Belena could meet him?

ANABELÍ: That is true.

ENCARNACIÓN: Remember that Belena had never been
able to get out of Cecilia where it was that she went in the
afternoon. Besides, once Cecilia had got mad and had called
her a harpy.

ANABELÍ: A harpy! What a nice thing to do!

ENCARNACIÓN: Nice, indeed.

ANABELÍ: And what about you? Didn't you try to talk with
Cecilia.

ENCARNACIÓN: But that girl is always in another world.
You try to get something out of her, and it's like talking to
the wall. Besides, we didn't want to make things bad for
Belena by giving away that she had confided in us. Belena
herself had asked us not to say anything. And if you don't
mind my telling you everything, Cecilia has a kind of
dislike for us, I can't think why.

MERCEDES: Between Jan and Guirlanda they had got it
into her head that we . . .

ENCARNACIÓN: Mercedes! The trouble is that Cecilia
already was not quite right in her mind. At times people
like that, a little touched, take a dislike to certain people, for
no good reason, just because.

ANABELÍ: That's true. And afterward?

ENCARNACIÓN: Afterward?

MERCEDES: Oh, Lord!

ENCARNACIÓN: Afterward what we were afraid would
happen, happened. It was one afternoon. We had arranged

that I would go with Belena to Dr Criscuolo's office—you must have heard of him, he's a famous heart specialist. Yes, poor Belena thought there was something wrong with her heart. She asked me to go with her because I had told her that we had known Criscuolo since we were children. I was to come by for her. And so I did. It was four in the afternoon. I remember that before we left Belena said to Cecilia: "I hate to go off and leave you alone." Can you imagine, it was as though she had a premonition, poor Belena. And I laughed and said to her: "But we'll be back in no time. Nobody's going to eat her." Dr Criscuolo took Belena around six. He told her there was nothing the matter with her heart. After that we went to have tea at *Los Dos Chinos*. We were sitting there, as pleasant as could be, when Belena began to get nervous, and tell me that the day before Cecilia had received a letter, and that she was terribly worried, because she suspected, from various things she had noticed, that her cousin was carrying on a love affair and so on, and so forth, and that we had made a great mistake in leaving her alone for so long. The long and the short of it was that, having barely swallowed my tea, I had to get up and go back to the house with Belena. When we got there it was dark. The street door was standing ajar. We went in. It was all dark. Belena turned on the light and we saw furniture with the drawers pulled out, an overturned chair, and cigarette stubs on the floor. Belena began to scream: "Cecilia, Cecilia," but there was no sign of Cecilia. I was scared out of my wits. "Let's call the police," I said. But Belena went on screaming: "Cecilia, Cecilia." We searched the whole first floor, and not a sign of Cecilia. Belena dragged me up the stairs. I didn't want to go with her, for I was sure we would find her in a pool of blood, her throat cut, stabbed to death. But Belena made me. The door of her bedroom was locked, and the key was in the keyhole on the outside. We opened the door, and there was Cecilia.

MERCEDES: Alive.

ENCARNACIÓN: What a piece of news! Of course she was alive. But the state she was in! She was shaking like a mad dog, her eyes had a wild look, her hair was all in disorder, and her clothes were torn. And so was the bed, if you see what I mean. All tumbled.

MERCEDES: Tell her about Belena.

ENCARNACIÓN: When she went into Cecilia's bedroom and saw that sight, Belena underwent a transformation. I won't forget her face as long as I live. She became ugly—I don't know if I am making myself clear. Such a hideous face that Cecilia shrank away and began to scream, as if she was afraid that Belena was going to punish her or kill her. It was all very strange. But aside from the expression on her face, Belena did nothing. She just stood there. And then she flew out of the room like a whirlwind. I followed her. She crossed the anteroom, and went into Guirlanda's bedroom, and I behind her. She began to go through all the drawers, and I too.

ANABELÍ: What were you looking for?

ENCARNACIÓN: Guirlanda's jewelry, the pounds sterling, the Peruvian soles, the Mexican gold, all the coins that Jan had collected, a veritable fortune.

ANABELÍ: They were gone.

ENCARNACIÓN: The whole lot. Belena stopped searching. She was beside herself. She bit her lips, her hands shook, sparks shot out of her eyes. How did I tell you she went, Mercedes?

MERCEDES:*Uuuh, uuuh,* like that, as though she was blowing through something.

ENCARNACIÓN: After that, without so much as looking at me, she rushed down to the first floor. I didn't know what to do. For a while I wandered around Guirlanda's bedroom and through the anteroom. I didn't venture to go into Cecilia's room. Finally I made up my mind and went to look for Belena. I found her in the kitchen, crying as I have never seen anybody cry in my life. When she saw me she stopped crying instantly, turned her back on me, and said sharply: "Encarnación, I beg of you, nobody is to know what has happened here. I ask it for Guirlanda's sake. And now go. Go and leave me alone." It seemed to me that grief had made her rather rude. But I forgave her. And as I don't need to be told a thing twice, I left that very minute.

ANABELÍ: My dear, let me ask you a question. Do you happen to remember if that day when whatever it was that happened, happened, was a Monday?

ENCARNACIÓN: Let me think. Criscuolo has office hours on Mondays and Thursdays.

MERCEDES: It wasn't a Thursday, for if it had been a Thursday, I would have gone to the Mission, and as it was I stayed at home.

ENCARNACIÓN: In that case, it was a Monday. How did you know?

ANABELÍ: No matter. But go on, my dear.

ENCARNACION: There's not much left to tell. When I went back the next day with this one, we found a Belena that was like a stone image; she hardly spoke to us, and when she did open her mouth it was to ask us again to say nothing. It disturbed us to see her like that.

ANABELÍ: Like that? How?

ENCARNACIÓN: Limp as a rag. She who was so proud. Oh yes, and when we asked how Cecilia was, she screamed at us that she didn't want to hear her name, and began to sob. I repeat, we were terribly upset.

ANABELÍ: And what about Cecilia?

ENCARNACIÓN: We didn't see her that afternoon. Two days later we went back, but Belena was no longer there. As for Cecilia, she had such a deranged look when she asked us in that we were horrified. She was talking utter nonsense, saying that her mother had gone out, and was taking a long time getting back, and that maybe she was lost and she ought to go out and find her . . . It broke your heart to listen to her.

ANABELÍ: So Belena deserted Cecilia when the girl needed her most.

ENCARNACIÓN: Yes, we, too, thought it very strange.

ANABELÍ: And you haven't seen her since?

ENCARNACIÓN: No, never.

ANABELÍ: Do you know where she lives?

ENCARNACIÓN: No.

MERCEDES: No.

ENCARNACIÓN: We tried to find that out from Cecilia, but it was useless.

ANABELÍ: So neither you nor Belena informed the police?

ENCARNACIÓN: My dear, what would we have gained by it.

ANABELÍ: You? On the contrary, you would have lost.

ENCARNACIÓN: What's that?

MERCEDES: Lost?

ENCARNACIÓN: What do you mean, lost?

ANABELÍ: You would have lost the opportunity to keep on going to Cecilia's house to steal things.

MERCEDES: What?

ENCARNACIÓN: I don't know what you mean, madam.

ANABELÍ: On the contrary, you know very well.

ENCARNACIÓN: Let me tell you that if that crazy thing has gone to you with tales . . .

ANABELÍ: No tales. Cecilia has told me nothing.

ENCARNACIÓN: If that's the case, come to the point, what are you talking about?

ANABELÍ: To come to the point, I'm talking about a number of ornaments from the dining room. To come to the point, I am referring to an otter stole. To come to the point, I'm talking about several of Guirlanda's dresses. I was the person who was locked in the bathroom yesterday.

ENCARNACIÓN: You?

MERCEDES: You?

ANABELÍ: Finally, to come to the point, I am talking about that doll.

ENCARNACIÓN: Oh, no, I beg your pardon. Belena gave me that doll.

ANABELÍ: And what right had Belena to give away things that belonged to her cousin without the latter's permission? So, excuse me. And that buddha.

ENCARNACIÓN: That I will not allow. That buddha was one of my mother's wedding presents.

ANABELÍ: I'm taking it anyway. In place of the fur stole.

ENCARNACIÓN: Oh, no. I'll call the police.

MERCEDES: The police.

ANABELÍ: Call them. I'll call them first. We'll see what you have to tell them and what I tell them.

ENCARNACIÓN: Don't raise your voice. My mother may hear you.

ANABELÍ: Then you set an example by lowering yours. And tell your sister to stop her sniveling.

ENCARNACIÓN: Mercedes, keep still.

ANABELÍ: And now, let's see: what else?

ENCARNACIÓN: Is there anything else?

ANABELÍ: Money, the money you stole from the poor thing. Or you've made her sign a will in your favor, forced legacies for which you can be sent to jail.

ENCARNACIÓN: But what are you saying?

MERCEDES: What is she saying?

ANABELÍ: Now, you listen to me. I forbid you to return to Cecilia's house. I'm going to be there, on the lookout. If you come back, on any excuse whatsoever, I'll have you arrested.

ENCARNACIÓN: That's enough, madam. For pity's sake, that is enough.

ANABELÍ: Have you understood me?

ENCARNACIÓN: Go, I beg of you.

MERCEDES: Go, go.

ANABELÍ: I am going. But let me repeat what I said.

ENCARNACIÓN: You don't need to.

MERCEDES: You don't need to.

ANABELÍ: In that case, good-by.

Still in the disguise of Anabelí Santos, exhausted, racked, all her strength drained away by the long performance she had put on before those two old hags (especially that last scene, when she felt as though she was smashing countless clay images with a rod of iron), Miss Leonides collapsed on her narrow bed, and without even the strength to blink, stared with glazed eyes at a rosette in the ceiling. On the floor, disjointed in an incredible posture, the doll whimpered. Farther off, the buddha smiled and meditated.

The afternoon slipped by, night came, the darkness wiped out the rosette in the ceiling, and Miss Leonides lay there as motionless as a felled tree.

Until—perhaps it was a dream, perhaps it wasn't—it seemed to her that Anabelí Santos was not a figment of her imagination, but was acquiring real dimensions, was there, alive, and conveying to her a kind of long admonition.

Yes, Anabelí Santos said to her: "All right, Leonides. You have discovered that Cecilia had one of those entanglements that disgust you so. Did you hear them, those two old parrots? And now you draw a line and tot up the sum: Cecilia is this, Cecilia is that, she doesn't deserve my affection, and, therefore, I'm washing my hands of her, just the way Belena did; I'm not going back there any more, the game is over. Leonides, you're doing like the others. Like her mother, like Fabian, like Belena, like all of them. They go to Cecilia, they take advantage of her (some in one way, some in another) and then they run away (the mother left for the other world, but basically it's the same thing). And you, why are you doing it? That business with Fabian has hit you hard. I understand it. You thought that the ruination of that house, that the derangement of Cecilia were the result of her angelic grief, and now those two mummies have come and whispered in your ear that that's not true, that you were mistaken, that it was all a ruse of the beast, a filthy mixture of sex, lust, rape, and robbery. And you shrink away in disgust from that mangy monkey. All right, but let's think things over. You're not going to compare Cecilia, I hope, with those women who kiss and carry on with men in public places, and when they see you go by in your loneliness and that hat of yours laugh insolently. Those women are always beautiful, tall, always sure of themselves (just the opposite of Cecilia). Those women don't shut themselves up in the house to nurse sick people, they don't shackle themselves to the bed of a dying woman who takes three years to die (not three weeks or three days). Their dead die alone, cursing them, while they hurry to embrace some nice-looking young fellow in a park, in an automobile, in a luxurious apartment. Whereas Cecilia is your fellow being, your sister in timidity and suffering.

After those three years with her dying mother, what do you think the world holds for her? The same snares as for you. For you, to run the scale along the tiles, talk to yourself, and put a bunch of nettles at Natividad González's door. And for her, to walk along the street looking like a Polish immigrant, and some street lout to see her and follow her. And then it's done. The trap opens and, before Cecilia realizes it, has snapped on her foot. She thought she had finally found a comrade, a smiling young friend, with whom to walk hand in hand under the trees, as she had seen so many boys and girls her own age do. And above all, someone well, someone strong, someone free from the bite of the horrible crab, and who did not smell of medicines, or age, or death, but of clean flesh and youth, and health. All this was what Fabian probably meant to Cecilia. And when Belena, that handsome, mature woman (one of those who embrace in public places) tried to interfere, she defended herself with her only weapon: silence. Silence and keeping Fabian away. For if Fabian met Belena, he would fall in love with Belena, and forget her. But in front of him she laid down all her arms. All of them, even her nails. And she confided to him that her father had left her a collection of gold coins, and that her mother had jewelry which nobody used now, that they were put away in cases, and even that there was money in all the drawers. And another day she said to him: 'On Monday I won't be able to come out. My cousin, who is old, and very bad' (she was lying, or maybe she wasn't) 'has to go to the doctor and I can't leave the house alone.' Fabian probably inhaled cigarette smoke, looked at his nails, and let a whisper out of the corner of his lips like a trickle of saliva: 'If you'd like, I can come to see you.' Then all of a sudden he slapped his leg, took off the mask of playmate, and with his lout's face bare, muttered: 'Jeez, I forgot. Not Monday. I'm on duty Monday.' For a day or two he tried to get around it, finally managed, and wrote that letter: *'Dear Cecilia. Yours, Fabian.'* Cecilia imagined that they would have tea together, they would look out of the window over Suipacha; perhaps, if he asked

her to, she would recite the verses about Anabel, Anabelí.
But inside the deep, soundless house Fabian became
transformed into another man, a livid man who roared,
threw himself upon her, dragged her to a bottomless pit,
cut her to pieces, dissolved her like a particle of earth in
water, and then left, went away, disappeared forever. And
she lost her mind (those women who are your enemies do
not lose their mind). And mad and lonely, she built a walled
nook where sex cannot enter, where the beast of the flesh
cannot slip through. It is a city consecrated to the angel. A
sanctuary where no other rite than the purest love can be
celebrated. And it is to you, to you alone, that she has
unbarred the entrance. What more do you want? For thirty
years you wandered from rejection to rejection. And now
that you had been admitted, as soon as you found out the
foundation of dross on which the city had been built, you
turned up your nose and left. Leonides, you are stupid.
Apparently you prefer this jail cell of a room. You prefer the
company of the periwinkle. Go look for Natividad González. And in the meantime I can see Cecilia, standing at the
door of her house, waving good-by with her hand. And on
that hand I see the short, broken nails, I see a blister, the
stigma of a burn, just a little red, nothing."

Anabelí Santos, that will do. Don't you see that the sheets
are beginning to burn under Miss Leonides. Don't you see
that she thinks she heard a noise, sits up, and only after a few
minutes have elapsed, does she realize that it's her own sob
she heard. Now she gets up, turns on the light, looks at the
alarm clock (but the alarm clock, unwound for so many
days, no longer tells the time, it tells eternity), opens the
door, and forgetting you and the meditating buddha and
the doll on the rack, rushes out like a cyclone.

Miss Leonides crosses an unknown city in the streetcar.
What time is it? She doesn't know. Nobody knows. Maybe
it's eleven at night, maybe it's four in the morning.
Impatience gnaws at her like a termite. She looks out of the
window without recognizing anything that she sees. The
streetcar reaches a corner that copies, with various old

props, the corner of Sarmiento and Suipacha. Miss Leonides gets off. Now she hurries down a long deserted corridor. In the distance she can make out the mass of the church. And across from it the house. And in the door, Cecilia. Cecilia, huddled on the doorstep like a beggar. Arms and legs interlaced as though embracing herself. She is looking toward Rivadavia. Looking toward the vast south where, hours before, Guirlanda Santos disappeared from view. It is very late, the city has gone to bed, but Cecilia waits on. Guirlanda Santos promised to return. And she waits for her.

Miss Leonides could not bear it any longer. She felt huge with love. She cried: "Cecilia!"

Her cry spread, bounced back from the walls of the long deserted corridor, awoke the doves of echo.

The knot of legs and arms comes undone as though slashed by a scimitar, the beggar gets to her feet with one bound, whirls around, sees Guirlanda, Guirlanda who has returned, runs toward her, toward Guirlanda with her hair coming loose, her cheeks glowing, her eyes gleaming, looking like a girl, looking a thousand years younger, looking well and lithe and beautiful. A store (closed) to the right, another store (closed) to the left, across the way the wall (sleeping) of St Michael Archangel; there is no witness to see how these two pitiful creatures rush toward one another, how they embrace, weep, and enter the house, Number 78, closing the door behind them, nor how the gargoyle faces of the bronze knockers beam and seem to smile.

Leonides Arrufat, Anabelí Santos, Guirlanda Santos, the three of them simultaneously and in turn laugh and cry and kiss Cecilia and exclaim:

"You'll never guess where I went. To see a famous doctor. And you'll never guess what he told me. That I am cured. You realize what that means, Cecilia? That now we don't have to live shut up in the four walls of this house. Now we can go out for walks, go to the movies and the theater. We'll have tea every day at a different tearoom, where there is music. And we'll buy ourselves things, lots of things, everything we want. But, what's the matter, Cecilia? What's wrong, Cecilia?"

Cecilia sways, a change comes over her face which seems to split up into several identical faces superimposed on one another without coinciding. Bent double, she throws up on the rug.

Miss Leonides picks her up in her arms (Guirlanda and Anabelí help her), carries her to the bedroom, lays her gently on the bed, undresses her, tucks her in, and is about to tell her that from now on. . . . But Cecilia, as though struck down by accumulated fatigue, has fallen asleep as soon as her head touched the pillow.

Guirlanda, Anabelí, and Leonides look thoughtfully at that yeasty face, that face like a loaf of bread that has fallen in the water and swelled without, at the same time, losing its shape.

Suddenly the three of them understood.

Several months went by. The constellations moved in their changeless orbits. Spring was followed by summer.

Miss Leonides would say: "Cecilia, my child," and she no longer felt as though she were using an artificial language. Cecilia would call out: "Mama, Mama," and Miss Leonides no longer noticed, beneath this call, the vacuum which before left it whirling in the air like a dry leaf. For the spirit, as well as the flesh, more than the flesh, makes its adjustments.

They went out walking, arm in arm. They sat down at a sidewalk table of one of the tearooms on Avenida de Mayo, slowly sipping their refreshments, watching the people go by. Or they went into one of the movie houses on Lavalle, watched the procession of those images which always passed too fast, came out as though they were drunk, and for the rest of the day talked about nothing but what they had seen. (To be sure, Miss Leonides realized that many times Cecilia had not made head nor tail out of the picture. But what difference did it make? She looked so happy sitting there, laughing and eating caramels!)

Together, always together. Now Miss Leonides wore gray, white, blue. Her cheeks filled out. She had put on weight. She looked more than ever like Guirlanda Santos ten years back (when Belena saw her alive for the last time). And beside her, neat, obedient, a pearl, the little doll with the face of a peasant and that blonde mop of hair trotted along on her mechanical stumpy legs.

"Dear Lord," prayed Miss Leonides, "don't take this happiness from me."

The house shone like a mirror. The smell of decay and medicine had been aired out. Between the two of them they prepared complicated, unheard-of dishes which they gaily gobbled up in the kitchen.

They celebrated Christmas with a banquet. Miss Leonides, giving free rein to long-repressed fantasies, decorated the dining room beyond recognition. On the table an imposing relief map of dainties was spread. They drank champagne. They laughed uproariously. Miss Leonides whirled through the measures of a dance by herself, throwing kisses to an imaginary audience. And, as always, they wound up crying.

"Dear Lord," Miss Leonides implored, "don't take this happiness from me."

But inexorable rust was already gnawing at that gilded structure.

Cecilia's face revealed, like the obverse and reverse of a coin, at times infinite happiness, at times a mute despair, and as these two expressions went with that sardonic smile which never left her lips, her countenance soon took on a tinge of shrewdness and malice, like those Roman emperors whose severe air is in contradiction to the sly mouth which seems to reveal a kind of perfidious inner gaiety. But at other times both sides of the coin became effaced, and in their place there appeared fleetingly the profile of a little girl who, alone in the night, hears the sound of approaching footsteps.

Every time this pathetic child took Cecilia's place, something clutched at Miss Leonides' heart.

"Dear God," she would pray, seized by a deep distress.

By the end of the summer, Miss Leonides' almost sole company was this terrified little girl who heard the noise of steps. It was useless for her to take her hands, press them against her breast, say to her:

"You wait and see, you wait and see, everything will be all right."

What was it that would be all right? Cecilia clutched desperately at the hands holding hers, with terror in her eyes at the same time that the hovering smile became more pronounced; she moaned in a kind of hoarse wail:

"I'm afraid, I'm afraid."

Perhaps in her dream she knew what Miss Leonides still ignored in hers.

She knew that, when the steps stopped and the visitor knocked, she must awake, emerge from her dream, open a door and go out. And that when the door closed behind her she could never come in again.

She knew that the doctor, a stranger whom Miss Leonides had found thanks to a bronze name plate on the door, would say in a sententious and final tone:

"We'll have to choose between the mother and the child."

And that Miss Leonides, horrified, would stammer:

"But, doctor, who's to make the decision? My daughter (dear, beloved Leonides Arrufat), my daughter is not in a state to make such a decision, you can see."

"I see, madam, I see," the doctor would answer, annoyed because they were making him enter into explanations. "But we can't save the two of them."

Perhaps she already knew what the doctor did not know. She knew that, contrary to his pedantic assertions, there would be nobody to save and nobody to condemn.

And she would have liked to tell Miss Leonides so, but she could not find the words, she could not find the way to decant, from one irreality to the other, the subterranean water of that premonition. And for that reason, with growing frequency, she moaned, she twitched with convulsive jerks, that repulsive little smile hovered about her lips as though trying to break through.

And all poor Miss Leonides could think to do was to repeat monotonously:

"You wait and see, you just wait and see, everything will be all right."

Until one night, during carnival, the footsteps halted, the big door swung open, and Cecilia, with a scream, emerged from the dream.

She was sleeping in her mother's bedroom, in her mother's bed. Beside her a strange woman, dressed like her mother, wearing her hair like her mother, was looking at her with eyes that seemed bursting from their sockets.

"Who are you?" she asked weakly, trying to sit up. But her strength dissolved and she had to let her head drop back on the pillow.

From a distance there came a noise that was like a stream of water running into an empty tank. And at the same time the stream of water produced a strident music.

"What is all that noise?" she asked, turning her eyes toward the window through which came a reddish glow.

She heard the stranger's voice answer:

"It's the parade up Avenida de Mayo, Cecilia."

She called her Cecilia, just Cecilia. The girl looked at her.

"Why have you done your hair the way she did? Why have you put on her blue dress which she was so fond of? Why did I try to make myself believe . . .? Or perhaps I myself asked you to, and I can't remember."

The stranger said nothing, folding her arms over her breast, as though trying to hide herself, bowing her shoulders with the air of a servant effacing herself before an imperious mistress.

"I know. You are my nurse. I have been sick all this time."

She touched her abdomen with her hands.

"Why is my body so swollen? Am I going to have a baby?"

Suddenly she seemed to enter a familiar landscape. She recognized it. Everything was in its place. And in this landscape, that gilded shadow, that frightening shadow, where was it?

"Where is Belena?"

She looked searchingly at the stranger, and the stranger stammered:

"She's not. . . . She doesn't live here any more. . . ."

Belena. There was something that had to do with Belena. Something unfinished. But she could not remember.

"Where has she gone?"

"I don't know, I don't know, Miss."

"And Encarnación and Mercedes?"

The stranger shrank still more into herself, huddled up, hunching her head between her shoulders.

"They don't come anymore either."

The familiar landscape. The solid ground underfoot. And overhead the sky like a pledge of eternity. Suddenly she remembered.

"Do you know?" she said, in a voice so abruptly adult that the stranger started and looked around in fright, as though she suspected it was some other person who had spoken to her. "Do you know why I got sick? Do you know everything?"

"Yes, Miss, I do. And I can't tell you how I pity you!"

She raised a hand. Pity her! This woman did not know that she was the daughter of Jan Engelhard, the sage, the wizard, the saint. Daughter and pupil. At his side she had learned to suffer and keep silent, and to purify herself in suffering like silver in the fire. But the time had come to reveal all.

"Who told you?"

"Encarnación and Mercedes, the last time they were here."

"No, they don't know it all. Listen to me. I don't want to die without first. . . ."

"Miss Cecilia!"

Die, yes, die. Chunks of rubble that fall to the ground like dry husks. And the living kernel, glowing in the light like a diamond.

"I know that I am going to die. I don't have much time. And you are the only person here with me. Listen to me."

The stranger heard this tale:

She was alone. Belena had left, with Encarnación, to see a doctor. Suddenly three men appeared in the dining room, where she was folding some tablecloths. They were young. Two of them didn't look to be more than twenty. The third one, tall and dark, was about twenty-five. They were wearing black leather jackets. And gloves. One aimed a revolver at her. She started to scream and they hit her. They dragged her through the house. They raided the pantry. They ate, they drank, they smoked. Then they took her upstairs. They seemed to know the layout of the rooms perfectly. In her room the two younger ones said to the other: "O.K., brother, it's your show." The other one laughed and then turned and looked at her. She struggled, she defended herself. She buried her teeth in a gloved hand. Then everything collapsed. The roofs, the walls, the bed, the shelf with the dolls. They had left. They had locked her in and had left. She could hear them talking. No, not she. Her head. But her head had come loose from her body, had rolled far away on the floor, cut off, detached. That head which was no longer hers had heard. Now that it was back on her shoulders again, now she knew what that guillotined carrion had then overheard. The three men were talking in her mother's room. One of them said: "Look, seventy pounds sterling." Another: "What time is it?" Another: "Five of six. Belena said that she wouldn't be coming back with the old woman till after seven." The same voice added, "When she gets back and sees that I stopped after the first act and didn't finish off the cousin for her, she's going to be as mad as hell." The first one: "Jeez, won't she squeal on you?" The other: "Let her, if she wants to. For I kept the photo. And let her explain to the police why she told the two old women that she had found it in one of the kid's dresses, and that she suspected that it might be the photo of some boy friend of the kid's, and that she was worried, and she even squeezed out some tears, and the photo is of her husband, who died a natural death a couple of years ago. Ah, no, she'll have to excuse me, but when it comes to blood, I'm out. I am sorry to deprive her of inheriting the cousin's property, which she planned to enjoy in my honorable company, but I'm satisfied with these leavings." The second one: "We, too." The third one: "Sure, kid, sure. We're in this share and share alike. As I said, if there's any killing, count me out. But she—what guts! But I'm tired of that bag. Not to mention the fact that she is forty-two, and I, unless there's been an error or miscount, am twenty-five." The first one: "Say, and what about the kid?" The other: "What about her?" The first one: "Won't she talk?" The other: "Let her. What's she going to say? What clue has she got? Nobody is going to suspect us. And anyway, Belena will take good care to queer her pitch. Because she knows that if they catch me, they'll get her, too. So she's going to take good care to cover up for me. And let her find herself another sucker. For she's not going to see hide nor hair of me again."

Her head had heard all this at the time. But not she. She lay mutilated in a corner of her bedroom. Until after she couldn't tell how long, the door opened and Encarnación and Belena came in. On her neck an artificial head was grafted, a vibratile head of a fetish which moved and talked of itself. With this automaton wedged between her shoulders, she could no longer think or reason. All she could do was to hide away in her warm, numb entrails, curl up like her own fetus, drift off in a deep morbid sleep in which Guirlanda Santos was alive. And it was from this sleep that she had just awoken.

But why was the stranger looking at her with that frightening face? Why did she rush out of the bedroom? Why did she come right back with a letter and say to her:

"Miss Cecilia, read this."

And she read: *"Dear Cecilia. I have just managed to get*

Monday off, so I can come . . . Yours, Fabian."
    She did not understand, she did not understand any of it.
"Where did you find this letter?"
    "In your room, Miss."
    "But I never received it. I don't know any Fabian."
    The eyes of the stranger did not let go of hers. And those
eyes were screaming a frightful revelation at her. Those
eyes had a name tattooed on them.
    It was hard for her to breathe, her head was whirling, a
thundering storm was brewing in her womb.
    "Belena," she managed to bring out.
    The stranger bent over her.
    "Where does she live?"
    "I don't know. I don't know. But find her. Bring her to
me."
    The stranger seemed turned to stone.
    "Belena," Cecilia's pale lips repeated, "Belena."
    A lightning flash burst in her eyes. Now would be when
the stranger would call that doctor.
    But she was already leaving. She was floating down a
murmurous river, full of birds, flowers, algae, fish. A cool
clear river that carried her farther and farther away toward
a plain as blue as the sea. Before sinking into this sea she
turned and made out the stranger who, from the distant
bank, seemed to follow her like a faithful dog. She smiled
at her, stretched a translucent hand toward her which
overcame the distance and reached that maternal face, and
asked her again, this time in a tone of inexpressible
sweetness:
    "Who are you, madam?"
    But she did not hear, she would never hear, the stranger's
answer.

Everything was now clear.
    If her face and the face of Guirlanda Santos had been cast
in the same mold; if Natividad González, that morning,
had covered her with insults; if she took that streetcar, and
gesticulated and laughed to herself; if Cecilia, sitting

beside her, saw her and saw her making those gestures; if she then stubbornly followed her through the city streets; if no accident, no chance prevented their meeting in the cemetery, and the flight to the house at 78 Suipacha, and the episodes that followed, it was because everything formed part of a vast ceremony, everything made up one of those intricate mechanisms of which we will never know who was the artificer—God or ourselves.

But fate never beckons to anyone gratuitously. If she had been included in the ceremony, it was because, at some determined moment, she was to pass from acolyte to minister and officiate at the final ritual act, the one with which the ceremony would end. She understood that this moment had arrived. Cecilia had laid her hands upon her, and she was now consecrated for the horrid rite.

She looked at Cecilia's face lying upon the pillow.

She looked at it with a kind of voraciousness, as though to impregnate herself in it. Stamp it on her soul like a tattoo on the skin. That face minute by minute became more beautiful. Death, wiping out its fatigue, gradually brought it to life. Until, wide-awake, it glowed like a jewel. Just as in the old fairy stories, the peasant girl had been turned into a princess. And Miss Leonides sank to her knees.

Afterwards she got up. She was possessed by an icy calm. She remembered:

ENCARNACIÓN: Just like Belena.

MERCEDES: Belena found it out through the newspaper.

First she would try that scheme. And then others, many, all, until she found her.

She went to an undertaking establishment. She went to the newspaper offices. She arranged for a notice to be published saying: "Cecilia Engelhard, R.I.P. Her bereaved family announces the passing . . . Funeral services at: 78 Suipacha."

The employees of the undertaking establishment prepared the funeral chapel in one of the downstairs rooms, laid out Cecilia in a black coffin, the infant in a tiny white one, placed close by the street door a mahogany urn, and fled from that somber mansion where there was nobody to be seen but the two corpses and a woman who was not weeping but in front of whom, without knowing why, they had to lower their eyes.

Then Miss Leonides took up her position beside a window and waited.

Outside, in the carnival afternoon, Suipacha drowsed.

Several hours went by, as long as days. Night came. Along Avenida de Mayo rainbows of lights sprang up, the music struck up, the procession began its uproar.

And Miss Leonides, standing beside the window, went on waiting. Only her lips moved, as though in prayer. The rest of her body had the lethargy of a crocodile. But from the depths of their orbits, her eyes gave off a gleam of silica. They did not take in the groups of people moving toward the procession. They were aimed, across the city, at a single spot, unknown and divined. And that glance instantly recognized the woman who had stopped before the door.

The woman hesitated for a second. Then she came in. She saw the mahogany urn. She saw, farther off, an open door and the gleam of the candles. She walked over to the door and went in. She saw the two coffins. She approached first one, then the other, she looked into their depths observing them as from a parapet. She seemed perplexed and a little frightened. At that moment she heard someone behind her call:

"Belena."

She turned around.

Her fine eyes, with their firmly etched contours, opened wide with amazement. She was about to cry out when she felt as if a wound had burst open between her breasts, and a burning, sticky liquid was running down her skin under her dress. A sudden drowsiness came over her. She tried to move her head, wave an arm, rid herself of that absurd sleep that was weighting her down, but was unable to, and fell heavily amidst the joyful flickering of the candles.

Miss Leonides then straightened up. A drop of sweat was

running down her cheek, which she wiped away mechanically with her hand which was trembling convulsively, looked at Cecilia for one last time, smiled at her, and went out.

In Guirlanda Santos' bedroom she laid the stiletto on the book shelf, took off the blood-stained clothes, put on her black dress, her black coat, the liturgical black turban, slipped the handbag which looked like a huge rotten fig under her arm, went down to the first floor, and without turning off any light, without closing any door, went out in the street and walked away.

A group of masked revelers greeted her with the dry lugubrious laughter of their ratchets.

Translated from the Spanish by Harriet de Onís

Bridging
Max Apple

Max Apple
(USA, b. 1941)

"If Sholem Aleichem lived among us today," E. L. Doctorow wrote, "he would root for the Detroit Tigers and be a member of the Chuck E. Cheese fan club, and he'd write his stories under the name Max Apple." It isn't fair to give a writer the name of another, more illustrious, colleague, but it is true that, separated by almost a century, in another tongue and another country, Aleichem and Max Apple share a sense of joy in the little ceremonies of everyday life, in the absurd and moving rituals of a community. In "Bridging," the joy comes from crossing over ritualized roles: the daughter becomes the father, the father becomes the daughter.

Apple has written two volumes of short stories—*The Oranging of America* and *Free Agents*—one novel, *Zip*, and a one-act play, *Trotsky's Bar Mitzvah*. He also compiled and introduced an anthology of American Southwest fiction, in which he justifies "regionalism," the writing from one particular territory in its endemic voice. If we replace "Southwest" for "Max Apple's country," the final lines of that introduction illuminate and enlarge Apple's own story about the "bridging" of so-called social boundaries: "There are no boundaries to regionalism; when you see the Southwest you are seeing everything. The local language and customs, the small matters that separate us, these things, properly noticed, become the bond that unites us."

Bridging

At the Astrodome, Nolan Ryan is shaving the corners. He's going through the Giants in order. The radio announcer is not even mentioning that by the sixth the Giants haven't had a hit. The K's mount on the scoreboard. Tonight Nolan passes the Big Train and is now the all-time strikeout king. He's almost as old as I am and he still throws nothing but smoke. His fastball is an aspirin; batters tear their tendons lunging for his curve. Jessica and I have season tickets, but tonight she's home listening and I'm in the basement of St Anne's Church watching Kay Randall's fingertips. Kay is holding her hands out from her chest, her fingertips on each other. Her fingers move a little as she talks and I can hear her nails click when they meet. That's how close I'm sitting.

Kay is talking about "bridging"; that's what her arched fingers represent.

"Bridging," she says, "is the way Brownies become Girl Scouts. It's a slow steady process. It's not easy, but we allow a whole year for bridging."

Eleven girls in brown shirts with red bandannas at their neck are imitating Kay as she talks. They hold their stumpy chewed fingertips out and bridge them. So do I.

I brought the paste tonight and the stick-on gold stars

and the thread for sewing buttonholes.

"I feel a little awkward," Kay Randall said on the phone, "asking a man to do these errands . . . but that's my problem, not yours. Just bring the supplies and try to be at the church meeting room a few minutes before seven."

I arrive a half hour early.

"You're off your rocker," Jessica says. She begs me to drop her at the Astrodome on my way to the Girl Scout meeting. "After the game, I'll meet you at the main souvenir stand on the first level. They stay open an hour after the game. I'll be all right. There are cops and ushers every five yards."

She can't believe that I am missing this game to perform my functions as an assistant Girl Scout leader. Our Girl Scout battle has been going on for two months.

"Girl Scouts is stupid," Jessica says. "Who wants to sell cookies and sew buttons and walk around wearing stupid old badges?"

When she agreed to go to the first meeting, I was so happy I volunteered to become an assistant leader. After the meeting, Jessica went directly to the car the way she does after school, after a birthday party, after a ball game, after anything. A straight line to the car. No jabbering with girlfriends, no smiles, no dallying, just right to the car. She slides into the back seat, belts in, and braces herself for destruction. It has already happened once.

I swoop past five thousand years of stereotypes and accept my assistant leader's packet and credentials.

"I'm sure there have been other men in the movement," Kay says, "we just haven't had any in our district. It will be good for the girls."

Not for my Jessica. She won't bridge, she won't budge.

"I know why you're doing this," she says. "You think that because I don't have a mother, Kay Randall and Girl Scouts will help me. That's crazy. And I know that Sharon is supposed to be like a mother too. Why don't you just leave me alone."

Sharon is Jessica's therapist. Jessica sees her twice a week.

Sharon and I have a meeting once a month.

"We have a lot of shy girls," Kay Randall tells me. "Scouting brings them out. Believe me, it's hard to stay shy when you're nine years old and you're sharing a tent with six other girls. You have to count on each other, you have to communicate."

I imagine Jessica zipping up her sleeping bag, mumbling good night to anyone who first says it to her, then closing her eyes and hating me for sending her out among the happy.

"She likes all sports, especially baseball," I tell my leader.

"There's room for baseball in scouting," Kay says. "Once a year the whole district goes to a game. They mention us on the big scoreboard."

"Jessica and I go to all the home games. We're real fans."

Kay smiles.

"That's why I want her in Girl Scouts. You know, I want her to go to things with her girlfriends instead of always hanging around with me at ball games."

"I understand," Kay says. "It's part of bridging."

With Sharon the term is "separation anxiety." That's the fastball, "bridging" is the curve. Amid all their magic words I feel as if Jessica and I are standing at home plate blindfolded.

While I await Kay and the members of Troop III, District 6, I eye St Anne in her grotto and St Gregory and St Thomas. Their hands are folded as if they started out bridging, ended up praying.

In October the principal sent Jessica home from school because Mrs Simmons caught her in spelling class listening to the World Series through an earphone.

"It's against the school policy," Mrs Simmons said. "Jessica understands school policy. We confiscate radios and send the child home."

"I'm glad," Jessica said. "It was a cheap-o radio. Now I can watch the TV with you."

They sent her home in the middle of the sixth game. I let her stay home for the seventh too.

The Brewers are her favorite American League team. She likes Rollie Fingers, and especially Robin Yount.

"Does Yount go in the hole better than Harvey Kuenn used to?"

"You bet," I tell her. "Kuenn was never a great fielder but he could hit three hundred with his eyes closed."

Kuenn is the Brewers' manager. He has an artificial leg and can barely make it up the dugout steps, but when I was Jessica's age and the Tigers were my team, Kuenn used to stand at the plate, tap the corners with his bat, spit some tobacco juice, and knock liners up the alley.

She took the Brewers' loss hard.

"If Fingers wasn't hurt they would have squashed the Cards, wouldn't they?"

I agreed.

"But I'm glad for Andujar."

We had Andujar's autograph. Once we met him at a McDonald's. He was a relief pitcher then, an erratic right-hander. In St Louis he improved. I was happy to get his name on a napkin. Jessica shook his hand.

One night after I read her a story, she said, "Daddy, if we were rich could we go to the away games too? I mean, if you didn't have to be at work every day."

"Probably we could," I said, "but wouldn't it get boring? We'd have to stay at hotels and eat in restaurants. Even the players get sick of it."

"Are you kidding?" she said. "I'd never get sick of it."

"Jessica has fantasies of being with you forever, following baseball or whatever," Sharon says. "All she's trying to do is please you. Since she lost her mother she feels that you and she are alone in the world. She doesn't want to let anyone or anything else into that unit, the two of you. She's afraid of any more losses. And, of course, her greatest worry is about losing you."

"You know," I tell Sharon, "that's pretty much how I feel too."

"Of course it is," she says. "I'm glad to hear you say it."

Sharon is glad to hear me say almost anything. When I

complain that her $100-a-week fee would buy a lot of peanut butter sandwiches, she says she is "glad to hear me expressing my anger."

"Sharon's not fooling me," Jessica says. "I know that she thinks drawing those pictures is supposed to make me feel better or something. You're just wasting your money. There's nothing wrong with me."

"It's a long, difficult, expensive process," Sharon says. "You and Jessica have lost a lot. Jessica is going to have to learn to trust the world again. It would help if you could do it too."

So I decide to trust Girl Scouts. First Girl Scouts, then the world. I make my stand at the meeting of Kay Randall's fingertips. While Nolan Ryan breaks Walter Johnson's strikeout record and pitches a two-hit shutout, I pass out paste and thread to nine-year-olds who are sticking and sewing their lives together in ways Jessica and I can't.

II

Scouting is not altogether new to me. I was a Cub Scout. I owned a blue beanie and I remember very well my den mother, Mrs Clark. A den mother made perfect sense to me then and still does. Maybe that's why I don't feel uncomfortable being a Girl Scout assistant leader.

We had no den father. Mr Clark was only a photograph on the living room wall, the tiny living room where we held our monthly meetings. Mr Clark was killed in the Korean War. His son John was in the troop. John was stocky but Mrs Clark was huge. She couldn't sit on a regular chair, only on a couch or a stool without sides. She was the cashier in the convenience store beneath their apartment. The story we heard was that Walt, the old man who owned the store, felt sorry for her and gave her the job. He was her landlord too. She sat on a swivel stool and rang up the purchases.

We met at the store and watched while she locked the door; then we followed her up the steep staircase to her three-room apartment. She carried two wet glass bottles of milk. Her body took up the entire width of the staircase. She passed the banisters the way semi trucks pass each other on a narrow highway.

We were ten years old, a time when everything is funny, especially fat people. But I don't remember anyone ever laughing about Mrs. Clark. She had great dignity and character. So did John. I didn't know what to call it then, but I knew John was someone you could always trust.

She passed out milk and cookies, then John collected the cups and washed them. They didn't even have a television set. The only decoration in the room that barely held all of us was Mr Clark's picture on the wall. We saw him in his uniform and we knew he died in Korea defending his country. We were little boys in blue beanies drinking milk in the apartment of a hero. Through that aura I came to scouting. I wanted Kay Randall to have all of Mrs Clark's dignity.

When she took a deep breath and then bridged, Kay Randall had noticeable armpits. Her wide shoulders slithered into a tiny rib cage. Her armpits were like bridges. She said "bridging" like a mantra, holding her hands before her for about thirty seconds at the start of each meeting.

"A promise is a promise," I told Jessica. "I signed up to be a leader, and I'm going to do it with you or without you."

"But you didn't even ask me if I liked it. You just signed up without talking it over."

"That's true; that's why I'm not going to force you to go along. It was my choice."

"What can you like about it? I hate Melissa Randall. She always has a cold."

"Her mother is a good leader."

"How do you know?"

"She's my boss. I've got to like her, don't I?" I hugged Jessica. "C'mon, honey, give it a chance. What do you have to lose?"

"If you make me go I'll do it, but if I have a choice I won't."

Every other Tuesday, Karen, the fifteen-year-old Greek

girl who lives on the corner, babysits Jessica while I go to the Scout meetings. We talk about field trips and how to earn merit badges. The girls giggle when Kay pins a promptness badge on me, my first.

Jessica thinks it's hilarious. She tells me to wear it to work.

Sometimes when I watch Jessica brush her hair and tie her ponytail and make up her lunch kit I start to think that maybe I should just relax and stop the therapy and the scouting and all my not-so-subtle attempts to get her to invite friends over. I start to think that, in spite of everything, she's a good student and she's got a sense of humor. She's barely nine years old. She'll grow up like everyone else does. John Clark did it without a father; she'll do it without a mother. I start to wonder if Jessica seems to the girls in her class the way John Clark seemed to me: dignified, serious, almost an adult even while we were playing. I admired him. Maybe the girls in her class admire her. But John had that hero on the wall, his father in a uniform, dead for reasons John and all the rest of us understood.

My Jessica had to explain a neurologic disease she couldn't even pronounce. "I hate it when people ask me about Mom," she says. "I just tell them she fell off the Empire State Building."

III

Before our first field trip I go to Kay's house for a planning session. We're going to collect wildflowers in East Texas. It's a one-day trip. I arranged to rent the school bus.

I told Jessica that she could go on the trip even though she wasn't a troop member, but she refused.

We sit on colonial furniture in Kay's den. She brings in coffee and we go over the supply list. Another troop is joining ours so there will be twenty-two girls, three women, and me, a busload among the bluebonnets.

"We have to be sure the girls understand that the

bluebonnets they pick are on private land and that we have permission to pick them. Otherwise they might pick them along the roadside, which is against the law."

I imagine all twenty-two of them behind bars for picking bluebonnets and Jessica laughing while I scramble for bail money.

I keep noticing Kay's hands. I notice them as she pours coffee, as she checks off the items on the list, as she gestures. I keep expecting her to bridge. She has large, solid, confident hands. When she finishes bridging I sometimes feel like clapping the way people do after the national anthem.

"I admire you," she tells me. "I admire you for going ahead with Scouts even though your daughter rejects it. She'll get a lot out of it indirectly from you."

Kay Randall is thirty-three, divorced, and has a Bluebird too. Her older daughter is one of the stubby-fingered girls, Melissa. Jessica is right; Melissa always has a cold.

Kay teaches fifth grade and has been divorced for three years. I am the first assistant she's ever had.

"My husband, Bill, never helped with Scouts," Kay says. "He was pretty much turned off to everything except his business and drinking. When we separated I can't honestly say I missed him; he'd never been there. I don't think the girls miss him either. He only sees them about once a month. He has girlfriends, and his business is doing very well. I guess he has what he wants."

"And you?"

She uses one of those wonderful hands to move the hair away from her eyes, a gesture that makes her seem very young.

"I guess I do too. I've got the girls, and my job. I'm lonesome, though. It's not exactly what I wanted."

We both think about what might have been as we sit beside her glass coffeepot with our lists of sachet supplies. If she was Barbra Streisand and I Robert Redford and the music started playing in the background to give us a clue and there was a long close-up of our lips, we might just fade into middle age together. But Melissa called for Mom because her mosquito bite was bleeding where she scratched it. And I had an angry daughter waiting for me. And all Kay and I had in common was Girl Scouts. We were both smart enough to know it. When Kay looked at me before going to put alcohol on the mosquito bite, our mutual sadness dripped from us like the last drops of coffee through the grinds.

"You really missed something tonight," Jessica tells me. "The Astros did a double steal. I've never seen one before. In the fourth they sent Thon and Moreno together, and Moreno stole home."

She knows batting averages and won-lost percentages too, just like the older boys, only they go out to play. Jessica stays in and waits for me.

During the field trip, while the girls pick flowers to dry and then manufacture into sachets, I think about Jessica at home, probably beside the radio. Juana, our once-a-week cleaning lady, agreed to work on Saturday so she could stay with Jessica while I took the all-day field trip.

It was no small event. In the eight months since Vicki died I had not gone away for an entire day.

I made waffles in the waffle iron for her before I left, but she hardly ate.

"If you want anything, just ask Juana."

"Juana doesn't speak English."

"She understands, that's enough."

"Maybe for you it's enough."

"Honey, I told you, you can come; there's plenty of room on the bus. It's not too late for you to change your mind."

"It's not too late for you either. There's going to be plenty of other leaders there. You don't have to go. You're just doing this to be mean to me."

I'm ready for this. I spent an hour with Sharon steeling myself. "Before she can leave you," Sharon said, "you'll have to show her that you can leave. Nothing's going to happen to her. And don't let her be sick that day either."

Jessica is too smart to pull the "I don't feel good" routine. Instead she becomes more silent, more unhappy looking than usual. She stays in her pajamas while I wash the dishes and get ready to leave.

I didn't notice the sadness as it was coming upon Jessica. It must have happened gradually in the years of Vicki's decline, the years in which I paid so little attention to my daughter. There were times when Jessica seemed to re-cognize the truth more than I did.

As my Scouts picked their wildflowers, I remembered the last outing I had planned for us. It was going to be a Fourth of July picnic with some friends in Austin. I stopped at the bank and got $200 in cash for the long weekend. But when I came home Vicki was too sick to move and the air conditioner had broken. I called our friends to cancel the picnic; then I took Jessica to the mall with me to buy a fan. I bought the biggest one they had, a 58-inch oscillating model that sounded like a hurricane. It could cool 10,000 square feet, but it wasn't enough.

Vicki was home sitting blankly in front of the TV set. The fan could move eight tons of air an hour, but I wanted it to save my wife. I wanted a fan that would blow the whole earth out of its orbit.

I had $50 left. I gave it to Jessica and told her to buy anything she wanted.

"Whenever you're sad, Daddy, you want to buy me things." She put the money back in my pocket. "It won't help." She was seven years old, holding my hand tightly in the appliance department at J. C. Penney's.

I watched Melissa sniffle even more among the wild-flowers, and I pointed out the names of various flowers to Carol and JoAnne and Sue and Linda and Rebecca, who were by now used to me and treated me pretty much as they treated Kay. I noticed that the Girl Scout flower book had very accurate photographs that made it easy to identify the bluebonnets and buttercups and poppies. There were also several varieties of wild grasses.

We were only 70 miles from home on some land a wealthy rancher long ago donated to the Girl Scouts. The girls bending among the flowers seemed to have been quickly transformed by the colorful meadow. The gigglers and monotonous singers on the bus were now, like the bees, sucking strength from the beauty around them. Kay was in the midst of them and so, I realized, was I, not watching and keeping score and admiring from the distance but a participant, a player.

JoAnne and Carol sneaked up from behind me and dropped some dandelions down my back. I chased them; then I helped the other leaders pour the Kool-Aid and distribute the Baggies and the name tags for each girl's flowers.

My daughter is home listening to a ball game, I thought, and I'm out here having fun with nine-year-olds. It's upside down.

When I came home with dandelion fragments still on my back, Juana had cleaned the house and I could smell the taco sauce in the kitchen. Jessica was in her room. I suspected that she had spent the day listless and tearful, although I had asked her to invite a friend over.

"I had a lot of fun, honey, but I missed you."

She hugged me and cried against my shoulder. I felt like holding her the way I used to when she was an infant, the way I rocked her to sleep. But she was a big girl now and needed not sleep but wakefulness.

"I heard on the news that the Rockets signed Ralph Sampson," she sobbed, "and you hardly ever take me to any pro basketball games."

"But if they have a new center things will be different. With Sampson we'll be contenders. Sure I'll take you."

"Promise?"

"Promise." I promise to take you everywhere, my lovely child, and then to leave you. I'm learning to be a leader.

The Dreaming Child
Isak Dinesen

Isak Dinesen
(Denmark, 1885-1962)

The child who wittingly (or unwittingly) dishonours his parents, and then must expiate this sin through sacrifice and suffering, has long haunted our imagination. Flaubert retold this story in "The Legend of St Julian the Hospitable," and Oscar Wilde in "The Star Child." In literature, expiation is an excuse for adventures: to achieve it, the child must complete a number of near-impossible tasks that will cleanse him of fault, and in doing so weave his own story. The Gothic sensibility which brought glamour to ruins and dead trees in the late eighteenth century took great delight in the purgatory of the innocent at fault. Like Frankenstein's monster, these children had disobeyed their creators and had to be punished. Baroness Karen Blixen-Finecke, who under the pen-name Isak Dinesen reinvented Gothic fiction, gave her "Dreaming Child" a different, more generous destiny. He is not punished, like Flaubert's hero; he is purged by experience.

Isak Dinesen was born in Rungsted, Denmark; after marrying her cousin she moved to Kenya, where they managed a coffee plantation. Their life is chronicled in her memoir *Out of Africa* (1937), but the book that made her famous was a collection of short stories written in English, *Seven Gothic Tales* (1934), from which "The Dreaming Child" is taken. A few of these gothic tales were written in Africa. In an interview shortly before her death, she told how she would speak to the Wakamba tribe in rhyme (a device they had never discovered) and try her stories on them. "Afterwards they'd say, 'Please, Memsahib, talk like rain,' so then I knew they had liked it, for rain was very precious to us there."

The Dreaming Child

In the first half of the last century there lived in Sealand, in Denmark, a family of cottagers and fishermen, who were called Plejelt after their native place, and who did not seem able to do well for themselves in any way. Once they had owned a little land here and there, and fishing-boats, but what they had possessed they had lost, and within their new enterprises they failed. They just managed to keep out of the jails of Denmark, but they gave themselves up freely to all such sins and weaknesses—vagabondage, drink, gambling, illegitimate children and suicide—as human beings can indulge in without breaking the law. The old judge of the district said of them: "These Plejelts are not bad people; I have got many worse than they. They are pretty, healthy, likable, even talented in their way. Only they just have not got the knack of living. And if they do not promptly pull themselves together I cannot tell what may become of them, except that the rats will eat them."

Now it was a queer thing that—just as if the Plejelts had been overhearing this said prophecy and had been soundly frightened by it—in the following years they actually seemed to pull themselves together. One of them married into a respectable peasant family, another had a stroke of luck in the herring-fishery, another was converted by the

new parson of the parish, and obtained the office of bell-
ringer. Only one child of the clan, a girl, did not escape its
fate, but on the contrary appeared to collect upon her young
head the entire burden of guilt and misfortune of her tribe.
In the course of her short, tragic life she was washed from
the country into the town of Copenhagen, and here, before
she was twenty, she died in dire misery, leaving a small son
behind her. The father of the child, who is otherwise
unknown to this tale, had given her a hundred rixdollars.
These, together with the child, the dying mother handed
over to an old washerwoman, blind in one eye, and named
Madame Mahler, in whose house she had lodged. She
begged Madame Mahler to provide for her baby as long as
the money lasted, in the true spirit of the Plejelts, con-
tenting herself with a brief respite.

At the sight of the money Madame Mahler got a rose in
each cheek; she had never till now set eyes on a hundred
rixdollars, all in a pile. As she looked at the child she sighed
deeply; then she took the task upon her shoulders, with
what other burdens life had already placed there.

The little boy, whose name was Jens, in this way first
became conscious of the world, and of life, within the slums
of old Copenhagen in a dark backyard like a well, a
labyrinth of filth, decay and foul smell. Slowly he also
became conscious of himself, and of something exceptional
in his worldly position. There were other children in the
backyard, a big crowd of them; they were pale and dirty as
himself. But they all seemed to belong to somebody; they
had a father and a mother; there was, for each of them, a
group of other ragged and squalling children whom they
called brothers and sisters, and who sided with them in the
brawls of the yard; they obviously made part of a unity. He
began to meditate upon the world's particular attitude to
himself, and upon the reason for it. Something within it
responded to an apprehension within his own heart: that he
did not really belong here, but somewhere else. At night he
had chaotic, many-coloured dreams; in the day-time his
thoughts still lingered in them; sometimes they made him

laugh, all to himself, like the tinkling of a little bell, so that Madame Mahler, shaking her own head, held him to be a bit weak in his.

A visitor came to Madame Mahler's house, a friend of her youth, an old wry seamstress with a flat, brown face and a black wig. They called her Mamzell Ane. She had in her young days sewn in many great houses. She wore a red bow at the throat, and had many coquettish, maidenly little ways and postures. But within her sunken bosom she had also a greatness of soul, which enabled her to scorn her present misery in the memory of that splendour which in the past her eyes had beheld. Madame Mahler was a woman of small imagination; she did but reluctantly lend an ear to her friend's grand, interminable soliloquies. After a while Mamzell Ane turned to little Jens for sympathy. Before the child's grave attentiveness her fancy took speed; she called forth, and declaimed upon, the glory of satin, velvet and brocade, of lofty halls and marble staircases. The lady of the house was adorned for a ball by the light of multitudinous candles; her husband came in to fetch her with a star on his breast, while the carriage and pair waited in the street. There were big weddings in the cathedral, and funerals as well, with all the ladies swathed in black like magnificent, tragic columns. The children called their parents Papa and Mamma; they had dolls and hobby-horses to play with, talking parrots in gilt cages, and dogs that were taught to walk on their hind legs. Their mother kissed them, gave them bonbons and pretty pet-names. Even in winter the warm rooms behind the silk curtains were filled with the perfumes of flowers named heliotrope and oleander, and the chandeliers that hung from the ceiling were themselves made of glass in the shape of bright flowers and leaves.

The idea of this majestic, radiant world, in the mind of little Jens merged with that of his own inexplicable isolation in life into a great dream, or fantasy. He was so lonely in Madame Mahler's house because one of the houses of Mamzell Ane's tales was his real home. In the long days, when Madame Mahler stood by her washtub, or brought

her washing out into town, he fondled, and played with, the
picture of this house and of the people who lived in it, and
who loved him so dearly. Mamzell Ane, on her side, noted
the effect of her *épopée* on the child, realized that she had at
last found the ideal audience, and was further inspired by
the discovery. The relation between the two developed into
a kind of love-affair; for their happiness, for their very
existence they had become dependent upon each other.

Now Mamzell Ane was a revolutionist, on her own
accord, and out of some primitive, flaming visionary sight
within her proud, virginal heart, for she had all her time
lived amongst submissive and unreflective people. The
meaning and object of existence to her was grandeur, beauty
and elegance. For the life of her she would not see them
disappear from the earth. But she felt it to be a cruel and
scandalous state of things that so many men and women
must live and die without these highest human values—yes,
without the very knowledge of them—that they must be
poor, wry and unelegant. She was every day looking
forward to that day of justice when the tables were to be
turned, and the wronged and oppressed enter into their
heaven of refinement and gracefulness. All the same she
now took pains not to impart into the soul of the child any
of her own bitterness or rebelliousness. For as the intimacy
between them grew, she did in her heart acclaim little Jens
as legitimate heir to all the magnificence for which she had
herself prayed in vain. He was not to fight for it; everything
was his by right, and should come to him on its own.
Possibly the inspired and experienced old maid also noted
that the boy had in him no talent for envy or rancour
whatever. In their long, happy communications, he
accepted Mamzell Ane's world serenely and without
misgiving, in the very manner—except for the fact that he
had not any of it—of the happy children born within it.

There was a short period of his life in which Jens made
the other children of the backyard party to his happiness.
He was, he told them, far from being the half-wit barely
tolerated by old Madame Mahler; he was on the contrary the

favourite of fortune. He had a Papa and Mamma and a fine house of his own, with such and such things in it, a carriage, and horses in the stable. He was spoiled, and would get everything he asked for. It was a curious thing that the children did not laugh at him, nor afterwards pursue him with mockery. They almost appeared to believe him. Only they could not understand or follow his fancies; they took but little interest in them, and after a while they altogether disregarded them. So Jens again gave up sharing the secret of his felicity with the world.

Still some of the questions put to him by the children had set the boy's mind working, so that he asked Mamzell Ane— for the confidence between them by this time was complete—how it had come to pass that he had lost contact with his home and had been taken into Madame Mahler's establishment? Mamzell Ane found it difficult to answer him; she could not explain the fact to herself. It would be, she reflected, part of the confused and corrupt state of the world in general. When she had thought the matter over she solemnly, in the manner of a Sibyl, furnished him with an explanation. It was, she said, by no means unheard of, neither in life nor in books, that a child, particularly a child in the highest and happiest circumstances, and most dearly beloved by his parents, enigmatically vanished and was lost. She stopped short at this, for even to her dauntless and proven soul the theme seemed too tragic to be further dwelt on. Jens accepted the explanation in the spirit in which it was given, and from this moment saw himself as that melancholy, but not uncommon, phenomenon: a vanished and lost child.

But when Jens was six years old Mamzell Ane died, leaving to him her few earthly possessions: a thin-worn silver thimble, a fine pair of scissors and a little black chair with roses painted on it. Jens set a great value to these things, and every day gravely contemplated them. Just then Madame Mahler began to see the end of her hundred rixdollars. She had been piqued by her old friend's absorption in the child, and so decided to get her own back.

From now on she would make the boy useful to her in the business of the laundry. His life therefore was no longer his own, and the thimble, the scissors and the chair stood in Madame Mahler's room, the sole tangible remnants, or proof, of the splendour which he and Mamzell Ane had known and shared.

At the same time as these events took place in Adelgade, there lived in a stately house in Bredgade a young married couple, whose names were Jakob and Emilie Vandamm. The two were cousins, she being the only child of one of the big shipowners of Copenhagen, and he the son of that magnate's sister—so that if it had not been for her sex, the young lady would with time have become head of the firm. The old shipowner, who was a widower, with his widowed sister, occupied the two loftier lower stories of the house. The family held closely together, and the young people had been engaged from childhood.

Jakob was a very big man, with a quick head and an easy temper. He had many friends, but none of them could dispute the fact that he was growing fat at the early age of thirty. Emilie was not a regular beauty, but she had an extremely graceful and elegant figure, and the slimmest waist in Copenhagen; she was supple and soft in her walk and all her movements, with a low voice, and a reserved, gentle manner. As to her moral being she was the true daughter of a long row of competent and honest tradesmen: upright, wise, truthful and a bit of a pharisee. She gave much time to charity work, and therein minutely distinguished between the deserving and the undeserving poor. She entertained largely and prettily, but kept strictly to her own milieu. Her old uncle, who had travelled round the world, and was an admirer of the fair sex, teased her over the Sunday dinner-table. There was, he said, an exquisite piquancy in the contrast between the suppleness of her body and the rigidity of her mind.

There had been a time when, unknown to the world, the two had been in concord. When Emilie was eighteen, and Jakob was away in China on a ship, she fell in love with a young naval officer, whose name was Charlie Dreyer, and who, three years earlier, when he was only twenty-one, had distinguished himself, and been decorated, in the war of 1849. Emilie was not then officially engaged to her cousin. She did not believe, either, that she would exactly break Jakob's heart if she left him and married another man. All the same, she had strange, sudden misgivings; the strength of her own feelings alarmed her. When in solitude she pondered on the matter, she held it beneath her to be so entirely dependent on another human being. But she again forgot her fears when she met Charlie, and she wondered and wondered that life did indeed hold so much sweetness. Her best friend, Charlotte Tutein, as the two girls were undressing after a ball, said to her: "Charlie Dreyer makes love to all the pretty girls of Copenhagen, but he does not intend to marry any of them. I think he is a Don Juan." Emilie smiled into the looking-glass. Her heart melted at the thought that Charlie, misjudged by all the world, was known to her alone for what he was: loyal, constant and true.

Charlie's ship was leaving for the West Indies. On the night before his departure he came out to her father's villa near Copenhagen to say good-bye, and found Emilie alone. The two young people walked in the garden; it was moonlit. Emilie broke off a white rose, moist with dew, and gave it to him. As they were parting on the road just outside the gate, he seized both her hands, drew them to his breast, and in one great flaming whisper begged her, since nobody would see him walk back with her, to let him stay with her that night, until in the morning he must go so far away.

It is probably almost impossible to the children of later generations to understand or realize the horror and abomination which the idea and the very word of seduction would awake in the minds of young girls of that past age. She could not have been more deadly frightened and revolted had she found that he meant to cut her throat.

He must repeat himself before she understood him, and as she did so the ground sank beneath her. She felt as if the

one man amongst all, whom she trusted and loved, was
intending to bring upon her the supreme sin, disaster and
shame, was asking her to betray her mother's memory and
all the maidens in the world. Her own feelings for him
made her an accomplice in the crime, and she realized that
she was lost. Charlie felt her wavering on her feet, and put
his arms around her. In a stifled, agonized cry she tore
herself out of them, fled, and with all her might pushed the
heavy iron gate to; she bolted it on him as if it had been the
cage of an angry lion. On which side of the gate was the
lion? Her strength gave way; she hung on to the bars, while
on the other side the desperate, miserable lover pressed
himself against them, fumbled between them for her hands,
her clothes, and implored her to open. But she recoiled and
flew to the house, to her room, only to find there despair
within her own heart, and a bitter vacuity in all the world
round it.

Six months later Jakob came home from China, and their
engagement was celebrated amongst the rejoicings of the
families. A month after she learned that Charlie had died
from fever at St Thomas. Before she was twenty she was
married and mistress of her own fine house.

Many young girls of Copenhagen married in the same
way—*par dépit*—and then, to save their self-respect, denied
their first love and made the excellency of their husbands
their one point of honour, so that they became incapable of
distinguishing between truth and untruth, lost their moral
weight and flickered in life without any foothold in reality.
Emilie was saved from their fate by the intervention, so to
say, of the old Vandamms, her forefathers, and by the
instinct and principle of sound merchantship which they
had passed on into the blood of their daughter. The staunch
and resolute old traders had not winked when they made
out their balance-sheet; in hard times they had sternly
looked bankruptcy and ruin in the face; they were the loyal,
unswerving servants of facts. So did Emilie now take stock
of her profit and loss. She had loved Charlie; he had been
unworthy of her love; and she was never again to love in

that same way. She had stood upon the brink of an abyss, and but for the grace of God she was at this moment a fallen woman, an outcast from her father's house. The husband she had married was kind-hearted, and a good man of business; he was also fat, childish, unlike her. She had got, out of life, a house to her taste and a secure harmonious position in her own family and in the world of Copenhagen; for these she was grateful, and for them she would take no risk. She did at this moment of her life with all the strength of her young soul embrace a creed of fanatical truthfulness and solidity. The ancient Vandamms might have applauded her, or they might have thought her code excessive; they had taken a risk themselves, when it was needed, and they were aware that in trade it is a dangerous thing to shy danger.

Jakob, on his side, was in love with his wife, and prized her beyond rubies. To him, as to the other young men out of the strictly moral Copenhagen bourgeoisie, his first experience of love had been extremely gross. He had preserved the freshness of his heart, and his claim to neatness and orderliness in life by holding on to an ideal of purer womanhood, in the first place represented by the young cousin whom he was to marry, the innocent fair-haired girl of his own mother's blood, and brought up as she had been. He carried her image with him to Hamburg and Amsterdam, and that trait in him which his wife called childishness made him deck it out like a doll or an icon; out in China it became highly ethereal and romantic, and he used to repeat to himself little sayings of hers, to recall her low, soft voice. Now he was happy to be back in Denmark, married and in his own home, and to find his young wife as perfect as his portrait of her. At times he felt a vague longing for a bit of weakness within her, or for an occasional appeal to his own strength, which, as things were, only made him out a clumsy figure beside her delicate form. He gave her all that she wanted, and out of his pride in her superiority left to her all decisions on their house and on their daily and social life. Only within their charity work it happened that the husband and wife did not see eye to eye, and that Emilie would give him a little lecture on his credulity. "What an absurd person you are, Jakob," she said. "You will believe everything that these people tell you—not because you cannot help it, but because you do really wish to believe them." "Do you not wish to believe them?" he asked her. "I cannot see," she replied, "how one can well wish to believe or not to believe. I wish to find out the truth. Once a thing is not true," she added, "it matters little to me whatever else it may be."

A short time after his wedding Jakob one day had a letter from a rejected supplicant, a former maid in his father-in-law's house, who informed him that while he was away in China his wife had a liaison with Charlie Dreyer. He knew it to be a lie, tore up the letter, and did not give it another thought.

They had no children. This to Emilie was a grave affliction; she felt that she was lacking in her duties. When they had been married for five years Jakob, vexed by his mother's constant concern, and with the future of the firm on his mind, suggested to his wife that they should adopt a child, to carry forward the house. Emilie at once, and with much energy and indignation, repudiated the idea; it had to her all the appearance of a comedy, and she would not see her father's firm encumbered with a sham heir. Jakob held forth to her upon the Antonines with but little effect.

But when six months later he again took up the subject, to her own surprise she found that it was no longer repellent. Unknowingly she must have given it a place in her thought, and let it take root there, for by now it seemed familiar to her. She listened to her husband, looked at him, and felt kindly towards him. "If this is what he has been longing for," she thought, "I must not oppose it." But in her own heart she knew clearly and coldly, and with awe of her own coldness the true reason for her indulgence: the deep apprehension, that when a child had been adopted there would be no more obligation to her of producing an heir to the firm, a grandson to their father, a child to her husband.

It was indeed their little divergences in regard to the deserving or undeserving poor which brought upon the young couple of Bredgade the events recounted in this tale. In summer-time they lived in Emilie's father's villa on the Strandvej, and Jakob would drive in to town, and out, in a small gig. One day he decided to profit by his wife's absence to visit an unquestionably unworthy mendicant, an old sea-captain from one of his ships. He took his way through the ancient town, where it was difficult to drive a carriage, and where it was such an exceptional sight that people came up from the cellars to stare at it. In the narrow lane of Adelgade a drunken man waved his arms in front of the horse; it shied, and knocked down a small boy with a heavy wheelbarrow piled high with washing. The wheelbarrow and the washing ended sadly in the gutter. A crowd immediately collected round the spot, but expressed neither indignation nor sympathy. Jakob made his groom lift the little boy onto the seat. The child was smeared with blood and dirt, but he was not badly hurt, nor in the least scared. He seemed to take this accident as an adventure in general, or as if it had happened to somebody else. "Why did you not get out of my way, you little idiot?" Jakob asked him. "I wanted to look at the horse," said the child, and added: "Now, I can see it well from here."

Jakob got the boy's whereabouts from an onlooker, paid him to take the wheelbarrow back, and himself drove the child home. The sordidness of Madame Mahler's house, and her own, one-eyed, blunt unfeelingness impressed him unpleasantly; still he had before now been inside the houses of the poor. But he was, here, struck by a strange incongruity between the backyard and the child who lived in it. It was as if, unknowingly, Madame Mahler was housing, and knocking about, a small, gentle, wild animal, or a sprite. On his way to the villa he reflected that the child had reminded him of his wife; he had a reserved, as it were selfless, way with him, behind which one guessed great, integrate strength and endurance.

He did not speak of the incident that evening, but he went back to Madame Mahler's house to inquire about the boy, and, after a while, he recounted the adventure to his wife and, somewhat shyly and half in jest, proposed to her that they should take the pretty, forlorn child as their own.

Half in jest she entered on his idea. It would be better, she thought, than taking on a child whose parents she knew. After this day she herself at times dwelt upon the matter when she could find nothing else to talk to him about. They consulted the family lawyer, and sent their old doctor to look the child over. Jakob was surprised and grateful at his wife's compliance with his wish. She listened with gentle interest when he developed his plans, and would even sometimes vent her own ideas on education.

Lately Jakob had found his domestic atmosphere almost too perfect, and had had an adventure in town. Now he tired of it and finished it. He bought Emilie presents, and left her to make her own conditions as to the adoption of the child. He might, she said, bring the boy to the house on the first of October, when they had moved into town from the country, but she herself would reserve her final decision in the matter until April, when he should have been with them for six months. If by then she did not find the child fit for their plan she would hand him over to some honest, kindly family in the employ of the firm. Till April they themselves would likewise be only Uncle and Aunt Vandamm to the boy.

They did not talk to their family of the project, and this circumstance accentuated the new feeling of comradeship between them. How very different, Emilie said to herself, would the case have proved had she been expecting a child in the orthodox way of women. There was indeed something neat and proper about settling the affairs of nature according to your own mind. "And," she whispered in her mind, as her glance ran down her looking-glass, "in keeping your figure."

As to Madame Mahler, when time came to approach her, the matter was easily arranged. She had it not in her to oppose the wishes of her social superiors; she was also, vaguely, rating her own future connection with a house that must surely turn out an abundance of washing. Only the readiness with which Jakob refunded her her past outlays on the child left in her heart a lifelong regret that she had not asked for more.

At the last moment Emilie made a further stipulation. She would go alone to fetch the child. It was important that the relationship between the boy and herself should be properly established from the beginning, and she did not trust to Jakob's sense of propriety on this occasion. In this way it came about that, when all was ready for the child's reception in the house of Bredgade, Emilie drove by herself to Adelgade to take possession of him, easy in her conscience towards the firm and her husband, but, beforehand, a little tired of the whole affair.

In the street by Madame Mahler's house a number of unkempt children were obviously waiting for the arrival of the carriage. They stared at her, but turned off their eyes, when she looked at them. Her heart sank as she lifted her ample silk skirt and passed through their crowd and across the backyard. Would her boy have the same look? Like Jakob, she had many times before visited the houses of the poor. It was a sad sight, but it could not be otherwise. "The poor you have with you always." But today, since a child from this place was to enter her own house, for the first time she felt personally related to the need and misery of the world. She was seized with a new deep disgust and horror, and at the next moment with a new, deeper pity. In these two minds she entered Madame Mahler's room.

Madame Mahler had washed little Jens and watercombed his hair. She had also, a couple of days before, hurriedly enlightened him as to the situation and his own promotion in life. But being an unimaginative woman and moreover of the opinion that the child was but half-witted, she had not taken much trouble about it. The child had received the information in silence; he only asked her how his father and mother had found him. "Oh, by the smell," said Madame Mahler.

Jens had communicated the news to the other children
of the house. His Papa and Mamma, he told them, were
coming on the morrow, in great state, to fetch him home.
It gave him matter for reflection that the event should
raise a great stir in that same world of the backyard that
had received his visions of it with indifference. To him
the two were the same thing.

He had got up on Mamzell Ane's small chair to look out
of the window and witness the arrival of his mother. He was
still standing on it when Emilie came in, and Madame
Mahler in vain made a gesture to chase him down. The first
thing that Emilie noticed about the child was that he did
not turn his gaze from hers, but looked her straight in the
eyes. At the sight of her a great, ecstatic light passed over his
face. For a moment the two looked at each other.

The child seemed to wait for her to address him, but as she
stood silent, irresolute, he spoke. "Mamma," he said, "I am
glad that you have found me. I have waited for you so long,
so long."

Emilie gave Madame Mahler a glance. Had this scene
been staged to move her heart? But the flat lack of
understanding in the old woman's face excluded the
possibility, and she again turned to the child.

Madame Mahler was a big, broad woman. Emilie herself,
in a crinoline and a sweeping mantilla, took up a good deal
of room. The child was much the smallest figure in the
room, yet at this moment he dominated it, as if he had taken
command of it. He stood up straight, with that same
radiance in his countenance. "Now I am coming home
again, with you," he said.

Emilie vaguely and amazedly realized that to the child the
importance of the moment did not lie with his own good
luck, but with that tremendous happiness and fulfillment
which he was bestowing on her. A strange idea, that she
could not have explained to herself, at that, ran through her
mind. She thought: "This child is as lonely in life as I."
Gravely she moved nearer to him and said a few kind words.
The little boy put out his hand and gently touched the long

silky ringlets that fell forward over her neck. "I knew you at once," he said proudly. "You are my Mamma, who spoils me. I would know you amongst all the ladies, by your long pretty hair." He ran his fingers softly down her shoulder and arm, and fumbled over her gloved hand. "You have got three rings on today," he said. "Yes," said Emilie in her low voice. A short, triumphant smile broke upon his face. "And now you kiss me, Mamma," he said, and grew very pale. Emilie did not know that his excitement rose from the fact that he had never been kissed. Obediently, surprised at herself, she bent down and kissed him.

Jens' farewell to Madame Mahler at first was somewhat ceremonious in two people who had known each other for a long time. For she already saw him as a new person, the rich man's child, and took his hand tardily, her face stiff. But Emilie bade the boy, before he went away, to thank Madame Mahler because she had looked after him till now, and he did so with much freedom and grace. At that the old woman's tanned and furrowed cheeks once more blushed deeply, like a young girl's, as by the sight of the money at their first meeting. She had so rarely been thanked in her life. In the street he stood still. "Look at my big, fat horses!" he cried. Emilie sat in the carriage, bewildered. What was she bringing home with her from Madame Mahler's house?

In her own house, as she took the child up the stairs and from one room into another, her bewilderment grew. Rarely had she felt so uncertain of herself. It was, everywhere, in the child, the same rapture of recognition. At times he would also mention and look for things which she faintly remembered from her own childhood, or other things of which she had never heard. Her small pug, that she had brought with her from her old home, yapped at the boy. She lifted it up, afraid that it would bite him. "No, Mamma," he cried, "she will not bite me, she knows me well." A few hours ago—yes, she thought, up to the moment when in Madame Mahler's room she had kissed the child— she would have scolded him: "Fie, you are telling a fib." Now she said nothing, and the next moment the child

looked round the room and asked her: "Is the parrot dead?"
"No," she answered, wondering, "she is not dead; she is in
the other room."

She realized that she was afraid both to be alone with the
boy, and to let any third person join them. She sent the
nurse out of the room. By the time Jakob was to arrive at the
house she listened for his steps on the stairs with a kind of
alarm. "Who are you waiting for?" Jens asked her. She was
at a loss as how to designate Jakob to the child. "For my
husband," she replied, embarrassed. Jakob on his entrance
found the mother and the child gazing in the same picture-
book. The little boy stared at him. "So it is you who are my
Papa!" he exclaimed, "I thought so, too, all the time. But I
could not be quite sure of it, could I? It was not by the smell
that you found me, then. I think it was the horse that
remembered me." Jakob looked at his wife; she looked into
the book. He did not expect sense from a child, and was
soon playing with the boy and tumbling him about. In the
midst of a game Jens set his hands against Jakob's chest.
"You have not got your star on," he said. After a moment
Emilie went out of the room. She thought: "I have taken
this upon me to meet my husband's wish, but it seems that I
must bear the burden of it alone."

Jens took possession of the mansion in Bredgade, and
brought it to submission, neither by might nor by power,
but in the quality of that fascinating and irresistible
personage, perhaps the most fascinating and irresistible in
the whole world: the dreamer whose dreams come true. The
old house fell a little in love with him. Such is ever the lot of
dreamers, when dealing with people at all susceptible to the
magic of dreams. The most renowned amongst them,
Rachel's son, as all the world knows, suffered hardships and
was even cast in prison on that account. Except for his size,
Jens had no resemblance to the classic portraits of Cupid;
all the same it was evident that, unknowingly, the shipowner and his wife had taken into them an amorino. He
carried wings into the house, and was in league with the
sweet and merciless powers of nature, and his relation to

each individual member of the household became a kind of aerial love affair. It was upon the strength of this same magnetism that Jakob had picked out the boy as heir to the firm at their first meeting, and that Emilie was afraid to be alone with him. The old magnate and the servants of the house no more escaped their destiny—as was once the case with Potiphar, captain to the guard of Egypt. Before they knew where they were, they had committed all they had into his hands.

One effect of this particular spell was this: that people were made to see themselves with the eyes of the dreamer, and were impelled to live up to an idea, and that for this their higher existence they became dependent upon him. During the time that Jens lived in the house, it was much changed, and dissimilar to the other houses of the town. It became a Mount Olympus, the abode of divinities.

The child took the same lordly, laughing pride in the old shipowner, who ruled the waters of the universe, as in Jakob's staunch, protective kindness and Emilie's silk-clad gracefulness. The old housekeeper, who had often before grumbled at her lot in life, for the while was transformed into an all-powerful, benevolent guardian of human welfare, a Ceres in cap and apron. And for the same length of time the coachman, a monumental figure, elevated sky-high above the crowd, and combining within his own person the vigour of the two bay horses, majestically trotted down Bredgade on eight shod and clattering hoofs. It was only after Jens' bed hour, when, immovable and silent, his cheek buried in the pillow, he was exploring new areas of dreams that the house resumed the aspect of a rational, solid Copenhagen mansion.

Jens was himself ignorant of his power. As his new family did not scold him or find fault with him, it never occurred to him that they were at all looking at him. He gave no preference to any particular member of the household; they were all within his scheme of things and must there fit into their place. The relation of the one to the other was the object of his keen, subtle observation. One

phenomenon in his daily life never ceased to entertain and
please him: that Jakob, so big, broad and fat, should be
attentive and submissive to his slight wife. In the world that
he had known till now bulk was of supreme moment. As
later on Emilie looked back upon this time, it seemed to her
that the child would often provoke an opportunity for this
fact to manifest itself, and would then, so to say, clap his
hands in triumph and delight, as if the happy state of things
had been brought about by his personal skill. But in other
cases his sense of proportion failed him. Emilie in her
boudoir had a glass aquarium with goldfish, in front of
which Jens would pass many hours, as silent as the fish
themselves, and from his comments upon them she gathered
that to him they were huge—a fine catch could one get hold
of them, and even dangerous to the pug, should she happen
to fall into the bowl. He asked Emilie to leave the curtains
by this window undrawn at night, in order that, when
people were asleep, the fish might look at the moon.

 In Jakob's relation to the child there was a moment of
unhappy love, or at least of the irony of fate, and it was not
the first time either that he had gone through this same
melancholy experience. For ever since he himself was a
small boy he had yearned to protect those weaker than he,
and to support and right all frail and delicate beings in his
surroundings. The very qualities of fragility and help-
lessness inspired in him an affection and admiration
which came near to idolatry. But there was in his nature an
inconsistency, such as will often be found in children of old,
wealthy families, who have got all they wanted too easily,
till in the end they cry out for the impossible. He loved
pluck, too; gallantry delighted him wherever he met it, and
for the clinging and despondent type of human beings, and
in particular of women, he felt a slight distaste and
repugnance. He might dream of shielding and guiding his
wife, but at the same time the little cool, forbearing smile
with which she would receive any such attempt on his side
to him was one of the most bewitching traits in her whole
person. In this way he found himself somewhat in the sad

and paradoxical position of the young lover who pas-
sionately adores virginity. Now he learned that it was
equally out of the question to patronize Jens. The child did
not reject or smile at his patronage, as Emilie did; he even
seemed grateful for it, but he accepted it in the part of a
game or a sport. So that, when they were out walking
together, and Jakob, thinking that the child must be tired,
lifted him on to his shoulders, Jens would take it that the
big man wanted to play at being a horse or an elephant just
as much as he himself wanted to play that he was a trooper
or a mahout.

Emilie sadly reflected that she was the only person in the
house who did not love the child. She felt unsafe with him,
even when she was unconditionally accepted as the
beautiful, perfect mother, and as she recalled how, only a
short time ago, she had planned to bring up the boy in her
own spirit, and had written down little memoranda upon
education, she saw herself as a figure of fun. To make up for
her lack of feeling she took Jens with her on her walks and
drives, to the parks and the zoo, brushed his thick hair, and
had him dressed up as neatly as a doll. They were always
together. She was sometimes amused by his strange, graceful, dignified delight in all that she showed him, and at the
next moment, as in Madame Mahler's room, she realized
that however generous she would be to him, he would
always be the giver. Her sisters-in-law, and her young
married friends, fine ladies of Copenhagen with broods of
their own, wondered at her absorption in the foundling—
and then it happened, when they were off their guard, that
they did themselves receive a dainty arrow in their satin
bosoms, and between them began to discuss Emilie's pretty
boy, with a tender raillery as that with which they would
have discussed Cupid. They asked her to bring him to play
with their own children. Emilie declined, and told herself
that she must first be certain about his manners. At the New
Year, she thought, she would give a children's party herself.

Jens had come to the Vandamms in October, when trees
were yellow and red in the parks. Then the tinge of frost in

the air drove people indoors, and they began to think of Christmas. Jens seemed to know everything about the Christmas-tree, the goose with roast apples, and the solemnly joyful church-going on Christmas morning. But it would happen that he mixed up these festivals with others of the season, and described how they were soon all to mask and mum, as children do at Shrovestide. It was as if, from the centre of his happy, playful world, its sundry components showed up less clearly than when seen from afar.

And as the days drew in and the snow fell in the streets of Copenhagen, a change came upon the child. He was not low in spirits, but singularly collected and compact, as if he were shifting the centre of gravitation of his being, and folding his wings. He would stand for long whiles by the window, so sunk in thought that he did not always hear it when they called him, filled with a knowledge which his surroundings could not share.

For within these first months of winter it became evident that he was not at all a person to be permanently set at ease by what the world calls fortune. The essence of his nature was longing. The warm rooms with silk curtains, the sweets, his toys and new clothes, the kindness and concern of his Papa and Mamma were all of the greatest moment because they went to prove the veracity of his visions; they were infinitely valuable as embodiments of his dreams. But within themselves they hardly meant anything to him, and they had no power to hold him. He was neither a worldling nor a struggler. He was a Poet.

Emilie tried to make him tell her what he had in his mind, but got nowhere with him. Then one day he confided in her on his own account.

"Do you know, Mamma," he said, "in my house the stairs were so dark and full of holes that you had to grope your way up it, and the best thing was really to walk on one's hands and knees? There was a window broken by the wind, and below it, on the landing, there lay a drift of snow as high as me." "But that is not your house, Jens," said Emilie.

"This is your house." The child looked round the room. "Yes," he said, "this is my fine house. But I have another house that is quite dark and dirty. You know it, you have been there too. When the washing was hung up, one had to twine in and out across that big loft, else the huge, wet, cold sheets would catch one, just as if they were alive." "You are never going back to that house," said she. The child gave her a great, grave glance, and after a moment said: "No."

But he was going back. She could, by her horror and disgust of the house, keep him from talking of it, as the children there by their indifference had silenced him on his happy home. But when she found him mute and pensive by the window, or at his toys, she knew that his mind had returned to it. And now and again, when they had played together, and their intimacy seemed particularly secure, he opened on the theme. "In the same street as my house," he said, one evening as they were sitting together on the sofa before the fireplace, "there was an old lodging-house, where the people who had plenty of money could sleep in beds, and the others must stand up and sleep, with a rope under their arms. One night it caught fire, and burned all down. Then those who were in bed did hardly get their trousers on, but ho! those who stood up and slept were the lucky boys; they got out quick. There was a man who made a song about it, you know."

There are some young trees which, when they are planted, have thin, twisted roots and will never take hold in the soil. They may shoot out a profusion of leaves and flowers, but they must soon die. Such was the way with Jens. He had sent out his small branches upwards and to the sides, had fared excellently of the chameleon's dish and eaten air, promise-crammed, and the while he had forgotten to put out roots. Now the time came when by law of nature the bright, abundant bloom must needs wither, fade and waste away. It is possible, had his imagination been turned on to fresh pastures, that he might for a while have drawn nourishment through it, and have detained his exit. Once or twice, to amuse him, Jakob had talked to him of China.

The queer outlandish world captivated the mind of the child. He dwelled with the highest excitement on pictures of pig-tailed Chinamen, dragons and fishermen with pelicans, and upon the fantastic names of Hongkong and Yangtze-kiang. But the grown-up people did not realize the significance of his novel imaginative venture, and so, for lack of sustenance, the frail, fresh branch soon dropped.

A short time after the children's party, early in the new year, the child grew pale and hung his head. The old doctor came and gave him medicine to no effect. It was quiet, unbroken decline: the plant was going out.

As Jens was put to bed and was, so to say, legitimately releasing his hold upon the world of actuality, his fancy fetched headway and ran along with him, like the sails of a small boat, from which the ballast is thrown overboard. There were, now, people round him all the time who would listen to what he said, gravely, without interrupting or contradicting him. This happy state of things enraptured him. The dreamer's sick-bed became a throne.

Emilie sat at the bed all the time, distressed by a feeling of impotence which sometimes in the night made her wring her hands. All her life she had endeavoured to separate good from bad, right from wrong, happiness from unhappiness. Here she was, she reflected with dismay, in the hands of a being, much smaller and weaker than herself, to whom these were all one, who welcomed light and darkness, pleasure and pain, in the same spirit of gallant, debonair approval and fellowship. The fact, she told herself, did away with all need of her comfort and consolation here at her child's sick-bed; it often seemed to abolish her very existence.

Now within the brotherhood of poets Jens was a humorist, a comic fabulist. It was, in each individual phenomenon of life, the whimsical, the burlesque moment that attracted and inspired him. To the pale, grave young woman his fancies seemed sacrilegious within a death-room, yet after all it was his own death-room.

"Oh, there were so many rats, Mamma," he said, "so

many rats. They were all over the house. One came to take a bit of lard on the shelf—pat! a rat jumped at one. They ran across my face at night. Put your face close to me, and I will show you how it felt." "There are no rats here, my darling," said Emilie. "No, none," said he. "When I am sick no more I shall go back and fetch you one. The rats like the people better than the people like them. For they think us good, lovely to eat. There was an old comedian, who lived in the garret. He had played comedy when he was young, and had travelled to foreign countries. Now he gave the little girls money to kiss him, but they would not kiss him, because they said that they did not like his nose. It was a curious nose, too—all fallen in. And when they would not he cried and wrung his hands. But he got ill, and died, and nobody knew about it. But when at last they went in, do you know, Mamma—the rats had eaten off his nose!—nothing else, his nose only! But people will not eat rats even when they are very hungry. There was a fat boy in the cellar, who caught rats in many curious ways, and cooked them. But old Madame Mahler said that she despised him for it, and the children called him Rat-Mad."

Then again he would talk of her own house. "My Grandpapa," he said, "has got corns, the worst corns in Copenhagen. When they get very bad he sighs and moans. He says: 'There will be storms in the China Sea. It is a damned business; my ships are going to the bottom.' So, you know, I think that the seamen will be saying: 'There is a storm in this sea; it is a damned business; our ship is going to the bottom.' Now it is time that old Grandpapa, in Bredgade, goes and has his corns cut."

Only within the last days of his life did he speak of Mamzell Ane. She had been, as it were, his Muse, the only person who had knowledge of the one and the other of his worlds. As he recalled her his tone of speech changed; he held forth in a grand, solemn manner, as upon an elemental power, of necessity known to everyone. If Emilie had given his fantasies her attention many things might have been made clear to her. But she said: "No, I do not know her,

Jens." "Oh, Mamma, she knows you well!" He said: "She
sewed your wedding-gown, all of white satin. It was slow
work—so many fittings! And my Papa," the child went on
and laughed, "he came in to you, and do you know what he
said? He said: 'My white rose.' " He suddenly bethought
himself of the scissors which Mamzell Ane had left him, and
wanted them, and this was the only occasion upon which
Emilie ever saw him impatient or fretful.

She left her house for the first time within three weeks,
and went herself to Madame Mahler's house to inquire
about the scissors. On the way the powerful, enigmatical
figure of Mamzell Ane took on to her the aspect of a Parca,
of Atropos herself, scissors in hand, ready to cut off the
thread of life. But Madame Mahler in the meantime had
bartered away the scissors to a tailor of her acquaintance,
and she flatly denied the existence both of them and of
Mamzell Ane.

Upon the last morning of the boy's life Emilie lifted her
small pug, that had been his faithful playmate, onto the
bed. Then the little dark face and the crumpled body seemed
to recall to him the countenance of his friend. "There she
is!" he cried.

Emilie's mother-in-law and the old shipowner himself
had been daily visitors to the sick-room. The whole
Vandamm family stood weeping round the bed when, in
the end, like a small brook which falls into the ocean, Jens
gave himself up to, and was absorbed in, the boundless,
final unity of dream.

He died by the end of March, a few days before the date
that Emilie had fixed to decide on his fitness for admission
into the house of Vandamm. Her father suddenly determined that he must be interred in the family vault—
irregularly, since he was never legally adopted into the
family. So he was laid down behind a heavy wrought-iron
fence, within the finest grave that any Plejelt had ever
obtained.

Within the following days the house in Bredgade, and its
inhabitants with it, shrank and decreased. The people were

a little confused, as after a fall, and seized by a sad sense of diffidence. For the first weeks after Jens' burial life looked to them strangely insipid, a sorry affair, void of purport. The Vandamms were not used to being unhappy, and were not prepared for the sense of loss with which now the death of the child left them. To Jakob it seemed as if he had let down a friend, who had, after all, laughingly trusted to his strength. Now nobody had any use for it, and he saw himself as a freak, the stuffed puppet of a colossus. But with all this, after a while there was also in the survivors, as ever at the passing away of an idealist, a vague feeling of relief.

Emilie alone of the house of Vandamms preserved, as it were, her size, and her sense of proportion. It may even be said that when the house tumbled from its site in the clouds, she upheld and steadied it. She had deemed it affected in her to go into mourning for a child who was not hers, and while she gave up the balls and parties of the Copenhagen season, she went about her domestic tasks quietly as before. Her father and her mother-in-law, sad and at a loss in their daily life, turned to her for balance, and because she was the youngest amongst them, and seemed to them in some ways like the child that was gone, they transferred to her the tenderness and concern which had formerly been the boy's, and of which they now wished that they had given him even more. She was pale from her long watches at the sick-bed; so they consulted between them, and with her husband, on means of cheering and distracting her.

But after some time Jakob was struck with, and scared by, her silence. It seemed at first as if, except for her household orders, she found it unnecessary to speak, and later on as if she had forgotten or lost the faculty of speech. His timid attempts to inspirit her so much appeared to surprise and puzzle her that he lacked the spirit to go on with them.

A couple of months after Jens' death Jakob took his wife for a drive by the road which runs from Copenhagen to Elsinore, along the Sound. It was a lovely, warm and fresh day in May. As they came to Charlottenlund he proposed to her that they should walk through the wood, and send the carriage round to meet them. So they got down by the forest-gate, and for a moment their eyes followed the carriage as it rolled away on the road.

They came into the wood, into a green world. The beech trees had been out for three weeks, the first mysterious translucence of early May was over. But the foliage was still so young that the green of the forest world was the brighter in the shade. Later on, after midsummer, the wood would be almost black in the shade, and brilliantly green in the sun. Now, where the rays of the sun fell through the tree-crowns, the ground was colourless, dim, as if powdered with sun-dust. But where the wood lay in shadow it glowed and luminesced like green glass and jewels. The anemones were faded and gone; the young fine grass was already tall. And within the heart of the forest the woodruff was in bloom; its layer of diminutive, starry, white flowers seemed to float, round the knotty roots of the old grey beeches, like the surface of a milky lake, a foot above the ground. It had rained in the night; upon the narrow road the deep tracks of the wood-cutters' cart were moist. Here and there, by the roadside, a grey, misty globe of a withered dandelion caught the sun; the flower of the field had come on a visit to the wood.

They walked on slowly. As they came a little way into the wood they suddenly heard the cuckoo, quite close. They stood still and listened, then walked on. Emilie let go her husband's arm to pick up from the road the shell of a small, pale-blue, bird's egg, broken in two; she tried to set it together, and kept it on the palm of her hand. Jakob began to talk to her of a journey to Germany that he had planned for them, and of the places that they were to see. She listened docilely, and was silent.

They had come to the end of the wood. From the gate they had a great view over the open landscape. After the green sombreness of the forest the outside world seemed un-believably light, as if bleached by the luminous dimness of midday. But after a while the colours of fields, meadows and dispersed groups of trees defined themselves to the eye, one by one. There was a faint blue in the sky, and faint white cumulus clouds rose along the horizon. The young green rye on the fields was about to ear; where the finger of the breeze touched it it ran in long, gentle billows along the ground. The small thatched peasants' houses lay like lime-white, square isles within the undulating land; round them the lilac-hedges bore up their light foliage and, on the top, clusters of pale flowers. They heard the rolling of a carriage on the road in the distance, and above their heads the incessant singing of innumerable larks.

By the edge of the forest there lay a wind-felled tree. Emilie said: "Let us sit down here a little."

She loosened the ribbons of her bonnet and lay it in her lap. After a minute she said: "There is something I want to tell you," and made a long pause. All through this conversation in the wood she behaved in the same way, with a long silence before each phrase—not exactly as if she were collecting her thoughts, but as if she were finding speech in itself laborious or deficient.

She said: "The boy was my own child." "What are you talking about?" Jakob asked her. "Jens," she said, "he was my child. Do you remember telling me that when you saw him the first time you thought he was like me? He was indeed like me; he was my son." Now Jakob might have been frightened, and have believed her to be out of her mind. But lately things had, to him, come about in unexpected ways; he was prepared for the paradoxical. So he sat quietly on the trunk, and looked down on the young beech-shoots in the ground. "My dear," he said, "my dear, you do not know what you say."

She was silent for a while, as if distressed by his interruption of her course of thought. "It is difficult to other people to understand, I know," she said at last, patiently. "If Jens had been here still, he might perhaps have made you understand, better than I. But try," she went on, "to understand me. I have thought that you ought to know. And if I cannot speak to you I cannot speak to anyone." She said this with a kind of grave concern, as if really threatened by total incapacity of speech. He remembered how, during these last weeks, he had felt her silence heavy on him, and had tried to make her speak of something, of anything. "No, my dear," he said, "you speak, I shall not interrupt you." Gently, as if thankful for his promise, she began:

"He was my child, and Charlie Dreyer's. You have met Charlie once in Papa's house. But it was while you were in China that he became my lover." At these words Jakob remembered the anonymous letter he had once received. As he recalled his own indignant scouting of the slander and the care with which he had kept it from her, it seemed to him a curious thing that after five years he was to have it repeated by her own lips.

"When he asked me," said Emilie, "I stood for a moment in great danger. For I had never talked with a man of this matter. Only with Aunt Malvina and with my old governess. And women, for some reason, I do not know which, will have it that such a demand be a base and selfish thing in a man, and an insult to a woman. Why do you allow us to think that of you? You, who are a man, will know that he asked me out of his love and out of his great heart, from magnanimity. He had more life in him that he himself needed. He meant to give that to me. It was life itself; yes, it was eternity that he offered me. And I, who had been taught so wrong, I might easily have rejected him. Even now, when I think of it, I am afraid, as of death. Still I need not be so, for I know for certain that if I were back at that moment again, I should behave in the same way as I did then. And I was saved from the danger. I did not send him away. I let him walk back with me, through the garden—for we were down by the garden-gate—and stay away with me the night till, in the morning, he was to go so far away."

She again made a long pause, and went on: "All the same, because of the doubt and the fear of other people that I had in my heart, I and the child had to go through much. If I had been a poor girl, with only a hundred rixdollars in all the world, it would have been better, for then we should have remained together. Yes, we went through much."

"When I found Jens again and he came home with me," she took up her narrative after a silence, "I did not love him. You all loved him, only I myself did not. It was Charlie that I loved. Still I was more with Jens than any of you. He told me many things, which none of you heard. I saw that we could not find another such as he, that there was none so wise." She did not know that she was quoting the Scripture, any more than the old shipowner had been aware of doing so when he ordained Jens to be buried in the field of his fathers and the cave that was therein—this was a small trick peculiar to the magic of the dead child. "I learned much from him. He was always truthful, like Charlie. He was so truthful that he made me ashamed of myself. Sometimes I thought it wrong in me to teach him to call you Papa."

"By the time when he was ill," she said, "what I thought of was this: that if he died I might, at last, go into mourning for Charlie." She lifted up her bonnet, gazed at it and again dropped it. "And then after all," she said, "I could not do it." She made a pause. "Still if I had told Jens about it, it would have pleased him; it would have made him laugh. He would have told me to buy grand black clothes, and long veils."

It was a lucky thing, Jakob reflected, that he had promised her not to interrupt her tale. For had she wanted him to speak he should not have found a word to say. As now she came to this point in her story she sat in silence for a long time, so that for a moment he believed that she had finished, and at that a choking sensation came upon him, as if all words must needs stick in his throat.

"I thought," she suddenly began again, "that I would have had to suffer, terribly even, for all this. But no, it has not been so. There is a grace in the world, such as none of us has known about. The world is not a hard or severe place, as people tell us. It is not even just. You are forgiven everything. The fine things of the world you cannot wrong or harm; they are much too strong for that. You could not wrong or harm Jens; no one could. And now, after he has died," she said, "I understand everything."

Again she sat immovable, gently poised upon the tree-stem. For the first time during their talk she looked round her; her gaze ran slowly, almost caressingly, along the forest scenery.

"It is difficult," she said, "to explain what it feels like to understand things. I have never been good at finding words, I am not like Jens. But it has seemed to me ever since March, since the Spring began, that I have known well why things happened, why, for instance, they all flowered. And why the birds came. The generosity of the world; Papa's and your kindness too! As we walked in the wood today I thought that now I have got back my sight, and my sense of smell, from when I was a little girl. All things here tell me, of their own, what they signify." She stopped, her gaze steadying. "They signify Charlie," she said. After a long pause she added: "And I, I am Emilie. Nothing can alter that either."

She made a gesture as if to pull on her gloves that lay in her bonnet, but she put them back again, and remained quiet, as before.

"Now I have told you all," she said. "Now you must decide what we are to do."

"Papa will never know," she said gently and thoughtfully. "None of them will ever know. Only you. I have thought, if you will let me do so, that you and I, when we talk of Jens—" She made a slight pause, and Jakob thought: "She has never talked of him till today"—"might talk of all these things, too."

"Only in one thing," she said slowly, "am I wiser than you. I know that it would be better, much better, and easier to both you and me if you would believe me."

Jakob was accustomed to take a quick summary of a situation and to make his dispositions accordingly. He waited a moment after she had ceased to talk, to do so now.

"Yes, my dear," he said, "that is true."

The Rock Garden
Sandra Birdsell

Sandra Birdsell

(Canada, b. 1942)

In 1981 Sandra Birdsell was a guest at a writer's colony in Sas-katchewan. She was talking to an older woman: the conversation itself is now forgotten, but one remark stuck in Birdsell's memory. The woman said simply: "I'm tired of being a mother." It then occurred to Birdsell, for the first time, that for some people parenthood was in fact an occupation which could be given up, like any other. For many months she thought about a story that would explore this theme, and which would also explore the criss-crossed relationships which establish themselves within a family. After many rewrites, her story became "The Rock Garden."

The Canadian Prairies provide Sandra Birdsell with a setting for her fiction, but there is no "local colour" in her stories. Her collections *Night Travellers* (1982) and *Ladies of the House* (1984) chronicle the everyday discoveries and quiet miracles of men and women in humdrum situations: most of them take place in Manitoba, but their reality can be recognized most anywhere. They are as ubiquitous as the Mexican stories of D. H. Lawrence or the Australian stories of Christina Stead, and justify her rep-utation as one of Canada's most subtle and accomplished writers.

The Rock Garden

I was one of four children who stood beneath the maple tree early one morning. We were on our way to school. Mika, our mother, had spit and licked and polished and we were fresh and as clean as was the day which smelled to me of lilacs. Above us, leaf buds, tight like babies' fists, began uncurling fingers one by one to the sun. It wasn't a day to argue. We stood beneath the tree looking down at a rock. The rock had appeared mysteriously overnight and we, like curious animals, sniffed and poked at it.

"I wonder where it came from," I said.

Truda, the third eldest, spoke. "It could have been a dog. A dog carried it in its mouth and dropped it."

Betty laughed at Truda and tickled the top of her head. "Silly."

I nudged the rock with my foot. It wouldn't budge and I was relieved, seeing in my mind the possibility of a garter snake curled beneath it, or thick slugs kissing the damp bottom of the rock with their sucky mouths.

I was the only black-haired child of the six Lafreniere children. My skin didn't blister and peel in the sun, but tanned to the colour of a netted gem potato, dusty and dry looking. My hair, straight and black, resembled Maurice's, my father's hair. I was the only child in our family who looked like a Lafreniere should look, fine-boned, tiny feet and hands, small black eyes. I was conscious of being different, and felt cocky and self-assured in this difference. "It looks like a rock," I said. "But it could be something else, you know. It could, for instance, be a fossilized dinosaur egg. It was dug up when they made the ring dike."

"Yes, it could be an egg," said the myopic Truda.

I could tell that Betty was stung by Truda's disloyalty; usually they were a team. "We'll be late for school," Betty said. "And then I'll get the blame for it. I'm the example." She gathered her books up from the grass and headed down the cinder-strewn driveway.

"If it's a dinosaur egg," Rudy said, always wanting to get to the truth of the matter, "then it might hatch, won't it? I think it will. And then it'll eat us up."

"It can't hatch," I told him. "It hasn't been fertilized." Put that in your pipe and smoke it, as my father would say. I took Truda and Rudy by the hand and led them down the dirt road where we traced our own footprints in the bottom of the deep ruts. Betty followed along behind us, neat and proper, never galloping, our perfect example.

After a time, we left the road and entered the coulee, a grassy dish of marshland that filled each spring with water which receded quickly, leaving behind twitch grass that grew waist-high, and spotted toads that leapt up before our feet.

"I am thee Count," a voice said in Draculan tones. "Let me bite your neck. Heh, heh, heh." Laurence Anderson's brown curly head parted the grasses as he stood up and came towards us. He carried a paper sack and wiped his palms against his white T-shirt, leaving behind grey smudges of something he'd been into.

"It's puke-face himself."

"Lureen!"

I knew Betty would tell Mother. Lureen swore, she'd say, her blue eyes wide with a pretended innocence. Lureen said: shit, piss and God. Exaggerating, because reciting the words was the only way Betty had the courage to do it too.

And Mother would believe her because Betty was her favourite child. Betty had memorized one hundred Bible verses and won a trip to church summer camp. Our mother respected those who could do what she couldn't.

Girls don't swear, she often said.

But they do on Father's side of the family, I argued.

Well, I guess. What can you expect, she said. There are no ladies in your father's family. None that I know of. They're coarse and hard. They paint their nails. They walk around in their war paint looking as though they've dipped their fingers in someone's blood. You want to be like that? I knew nothing of my father's family except what my mother told me. But, yes, that sounded exciting.

Why don't girls swear? Because, Mother said when she didn't want to talk to us, just because. Because I say so. And then, exasperated, it gives boys the wrong impression, you know. That you aren't to be respected. That you're Fair Game. Like a female dog in heat.

What is Fair Game? I wondered, and imagined a prairie chicken flapping up from the grass in the coulee. I was twelve years old, I knew what the spring dance of the dogs meant and I thought that she was coarse and hard for referring to it. But what was Fair Game?

Sometimes my mother would say, men, who needs them? In the same derogatory way she discussed my uncles' wives. She would say, Lureen, you would be "wery vise" to forget about boys until you have an education.

By education, Mother meant grade twelve, which, to me, seemed a preposterous length of time to wait for boys, an indication of her being so out of touch with reality, that her opinion couldn't be trusted. A person whose English was so faulty that they said, "wery vise," lost their credibility. Piss, shit and God are nothing to get excited about, my father would say with a laugh.

I began to hum because I knew it annoyed Laurence. "Twit," he said, not looking at me directly. He fell into step with Betty. "Wait until you see what I found," he said to her.

I wanted to fling mud at him. A solid blow to his shaggy head. Wham! It made me angry the way he followed Betty around when it was so obvious to me that I was better-looking. I watched as Laurence held open the paper bag and Betty looked inside it. Since Betty's new breasts, Mother's objections to their friendship had grown stronger. If I went to her and told her that they had met in the coulee, that would be that. But I wouldn't do that because I was beginning to use Betty's sins against her, to realize that there was something to my mother's admonition that sisters should be friends.

"What is it?" There was fear in Betty's voice. "Where did you find that awful thing?"

Laurence closed the bag quickly at the word "awful" and clutched it against his chest.

"I found it where they're digging," he said. "It's mine now. I'm going to keep it."

Betty looked frail and meek against the tall, sharp-bladed grasses. Her hair was wound about her head in a golden crown of tight braids which made her neck look thin, too thin to support so large a head. "But why would you want to?" she asked. "It looks real, like a real person's—"

"It is," said Laurence. "It's a human skull."

"But it must be wrong, you should get rid of it, bury it or something."

Let me look, I wanted to say, but they had joined themselves against me, turned their backs and were lost in their own conversation. I wanted to look inside the bag, force myself to touch, hold in my hands, whatever it was that frightened Betty, to show Laurence that he'd made a mistake in choosing Betty over me.

Weeks later, the lilacs had finished blooming and were just rust-coloured flecks on the ground, and now there were seven buff-coloured, pumpkin-sized rocks on the ground beneath the maple tree. Truda had wised up by then, and decided that the rocks weren't dinosaur eggs. "Maybe Mother laid them, like a chicken," she said once. That morning, when another stone had been added by mysterious circumstances to the growing mound of them beneath the rope swing, Truda called me over to examine the new rock and said, "Look at that, she laid another egg."

Rudy was there too. He was pumping fruitlessly on the rope swing, trying to gain some height, but his feet kept glancing off the stones, making the swing career wildly, bringing his shins too close to the rough bark of the maple tree. "Damn," Rudy said. "I don't think it's fair that we can't use the swing."

"Do something," Truda pleaded, her heavy thick glasses slipping down her nose and her myopic grey eyes clouded and pleading.

I decided to do something about the stones. I marched into the house and faced my father who had his day off from the barbershop and was sprawled in the maroon easy chair with his bare feet propped up on the hassock. He hid behind a magazine so he wouldn't have to take note of the multi-coloured and malodorous piles of dirty laundry Mother sorted in the living and dining room every Monday.

Why do you have to do the laundry on my day off for God's sake, he complained. And I agreed fully, it was inconsiderate.

Because, she said. Just because I have to. Monday is washday. I can't help it if it also happens to be your day off.

Father looked at me overtop his *Game and Fish* magazine. "How should I know where the rocks came from? I'm not the chief cook and bottle washer around here." He tried to tease me from my seriousness. "Serious, serious," he'd say. "That's your mother's department." His small black eyes reflected light in a curious way, making him look as though he were about to burst into tears or laughter. I could never tell which.

"Why don't you ask your mother where the rocks came from? She should know."

Everything in the yard and the two-storey frame house belonged absolutely to us, the children. Mother had always arranged everything according to the patterns of our play. So the rocks were encroaching on our territory. I went to the kitchen where she folded diapers at the table. The washing machine sloshed and chugged another load clean in the back porch. There were two stacks of diapers, Peter's and Sharon's, white unspotted flannel, smelling of the reedy wind that blew in from the coulee.

"What rocks?" Mother asked.

"You know. Under the swing. Those rocks."

"They're mine." Her voice snapped the sentence shut the same way her strong white teeth nipped at knots in laces. You could ask Father anything and get an interesting, amusing answer, but not Mother. She was as serious as a mousetrap.

"What are they for? We can't use the swing anymore."

"Swing, fling. You're too old anyway. And you don't really care about the others, you just want to stir up trouble. I know you." She flicked a diaper and folded it into the shape of a kite, triple folds for Peter, because a boy pees the front. "Anyway, you have the rest of the yard to do what you want."

"It's our yard."

"I beg your pardon?"

"You should give us a reason, at least. You should tell us what the rocks are for."

"I don't have to tell you anything, missy," she said. "You only want reasons so that you can argue."

The sun moved behind the clouds for a moment and the yellow kitchen walls lost their sheen as the shadow came and fell on Mother's face, making her deeply set hazel eyes sink even further back into their bony sockets.

"O Lord," she said. "Please don't let it rain today."

"Why not?" I asked, grateful that she had been diverted from the tone of "I beg your pardon."

"You think I like mud from one end of this house to the other?"

The cloud passed and the room shone once again, but it seemed to me that pieces of the shadow lingered in her eyes. A creeping uneasiness made me close the screen door behind me gently.

That same evening as the garden arose silently from the black earth behind the chicken wire fence, I awoke to the sound of the latch on the screen door. I thought it was Father coming home from the hotel. But instead of my father's heavy step in the kitchen, there were light footsteps on the sidewalk at the side of the house and then silence. I looked out across the coulee and imagined Laurence crouching in the tall weeds, like a prairie chicken about to spring up. The moon was a silver disc, licked and pressed onto a black broadcloth sky. The night breezes fanned the tops of the grass in the coulee and sounded like the whispering of a single voice.

Let me bite your neck.

Mother stepped out from beneath the maple tree and crossed the yard to the driveway. She left the yard and walked down the centre of the road, head bent into the darkness. The moon revealed the fish-white muscles in her calves. Mother's knotted tanned arms, her strong back, the muscles in her legs made her look chunky and shorter than she really was. She could carry a hundred-pound sack of flour in her arms. A dog barked in the distance and Mother vanished into the inky darkness. I knelt beside the window to wait.

When I awoke, my knees were stiff from kneeling. The wind had fallen. From Main Street came the insistent toot of a car horn. At the end of the street there was another sound. The sound was a needle-thin one, yet musical, like a violin being plucked instead of bowed. A blotted figure emerged from the darkness and gradually came to the light. The plucking sound was Mother's voice raised softly in a song. She came to the light. Her hair was unwound and flowed in a brown cascade of ripples across her shoulders. She carried a rock in her arms. She turned in at the driveway beneath the window. Still singing lightly, she strode across the yard and laid the stone gently down among the others.

Weeks later, the sweet peas had climbed to their glory on the chicken wire fence surrounding the garden and the bees droned above the profusion of pea blossoms. I was behind

the sweet peas, hoeing the potato patch. I was unhappy.
Laurence had put his hand on Betty's breast in the coulee.
They thought I hadn't seen. I hadn't told anyone although I
was burning with the desire to do so. I heard a noise and
looked up. Laurence was there, behind the tree out of sight,
should anyone look out the window. He played with his
knife. He held the blade at the end and then flung it,
making the blade turn once in mid-air before it cut into the
tree.

"That's easy," I said. "I can do that." I'd dropped the hoe,
come to watch.

"You think you're so tough," Laurence said.

"I don't think. I know I am."

"God, you make me sick." He bent to pick up the knife
which had bounced off the bark and stuck into the ground.

I beat him to it, grabbed the knife before he'd had the
chance to reach for it.

"Give it to me."

"Make me."

His hand was strong on my wrist, chapped and raw-
looking like his mouth; it felt like sandpaper as he twisted
my skin red. I felt tears forming. They were going to squirt
forward onto my cheeks in a second and betray me if I didn't
do something. I made a fist with my free hand, punched him
hard in the middle of his dirty T-shirt. Woof, he said,
sounding like a dog, and let go of me.

"Here's your stupid knife." I threw it onto the rock pile.
My wrist ached. I walked away from him rapidly and
entered the house. I could hear Mother moving about in the
rooms upstairs.

"If you've got nothing better to do, you could give me a
hand," she said.

I sat cross-legged on the floor beside the bed as Mother
changed the linens. I let my head drop so that my hair fell
forward and hid my face. The effect I hoped to achieve was a
look of despair or dejection.

"What is it?"

It worked. I sighed deeply.

"Well, out with it."

"I don't know—it's just that he follows her around. As though she were a bitch in heat. We can never go anywhere without him."

"What did you say?"

"I said, I'm fed up. Everywhere we go, there he is. It's like we're Fair Game."

The colour fled from Mother's cheeks. "Who's following you around?"

"Laurence. He's here again. And yesterday, when I went to school I saw him and Betty. He—they were necking."

Mother's shoulders sagged. She dropped a sheet and rushed over to the bedroom window. "Oh, this is no good," she said. "I don't like the sound of this at all."

She clattered down the stairs and then the front door rattled on its hinges. I got up from the floor and went over to the window and stood looking down at Laurence and Betty. I saw Mother run across the yard toward them. She hopped from foot to foot when she reached the pile of rocks.

"But Mother," Betty protested. "He's just fixing the swing. He's moving the ropes up so the little ones can use it."

"I'll fix him. Just you let him come around again and I'll fix him." Mother turned to Betty and shook her finger. "Really, you'd think you'd have more pride." She sputtered and glanced up at the bedroom window where I watched. "Don't you want more than that for yourself?"

I parted the curtains and smiled at the sight of Laurence retreating, edging backwards from the yard.

"Wait," Mother said and held out her hand. "Give me your knife."

Laurence removed it from its leather sheath. The blade shone as it crossed the space between them. She grabbed it from him and, teetering up the stony mound of rocks beneath the tree, she cut through the ropes of the swing with saw-like motions. Betty ran into the house with her hands covering her face.

I saw the tanned V at Mother's throat rising and falling

rapidly as she stood looking down the road where Laurence
had gone and then back at the house. And then, as though
she had come to some decision, she strode over to the
icehouse and returned moments later pushing the wheelbarrow, which held a pail of whitewash and a paint brush.
Betty rushed into the bedroom and threw herself onto the
bed, crying loudly.

Mother stood beneath the maple tree with her hands on
her hips. "Alright," she said loudly. "Alright, okay. You
can't change a thing. No amount of harping will change
anything. They'll do what they want to do in the end
anyway. I'm butting my head against a stone wall." She
pried open the pail of whitewash. "Don't take my advice.
See what you get in the end." She stirred the thick paint and
then dipped the brush into it. "Life is too short to butt your
head against a stone wall." She began to paint a large rock a
brilliant white. "And what do you get for it? Let them learn
the hard way." She continued to complain bitterly as she
finished painting the rock and set it aside. She rolled
another stone down from the pile and began to paint it also.

An hour passed. Betty came to the window to watch what
was happening below. We heard Peter the baby down in the
kitchen banging impatiently on the tray of the highchair
and the clatter of pots as Sharon amused herself in the
cupboards. Mother continued to paint rock after rock and to
place them into a large circle. I sent Truda and Rudy
outside to make polite restrained overtures at conversation
in order to jar Mother from her strange behaviour, but her
sour expression sent them scurrying back into the house.

At a quarter to twelve, Father came walking up the
sidewalk for his lunch. He stood waiting as Mother wheeled
a load of dirt through the garden towards him.

"It's a funny time to start that job," he said, glancing at
his watch.

"It's now or never."

Father shrugged. "Suits me. But what's for lunch?"

Mother looked up angrily. "Why don't you have a look?"

He came back out minutes later. "There's nothing

prepared," he said, sounding injured and puzzled.

"I know."

"Why not?"

"Because," she said quietly and then once again, louder, "because. Just because. I don't know why. I'm tired of answering stupid questions. Make your own lunch."

"Listen here," Father said, his voice rising above its accustomed gentle gone. "The babies are in there alone. Their diapers are dripping."

"And does that bother you?"

"Of course, what do you think? Something could happen to them."

Mother grunted as the wheelbarrow tilted suddenly from her grasp and fell onto its side. "Well, change them then," she said. "They're your babies too."

"What's the matter?" he asked, lowering his voice. "Is it—are you in the family way?"

Mother stopped shovelling and looked him straight in the eye. "Yes. I'm always in the family way. And I'm tired. I'm tired of being a mother."

What? Tired of being a mother? It was an astounding thought. In the same way I grew tired of playing 7-up against the house, or sick of my best friend, so that I picked a fight in order to cut myself off from her, Mother was tired of us, her children?

Father turned from her in disgust. "Is that all?" he said. "Who doesn't get tired? What if I should say the same thing, eh? Where would you be?"

Absolutely, I agreed, where would you be without him? Where would any of us be?

"I would change places with you in a flash. You stay home, I'll go to work."

Father edged away from her. I had to do something. I knocked on the windowpane. "We're hungry," I said, reminding them both of their parental duties.

He looked up, startled. "What do you expect me to do about it?"

"Peter needs a bottle."

"I don't know what's going on here," Father said. "But I do know that I've got five heads waiting to be cut. So I'm going to grab a bite to eat at the hotel and then I'm going to get back to work. Somebody's got to work around here," he said loudly, for Mother's benefit.

"Oh, you're useless," she said. "You can go to the hotel. You couldn't look after a dog."

Father stared at her, shocked, and then retreated quickly.

"That's not fair," I said to my sister, "she's always so bloody unfair to him." Father had all the money. In case of marital breakdown, I wanted to be where the money was. So my sympathies in any of their arguments rested with him.

"I wouldn't know what's fair," Betty said. "Someone has to look after the kids today and I guess that leaves me." She went downstairs.

The sun passed centre sky and the birds stopped singing. I nibbled at the sandwich Betty had brought to me, but my stomach was tight and the food tasted flat. So, Mother was tired of being a mother, eh? The idea was like a thunderstorm. I was unsettled by the sound of it. I didn't know how she could be so selfish.

Wet stains spread across my mother's back and from beneath her armpits, as she began to form a smaller circle of rocks on top of the larger one. Her hair was pasted in strands against her white neck. She looked to me like a sweaty, irritable child. Back and forth she went, scooping up the black dirt, wheeling it across the yard to the tree, dumping it, shovelling it into place, raking it smooth, back and forth, with a bulldog determination. And then, on one of her trips, she stumbled, broke her stride and fell beneath the weight of the dirt in the wheelbarrow. She landed flat on her back. She looked like a beetle squirming to right itself. The more she floundered, the more exposed she became. Her blue cotton shift worked upwards, baring her thighs and then the white cotton V of her crotch.

My breath caught in my throat at the sight of my mother sprawled on the ground, at the sight of her vulnerability, that cotton mound between her legs.

She struggled upright, brushed dirt from her legs, her dress. I urged her to come inside. I wanted her to give up this silly project, wash her hands, or take up the broom and become a mother again. But she didn't. When she'd finished brushing herself off, she took up the handles of the wheelbarrow and began to fill in the second circle with earth.

She was forming the last, smallest circle when the sun began its falling behind the house, casting long pale shadows across the grass. Betty stood in the doorway of the bedroom with diaper pins in her mouth and a towel draped over her shoulder.

"I need a hand," she said.

"It's not our job," I said. "It's her job. Let her come and do it. She doesn't care if we starve, she only cares about herself." But my heart wasn't in it.

Betty threw the towel at me. "There's enough babies around here already without you becoming one too. Help me get them washed and into bed."

Together we bathed the children and put them into bed. We took turns reading stories to them to take their minds off their mother who wouldn't come inside and be a mother.

I listened to Betty's flat monotone voice reading, wooing the babies to sleep. Part of what happened was my fault. If I hadn't told on my sister, none of this would have happened. I would make tea, arrange a tray of food and lure her back inside. I might even begin to help around the house. Maybe finish changing the linens on the bed. Might not complain when asked to wipe the dishes.

I heard the door of the icehouse being closed. I crept to the window, looked down to see Mother scraping her shoes on the footscraper. I beckoned Truda and Rudy from the bed. They tiptoed to the window. I instructed them to say goodnight. I arranged them side by side. They cleared their throats. One, two, three—now.

"Goodnight Mother."

She'd have to answer. She'd say, "Don't let the bed bugs bite." And then they would reply. "Oh no, we'll hit them black and blue with our shoes." We waited. No answer. I nudged them again. "Goodnight," they called once more. Their voices, clear in the moisture-laden air, were fruity and sweet.

Still no answer.

The screen door flapped shut. There was a long silent time. Then we heard the kitchen chair creaking beneath her weight and then the sound of her shoes dropping one after the other to the floor.

I'll memorize Bible verses, I vowed silently. I'll follow Betty's example. Then I stopped breathing, listened, as there came another sound from below. It was the dry swishing sound of the broom being swept briskly across the kitchen floor.

I began to breathe once again. "She's back. Listen, she's sweeping the floor." I sat down beside Betty who had gathered her knees up and rocked back and forth in the centre of the bed.

My body felt weak, overpowered by the flooding of relief. The crisis was over. "I'll make tea," I said, "if you help me get together a plate of food for her."

"Are you crazy?" Betty said. "After what she did to Laurence? You go ahead and do that if you want to, but I couldn't care less."

I went back to the window to think about this new development. The rock garden glowed strangely in the falling light. Beside it on the ground were the ropes from our swing, curled like two large question marks. The rocks' pink glow dimmed slowly to a violet and then at last, a dull grey. My resolutions faded gently. Oh well, I told myself, she's used to making her own tea anyway. If I offered to make it, the shock would kill her.

"I know what you mean," I said. "What she did to Laurence was awful. I almost died. And it wasn't fair, either. He was only trying to help. She's so unfair."

"She's a witch," Betty, my example, said, "a frigging witch."

The first of the whispering sounds swept in from the

coulee, gently puffing the curtains in and out like a frog's throat. I felt a slight chill. The sounds brought with them mystery, uncertainty.

Let me bite your neck.

I knew my mother had some of the answers to the mysteries. But the pull of an alliance between sisters was stronger. It was better than being on your own with a person who could suddenly grow tired of being your mother.

"Piss, shit and God," I said. "A mean witch." I stepped out and away from my mother. Suddenly, I was afraid.

The Other Son
Luigi Pirandello

Luigi Pirandello
(Italy, 1867-1936)

Though Pirandello is mainly known for his extraordinary contribution to the theatre, many of his plays are dramatizations of short stories that he wrote during his early career, mostly between 1900 and 1918. This was the most difficult period in Pirandello's life. His wife, the daughter of a business associate of his father, became dangerously insane and had to be committed to an asylum; at the same time, Pirandello's family lost all their possessions in a flood in Sicily, leaving him practically destitute.

Pirandello's stories, collected after his death under the title of *Novelle per un anno ("Tales for Every Day in the Year"*: there were 365 of them), contain the themes of insecurity and dissociation from reality that are the trademark of his theatre. He felt that the many aspects of the human soul could best be represented by the action of the stage, where he juggled with the several levels of reality allowed by live drama; but he achieved this same effect in his prose, with more power and conviction than he himself was willing to admit. "The Other Son" stages struggle in at least two realities: that of the son, grappling with the idolized example of his sibling, and that of his mother, for whom the truth is unseen and unapproachable. In 1934, Luigi Pirandello was awarded the Nobel Prize for Literature.

The Other Son

"Is Ninfarosa in?"

"Yes, knock at the door."

Old Maragrazia gave a knock and settled herself down quietly on the rickety steps in front of the door.

Those steps were her natural seat—those and many other front-door steps—for she spent her time sitting huddled before the door-way of one or other of the cottages of Farnia, either asleep or dissolved in silent tears. When a passer-by threw a copper or a piece of bread into her lap, she scarcely roused herself from her sleep or dried her tears: she kissed the copper or the bread, crossed herself and continued weeping or dozing.

She was a bundle of rags—thick, greasy rags—always the same, in summer or winter, tattered, torn and faded, and stinking foully of sweat and the filth of the streets. Her sallow face was covered with a close network of wrinkles and her eyelids gaped open, bloody and horrible, inflamed by the incessant flow of her tears. But from between those wrinkles, though the blood and tears, there shone a pair of bright eyes—eyes that seemed to peer out across a great distance—the eyes of a long-forgotten childhood. The flies settled hungrily on those eyes, but she remained so deeply absorbed in her sorrow that she did not drive them away or

323

so much as notice them. Her dry and scanty hair was parted
on the top of her head and ended in two matted locks
hanging above her ears, whose lobes were torn by the
weight of the massive earrings she had worn in her youth. A
deep black furrow started at her chin and ran down her
flabby throat, until it disappeared in her hollow breast.

The women sitting at their thresholds paid no attention
to her any more. They spent almost the whole day there,
chatting in front of their cottages—some patching clothing,
others preparing vegetables or knitting, all occupied with
some task. The dwellings were house and stable combined,
lighted only by the doorway, and paved with cobble-stones
the same as the streets. On one side was the manger, with an
ass or a mule, kicking to keep off the persistent flies; on the
other side was the bed, towering up like a monument. Each
room contained also a long black chest of pine or beech-
wood, which looked as if it were a coffin, two or three
straw-bottomed chairs, a kneading trough and some agri-
cultural implements. The rough and sooty walls were
decorated with a few common halfpenny prints, repre-
senting the particular saints dear to that countryside. In the
street, which reeked with smoke and manure, sunburnt
children played—some stark naked, others in little dirty,
tattered shirts. Hens scratched about among the children;
young pigs, caked in mud, sniffed and grunted, digging
into the heaps of garbage.

That day, the women were discussing the latest party of
emigrants which was to leave the next morning for South
America.

"Saro Scoma is going," said one of them. "He's leaving
behind him his wife and three children."

"Vito Scordia," added another, "leaves five and his wife,
who is pregnant."

"Is it true," asked a third, "that Carmine Ronca is taking
his twelve-year-old son who had already started working in
the sulphur mines? Blessed Virgin! he might at least have
left the boy with his wife. How will that poor woman
manage for help now?"

"How they cried all night long in the house of Nunzio Ligreci . . ." called out a fourth woman in pitiful tones from farther up the street. "What tears they've shed—Nunzio's son, Nico, who's only just returned from his military service, has decided to go too."

At this piece of news, old Maragrazia pressed her shawl over her mouth to prevent an outburst of sobbing, but the vehemence of her grief caused an endless flow of tears to well up from her inflamed eyes.

Fourteen years before, her two sons had also left for America. They had promised to return after four or five years, but they had prospered there—especially the elder one—and they had forgotten their old mother. Every time a fresh body of emigrants was to leave Farnia, she went to Ninfarosa to get her to write a letter for her, and begged some member of the party to be so kind as to deliver it personally to one or other of those two sons. Then, as the party of emigrants—heavily laden with sacks and bundles—set out for the nearest railway station, the old woman joined with the mothers, wives and sisters who, with tears and cries of despair, followed after along the dusty high-road. As she walked, on one of these occasions, she gazed steadily at the eyes of a young emigrant, who was making a great show of noisy cheerfulness, in order to discourage manifestations of grief from the relations who accompanied him.

"Mad old crone!" he shouted at her. "Why are you looking at me like that? D'you want to make my eyes drop out?"

"No, my fine fellow! I envy you those eyes, because, with them, you'll see my sons. Tell them the state I was in when you left here, and say that if they delay any longer they won't find me alive. . ."

The gossips of the neighbourhood were still going through the list of those who were leaving the next day. Near by, an old man lay on his back in the lane, his head pillowed on a donkey's saddle, listening to the chatter and quietly smoking his pipe. Suddenly he folded his great horny hands across his chest, spat and said:—

"If I were king, I should not allow one single letter to be sent from over there to Farnia any more."

"Three cheers for Jaco Spina!" exclaimed one of the women. "And how would the poor mothers and wives manage without any news or help?"

"They send too many letters—that's the trouble," the old man muttered, and spat again. "The mothers could go into service and the wives could go to the bad. . . . Why don't those fellows mention in their letters the hardships they find over there? They only describe the good side of things, and every letter that comes calls up these ignorant lads and carries them off. Where are the hands for working our fields? At Farnia, the only people left are old men, women and babies. I've got some land and I have to watch it going to ruin. What can I do with only a single pair of hands? And still they go and still they go! Rain on their faces and wind on their backs, say I. I hope they'll break their necks, the damned fools!"

At that moment Ninfarosa opened her door. It was as if the sun had suddenly appeared in the little street. She was dark, with rich colouring, sparkling black eyes and bright red lips. Her form was slender but strong, and she exhaled a kind of wild gaiety. A large red and yellow spotted handkerchief was knotted over her shapely bosom and in her ears were thick golden rings. Her hair was black and curling, and she wore it drawn back without a parting, fastened on to the nape of her neck in a shining coil wound round a silver dagger. A deep dimple in the middle of her well-rounded chin gave her a humorous look and added still further to her fascinations.

Left a widow after barely two years of marriage, Ninfarosa had been deserted by her second husband, who had gone to America five years ago. No one was supposed to know it, but, at night, one of the leading residents of the village visited her, entering through the orchard and the back door. And therefore the neighbours—who were respectable, God-fearing women—looked askance at her, while they secretly envied her luck. They had another grudge against her, for it was said in the village that, out of revenge for being deserted by her second husband, she had written several anonymous letters to the emigrants in America, making slanderous charges against some of the unfortunate women.

"Who's that preaching?" she asked, coming out into the lane. "Oh, it's Jaco Spina! It would be much better, Uncle Jaco, if only we women remained at Farnia. We'd cultivate the fields."

"You women," the old man muttered in husky tones— "You women are only good for one thing." And he spat.

"For what thing, Uncle Jaco? Go on, say it."

"For weeping—and for one other thing."

"Ah! That makes two things then. I do not weep, you see."

"Yes, I know that, my girl. You didn't even weep when your first husband died!"

"But if I had died first, Uncle Jaco," retorted Ninfarosa promptly, "d'you think he wouldn't have taken another wife? Of course he would! But look here—see who weeps enough for all of us—Maragrazia."

"That depends," murmured Jaco Spina, stretching himself out again on his back. "Since the old woman has water to get rid of, she gets rid of it from her eyes too." The women laughed. Roused from her abstraction, Maragrazia cried:—

"I have lost two sons, handsome as the sun, and you would not have me weep?"

"Handsome indeed! Yes, very handsome, and worth weeping over—" said Ninfarosa. "There they are over there, swimming in abundance, and they leave you here to die—a beggar."

"They are the sons and I am their mother," replied the old woman. "How can they realise my grief?"

"Well, I don't know the reason for so many tears and all this grief," replied Ninfarosa, "when it was you yourself— people say—who worried them and plagued them until they went off."

"I?" exclaimed Maragrazia, utterly amazed. Beating her

fist against her chest, she rose to her feet. "I? Who said so?"

"Somebody or other said it."

"A shame! A shame on them—I! My sons? I who . . ."

"Oh, don't mind her!" interrupted one of the women. "Can't you see she's joking?"

Ninfarosa indulged in a long laugh, swaying her body contemptuously from the hips; then, to make up to the old woman for her cruel jest, she asked in a kindly tone:—

"Well, well, Granny, what is it you want?"

Maragrazia put a shaky hand to her bosom and pulled out a badly crumpled sheet of paper and an envelope. She showed them to Ninfarosa with a look of entreaty.

"If you would do me the usual favour. . . ."

"What? Another letter?"

"If you would be so good. . . ."

Ninfarosa sniffed; then, knowing that it would be impossible to get rid of the old woman, she invited her into her house.

This house was not like the others in the neighbourhood. The large room was rather dark when the door was shut because its only other light was from a grated window above the door, but it was a white-washed room with a brick floor, and all was clean and well-kept. There was an iron bedstead, a wardrobe, a marble-topped chest of drawers and a small inlaid walnut table—humble furniture, it is true, but clearly Ninfarosa could not have afforded the luxury of purchasing it herself, out of the very uncertain income she earned as a village dressmaker.

She took her pen and inkstand, placed the crumpled sheet of paper on the top of the high chest of drawers and prepared to write, standing up.

"Be quick, out with it!"

" 'Dear sons'," the old woman began to dictate.

" 'I have no longer any eyes to weep with. . . .'," continued Ninfarosa, with a weary sigh. She knew the usual formula for these letters.

The old woman added:—

" 'Because my eyes are inflamed by the longing to see you

at least for one last time. . . .'."

"Get on, get on!" urged Ninfarosa. "You must have written that to them quite thirty times, at the very least."

"Well, you write it. It's the truth, my dear, don't you see? So now write: *'Dear sons'. . . .' "*

"What? All over again?"

"No. This time it's something different. I thought it out all last night. Listen: *'Dear sons: Your poor old mother promises and vows'*—yes, like that—*'promises and vows before God, that if you return to Farnia, she will make over to you, during her life-time, her cottage.' "*

Ninfarosa burst out laughing. "That cottage! But since they're already so rich, what d'you expect them to do with your four walls of wattles plastered with mud? Why, they'd collapse if one blew on them!"

"Well, you write it," repeated the old woman obstinately. "Four rough bits of stone in one's own country are worth more than a whole kingdom outside. Write it, write."

"I have written it. What else would you like to add?"

"Just this—*'that your poor Mamma, dear sons, shivers from the cold now that the winter is starting. She would like to have some kind of a dress made but cannot afford to do so; would you be so kind as to send her at least a bank note for five lire, so that. . .' "*

"Enough, enough, enough!" said Ninfarosa, folding up the sheet and putting it into the envelope. "I've written it good and proper. That's enough."

"Also about the five lire?" asked the old woman, surprised at the unexpected speed with which it had been finished.

"Yes, yes, everything, also about the five lire, my Lady."

"Written it properly? Everything?"

"Ouf! Yes, I tell you."

"Be patient . . . be a little patient with this poor old woman, my daughter," said Maragrazia. "What can you expect of me? I am half stupid nowadays. . . . May God and his beauteous and most holy Mother requite you for the favour."

She took the letter and placed it in her bosom. She had

decided to entrust it to the son of Nunzio Ligreci, who was leaving for Rosario in Santa Fe, where her sons were. She went off to find him.

•

By evening, the women had gone back into their cottages and almost all the doors were shut. Not a soul was to be seen in the narrow lanes, except the lamp-lighter going his rounds, ladder on shoulder, to light the few small kerosene-oil lamps, whose sparse and feeble glimmer gave a still more gloomy aspect to those silent, deserted ill-kept alleys.

Old Maragrazia walked along, stooping low. With one hand she pressed the letter to her bosom, as if she hoped to transmit to that piece of paper the warmth of a mother's love. She employed the other hand in frequent scratching of her back and head. With each fresh letter, hope revived strongly within her—hope that at last she would succeed in touching the hearts of her sons—in calling them back to her. Surely when they read her words, eloquent of all the tears which she had shed for them during the past fourteen years, her handsome sons, her sweet sons would be unable to stand out against her entreaties any longer. . . .

But on this occasion, as it happened, she was not thoroughly satisfied with the letter which she carried in her bosom. It seemed to her as if Ninfarosa had dashed it off too hurriedly and she did not feel at all sure that she had put in the last part properly—the part about the five lire for the dress. Five lire! Surely it would mean nothing to her sons— her rich sons—to pay five lire for clothing for their old mother, who suffered so dreadfully from the cold. . . .

Meanwhile, from behind the closed doors of the cottages, there came the sound of weeping—mothers weeping for the sons who would leave them in the morning.

"Oh! sons, sons," groaned Maragrazia to herself, pressing the letter more firmly to her breast—"How can you have the heart to go? You promise to return and you do not come. . . . Ah, poor old women, do not trust their promises! Your sons, like mine, will never come back . . . they will never come back. . . ."

Suddenly, she stopped beneath a lamp-post, hearing footsteps in the lane. Who was that?

Ah! It was the new parish-doctor—that young man who had recently come and who, they said, would soon be leaving, not because he had failed to do good work, but because he was in the black books of the few big gentlefolk of the village. The poor, on the other hand, had all taken to him at once. He was only a boy to look at, but he was an old man, as far as sense and learning went. People said that he, too, meant to leave for America. But then he no longer had a mother—no, he was alone.

"Doctor," asked Maragrazia, "would you do me a favour?"

The young doctor stopped under the lamp-post, taken by surprise. Walking along, deep in thought, he had not noticed the old woman.

"Who are you? Oh, you are . . . Yes, of course, you're . . . "

He remembered then that he had seen that bundle of rags on several occasions in front of some cottage door.

"Would you do me the favour, Doctor, of reading me this little letter, which I have to send to my sons."

"If I can see to read it," said the doctor, who was short-sighted. He settled his glasses on his nose.

Maragrazia drew the letter from her bosom, held it out and waited in expectation that he would begin to read the words dictated to Ninfarosa—"Dear sons"—but no! either the doctor could not see to read the writing, or he was unable to decipher it.

He put the paper close to his eyes, moved it away to get more light on it from the street lamp, turned it over from one side to the other, and finally said:

"But what is this?"

"Can't you read it, your Honour?" enquired Maragrazia timidly.

The doctor started laughing.

"But there's nothing to read—there's nothing written on it," he said. "Four scrawls, drawn down zigzag with the pen. Here, you look at it."

"What!" exclaimed the old woman in consternation.

"It is so. Just look! Nothing! There's nothing written down at all."

"Is it possible!" cried the old woman. "How? Why, I dictated it to her, to Ninfarosa, word by word, and I saw her write."

"She must have pretended to, then," said the doctor, shrugging his shoulders.

Maragrazia remained a moment as if petrified. Then, giving herself a violent blow on the chest, she broke out in a torrent of words:—

"Ah! the wretch! The vile wretch! Why did she deceive me! So that's why my sons don't send me any answer. They've never had a line from me. . . . She's never written anything of what I dictated. . . . That's the reason! So my sons know nothing of my condition—they don't know that I'm at death's door through pining for them. . . . And I was blaming them, Doctor, whilst all the time it was she—that vile wretch there—who's been making a mockery of me! My God! my God! How *could* anyone behave so treacherously to a poor mother, to a poor old woman like me? Oh! what a thing to do . . . what a thing to do. . . . Oh! ———"

The young doctor was full of sympathy and indignation, and tried to comfort her in her distress. He made her tell him who Ninfarosa was and where her cottage was, so that next day he could give her the scolding she deserved. But the old woman still went on excusing her absent sons for their long silence; she was overcome with remorse to think that she had blamed them during so many years for deserting her. She was quite convinced now that they would have returned, would have hastened back to her, if a single one of the many letters which she had believed she had sent had really been written and had reached them.

To cut the scene short, the doctor had to promise that he would write the sons a long letter on the following morning.

"Come, come, don't despair like that! Come to me in the morning. Not now—it's time to sleep. Come in the morning. Go to sleep now."

But it was no use—about two hours later, when the doctor passed back along the lane, he found her still there, weeping inconsolably as she squatted under the lamp-post. He scolded her, made her get up and told her to go straight home, at once, as it was now very late.

"Where do you live?"

"Ah! Doctor. . . . I have a cottage down there, at the end of the village. I told that vile wretch to write to my sons that I would make it over to them during my life-time if they would only return. She started laughing—the hussy—because it is nothing but four walls of wattle plastered with mud, she said. But I ———"

"Very well, very well," the doctor cut her short again. "You go to bed now, and tomorrow we'll write about the cottage also. Come along, I'll accompany you."

"God bless your Excellency! But what are you saying, Doctor? Accompany me? No, your Honour, you go on in front. I'm a poor old woman and I walk slowly."

The doctor said good-night to her and went off. Maragrazia followed him at a distance. When she reached the door where she had seen him go in, she stopped, pulled her shawl over her head, wrapped it well round her and sat down on the steps in front of the door, to spend the night there, waiting.

At dawn she was asleep when the doctor, an early riser, came out for his first round of visits. As he opened his door, the old woman rolled over at his feet, for she had gone to sleep leaning against it.

"Good heavens! Is that you? Are you hurt?"

"No. . . . Your Honour pardon me . . ." she stammered, struggling to her feet with difficulty, for her hands and arms were still enveloped in the shawl.

"Have you spent the night here?"

"Yes, Sir. . . . It's nothing; I'm used to it . . ." the old woman said, excusing herself. "What can you expect, young gentleman? I cannot keep calm. . . . I cannot keep calm after the treachery of that wretch. . . . I should like to kill her, Doctor! She might have told me that she found it a

nuisance writing for me, and I should have gone to
someone else. I could have come to your Honour, who is so
kind. . . ."

"Yes, yes, you wait here a little," said the doctor, "I'm
going now to that good woman. Then we will write the
letter. Just wait."

And he hurried away in the direction the old woman had
pointed out the night before.

When he asked a woman in the lane which was Ninfarosa's house, he discovered that it was Ninfarosa herself to
whom he was speaking.

"Here I am, I'm the person you want, Doctor," she said
with a smile and a blush, and asked him to come in.

She had seen him pass by on several occasions—that nice,
boyish-looking doctor. As she was always in good health
herself and not able to pretend that she was ill, there was no
excuse for calling him in. She was delighted, therefore, at
his visit, though rather surprised that he had come of his
own accord to speak to her. As soon as she knew the reason
for his call and saw that he was worried and annoyed, she
assumed a submissive, but seductive, air. Her expression
showed how grieved she was at his displeasure—his quite
unjustifiable displeasure. The moment she could get a
word in, without being so ill-bred as to interrupt him, she
began:—

"I beg your pardon, Doctor,"—and as she spoke she half
closed her handsome dark eyes, "but are you seriously
upset because of that old madwoman? Here in the village
everyone knows her, Doctor, and no one pays any attention to her now. Ask anybody you like and they'll all
tell you she's mad, quite mad, for the past fourteen years,
ever since her two sons left for America. She will not admit
that they've forgotten all about her—which is the truth—
but persists in writing, again and again. Well, just to
satisfy her—you understand—I make a pretence of writing
a letter for her; then those who are leaving pretend that
they will deliver it, and she, poor woman, is taken in.
Why, if everyone behaved the way she does, my dear

Doctor, the world would be in a pretty state. Look here, I also have been deserted—deserted by my husband. Yes, Doctor! And d'you know what cheek the fine gentleman had? He sent me a portrait of himself and his girl over there! I can show it to you. They were taken with their heads resting one against the other and their hands clasped—allow me, give me your hand—like this, d'you understand? And they're smiling, smiling in the face of whoever looks at them—that is in my face, if you please! Ah, Doctor . . . all the pity is lavished on those who go, and none on those who stay behind. I have wept too, you see, in the early days. Then I pulled myself together and now—now I manage to get along and I enjoy myself too, when I get the chance, seeing that the world is made the way it is. . . ."

The young doctor was becoming quite nervous, overwhelmed by the fascinating friendliness and sympathy of this handsome creature. He lowered his eyes and said:—

"But—you perhaps have enough to live on, while that poor woman, on the other hand ———"

"What? She?" cried Ninfarosa vivaciously. "She could have enough to live on, too, if she wished—well prepared and put into her mouth—only she doesn't wish it."

"What?" asked the doctor, looking up again in surprise.

Ninfarosa burst out laughing at the expression of amazement on his handsome face. Her beautiful smile revealed a set of strong, white teeth.

"Yes, indeed!" she said. "She doesn't wish it. She has another son—the youngest—who would like her to live with him and would see that she lacked nothing."

"Another son? That old woman?"

"Yes, Sir. He's called Rocco Trupia. She won't have anything to do with him."

"But why?"

"Because she's quite mad—haven't I told you? She weeps day and night for those who have deserted her, and she won't accept even a crust of bread from the other son, who clasps his hands and implores her. . . . She takes from strangers—yes. Not from him."

Unwilling to display further astonishment and anxious to conceal his increasing nervousness, the doctor frowned and said:—

"Perhaps he's treated her badly—the other son."

"I don't think so," said Ninfarosa. "He's a rough man, I admit, and always on the grumble, but he's not bad at heart. He is a worker, you see—work, wife and children are the only interests he has. If your Honour would like to satisfy your curiosity, you haven't far to go. Look, follow this road for nearly a quarter of a mile, and just outside the village, on the left, you'll find what's called the 'House of the Column'. That's his place. He's rented a fine field, which brings him in a good return. Go there and you will see that the facts are as I tell you."

The doctor rose; the conversation had excited him and the balmy air of the September morning added to his cheerfulness. More interested than ever in the old woman's case, he said:—

"I am certainly going."

Ninfarosa put her hands behind her neck to readjust the coil of hair about the silver dagger; with an invitation in her half-closed smiling eyes, she replied:—

"A pleasant walk then. I am always at your service."

After mounting the steep slope, the doctor paused to regain his breath. There were a few poor cottages on either side and then the village ended. The lane came out on the provincial highway which ran dead straight and deep in dust for more than a mile along the wide plateau. The road was bordered by fields, most of which had been cropped with grain and were now a mass of yellow stubble. On the left, a splendid solitary pine tree, looking like a gigantic umbrella, formed the goal of the young gentlemen of Farnia in their usual afternoon stroll. At the very end of the plateau rose a long range of bluish mountains, behind which dense white clouds, that looked like cotton-wool, lurked as if in ambush. Every now and then, one of them would leave the others and travel slowly across the sky, passing over Monte Mirotta, which rose behind Farnia. During its passage, the mountain below it was wrapped in a sombre purple shadow, then suddenly brightened again. The deep silence of the morning was broken from time to time by the sound of shots; the larks were just arriving, and peasants were shooting at them and at the turtle-doves as they passed over the plain; each shot was followed by a long and savage outburst of barking from the watch-dogs.

The doctor walked briskly along the road, looking around him at the dry fields which lay waiting to be ploughed as soon as the first showers had fallen. Farm-hands were scarce, however, and the whole country-side presented a sadly neglected appearance.

He perceived below him the 'House of the Column', so-called because one corner was upheld by the column of an ancient Greek temple, broken off at the top and badly worn away. The house was really only a wretched hovel—a '*roba*' as the Sicilian peasants call their rural dwellings. It was screened at the back by a thick hedge of cactus and in front of it stood a couple of large conical straw-ricks.

"Ho there! Anyone in the *roba*?" shouted the doctor, who was afraid of dogs; so he waited in front of a small rickety gate of rusted iron.

A well-grown boy of about ten appeared; he was bare-footed, with a tousled mop of reddish hair, faded from the sun. He had the greenish eyes of a young wild animal.

"Is there a dog here?" the doctor asked.

"Yes, but he won't do anything; he's quite quiet."

"Are you Rocco Trupia's son?"

"Yes, Sir."

"Where is your father?"

"He's over there, unloading the manure from the mules."

The boy's mother sat on the wall in front of the *roba*. She was combing the hair of her eldest child, a girl of about twelve, who was sitting on an overturned iron pail with her baby brother, a few months old, in her lap. Another small urchin was rolling about the ground among the hens, who showed no fear of him; the handsome cock, however, had taken offence and was stretching out his neck and shaking his crest with annoyance.

"I should like to speak to Rocco Trupia," the young doctor called to the woman. "I am the new parish-doctor."

She remained a moment staring at him, worried, unable to think what business a doctor could have with her husband. She had been suckling the baby and her bodice was still open: she pushed her coarse shirt inside, did up the buttons, and rose to get a chair for her visitor. He declined the offer, however, and stood petting the child on the ground, while the other lad ran off to summon his father.

A few minutes later, there was the scraping sound of heavy, hob-nailed boots, and Rocco Trupia appeared from among the cactus plants. He had long bow-legs and walked with a stoop, one hand held behind his back, in the usual manner of the peasants.

His large, flat nose and the excessive length of his upper lip, clean-shaven and up-turned, gave him a simian look: he was red-haired and his pale face was dotted with moles; from his deep-sunk, greenish eyes flashed side-long, shifty glances.

He greeted the doctor by raising his hand and pushing his black knitted cap slightly back from his forehead:

"I kiss your Honour's hand. What are your orders?"

"It's this way," began the doctor. "I have come to speak to you about your mother." Rocco Trupia changed countenance.

"Is she ill?"

"No," the doctor hastened to add. "She is in her usual condition; but she's so old, you see, old and ragged and neglected. . . ."

Whilst the doctor was speaking, Rocco Trupia's agitation increased, until at last he could restrain himself no longer.

"Have you any other orders to give me, Doctor? I am at your service. But if your Honour has come to speak to me about my mother, you must excuse my saying good-bye to you and returning to my work."

"Wait! I know that it's not your fault that she is in want," said the doctor, trying to stop him from going. "I have been told that you even ———"

"Come here, Doctor." Rocco Trupia pointed suddenly to the door of the *roba*. "It's only a poor man's house, but if your Honour is a village doctor, you must have seen many that are no better. I want to show you the bed always ready—you see—always prepared for that . . . good old woman. She is my mother, so I cannot speak of her in other terms. Here are my wife and children, who can assure you that I have always ordered them to serve that old woman and to respect her as they would the Blessed Virgin. For one's mother must be held sacred, Doctor. What have I done to that mother of mine that she should put me to such shame before the whole village and make people think God only knows what of me. . . . It's true that from my babyhood I was brought up in the home of my father's people and that I have no call to respect her as a mother, because she has always been cold towards me. Yet I have respected her and wished her well. When those wretched sons of hers left her for America I hastened to her, to bring her here as mistress of my house. No, your Honour! She must play the beggar-woman in the village, make an exhibition of herself and bring disgrace upon me. I swear to you, Doctor, that if one of those wretched sons of hers returns to Farnia, I will kill him for the disgrace and the bitterness I've endured these past fourteen years on their account. . . . I will kill him, as true as I stand here talking to you in the presence of my wife and these four little ones. . . ."

Rocco Trupia was shaking with rage. His face had grown paler, his eyes were bloodshot, and he passed his hand across his mouth to wipe the foam off his lips.

The young doctor stood looking at him with indignation. "I see," he said, after a pause. "So that's why your mother refuses to accept the hospitality you offer. It's because of the hatred you foster against your brothers. That's clear."

"Hatred?" exclaimed Rocco Trupia, clenching his fist

and bringing it out from behind his back. "Yes, hatred *now*, Doctor. I hate them because they've caused so much suffering to my mother and to me. In the old days, when they were here, I loved them and looked up to them like elder brothers. And they, in return for it, behaved like Cain towards me. Just listen, Doctor. They would not work and I worked for the lot of us. They used to come here and tell me there was nothing to cook that evening and that mother would go supperless to bed, and I gave. . . . They got drunk, they squandered money on low women, and I gave. . . . When they left for America, I bled myself white for them— here is my wife who can tell you about it."

"Then why?" repeated the doctor, almost to himself.

Rocco Trupia gave a wry smile.

"Why? Because my mother says that I'm not her son."

"What?"

"Get her to explain it to you, Doctor. I have no time to lose; the men are waiting over there for me with the mules laden with manure. I have to work. . . . I can't bear to talk of it. Get her to tell you about it. I kiss your hands."

And Rocco Trupia went away as he had come, stooping, his long legs bowed, and one hand held to his back. The doctor's glance followed him for a moment, then he turned to look at the little ones who were mute with fright. He saw the wife clasp her hands together as she closed her eyes in her distress and said with a sigh of resignation:—

"We must leave it in God's hands."

•

On his return to the village, the doctor was still more anxious to get to the bottom of that strange and incredible case. The old woman was there, seated on the steps in front of his door, just as he had left her. He spoke rather sharply to her when telling her to come in.

"I have been to have a talk with your son at the 'House of the Column'," he said. "Why did you conceal from me the fact that you have another son here?"

Maragrazia looked at him, first in confusion, then almost in terror. Passing her shaking hand across her forehead and hair, she replied:—

"Oh, young Sir, I get into a cold sweat if your Honour speaks to me of that son. Please don't mention him to me, for pity's sake."

"Why not?" asked the doctor angrily. "What has he done to you? Speak out!"

"He has done nothing," the old woman hastened to answer. "That I must give him credit for, in all conscience. On the contrary, he has always behaved respectfully to me. But I . . . I . . . do you see how I tremble, my dear young Sir, as soon as I speak of it? I cannot speak of it! It's because— because—that man—is not my son, Doctor!"

The young practitioner lost his patience.

"What do you mean—he's not your son? What are you saying? Are you stupid or quite mad? Did you or did you not give birth to him?"

The old woman bent her head before that outburst, half-closed her bleeding eyelids and replied:—

"Yes, Sir, I am stupid, perhaps. Mad—no! Would to God that I were mad! Then I should no longer suffer so. . . . But there are some things that your Honour cannot know, being still only a lad. I have white hair, I have suffered for a long time, I have seen many things, many things. . . . I have seen things, my dear young Sir, of which your Honour can have no conception."

"What have you seen, exactly? Speak!"—the doctor urged her.

"Terrible things! Horrible things!" the old woman lamented, shaking her head. "In those days your Honour was not born or thought of. I saw them with my own eyes—my eyes which since then have shed tears of blood. . . . Has your Honour heard speak of a certain Canebardo?"*

"Garibaldi?" asked the doctor, taken aback.

"Yes, Sir. Canebardo. He came to our parts and made the towns and country-side rebel against every law of God and man. Have you heard speak of him?"

---

*Sicilian corruption of the name Garibaldi.

"Yes, yes, go on! What was Garibaldi got to do with it?"

"He has got to do with it because your Honour should know that when he came here—that Canebardo—he gave orders to open all the prisons in all the towns. Well, your Honour can imagine what hellish furies were then let loose in our country—the worst robbers, the worst assassins, bloody wild beasts, maddened by many years of prison! Amongst them there was one called Cola Camizzi—he was the fiercest of them—a brigand chief who killed his victims as if they were flies, just for amusement, to test his powder, as he said—to see if his gun was properly loaded. He settled down in the open country, came in our direction and passed through Farnia with a band of followers he had collected among the peasants. He wasn't satisfied with their number, but wanted more and he killed all those who refused to join him. I had then been married a few years, your Honour, and already had those two sons who are over there in America— my darlings. We were living in the farm of Pozzetto, which my husband—peace be on his soul—had rented. Cola Camizzi passed by and carried him off, too—he took my husband off by force. . . . Two days later, I saw him come back, looking like a corpse—he did not seem the same man. He could not speak, his eyes were full of the horrors he had seen, and he hid his hands—poor fellow—from loathing of what he'd been compelled to do with them. . . . Ah! my dear young Sir, my heart was pierced by terror when I saw him looking like that. 'My boy!' I called out to him—peace be on his soul—'My boy, what have you done?' He could not speak. 'Have you run away from them, my boy? If they catch you, what will happen? They will kill you!'" My heart—my heart told me what would happen. . . . He stayed there for some time, sitting silent, close to the hearth, looking at the floor, his hands always hidden like this—under his jacket— and his eyes like those of a madman. Then he said: 'Better dead.' That was all he spoke. He stayed hidden for three days; on the fourth he went out—we were poor and had to work. He went out to work in the fields. The evening came— he did not return. I waited. Oh God! how I waited—But I

knew already, I had already pictured it all to myself. . . .
However, I thought, 'Who can say? Perhaps they have not
killed him—perhaps they have only taken him away again.'
Six days later I came to know that Cola Camizzi and his
band were in the Montelusa Manor, the property of the
Liguorian monks who had run away. I walked there,
almost out of my mind. It was a day of terrible wind, young
Sir, such as I have never seen in my life. Have you ever *seen*
the wind? Well, that day, you could really see it! It seemed as
if all the souls of the murdered ones were calling on men
and on God for vengeance! I started in that hurricane and
was carried along by it, almost torn to bits, and my screams
were louder than its roar. I flew. I took scarcely an hour to
reach the monastery, very high up, in a grove of black
poplars.

"It had a large court-yard surrounded by a wall. The
entrance was through a little door on one side, half
hidden—I still remember—by a large clump of caper
bushes which had their roots in the wall. I took a stone so as
to knock louder. I knocked and knocked, but they would
not open. I went on knocking, until at last they did open.
Ah! God, what did I see then! ———"

Maragrazia stood up, her face distorted by horror, her
bleeding eyes staring wide. She stretched out one hand, her
fingers cramped like claws. Her voice failed her, she could
not go on.

"In the hands . . ." she said at last, "in the hands . . . of
those assassins . . . in their hands. . . ."

She stopped again, almost choked, and moved her hand
making the gesture of throwing something.

"Well?" asked the doctor with a shiver.

"They were playing . . . there, in that courtyard . . . at
bowls . . . playing with men's heads . . . black and covered
with earth . . . they grasped them by the hair . . . and . . . and
one of the heads was my husband's . . . Cola Camizzi himself
was holding it . . . he showed it to me. I uttered a scream
which tore my throat and chest, a scream so loud that the
murderers themselves shuddered at it. Cola Camizzi seized

me by the neck to make me stop, but one of his men rushed at him furiously and then four or five or, maybe, ten others took courage from the first one's example and joined in, attacking him from every side. They too had had enough of the savage tyranny of that monster and revolted against him, Doctor, and I had the satisfaction of seeing his throat cut there, under my very eyes, by his own companions—that dog of an assassin!"

The old woman sank into her chair, panting and exhausted, a prey to a convulsive fit of trembling.

The young doctor watched her with a look of mingled pity, disgust and horror. When his feeling of nausea had passed and he was able to think calmly again, he still failed to understand what connection that ghastly story could have with the case of the other son. He asked her to explain.

"Wait!" replied the old woman, as soon as she regained her breath. "The one who came to my defence and started the revolt was called Marco Trupia."

"Ah!" exclaimed the doctor. "So that Rocco . . ."

"His son," replied Maragrazia. "But think, Doctor, think! Could I have become the wife of that man after what I'd been through? He insisted on taking me; for three months he kept me with him, he tied me up and gagged me, because I screamed and bit. . . . After three months the authorities got hold of him and shut him up in prison, where he died soon after. But I was left pregnant.

"Ah! young Sir, I swear to you that I wanted to tear out my inside—it seemed to me that I was doomed to give birth to a monster! I felt that I could never even touch the child. At the thought that I might have to suckle him, I screamed like a madwoman. I nearly died when he was born. My mother (peace be on her soul!) looked after me and did not even let me see the baby, but took him straight off to the father's family, where he was brought up. . . . Now, do not you think, Doctor, that I can rightly say that he is not my son?"

Absorbed in thought, the young doctor did not answer for a moment; then he said:—

"But he—after all—your son, what fault is it of his?"

"None!" replied the old woman, "and never, never have my lips uttered a word against him. Never, Doctor, quite the contrary, I assure you. But what can I do if I cannot bear the sight of him, even at a distance? He is the living image of his father, my dear young Sir, in features, in build and even in his voice. I begin to tremble, as soon as I see him, and I get into a cold sweat! I'm no longer myself; my blood revolts, you see. What can I do?"

She stopped a moment, wiping her eyes with the back of her hand; then, fearing that the party of emigrants would leave Farnia without the letter for her real sons—her adored sons—she plucked up courage and roused the doctor from his abstraction, saying:—

"If your Honour would do me the favour you promised. . . ."

With an effort the young man shook off his thoughts, moved his chair up to the desk, and told her that he was ready. Then once again she began to dictate in the same whining tone:—

"Dear sons . . ."

Translated from the Italian by Arthur and Henrie Mayne

Indian Camp
Ernest Hemingway

Ernest Hemingway
(USA, 1899-1961)

Morley Callaghan, who met Hemingway in Paris, quotes him as saying: "Always remember this. If you have a success, you have it for the wrong reasons. If you become popular it is always because of the worst aspects of your work. They always praise you for the worst aspects. It never fails." What Hemingway called "the worst aspects" were the superficial characteristics of his work: the dangerous heroes, the staccato style. Ignored by most readers were the facts that the heroes always failed physically, that the style dealt with difficult, unadorned truths. Hemingway the storyteller always seems to outshine Hemingway the thinker.

"Indian Camp" is one of the Nick Adams stories set in Michigan. Hemingway wrote most of them in Paris, in the twenties, in "a good café on the Place St-Michel," sitting at one of the tables with his lead pencil and notebook. "After writing a story," he says in *A Moveable Feast*, "I was always empty and both sad and happy, as though I had made love, and I was sure this was a very good story, although I would not know truly how good until I read it over the next day."

"Indian Camp" is not only a good story; it is also a miniature essay on childhood and learning. And in this anthology, it is one of the very few stories about a *happy* relationship between a father and his son. Unhappiness in writers—as has often been noted—seems to breed more fiction than happiness.

Indian Camp

At the lake shore there was another rowboat drawn up. The two Indians stood waiting.

Nick and his father got in the stern of the boat and the Indians shoved it off and one of them got in to row. Uncle George sat in the stern of the camp rowboat. The young Indian shoved the camp boat off and got in to row Uncle George.

The two boats started off in the dark. Nick heard the oarlocks of the other boat quite a way ahead of them in the mist. The Indians rowed with quick choppy strokes. Nick lay back with his father's arm around him. It was cold on the water. The Indian who was rowing them was working very hard, but the other boat moved farther ahead in the mist all the time.

"Where are we going, Dad?" Nick asked.

"Over to the Indian camp. There is an Indian lady very sick."

"Oh," said Nick.

Across the bay they found the other boat beached. Uncle George was smoking a cigar in the dark. The young Indian pulled the boat way up the beach. Uncle George gave both the Indians cigars.

They walked up from the beach through a meadow that

was soaking wet with dew, following the young Indian who carried a lantern. Then they went into the woods and followed a trail that led to the logging road that ran back into the hills. It was much lighter on the logging road as the timber was cut away on both sides. The young Indian stopped and blew out his lantern and they all walked on along the road.

They came around a bend and a dog came out barking. Ahead were the lights of the shanties where the Indian barkpeelers lived. More dogs rushed out at them. The two Indians sent them back to the shanties. In the shanty nearest the road there was a light in the window. An old woman stood in the doorway holding a lamp.

Inside on a wooden bunk lay a young Indian woman. She had been trying to have her baby for two days. All the old women in the camp had been helping her. The men had moved off up the road to sit in the dark and smoke out of range of the noise she made. She screamed just as Nick and the two Indians followed his father and Uncle George into the shanty. She lay in the lower bunk, very big under a quilt. Her head was turned to one side. In the upper bunk was her husband. He had cut his foot very badly with an ax three days before. He was smoking a pipe. The room smelled very bad.

Nick's father ordered some water to be put on the stove, and while it was heating he spoke to Nick.

"This lady is going to have a baby, Nick," he said.

"I know," said Nick.

"You don't know," said his father. "Listen to me. What she is going through is called being in labor. The baby wants to be born and she wants it to be born. All her muscles are trying to get the baby born. That is what is happening when she screams."

"I see," Nick said.

Just then the woman cried out.

"Oh, Daddy, can't you give her something to make her stop screaming?" asked Nick.

"No. I haven't any anesthetic," his father said. "But her

screams are not important. I don't hear them because they are not important."

The husband in the upper bunk rolled over against the wall.

The woman in the kitchen motioned to the doctor that the water was hot. Nick's father went into the kitchen and poured about half of the water out of the big kettle into a basin. Into the water left in the kettle he put several things he unwrapped from a handkerchief.

"Those must boil," he said, and began to scrub his hands in the basin of hot water with a cake of soap he had brought from the camp. Nick watched his father's hands scrubbing each other with the soap. While his father washed his hands very carefully and thoroughly, he talked.

"You see, Nick, babies are supposed to be born head first but sometimes they're not. When they're not they make a lot of trouble for everybody. Maybe I'll have to operate on this lady. We'll know in a little while."

When he was satisfied with his hands he went in and went to work.

"Pull back the quilt, will you, George?" he said. "I'd rather not touch it."

Later when he started to operate Uncle George and three Indian men held the woman still. She bit Uncle George on the arm and Uncle George said, "Damn squaw bitch!" and the young Indian who had rowed Uncle George over laughed at him. Nick held the basin for his father. It all took a long time.

His father picked the baby up and slapped it to make it breathe and handed it to the old woman.

"See, it's a boy, Nick," he said. "How do you like being an intern?"

Nick said, "All right." He was looking away so as not to see what his father was doing.

"There. That gets it," said his father and put something into the basin.

Nick didn't look at it.

"Now," his father said, "there's some stitches to put in.

You can watch this or not, Nick, just as you like. I'm going to sew up the incision I made."

Nick did not watch. His curiosity had been gone for a long time.

His father finished and stood up. Uncle George and the three Indian men stood up. Nick put the basin out in the kitchen.

Uncle George looked at his arm. The young Indian smiled reminiscently.

"I'll put some peroxide on that, George," the doctor said.

He bent over the Indian woman. She was quiet now and her eyes were closed. She looked very pale. She did not know what had become of the baby or anything.

"I'll be back in the morning," the doctor said, standing up. "The nurse should be here from St Ignace by noon and she'll bring everything we need."

He was feeling exalted and talkative as football players are in the dressing room after a game.

"That's one for the medical journal, George," he said. "Doing a Caesarian with a jackknife and sewing it up with nine-foot, tapered gut leaders."

Uncle George was standing against the wall, looking at his arm.

"Oh, you're a great man, all right," he said.

"Ought to have a look at the proud father. They're usually the worst sufferers in these little affairs," the doctor said. "I must say he took it all pretty quietly."

He pulled back the blanket from the Indian's head. His hand came away wet. He mounted on the edge of the lower bunk with the lamp in one hand and looked in. The Indian lay with his face toward the wall. His throat had been cut from ear to ear. The blood had flowed down into a pool where his body sagged the bunk. His head rested on his left arm. The open razor lay, edge up, in the blankets.

"Take Nick out of the shanty, George," the doctor said.

There was no need of that. Nick, standing in the door of the kitchen, had a good view of the upper bunk when his father, the lamp in one hand, tipped the Indian's head back.

It was just beginning to be daylight when they walked along the logging road back toward the lake.

"I'm terribly sorry I brought you along, Nickie," said his father, all his postoperative exhilaration gone. "It was an awful mess to put you through."

"Do ladies always have such a hard time having babies?" Nick asked.

"No, that was very, very exceptional."

"Why did he kill himself, Daddy?"

"I don't know, Nick. He couldn't stand things, I guess."

"Do many men kill themselves, Daddy?"

"Not very many, Nick."

"Do many women?"

"Hardly ever."

"Don't they ever?"

"Oh, yes. They do sometimes."

"Daddy?"

"Yes."

"Where did Uncle George go?"

"He'll turn up all right."

"Is dying hard, Daddy?"

"No, I think it's pretty easy, Nick. It all depends."

They were seated in the boat, Nick in the stern, his father rowing. The sun was coming up over the hills. A bass jumped, making a circle in the water. Nick trailed his hand in the water. It felt warm in the sharp chill of the morning.

In the early morning on the lake sitting in the stern of the boat with his father rowing, he felt quite sure that he would never die.